I0584727

INTENSITY

Jewels Harris

Copyright © 2021 Jewels Harris

All rights reserved. No part of this book may be reproduced, stored, or transmitted by any means—whether auditory, graphic, mechanical, or electronic—without written permission of both publisher and author, except in the case of brief excerpts used in critical articles and reviews. Unauthorized reproduction of any part of this work is illegal and is punishable by law.

ISBN: 978-1-63950-061-1 (sc)
ISBN: 978-1-63950-062-8 (e)

Because of the dynamic nature of the Internet, any web addresses or links contained in this book may have changed since publication and may no longer be valid. The views expressed in this work are solely those of the author and do not necessarily reflect the views of the publisher, and the publisher hereby disclaims any responsibility for them.

Writers Apex

Gateway Towards Success

8063 MADISON AVE #1252
Indianapolis, IN 46227
+13176596889
www.writersapex.com

ACKNOWLEDGEMENT

To Debbie, I want to express my gratitude for all your valuable support and encouragement as I endeavored to finish this book. Thank you, thank you, friend. I'm grateful to Sherry Brown who was there for me as well. Thank you, for your ongoing support and friendship throughout this writing challenge.

ACKNOWLEDGMENTS

DEDICATION

This book is first of all dedicated to an American hero named Robert Stricker. He was injured in the line of duty as an officer of the law and later on selected to be a part of an elite task force unit in the state where he lives. I want to also dedicate this book to all the men and women who have served in the armed forces to defend and protect our nation. I especially want to thank the wounded warriors who have fought in the last few wars such as; Desert Storm, the Iraq War, and Afghanistan. These people are the true heroes and I appreciate all their efforts to prevent further terrorists attacks on American soil.

"There are only two ways to live your life.
One is though nothing is a miracle.
The other is as though everything is a miracle."
—Albert Einstein

CHAPTER
One

There it was again, that annoying, unsettling dream. The first time he had this dream, he'd seen someone walking along a dirt road in a barren landscape containing little foliage and the only thing to see were heat waves rising from the scorched earth. The next thing he recalled about the dream was seeing a person take a step forward and then hesitate as if there was some kind of danger ahead. Suddenly, in this dream an explosion seemed to shake the earth beneath the man's feet causing his body to be propelled backwards through the shattered space. The last thing Jake recalled seeing in the scene was that man's body falling to the roadway as dust and dirt swirled around the crumpled figure and he had a sense that this person was dead. Then his compelling dream ended.

The second time he had this strange dream, it almost seemed as if he was experiencing the effects of that person's body being hurled through the air by a tremendous force. Why did this dream seem so real to him? Barely awake that particular morning, he'd dreaded getting out of bed or even going to his college classes. Jake didn't like having the same dream twice in one month. He attributed this vivid dream to the result of eating ice cream late at night and so he planned to forgo desserts for awhile. Anyway, he was the kind of person who didn't believe in signs or pay attention to superstitious revelations. After all, people had dreams all the time, right? He told himself to chalk it up to an over active imagination.

As Jake ran along the river path during this early morning hour, his thoughts returned involuntarily to that same vivid dream of a man dying. The reoccurring dream made no sense to him and yet, for some strange reason, he began to wonder if this dream might pertain to his own future. A vague sense of dread pervaded his thoughts momentarily and then he chose to turn his attention to what was at hand. He needed to focus on his plan to enlist in the Marines as soon as he completed his last semester of community college. His father had retired from his supervisor/builder vocation and purchased a small business where teens and young adults could be trained in the art of self-defense. His father's business had taken off within the first two years and so now there was a need to hire another employee to help carry the work load. His father had made a few hints to him recently in the hopes that Jake would consider working full time for him.

Sure he'd enjoyed working part-time in his dad's thriving business these past two years, but he didn't want to rely on his dad for a job anymore. He suspected that his parents hated listening to him talk about enlisting because they were aware of the dangers of war. Once he'd been in the Marines for awhile, his hope was to rise to the rank of a sergeant so he could train others in survival skills that would keep them alive. He'd always been a hard worker and now his passion was to serve his country. His dream was to be involved in Special Forces one day. Was he being too unrealistic about this goal? He paused momentarily and thought to himself, *geez, maybe I've watched too many war movies in the last few years, get a grip, Walker!*

Jake stopped on the narrow beaten path to watch the river as it pulsated and flowed over the larger rocks. The rushing water sparkled before his eyes as if there were a myriad of delicate, tiny water sprites dancing to the unique music of nature just as they'd done for decades. He marveled at the continuous flow of water no matter what time of the year he found himself running along his favorite path. Yes, he knew that mountain snow runoff was the main source of this water supply, but even in late August the water level was still in abundance. Then his thoughts drifted back to that unusual vision of a person's body being sent upward by an unknown force. It was as if he was viewing a western scene where a cowboy had been shot and the impact of a bullet had propelled the person backwards through the air. Once again, he tried to figure out the reason for this odd dream or if it even concerned him.

Jake knew what his mother would say if she heard about his dream. He was certain that she'd think of it as a possible warning dream and then she'd tell him to be more cautious and careful. He dismissed his mother's concerns for his well-being and stretched his arms out to his side as if to tell the world that it would not conquer him, for without a doubt, he was capable of handling himself in any situations. At the age of twenty-two, he thought he was unstoppable; he was a force to be reckoned with in his own mind and therefore, no amount of fear factor or people's negative, discouraging words would keep him from the plan to enlist. He was born to accept a challenge and he didn't hesitate to volunteer for any tough assignment. Even in high school, he'd taken on his coach, Reed Hanford's, challenge to become the best in his endeavors on and off of the football field. Yes, he'd stick to his ultimate plan: he wanted to be a part of an elite team in the Marine Corps.

At that moment, a flock of Canadian geese flew overhead squawking noisily and so Jake let out a military hoorah yell like he'd seen a soldier do in a recent movie. Feeling much better about his life, he continued on his run towards the hill overlooking his old high school where he'd often stopped to relax and think as a teen. He contemplated telling his folks about his decision to enlist in the Marines, but he was dreading their response to the news. He'd heard them discussing their opinions about young men enlisting in the military. His mother had said that she felt like there were enough US soldiers stationed in Middle Eastern countries to take care of the problems. Ever since 2001, and the attack on NYC twin towers, Jake had wanted to go into the military and do his part to protect America.

Now after two years of waiting and thinking about this plan, his mind was made up and he just wished his father would support him in this decision. Of course, he realized why his folks weren't encouraging him to join the military service; it was mainly because of the serious possibility that their only son might be killed overseas. He understood their valid concerns even though he was not a parent. Jake had watched the nightly news and seen the list of men killed in action scroll across the bottom of the news reports. Despite the dangers and the unknown, he still wanted to enlist and do his part to thwart another attack by the terrorist organization.

Jake plopped down onto the grassy knoll to think about his future. While he was sitting there feeling the cool breeze brush across his face, he recalled having another strange vision. Just as he'd been close to waking up one early morning in March, there had been a quick image of a woman's face which had flashed before his eyes. It seemed like this person's face was now inadvertently lodged in the crevasses of his subconscious. It couldn't be considered a dream since this vision had been so brief. It had happened like this: In his mind's eye he'd seen a woman with brown hair. Her eyes were compelling and there was a distinct impression that she carried pain or sadness in her eyes. He didn't recall anything about her form, but as he closed his eyes, he could still see her features and they seemed to haunt him. Jake had a weird sense that maybe he was in this next part where the woman was tumbling downward and someone reached out to catch her and then the vision ended abruptly. This morning as he'd stumbled out of bed and his feet had hit the cold vinyl floor in his room, he'd recalled the same image of the woman's face with those soulful eyes. What was this all about he wondered. Had the Mexican food he eaten the night before been too spicy for his system? How could he prevent these strange dreams or visions from disrupting his sleep? Maybe he should try going for an exhausting long run in the evening to solve his sleep problem.

He made an effort to dismiss this sad, unknown woman from his mind since he had no clue as to why that vision had returned to peak his interest again. The distinct image of a dark-haired woman wasn't someone he'd recalled seeing around town or on the college campus. At one point soon after having this perplexing vision, he'd decided to share this troubling image with his psychology professor, Mr. Morton, to see what it could mean. The professor didn't offer anything conclusive or helpful, but he did mention in passing that sometimes weird dreams have nothing to do with real life. While pondering the man's words, Jake thought about his grandmother, Eunice. She had given him some advice once. She was a praying woman and she felt that Jake needed to pay attention to his dreams because she believed he'd been given a gift. Since this image of a woman had no connection to his immediate world he forced himself to forget about the peculiar vision. And yet, he couldn't seem to forget about his grandmother's words. What could possibly be the purpose of dreams or visions if he couldn't understand them? What was it his grandmother had mentioned to him? Oh yeah, she'd quoted Walt Disney who said this: "All your dreams can come true if you have the courage to pursue them. *No, that wasn't the right quote*, he thought to himself.

Oh now I remember, it was what a successful basketball coach named John Wooden had said, "You can't live a perfect day without doing something for someone who will never be able to repay you." Jake didn't know anyone who needed an act of charity or help from him so he dismissed this idea and his thoughts turned to the swimming hole on this same river and the good times he'd had with teenage friends. Maybe he should try to get together with his buddy, Mark, to shoot some hoops or spend some time on the golf course. Those types of activities usually helped to clear his head.

As he jogged back towards his place, he recalled hearing a bible story where a lad had been given a dream about his future. This same youth had spent most of his young adulthood in misery and loneliness until he was finally released from an Egyptian prison. He recalled not understanding this story much at the time. Why would he keep getting these unusual dreams in his sleep? What was the purpose for a dream's reoccurrence he wondered? Once again Jake told himself to forget about the illusive dreams and the recent vision of a woman. He needed to live in the real world. A good lunch of lasagna leftovers would ease his troubled mind along with some chocolate ice cream for dessert. After all he had the rest of his life to figure this problem out! What's the point of getting dreams or visions he wondered? Surely it was not his responsibility to discover who the people in his dreams were or why he should even cared.

Later that evening while he sat on the porch watching the stars overhead and feeling the cool breeze wafting over his skin, he remembered the angelic presence that had come into his hospital room as a youngster when he'd been very ill. He recalled the strange words that had penetrated his mind and left a viable impression on his soul. The first part of the promise he'd been given from the angel figure had come true that same night. While lying there on his sick bed, he'd heard these unforgettable words pierce his soul. *You will live and not die and one day you will be there for someone who will need your help.* He'd survived that awful illness as well as the complication of pneumonia at the age of eight. He'd been perfectly healthy and active since that time and so he wondered about the last part- -could there still be some unique purpose for his life. If the second part of the angel's promise was true then how would he know who to help? Jake needed an answer and yet, no further insight was coming to him. He wondered if maybe he'd misunderstood the strange words directed at him that night in the hospital.

CHAPTER
Two

I t was 1978, and a section of Handley, Illinois was getting a makeover. Some of the older businesses located on Main Street in the downtown section of this thriving community needed a change to bring in more customers. The remodel job had been estimated to take at least eight months to finish as it included four buildings, a real estate office building, and a coffee shop at the end of the street. The Edwards construction company had been awarded the contract and their supervisor, Matt Walker, had begun tearing off the dilapidated siding on the first building; he hoped to get most of the outside work done by the end of November. Town folk and small clusters of teenagers could be seen on the weekends heading down this particular street in order to observe the progress which had been going on for the last two months in their fine city. Some folks stopped by habit in front of the coffee shop entrance thinking to go inside and order a hot espresso or vanilla latte only to be disappointed that it was still not open to business. The construction crew did their best to keep working in spite of the large number of people passing by each day.

In this same locale a dark-haired, energetic youngster named C. J. lived with his parent's, Matthew and Rebecca, and his older sister, Jillian. Outside of their home on this warm spring day, a strong breeze began to stir the leaves of the slender, white birch trees that faced this ranch-style house and with it came a promise of cooler weather. This house situated on Arlington Street had a fresh coat of white paint applied to the outside and four new green window shutters had been added for an accent color. There were attractive, deep lavender colored petunia flower baskets hanging from each metal brackets neatly placed in front to greet all who came up the pathway leading to the home. The front entry door had an intricately designed inlayed window of fine beveled glass which easily caught one's eye. In the top branches of a maple tree one could see a red-breasted robin busily gathering twigs as it worked to build a nest. A passing black Labrador and his owner jogged down the same street right then. Overtop of this busy street there was a telephone pole line where a rangy, grey squirrel could be seen darting along the electrical wire in order to reach a nearby maple tree. The nervous animal stopped briefly to observe the dog below and then it scampered away. A monarch butterfly landed delicately on the lilac bush situated on the side of a neighboring house with a sloping driveway.

A wooden sign with the occupant's last name and the letters, Established in 1970 had been attached to the siding of the home. There was an attractively painted welcome sign with black lettering near the front door. Inside this one-level home in the thriving city of Handley, Illinois, an average American family was beginning their day. The owner of this fine home, a trim and well built individual strode into the kitchen area with his jacket, thermos, and blue prints in hand looking rather rushed and harried. His slender, attractive wife, Rebecca, smiled as she heard him come into the room so she turned to give her husband a hug. He reciprocated with a gentle kiss on her lips and then he pulled his wife into his arms for a longer hug and kiss.

"Good morning, sweetheart." He said.

"Yes, it is a wonderful morning now that I've had my coffee and seen the sun rising over the trees in our backyard. It promises to be a good day. Do you want me to make pancakes or waffles for breakfast?" She asked him.

"No nothing today, I'm meeting Mr. Emerson at the work site to go over the problems we're having with the subcontractor, Dave Barnett. That guy didn't order the right windows like I wanted and now we're behind schedule again." Her tall, handsome husband laid down his paperwork and briefcase on the table and rubbed his eyes as he reached for a glass from the cupboard. "We need to get the front siding of the first building finished and closed up before the weather changes and the rain ruins things." He said.

"Well, that doesn't sound good Matthew. I hope you can finish on time tonight." She said.

"Why, am I forgetting something that you've scheduled with the family?" He asked.

"My sister, Cathy, is coming over tonight to celebrate your son's eighth birthday a week early. Since Doug, Deborah, and little Daniel are still in Shreveport Bay, visiting with Duke and his family they might be late for our gathering. They went fishing for halibut and promised to bring us some fish for our freezer. And speaking of family, I need you to pick up some steaks for tonight." Rebecca mentioned.

"I'm glad you reminded me that they are coming tonight. Stopping at the meat market will make me late." Matthew replied.

Flustered and annoyed with an errand to do after work, he turned to face his wife with his hands on his waist as if to say, how can I go to the market and still be on time? Her husband glanced over at the wall clock to check the time and she could tell he was perturbed with her.

"Well, my other sister is coming here as well. She finally got her first book published and she wants to share her news with the family. She submitted her drawings to the publisher and they might use them as well. So we're having the special meal to bless her at the same time that we celebrate Cole Jacob's birthday."

"Fine, so what time are you planning to sit down to eat." Matthew asked.

"I need you to be here by six-thirty. It doesn't take too long to cook steak. The rest of the meal will be done. Thanks for helping me out."Rebecca said.

Overhearing his parent's conversation, their son stood up and hollered his request. "Mom, can we have hot dogs too?" Then without waiting for an answer he went back to building his 'Hot wheels' race track.

"Yes, you can have your favorite food item, hot dogs. I'll also make some macaroni and cheese for you and your cousin, Daniel to go with dinner."

"Honey, can we talk about cutting down the tree in our backyard this weekend? Rebecca asked.

"I need to leave right now or I'll be late for the meeting." A look of exasperation crossed his face as he set his water glass on the counter. "Have a great day with your sister."Matthew said

He raced out the door muttering under his breath. Loading a few items in his work truck, he backed out the driveway with one thought in mind to beat the rush hour traffic that could make him late. He wanted to arrive at the work site before his crew showed up waiting for his orders. He was worried about the delay of the windows he'd ordered for this construction job because the weather in Illinois was unpredictable this time of the year and he couldn't afford more problems if the rains came. He didn't need the headache of water getting inside the building they were working on.

Their teenage daughter, Jillian, was scrambling to get ready for her first day as a hostess at Mitchell's Restaurant on Main Street. She'd have to take a detour to get to her job today since her father's construction work was still going on nearby. She could hear her mother humming her favorite tune, "Amore" while she cleared some of the morning dishes. Her eight year old brother, C. J., was happily playing with his Lego's building blocks and shiny Hot Wheel cars in the living room when she heard her father's truck leave. She searched her bedroom looking for her backpack and finally spotted it on the sofa. Turning around to head back to her bedroom, she almost tripped over her brother's Lego toys as she hurried past him.

Rebecca finished drinking her coffee and the remaining blueberry muffin. She looked out the back window of her kitchen and spied another bluebird flying towards their tree. She wondered if she should scattered a few bread crusts out back for the birds since she loved watching them search for food in her yard. All of a sudden the noise from a neighbor's dog barking out front reminded Rebecca that her sister would be arriving shortly so she went in search of her youngest child to make sure he was presentable. As she entered the living room to her dismay her young son had setup his race track and there were plenty of 'Hot wheel' cars scattered everywhere.

"C.J., I told you Aunt Cabbie was coming this morning. Hurry up and put away your toys and then get dressed for the day." She exclaimed. Rebecca could feel the tightness building in her neck muscles from this added stress. She loved her son, but was annoyed that he'd chosen to bring his mess into her living room today.

"Ah, Mom, Aunt Cabbie doesn't mind my toys being on the floor," He called out and continued building a Lego car garage next to the race track. "Besides, she can help me figure out how to make a cool ramp for my cars when she gets here." He retorted glibly.

"Well then, you'll be staying indoors all day because there's no going outside in your pajamas. So what's your choice going to be young man?"

"Mom, make C.J. move all of his toys into his bedroom so I don't trip over them all. We should call him Mooch the Messy' since he leaves stuff everywhere. Gosh, when is he going to start using her actual name which is Aunt Cathy?"

"Be quiet, bossy girl." He muttered greatly annoyed with his older sibling's demands.

"Well, I believe your aunt likes her nickname. Remember when your brother was barely three and he tried to pronounce her name, it sounded more like, Cabbie. For some reason the name fits her. I even find myself calling her by this nickname occasionally. It was adorable then and since she hasn't asked him to change it then deal with it!" Rebecca remarked. She smiled graciously at her daughter as she recalled her young son's first attempts at talking.

"Remember how your little brother couldn't say Jillian either; instead he'd said, Jelly' so we all tagged you as our loveable, 'Jelly bean' girl."

"Ha Ha Ha! Okay Mom, I have to go to work. Tell Aunt Cathy I said hello and give her big hug too."

"I will, love you. Have a great day at work, dear." She said.

An hour later, Rebecca's older sister, Cathy Harper, arrived out front of their home. She parked her Nissan car, locked the doors, and carried two bags of food snacks up the front steps and knocked twice on the door. She was an attractive, petite lady who walked with a spring in her step and a smile on her face. Everyone felt like there was a party happening when she walked into the room. The family members often made the comment that she really loved life and had an adventurous soul.

"Hello sis. They hugged and chatted briefly. Then Aunt Cathy went in search of her nephew.

"C.J., where are you hiding?" I need to give you a bear hug. Where are you?"

"Hi, Aunt Cabbie, I'm right here in my bedroom. Mom made me put away all of my toys and now I'm picking up my clothes." He responded with a disgruntled voice. Standing up with his arms wide open to receive a big hug, he chuckled when she tickled him and planted a kiss on his head. "Can you play with me after I clean up my room?" He asked.

"Sure thing, Tiger!" She gave him a big huge and a smile. "How's my favorite super galactic space- warrior?" She asked.

"I'm fine. I was going to show you what I made this morning, but Mom told me to clean it up. Hey, do you want to help make a ramp for my race cars outside after I get dressed?"

"I might come outside after I visit with your mother awhile." His aunt replied with a smile. "Say, did you ever find the other light saber which I need to defeat the dragon-master, Zorba?" His aunt asked playfully.

"Ah, no my room is kind of a mess right now, but I'll look for it later. You can use my wooden sword for now. If you need super powers then just tap your sword on my light saber for two minutes to gain electro-magnetic power." He replied with his usual flair for made up words.

Heading back to the kitchen, the two sisters began chatting merrily about Jillian's new job and their summer plans. Soon Rebecca was eagerly digging into the bulging bag of goodies lying on the counter. She sighed loudly with oh's of delight at the sight of red licorice, cashew nuts, and a box of raspberry chocolate bars for her to enjoy. She knew the bag of pretzels and the string cheese had been purchased for Cole Jacob.

Within minutes of finishing off his snack, this young Jedi-warrior asked for permission to head out back to find his scooter and a BMX bike in the garage. Hoping to discover the missing light saber while searching for his helmet, he waded past tool boxes, two adult bikes, and an assortment of baseball gear, but there was no sign of the second light-saber. He couldn't find his helmet anywhere in the clutter of boxes and stuff so he jumped onto his scooter without the protective gear. With one foot on the platform of the scooter and the other foot pushing on the paved driveway, he sailed gleefully down the sloping pavement and into the street. Then he hurriedly turned his scooter around and pushed it back towards the sidewalk before his mother could notice that he'd been out in the street.

After catching up on all the family news with her sister, Cathy drifted outside to look for her young nephew. She looked forward to seeing her other sister, Debbie, later tonight when the other family members arrived for the party. She always enjoyed spending time with her nephew and taking part in his activities. While watching him race back and forth exuberantly on the sidewalk in an effort to outperform his last ride, she thought of an intriguing idea for him to consider.

"Hey, C.J. let's make a ramp for you to jump over with your scooter or bike." She said.

"That's a great idea, Aunt Cabbie. There's plywood next to the garage. What else do we need to make a ramp?" He asked.

"We have to find two blocks of wood to put underneath the plywood board and then it will be ready to ride on with your bike. I use to ride my bike over a ramp when I was your age." She said.

CHAPTER
Three

After making the bike ramp, she watched her nephew raced down the sidewalk until he reached the wooden ramp. Then she held her breath as he managed to guide his bicycle onto the ramp and soar into the air. Fortunately, he stayed in the center of the piece of plywood and then made the landing without crashing onto the pavement. She smiled at her young nephew who waved jubilantly at her as he turned his bike around to try again. She was glad that she'd come over early to spend time with him before the relatives arrived.

Twenty minutes later, the bike moved closer to the edge of the wooden ramp and he lost control and tumbled awkwardly to the ground. She examined his bruises and cut wrist and then insisted that her nephew go inside to rest for a bit. While relaxing on the sofa, he asked for a drink of milk, a few crackers and a slice of cheese to satisfy his appetite. After finishing his snack, he was ready to show his aunt his new Leggo set. Aunt Cathy spent the next half hour building things with her nephew and admiring his construction skills.

That evening with the family and relatives all gathered around the dinner table, Rebecca brought out the chocolate cake along with some cupcakes for the two boys. Everyone was in a good mood that night, even Jillian. Matthew loved having Douglas over to talk about their jobs and his favorite football team, the Pittsburg Steelers.

"What do you think about the Steelers team this year? The main guy is one of the premier quarterbacks in the eastern division, don't you agree?" Matthew asked his relative.

"We'll see since the season has barely begun. I suppose if he doesn't get injured and he runs the ball more then maybe they'll have a good chance of making it to the playoffs." Doug quipped.

"True, having a quarterback who can run the ball into the end zone really helps the team. Did you see that last game against Minnesota Vikings? The Pittsburg Steelers offense destroyed the Viking's defense. What a great win for them." He stated.

"So how about a friendly wager on the next two games?" Doug questioned.

"Sure, I'm in for ten bucks that says the Patriots win their next football game against the LA Rams and the Pittsburg Steelers will probably beat the Saints team this time!" He said.

Little Daniel came racing into the dining room to grab his second chocolate cupcake. Aunt Cathy reached for the youngster and asked him for a hug and the lad responded to her request with a big grin. Then he followed his older cousin back outside to play the game of ninja warriors.

"Okay folks, its official. Daniel James is my second favorite nephew."

"Oh, you know you love all children. I've seen you play with the kids you meet at the park or at the lake when we are swimming or wading in the shallow end. No one else brings a water balloon to play a game of ' keep away' in the lake and then invites all the youngster to join in the crazy fun of trying to catch the silly water balloon and not let it break." Debbie retorted with a smirk on her jovial face.

"That's the truth. It's a proven fact that where ever Aunt Cathy is, it seems that children of all ages are drawn to her side. They follow her around like frolicking, happy puppy dogs eager to adopt her and join in her antics. She can get children of all ages to talk to her." Jillian remarked.

"People have started calling her the pied piper of children." Rebecca joined in the fun.

"I've even seen some kids when she tells them she has to go home they start to whine and beg her to stay longer." Douglas remarked glibly.

Soon everyone was laughing and making more remarks than were necessary to prove their point. Cathy Harper smiled and seemed to enjoy their lighthearted teasing. Two hours later, Matt and Rebecca were saying goodnight to the family members as they walked everyone out to their prospective vehicles.

CHAPTER
Four

Two months later, Cathy Harper received an unusual phone message from her sister, Rebecca, when she returned home after shopping for groceries. The message said they were at Madison Children's Hospital in the nearby bigger city of Mendon Falls. When she called Rebecca back she heard the alarm in her sister's voice.

"He had complained of some pain in his abdomen this week. Then he had some flu-like symptoms for three days so I took him to Dr. Sampson and now we're up here with a different doctor." She paused for a moment and then continued speaking.

"I'm dreading this next meeting with the doctor. The test results will hopefully give the doctors a definitive plan as to how to treat C.J. I've never like being in a hospital and I hope this is something easily treated. I just wanted to be handed a prescription or antibiodities so we take him home later today."

"Yes, that would be good. I don't understand why they insisted he be admitted to the hospital? Couldn't they just administer the medicine and run a test in the clinic here in Handley."

"Well, they did a test early this morning and then they sent him to Doctor Henshaw who is a specialist."

"That doesn't sound real good. I can drive over and stay with you two until we learn the final results and their prognosis."

Alarmed by the disturbing news about her sick nephew, Cathy Harper grabbed her purse, car keys, and a water bottle as she headed outside. Climbing into her car she wondered if she should bring some snacks to her sister. She decided to wait and find out if Rebecca needed something and she could drive to a local market for food items. Upon reaching the hospital, she locked her car and headed for the exit of the parking garage. While walking in search of the information desk, she couldn't help but notice a few people looking as if they were lost in the big hospital too. She tried to dismiss the negative thoughts pounding in her head as she left the elevator in search of her nephew's room on the fifth floor. Remembering the nurses' instruction to scrub her hands for twenty seconds before entering his room, she paused to clean up and say a quick prayer. Having never been in this kind of situation, she didn't know exactly how to encourage her family members. Jillian was the first person she saw as she stepped inside the quiet, stark white hospital room. Her niece walked over wearing a solemn face and gave her aunt a big hug. Rebecca stood up and produced a half-hearted smile and then she motioned for her sister to follow her out into the hall to talk.

"The doctor gave us the test results; it's not an ulcer. They are telling us that he has a tumor in his stomach." Rebecca said.

Her sister stood there in shock as she tried to comprehend the words coming from her sister. "I can't believe this is happening. Are they saying this growth is bad? What is the prognosis at this point?"

"I'm not sure of a prognosis at this moment, except that the doctor told us that it's malignant. So he will have to undergo chemotherapy treatment to keep the tumor from growing or spreading. Rebecca mentioned this news in a hushed voice so as to not disturb the nurses working at their station nearby. "I'm literally in shock. If this treatment doesn't cure him, then the tumor could multiply and spread into other organs in his body. Sis, what am I'm going to do? I know nothing about this disease or how long we might have to stay here." She exclaimed. "Besides that, the doctor also mentioned that if the chemo doesn't stop the tumor from growing then they will have to perform surgery."

Seeing the tears beginning to well up in her younger sister's eyes, she quickly reached out and hugged her until the crying subsided. "The doctor said they need to proceed with the normal protocol in this situation which is two weeks of chemo and then they plan to remove the growth. They are concerned about more tumors being found in a section of his large intestines."

"I'm so sorry, sweetheart. I promise to be here for you. You can call me anytime, day or night this coming week. If there is anything I can do to help you through this scary situation please let me know. Let's go to the cafeteria for some hot tea while Jillian can stay with him. We can get some hot soup. That always helps you, remember Momma's special answer to life's difficulties and any flu virus which we kids may've caught. She used to make us hot tea with lemon juice and honey or chicken noodle soup when we weren't feeling well."

"Okay, maybe you're right; I can use tea and hot soup. Matthew won't be here for another hour because he was out of town for company business in Chicago. He'd gone to watch the Red Sox's play earlier today, but now he's flying home to be with us." Rebecca mentioned.

"Does he need me to pick him up at the airport?" Cathy asked.

"No, he decided to leave his truck in long-term parking so he has a vehicle. I'm glad he is coming. We need him to stay here for awhile and then I can go back home and pack some clothes since I plan to stay here until C.J. is well again. Everything in our life is on hold right now. I feel numb and afraid and I'm not sure what to say to my son at times." Rebecca whispered.

She started to weep quietly. Her tears dropped down into the remainder of her soup. Cathy stood up and went around the cafeteria chairs to try and comfort her sister with a hug. Neither woman cared if anyone was watching their display of emotions. It wasn't easy for Rebecca to be so vulnerable, but at this moment she felt raw and as if she needed to be real with her sister.

"I just can't believe this is happening. It seems so unbelievable!" Rebecca exclaimed.

"Let's not think about that right now. I'm going to believe that the doctors can help him beat this disease. Let's see about getting some more tea or coffee. Tell me how is Jillian's doing at her job?"

"She seems to be doing fine. She is growing up so fast! I am thankful that she is thinking about applying for a scholarship for college after she finishes this year. I'm grateful that she is a safe driver and she isn't dating anyone seriously right now. I couldn't handle anymore problems now!" Rebecca exclaimed.

After taking a brief stroll around the hospital grounds, the two sisters headed back up to the fifth floor to check on their little patient. Jillian was relieved to have them back to watch over her sick brother. She chatted briefly with her aunt and then kissed her brother once more on the cheek and said goodbye since she had to go to work. Cathy Harper sat beside her nephew's bed for the next hour reading a magazine so Rebecca could get some rest. Eventually, her nephew woke up and glanced over at his aunt. He moaned twice and then mumbled something inaudible. She moved closer to hear his words.

"Aunt Cabbie', I don't feel so good. Can you bring me my superhero cape the next time you come here for a visit?" He asked his aunt.

"I can bring it to the hospital in a day or so."

"Good I miss playing Star Wars games with you. I want to go home soon."

"I know, your daddy is going to be here soon. We all love you very much. The doctors are going to take good care of you. You're a brave young man." She remarked.

"Okay, I just want to sleep now." He whispered as he closed his eyes again.

Fear pierced her soul in that moment as it sounded as if he'd resigned himself to being ill. She wondered if he was scared by all the seriousness of this place. Maybe he was worried about the next test which the doctor was planning to do.

Two days later, before driving over to the hospital, she stopped by her sister's place to retrieve the superman cape and a ring which according to her young nephew contained super magical powers. She finally located the desired items lying underneath his bed. Cathy then drove back to the children's hospital located in the larger neighboring city of Mendon Falls. Holding her nephew's cape in one hand, she pushed the UP button for the hospital elevator. When the elevator door opened she stepped inside and waited for the door to close. Standing there in the elevator, she couldn't help wondering if it was going to take more than the chemo drugs to save her sick nephew. Then she remembered something she had spoken to her nephew a few months before this. *Tiger, it's going to take more than just your superhero cape and a magnetic lightning ring to defeat the evil monster, Jarbo and his fiery dragon this time. You need a powerful laser sword to destroy the wicked dragon-master!!* The more she thought about her recent words, the more she came to the realization she needed to take her own advice this time.

So while standing alone in the empty elevator she spoke aloud a verse in the Book of Psalm she'd learned as a girl in Sunday school. "You will not die, but you will live and tell about the deeds of God." From that moment on she was determined to speak out life changing truths and declarations for her hurting nephew. Instead of rehearsing the doctors' words of weakness, tumors, and possible death, she'd begin to believe for health for her nephew. He would need a miracle. She believed in miracles because of the one time when her own life had been spared from almost having a head on collision. A teenager driving his car recklessly nearly hit her, but at the last second he steered clear enough to avoid crashing headlong into her car. No one could dissuade her from believing that she had a guardian angel after that frightening experience. She made a mental note to call her other sister, Debbie, to ask her to pray too.

Pushing the door of his room open, she discovered her nephew sitting up in the stark white hospital room waiting for her. He reached eagerly for his bright red cape and tied it around his neck; the contrasting red color next to his blue-grey gown gave her cause to smile. She hugged Rebecca and told her she'd be staying with her nephew for a few hours. She encouraged her sister to take a leisurely stroll outside of the hospital in order to enjoy the afternoon sunshine and get some dinner at a real restaurant. After her sister left, she moved a chair closer to her nephew's bedside and gave him a big smile.

She didn't know what to say to him at first, but then she decided to ask him a question.

"Sweetheart, what can I do to help you feel better while I'm here today?" Aunt Cathy asked.

"Auntie, will you tell me a story? I'm bored sitting here every day with not much to do but wait for the nurses to poke me or give me more medicine to swallow. I don't like being so sick or having to stay here so long. I want to go home."

"Goodness, I wouldn't want to be stuck here either. Let me think for a minute about a good story to share with you." She said.

His aunt thought for a few minutes and finally smiled broadly for his benefit. She got up and went to the cupboard, opened it up, and reached in to retrieve an extra pillow. Then she positioned the pillow behind her back to get more comfortable as she began her narrative.

"Ah, okay Tiger' here goes. Many years ago in the 1960s, long before you were born, life in America was entering the age of space and flights to the moon. It was a time of peace and prosperity in the land. This story happened about twenty years before you were born to your parents. There was a boy who loved to plan exciting adventures. He often dreamed of being a star gazer who would someday fly to another galaxy with his acquired powers to fight the evil leader named Harmst Wahkkin. This young, powerful hero reminded me of Superman and how he helped people here on planet earth." Pushing the pillow up higher, she settled once again in the chair and smiled at her nephew's interest in her story telling.

"I shall call the boy in my story, the 'Light star' hero."

"Is that his real name, Aunt Cabbie?"

"No, his actual name is Destin Morgan. This young lad loved to pretend that he could fight anyone who was threatening to destroy his family, his friends, or his planet home."

"How old was this kid named Destin?"

"He's a year older than you are."

"Well, this story is about a ten year old kid who believed he could do amazing feats that other humans couldn't do. You see, he'd discovered that he had this unique ability to perform supernatural things which usually comes from beings who live on a different planet realm."

"Cool, I like this story. Is this a true story because you said this happened like twenty years before I was born in America?" He said.

"Actually, this could have happened to a boy somewhere in our world I suppose. So now how about you settle back on your pillow and just listen as I tell you my story." Cathy Harper said.

"Okay, Aunt Cabbie. I'm feeling a little bit tired."

"Well, this boy named Destin the 'light star hero' went on a super cool flight in a supersonic rocket ship heading to Saturn to track down a war lord named Xnomar."

"But I thought you said this bad guy's name was Jarbo."

"Well, that was the first leader's name and he told everyone that he had decided to join forces with this second bad dude."

"Oh, I see. Okay, go on then because I like the story!"

"Well, you see this second wicked dude of the galaxy wanted to rule the universe and control every planet for his own use. Destin, our young hero had learned where this evil henchman was located on his last trip and so now his plan was to destroy this misguided ruler with his laser blaster. Destin would just need to get close enough to launch a surprise attack on the evil forces. He knew these dangerous men were determined to remove every person who stood in their way to gain world dominance. The warlord's aircraft had a weapon that hurled meteor-like rocks at other planes and rocket ship which entered the air space territory called Galaxy of Temarus." She continued telling her made up narrative for the next fifteen minutes until she happened to notice that he'd fallen asleep. She smiled and tucked the bed sheets around his frail body and gave him a slight kiss on top of his tousled hair.

Cathy stayed beside his bed as she read an interesting novel which she'd tucked into her purse before leaving her house. When Rebecca returned, she was glad to see her son sleeping. After talking quietly for a few minutes, Cathy said goodbye and headed out to the garage parking area to find her car. She would call her sister in a few days to ask a few more questions about the doctor's prognosis. In the meantime she tried not to worry about her nephew.

Two weeks later, Cole's situation became dire. The doctors were not able to operate on his stomach since his fever had spiked. His red blood cells were at a dangerously low level and he would need a blood transfusion before they even attempted to operate and remove the tumor. The doctor came to the boy's room and asked the parents to step outside and walk with him to a conference room for an update. Once they were settled in the quiet room, the doctor proceeded to share his information with them.

"This is our concern to date. The test results show that he has pneumonia and his fever has spiked. I'm putting him on stronger antibioditics to help your son fight off this infection in his lungs. Our consulting physician, Dr. Branson, agrees with me. Do you folks have any questions you would like to ask me?" The physician asked.

"Well, yes I do have one question, Doctor Henshaw. When can we expect our son to recover from this infection now that he's on different antibioditics?" Rebecca asked.

"In a normal situation the meds will take affect by forty-eight hours. With your son's case we are hopeful that he will get better within four days after receiving the medication. His body was in a weakened state when he came in here. So we will simply watch and see how he does."

"So you're saying that our son could get worse? Matt asked the doctor.

"Well, we've seen this kind of illness occur with patients who have a weakened immune system. However, once your son is through the first two to four days of this new medication, he will have to use the spirometer device regularly. This is an important method we use in the hospital to protect our patients from further complications. The nurses on duty will be monitoring his vitals and any problems or symptoms that may arise."

"How can I help since I will be staying here in his room for these next two weeks? Rebecca asked the doctor.

"After the nurse shows you how to administer the medical device called an incentive spirometer you will need to make sure he uses this particular medical device every four hours. This will help your son by opening up his lungs and keeping them free from troubling fluid buildup. The goal is to make sure your son breathes into this device in order to keep his lungs clear. That's your new assignment. Can you handle this task and make sure your son follows our instructions?" the doctor looked down at his clipboard and scanned the numbers and notes at the bottom of the page. "Each case can be different and the fact that your boy is young gives us hope that he will be able to beat this complication and soon be on the road to recovery. Once his blood count is back up to a normal level and there is no more fever or further complications, then we can proceed with the surgery to remove the tumor."

"Yes, I will keep an eye on him and remind him of the importance of using this medical device." Rebecca replied.

"Okay, well thank you doctor for keeping us informed of our son's situation." Matthew said.

The worried couple left the conference room and walked back down the hall both lost in their own thoughts. Rebecca was beginning to feel emotional and anxious after the doctor's consultation. Her son seemed so pale and helpless lying there in his hospital bed as they checked in on him. She felt a desperate ache in her heart at hearing this recent information. It had been difficult to know what to say or not say to her son and now he would have to wait for the surgery. Heartsick and discouraged, she closed his door quietly and turned to say something to her husband, but instead began to cry. Matthew placed his arm around her and buried his head in her thick black hair and started to cry as well. Where was God in this awful situation? It seemed that their son was very weak and even though he was under doctor's care, this didn't guarantee his recovery. He felt so bewildered, sad, and even frustrated because there was nothing he could do for his young son.

CHAPTER
Five

Two days later, young Cole Jacob was restless and feverish. He was awakened by the discomfort and pain in his abdomen. Suddenly, a brilliant light and a strong presence came into his hospital room. He looked at the end of his bed and saw a figure standing there watching him in the darkened room. He wondered if he was dreaming and yet, the figure didn't appear to pose a threat to him so he relaxed and watched the tall ethereal figure that was literally surrounded in a glowing light. The angelic presence, standing magnificently at the foot of his bed, appeared to be wearing mostly white clothing which captured his attention. The rather unusual, intriguing figure looked at him with a gentle countenance that seemed to radiate an aura of peacefulness as this individual stood there only a foot from his bed. He thought that if he blinked or closed his eyes for a moment the large presence might disappear and so he kept his eyes transfixed on the dynamic individual. He moved his hands ever so slightly as he waited for the angelic being to say something. The dazzling figure came closer and placed one large hand on the boy's chest and the other hand upon his painful stomach area. Cole winched at first, but then he felt a strong heat radiating from the hands of this angelic figure. Suddenly, it felt as if the same warm heat was moving gently into his abdomen and chest cavity. Gradually, the warmth from the angel's hands became hot and it frightened him a little. Then this unusual visitor spoke directly to him.

Cole, you will get well. God has a good plan for your life. One day you will help someone who needs you and then you will understand this: your purpose in the future will involve helping those who need your excellent protection.

Young Cole, or C.J. as his family called him, considered the intriguing phrases as he thought about the word 'purpose'. He was not familiar with this word or how it might apply to his life and so he concentrated on this new feeling of peace which seemed to permeate his entire being. Did this unique individual with such a marvelous presence have the power to remove pain and a fever from his body? Who was this stranger and how did he get access to his hospital room at night? He wished that the angelic presence would return and stay with him through the night. Then while lying in the bed he had an open vision. In this new scene which moved like a video clip before his eyes, he saw a boy with brown hair wearing strange clothing and walking on a glowing long pathway which seemed to stretched out in front of him. The boy in the vision turned back to wave and smile at him before continuing to walk on the strange glistening pathway which seemed to travel up through the star-lit sky towards a bigger, brighter star- shaped planet. Then the celestial vision ended. He lay there transfixed by this unusual sight and he wondered what it all meant. Did the boy going on that unusual pathway towards the stars represent him he wondered? A special atmosphere of peace and tranquility permeated his darkened room and then ten minutes later he realized his body felt cooler and there was no pain when he moved or shifted his weight. Moments after this new experience, Cole fell asleep without any trouble. When he woke up the next morning he called out for someone to bring him some breakfast because he was feeling hungry. The nurse on duty came into his room and checked his temperature. It was normal, 98.6 so she went to wake up his mother who was sleeping soundly in a room next to his.

"What's wrong? Is my son's fever getting worse?" Rebecca questioned.

"Surprisingly the answer is no. He's doing much better this morning and I will inform the doctor about this new development. If you'd like we can see about giving your son a small cup of warm broth first and then in another hour or so he can try a protein drink. We will watch and see how his stomach handles the liquid first before giving him solid food. The doctor isn't scheduled to examine your son until nine-thirty this morning. That's when he starts his normal rounds here." The nurse mentioned.

"That's so good to hear. I can imagine he'd like to eat something since he's saying that he's hungry." Rebecca stated.

Within the hour, the doctor entered Cole's room after learning of the remarkable change in his temperature. Normally, it takes a week or so for a person's system to recover from pneumonia the nurse had informed Rebecca earlier. Along with this astounding fact, the doctor also was amazed that when he placed his hands on the boy's stomach and intestines there had been no complaints of pain or distress from the lad. The doctor asked Rebecca to step outside so he could talk with her.

"I want to run one more blood test and also take another x-ray of your son's lungs to be sure everything is normal before we talk about stopping the chemotherapy treatment. I am amazed at his sudden recovery." The doctor informed her.

Rebecca called her husband first to give him the doctor's report. Then she called her two sisters and left a message on their phones. The next day, her sister, Cathy, called her to find out more details about her nephew's apparent recovery.

"Tell me again what the doctor has said about my nephew!"

"Well, he wants to run another test to try to rule out any other hidden problems, but Cole has no apparent signs of discomfort or pain. The fever is completely gone too. The doctor wants to have a second x-ray taken of his lungs to determine if there is no residual infection still lingering there. He doesn't understand what has happened with our son, but he believes the second ultra sound test of his abdomen will show him something conclusive. Plus, the x-ray of his chest will show us what is going on in his lungs."

"Well, I am hoping this is the miracle we have been asking the good Lord for." her sister declared.

"Oh for sure! You know after Matt and I'd prayed for C.J., this unusual peace came over me. I felt like I could believe that he would recover from the pneumonia and that he'd eventually walk out of this hospital before long. Is that a weird thing for me to say? I mean everything seems so negative for our son's health three days ago and now the doctor isn't even discussing the plan to do a surgery to remove the malignant tumor. I had been feeling nothing but despair and turmoil for the last three weeks and as of this afternoon; I'm feeling so relieved and hopeful again."

"I feel the same way you do, Rebecca. I have been making a statement of faith that C.J. will recover completely and maybe this is a miracle from heaven." Cathy exclaimed enthusiastically.

"Oh and you may not believe this, but Cole said something rather unusual to me. After the doctor had left his room, he informed me that he was visited by an individual and he saw a bright light around this person standing next to his bed. He informed me that this tall figure moved closer and then laid his hands on Cole's stomach and chest. After the visitor left, he became aware of a strange sensation emanating throughout his body and surprisingly, all the pain, fever, and weakness left him. After this short visit, this person or heavenly figure disappeared. Do you believe he really had an encounter with an angel like he is saying?" Rebecca queried.

"Well, it's quite possible. I've been told that angels are messengers of God sent to earth to protect children and to help assist those who chose to believe in God's divine plan."

"Well, I certainly don't believe that my son would tell me a tall tale about a stranger who entered his room last night and spoke to him. All I know is that I must've sleep through it all. I wished I could've seen this heavenly visitation. He believes that an angel touched him and healing occurred during that unusual visit. Can you believe this? I guess we will have to wait and see what the test results show us." Rebecca declared.

Three days later, the doctor confirmed what young Cole already knew which was that he was completely healed from the malignant tumor in his stomach as well as the serious infection in his body and lungs. They said the cancer was in remission and they would proceed with the plans to release him from the hospital within the week if his body continued to show no signs of infection. Each time the doctor pressed his hand on Cole's stomach or abdomen there was no apparent discomfort or complaint which astounded the medical team. Learning that her nephew's lungs were clear of fluids or pneumonia gave her reason to rejoice. Her sister had also mentioned that the doctor planned to keep a watchful eye on his vital signs and blood levels for the next few days, but for the first time since Cole had been admitted to the hospital, the family could relax and feel excited about the idea that they'd be taking their him home to rest. This was great news! Aunt Cathy was ecstatic over this new development. She in turn called her other sister, Debbie, and shared the good news with her. They talked about having a homecoming party for their nephew once he was settled in his own bedroom and familiar surroundings. Together the two sisters laughed and rejoiced at hearing such good news.

CHAPTER
Six

I t was an overcast day in this part of the world and the sun was hiding behind an ominous grey cloud cover. This region has been known to produce a strong wind that comes from the northeast and it would probably blow the clouds away by noon he reminded himself. Either way, Jake wasn't looking forward to another scorching day like yesterday. However, the temperature was expected to climb steadily into the high 90s by Saturday and he wished he could leave the area before then. The forecast was the least of his worries as he guided their newest recruit, Blue Boy', along the sun-baked dirt road in this god-forsaken region. This new canine needed another week of practice drills before he handed the animal over to the soldier taking his place for four days. Jake gave the dog another pat on its head as he refocused his attention on the section of highway ahead. He took his helmet off for a moment as he listened to the rumbling noise of the heavy military vehicle coming down the road. The transport vehicle sounded like the noise of a B 787 taxing down the runway as it readied for lift off. He replaced his helmet onto his head and sighed deeply. It was the year 2004, and the place where Jake had been reassigned for the last part of his tour of duty had been under siege for months.

Jake was now a part of the war time solution to protect his country's national security. Nearly three years prior to this, America had been attacked in 2001, and now they were at war with the Taliban forces in the region. Jake was hoping to have this bomb sniffing dog ready to work with Private Johnson before leaving for his R & R trip in three days. He knew that a weekend stay in Kuwait would be much better therapy for his sleep problems as well as his nerves. And that's why he'd agreed with his captain to go there instead of to Kandahar. He needed to get away for a few days of rest and relaxation and where there wouldn't be any conflict or a militant strike on one of the American convoys. Last month when one group was scouting a new area, that team had to turn around when some insurgent's fired a rocket launcher at them. Luckily this time, the missile had struck more of the ground than the supply truck that day. Fortunately, no US soldiers were injured in this incident as the driver sped away. However, Jake knew that if they didn't locate this small group of militants they could suffer from a second attack in the future.

He needed a break from the war zone if he was going to make it for the next six months of his stay in this desert environment. He wiped his brow with the sleeve of his camouflage shirt and then reached back up to scratch his sweaty neck. Sgt. Jake Walker was a tall man of six feet with wavy black hair and piercing blue-grey eyes. Those who knew the sergeant spoke well of him and said that he had a confidence and strength about him. He wasn't aware of what the other men were saying about him because he kept to himself mostly ever since the death of his good friends, Josh Harrison and Micah Anders. Josh and he had been making plans to work together after their tour was finished and they'd been back stateside for good. That plan would not happen now and he was still miserable and angry about his friend's deaths. He was much more hesitant to make close friends after this. Walker shifted his body weight to one foot briefly as he studied the terrain to the right side of the town. He felt uneasy about the lack of activity in the nearby shops as they passed the last intersection of town. Trying to shake off a foreboding feeling, he adjusted his M-16 on his left shoulder and pulled on the dog's leash to speed up the pace until they were ten yards ahead of the vehicle. His mind reverted back once more to the rumbling of the Humvee motor and its heavy tires as it rolled across the sun-baked road just ten miles out from the center of the town of Fallujah in Afghanistan. So far he hadn't seen anything to disturb the quiet morning travel and he was starting to wish he had a nice hot cup of coffee to placate his growling stomach noises.

Within moments of passing a local mercantile shop situated next to a larger abandoned building, Sgt. Walker sensed his bomb sniffing dog begin to strain on his leather leash. Blue Boy' move forward with his nose to the ground and then he barked at the man sitting in front of a small shop fifty yards from the side of the road. The dog strained on his lease and pulled as if to drag his partner with him. It felt as if Jake suddenly had a large steelhead hooked on his line ready to run on ahead of him as the line whizzed out from his fishing reel. He recalled the thrill of fighting against his first determined fish's powerful tug on his wet line. Smiling at the youthful memory, he wanted to be back fishing on Soule Lake near his Uncle Henry's favorite outdoor spot instead of guiding the bomb-sniffing dog in areas where IEDs might be planted. It was his job to locate any potential dangers and prevent serious damage to their vehicles and that's what he'd do today.

"Hey Sarge, what does your new canine smell this time?" Private Hodges asked as he stopped walking and turned towards the dog. "Does he always bark at the local Afghani's?" The private loosened his helmet strap and pushed the front edge of his helmet up above his forehead to wipe the dust and grime away. "Yesterday the only thing this canine recruit found was a pile of metal and old shrapnel pieces some kid must've hidden in the ground as a decoy." The soldier stated glumly.

"No Private First Class Hodges, Blue Boy' does not bark at everything that he sees. Just keep your eyes peeled for insurgents behind those nearby buildings while I inspect this section of the road a little closer. Blue boy is getting to be a reliable source in finding bombs so quit making fun of his nose or the wasted time digging up decoys. We can never be too cautious when checking for IED's. Even if we've cleaned up a road heading out of town, they can still plant another bomb within thirty feet of the last site." Jake Walker stated as he turned his thoughts back to the task at hand.

Sergeant Walker radioed his driver and crew to halt briefly while he checked the ground to see if it had been recently dug up by the local insurgents. Then he motioned to Private Hodges to come up next to him. The twenty- year old Marine hustled up to await the next orders.

"Hodges, grab that white rod that has an orange flag attached to it. The one we use to mark an area. It's inside the side panel of the Humvee. Plus, we need the tape measure I showed you to use for this task. After you've done that wait for the next crew to come along and remind him to dig at least four feet away from the center of this flagged spot." He said.

"Yes sir." Private Hodges ran over to the vehicle and hustled back to the section of the road needing to be properly secured at that spot. The soldier began his task of placing the slender white rod carefully into the ground and then he measured off the area correctly. Sgt. Walker strode briskly with his canine partner towards the back end of the vehicle and loosely wrapped the dog's leash to the bumper of the military vehicle. He then ordered the canine to sit and wait for him there. Next, he radioed the transport driver, Private Anthony Rizzo, to roll ahead a few more feet and wait until he gave further instructions. Jake rubbed his hand across his two day old stubble of beard growth and then without giving any thought to his long time habit, he tightened his helmet strap to make sure it was secured better. This small act was something he did unconsciously each time before calling to report a possible roadside bomb.

The sun had burnt off the thin layer of cloud formation and the intense heat was radiating off of his helmet and sunglasses. As he stood in the road watching the young soldier in the process of marking a site, he remembered another day when he'd been stationed near Kandahar some months before his assignment to this region. At that time he'd been teaching a group how to clear a site some two miles outside of their base camp. This area had been designated as a place where the military set up fake land mines and improperly disguised IED locations. Since this designated sector was set aside for mainly training purposes, it was considered a safe enough area for the military to teach the men how to spot, stake out, and dismantle or blow up fake land mines. There were armed soldiers posted at different locations around the perimeter of that site and the unit had learned the methods quickly.

The last day of training, Jake had awoken with a throbbing headache and he'd been ordered to stay back at base camp to rest and then to help get things ready for new recruits coming in later that afternoon. He grumbled about this change in plans, but he knew that potentially his headache could turn into a nasty migraine and so he complied begrudgingly.

Later on that same fateful morning, Jake felt another stabbing pain pulsated through his neck and head area making him feel nauseated. Rather than risk the chance of heaving up his breakfast, he'd asked permission to stop and go lay down for an hour. Not getting much relief, Walker reached into his backpack to grab a few more Advil pills, swallowed them with a swig of bottled water, and then put on his shirt and boots to rejoin the work crew who were getting some further instructions from Cpt. Dan Reynolds. He knew that their team's bomb sniffing dog, 'Tank, was in the capable hands of Private first class Johnson for that day's mission. His good buddy, Harrison, had been sitting up topside manning the vehicle's machine gun when the team left the camp so Jake was confident they'd be able to handle any kind of trouble. Harrison had been in his same unit during the six months of boot camp and they'd quickly become fast friends. After that initial training time, they had both been deployed to the same area near Kandahar. They'd usually spent their days off playing poker, shooting hoops or tossing a football around with a few other guys such as Anders, Johnson, and Rhyker from their unit. He'd do anything for his buddies, but on this day his CO hadn't released him to go with his group and for some odd reason this had disturbed him.

His mind went back again to that day in February and how he'd felt apprehensive about his buddies leaving without him on that particular mission. An hour after they'd departed from the base camp, he recalled hearing the faint sound of an explosion some distance from the compound. The thing they'd all dreaded had happened. Feeling that annoying pain again in his gut, Jake had stopped what he'd been doing and raced over to his tent to retrieve a PRC-126 two-way radio. He'd turned it on and set the dial to the correct frequency in order to listen to the chatter. It sounded as if something had been hit by either a rocket launcher or an IED bomb placed beneath the road surface by the local insurgents. He wondered if the intense pain in his stomach was his body's way of trying to get his attention. His grandmother had once said that she'd get awful pains in her stomach if one of her children was in serious danger. She'd learned to pray fervently for their safety and she was always rewarded by her heavenly Father. Could this headache and stomach pain be similar to that unusual way of reminding him to pray for his friend's safety? Sadly, Jake had ignored this type of warning discomfort.

Now a certain unexplainable fear was gripping him as he wondered what kind of trouble was facing his unit. He'd turned the small radio volume up higher as he grimaced again from the pain in his stomach. Back then he remembered wondering if he'd suffered from bad mess hall food, but now he attributed it to the sense of an impending attack on his fellow soldiers. Jake dreaded hearing that his friend, Josh Harrison, and their unit had been involved in a surprise sniper attack. He'd agonized over those worrisome thoughts as he'd waited back at the base camp and tried to stay busy.

At the present moment, Jake Walker toke a swig of water from his canteen, shook his head in an effort to clear it of the sad losses. Unfortunately, the distinct memories continued to replay in his mind about what had actually transpired that day. Back then he'd learned that the vehicle located in the western section of the village had hit a bomb device planted in the road and it had caught fire! He knew they'd be requesting a medic and the rescue team to rush to some four mile past the city's checkpoint site. He'd felt a strong urge to leave the training grounds and catch a ride to join the fight, but instead, he'd gone to ask for permission to use a jeep to go help his unit. Lt. Reynolds had listened to his request and then briskly ordered Jake to go back to his tent and wait there for further information. He'd promised Walker that he'd personally attend to this matter and get back to him as soon as he found out more about the action and situation.

Jake recalled how anxiously he'd waited that day as he paced inside and out of his tent until he'd finally seen the officer's jeep pull back into camp in a cloud of dust and dirt. He headed over to question the driver and the officer about the incident.

"Walker, I'm sorry to inform you that two men from your unit were killed in the explosion. The driver, Private First Class Anders and another soldier named Harrison who was manning the turret gun on top didn't make it. Sgt. Jed Williams was wounded, but he is alive. He was the one who'd managed to radio the information over to headquarters to tell us about the IED hit. He'd been walking behind the vehicle and so he survived the initial blast and fire explosion."

"What about Private Johnson and his canine companion named Tank, Sir?" Jake asked anxiously. They were supposed to be walking on one side of the truck as it headed out of camp and maybe they were spared any serious injury."

"From what I could learn from the medical guys helping this team, I was informed that the foot soldier was injured by some metal shards and shrapnel flying through the air. He is in the medic unit now in critical condition. Apparently, the bomb-detecting canine died on the scene. Walker, I'm truly sorry for your loss. It's a rotten war, soldier!

Lt. Reynolds placed his hand on Walker's shoulder for a brief moment and then gripped him firmly as if to impart some fortitude into him. Then the captain spoke from the depths of his own aching soul. "I understand your grief concerning this recent attack and our losses, Walker. We will need to make a request for another dog to replace this canine loss. This will take two weeks I imagine. We will need to figure out a different route out of camp to prevent this kind of tragedy from happening again. I know I can count on you doing your best to take Johnson's place on this team in the weeks to come, but for now, get some rest. I need you to take charge of your men tomorrow so try to get plenty of sleep tonight, soldier."

"Yes, Sir, I will try. I think I should stop by the Mash Unit after dinner to request a sleeping pill from the doctor." He said.

Walker turned reluctantly back around to head over to his tent where once inside and by himself, he'd sat down on his army cot as the news began to sink in. He remembered distinctly placing his head in his hands and groaning as he'd tried to fight back the waves of sadness and disbelief enveloping his soul. He'd found it difficult to believe that he had lost his two buddies. Finally, overcome with the reality of his friend's deaths Walker had lost control of his emotions as he expressed a few angry curse words and then let out a harsh yell of agony. He'd dropped to his knees on the ground as his mind reeled from the reality of this wartime loss. He would never laugh or talk with his good buddies again. They'd never again drink a cold beer to celebrate a victory on or off the court. A feeling of despair seemed to rumble inside of him and then without any warning, his chest muscles began to shake with heavy convulsions of intense emotions until he bent over and shook with overwhelming sorrow. A few soldiers milling outside could hear his muffled cries of anguish coming from inside the tent so they chose to remain on the perimeter smoking or talking quietly. After some time, he'd fallen into a restless sleep on the floor next to his army cot. The men who came inside the tent that night left him where he lay knowing it was best to not try to wake him.

Jake's mind went back to how he'd woke up in the pitch black tent and stumbled back into his cot in a stupor where he'd slept until dawn. That grievous loss had left a bitter taste in his mouth and a determination to get restitution against those who taken the lives of his friends. As the weeks went by, Jake learned something new when his superior officer required him to talk to their company chaplain. He learned that day that he was suffering from what his chaplain referred to as 'survivor guilt'. In other words, the person who didn't die with the others felt like they should've died and they can't explain their feelings or extreme grief to even themselves. Jake had done his best to stuff his feelings and forge ahead by doing his duty ever since the death of his two buddies. The only way he knew to do this was to focus his time in Afghanistan on just one objective: taking out the enemy with a vengeance. And yet, the memories of that fateful day with its tremendous losses continued to plague him. Try as he might, nothing seemed to alleviate the flashbacks or the nightmares now taking over his dismal life. He felt alone in this struggle to maintain his peace of mind and any hope of surviving this war.

CHAPTER
Seven

S gt. Walker shifted his attention back to the present. He needed to keep a watchful eye on the soldier as the man poked and prodded the dry ground with a metal rod. He rubbed his eyes in an effort to clear his head from the past memory of losing his two buddies during a conflict. Jake was still dealing with the fact that he was alive because he'd stayed back at the base camp that fateful day when his unit had been attacked. However, nothing had prepared him for the constant feelings of guilt and remorse. If he'd gone on the mission with his buddies, maybe he could've prevented their deaths somehow. In order to lead the next mission, he'd been told by his CO that he had to attend two more sessions with Chaplain James Herron. Back then Jake had made significant progress by meeting with the chaplain and working on his feelings of grief or what the chaplain had called 'survivor's guilt'. He was grateful to the chaplain for his wisdom and the reality check. He was also glad when the commander had finally released him to rejoin his unit for the next assignment. Jake didn't like sitting around camp; he needed to be back in active duty to be happy. For the remainder of his time in Afghanistan, he'd made an effort to hide his feelings. He used his alone times to curse at the insurgents and Taliban forces. This always made him feel better.

Walker shifted his weight from the left foot to his right as he attempted to focus his attention back to the present and the mission at hand. His buddies were gone and there was no amount of wishful thinking that could bring them back. He recalled his CO sprouting off a weird quote from someone which was almost funny. "A bad attitude is like a flat tire. If you don't change it, you'll never go anywhere." Well, he knew he wanted his lousy attitude to change for the better. He realized that his moodiness was unhealthy. His anger had made him feel nothing but hatred for the enemy and for this desolate dry land he found himself stuck in for way too long! It was becoming more apparent that he had to get rid of his irritableness and quick temper. In fact, one day he'd found himself cussing out a young recruit for something trivial. Suddenly, Walker's radio crackled with a slight vibrating noise and then he heard the driver, twenty-two year old Anthony Rizzo from Yonkers, New York talking on the two-way radio.

"It's getting hot inside this steel bucket of bolts! Is Hodges finished with his task out there?"

"Okay, Rizzo, keep your shirt on. Hold your position for two more minutes until Hodges has finished marking the probable bomb site." The sergeant barked back.

Walker would need to check Hodges work as well and remind the next team due to arrive shortly to be sure and dig approximately four feet away from the center rod with the orange flag. He scanned the horizon of low rolling foothills looking for any sign of danger. Seeing nothing, he then barked another order to Private Hodges about the safety measures and reached down to pat 'Blue Boy' on the head. He'd come to rely on this Blue Heeler dog more and more with each passing day.

He'd promised his canine partner, Blue Boy', a handful of doggie treats once they'd returned to the military compound. The next thing he did was to turn and observe the few Afghani men who'd come out of the coffee shop to watch his unit's activities. Neither of the locales had weapons in their hands so he turned to move towards the front of the vehicle to holler another order to the foot soldier. Suddenly a gun shot rang out which shattered the eerie silence of that day. Then simultaneously, more bullets struck the glass windows of the vehicle, the side panel, and a back tire causing the vehicle to jerk and falter as the tire slowly deflated. Walker hit the harden ground and initiated a fast army crawl in the dirt until he'd reached the backside of the vehicle. With the humvee's as a barrier, he could stand up to move around and reach over to pull the dog's leash free from the back bumper. He swore under his breath as he loosened the rope and pulled the dog closer to him. As he considered the situation briefly, he made a quick decision to move away from the military vehicle.

Jake Walker ordered Blue Boy to come with him as he hustled over to crouch behind a chipped plaster wall that was connected to an adjoining building. Sgt. Walker turned his head to watch the driver turn the vehicle sharply to the left to avoid hitting Private Hodges who was now lying face down in the road. As Walker glanced back again, he could tell that the point man was seriously injured and bleeding from one or more gunshot wounds. He stayed where he was next to the wall as he watched Rizzo put the vehicle into gear to move ahead three feet and out of the direct line of fire from the insurgents situated inside of a large two story building. Then a Marine inside of the Humvee began to return fire through a gun port opening.

Realizing they might get pinned down by possible crossfire, Walker called for backup and gave them his position and coordinates. "We got a man down and we're receiving gunfire. We need a medic here now!" Once Jake had radioed his demands to headquarters, he turned the channel of his radio to shout a demand to the driver inside of the vehicle.

"Get out of the Humvee now! And tell the guy who is with you to stop firing and evacuate the vehicle too! That's an order, private!" Sgt. Walker growled into his radio set.

Throwing open his door, Private First Class Rizzo scrambled out of the vehicle and knelt beside the injured man. He grabbed a pant leg to pull the wounded Hodges around to the other side of the vehicle. Then Rizzo was joined by the other Marine who'd managed to scramble out of the vehicle and Sgt. Walker could hear the driver instruct this same soldier to return fire while he examined Private Hodges injuries. Rizzo bent down to access Hodges' injuries and discovered that one bullet had hit the soldier just below the collar bone area while a second bullet had tore into his upper leg. It was becoming apparent to the Rizzo that the sniper's bullet may've hit a main artery in the soldier's thigh and the man could lose more blood if they didn't do something soon. Looking around for something other than his own thick shirt material, Rizzo's hand grazed his own belt buckle. Jake turned away from firing his rifle for a minute to glance over as Private Rizzo quickly pulled the leather belt out of the loops of his military grade pants, wrapped it around the top portion of Hodges leg, and then clinched it tight just above the open wound in order to stop the blood flow.

As Sgt. Walker fired off two more rounds at the militants, he glanced back towards the Humvee to suddenly notice a lone Marine in a vulnerable position with his hands gripping the machine gun and firing still. Knowing that this soldier was partially exposed to enemy gunfire, Walker shouted at the man.

"Rhyker, get out of there before they blow this stalled vehicle to bits with you in it!" He demanded.

"Alright, I'm coming." Nick Rhyker yelled.

Nervously he stood up to see Rhyker release his hold on the turret machine gun and then slide down off the side of the vehicle. Sgt. Walker continued giving fire coverage for his team as he aimed at the main target building across the way. Meanwhile, Rhyker knelt down beside the others as he pulled his handgun out of his belt to defend himself. The team could hear the second unit arriving some fifteen yards back from them on the same dirt road.

"The transport truck and medic has arrived. We need to move this injured man and fast or he's going to die here." Rhyker informed the men.

"Yeah, let's do it, I'll grab his shirt at the shoulders and pull him while you give us enough cover to make it to the other vehicle. Go! Go now!" Private Anthony Rizzo growled with an emphasis on the word, NOW.

Rhyker reached down with one hand and grabbed the injured soldier's backpack to help lift him as he unloaded his handgun at the militants emerging from the smaller building. Fortunately for the Americans, the insurgents stopped firing and quickly retreated back inside of the open doorway.

The driver and the one soldier who'd escaped from inside of the Humvee were able to hustle to safety as they crouched down behind the second transport truck. The medics yelled from inside the back end of the transport to lift the injured man up and slide him over so they could hook him up to the IV line. Rizzo stayed there to protect the medical team in case any attackers decided to head towards their location. Nick Rhyker hastened along the plaster wall to where he'd last seen the sergeant standing. Upon reaching the mercantile store, he slipped inside to locate an access door. After a few moments, he was able to join the sergeant who was preparing to enter the abandoned building across the way.

During those few minutes, Walker had spotted the glint of a rifle barrel protruding from an open window on the second floor of a taller building just across the cobblestone alley. From his position he couldn't draw a bead on anyone who might decide to poke their head out the window. Reaching into his backpack, he grabbed a hand grenade and pulled the pin to activate the small device. Then he stepped outside of the doorway and threw the grenade with all his strength in order to send it up towards the specific target. The grenade sailed through the air and landed inside the building with an explosive force. After hearing the blast there was complete silence and Walker smiled at his success in silencing that particular enemy fire.

Sgt. Walker grabbed the leash of the Blue Heeler dog and signaled to Nick Rhyker to follow him as they advanced further into the shadowy alleyway. Walker signaled his intentions to go first and scout out the upper level where the gunfire had first erupted. Private Rhyker followed behind within seconds of hearing the all-important word, 'CLEAR'. In the background they could hear Anthony Rizzo firing his weapon at the Afghani's intent on shooting a couple of Marines seen moving around the second military vehicle. The militants figured they were safe in their fortified position on the second floor of that taller building. With another surge of rapid-fire gunshots from the M-16s and Russian made rifles, the militants were attempting to pin the American soldiers down. Jake and Rhyker could hear the enemy firing above them as they cautiously proceeded up the final steps leading to an open hallway. Sgt. Walker held the dog's leash firmly in his left hand as they both proceeded stealthily towards the sound of gunfire. Upon reaching the top of the stair well, Walker raised his hand to indicate a pause and then he inched his head around the corner to look for any movement ahead.

Fortunately for these two Marines, there was no one guarding the hallway so they move cautiously towards the first doorframe. Walker waited while his dog sniffed at that door and when the animal's sensitive ears didn't pick up any sound of movement in that room, the canine continued forward. The Marines heard nothing to alert them at that first doorway and so Jake motioned to his companion to check it. The Marine slowly turned the door knob and looked inside to see only a dead terrorist lying slumped next to the open window. This must've been the guy who was killed by the recently tossed hand grenade. Seeing no other person in that first room, they carefully and quietly approached the next door frame in the same long hallway.

Sgt. Walker gripped the dog's restraint leash in his gun hand while giving a specific signal to let Rhyker know his plan. He pointed with two fingers down towards the floor to signify that he was intending to go low through the open doorway and thus, Rhyker would be firing from a normal stance once they both found their intended targets. He looked in through the open doorway to see the interior of the room which contained a handful of militants. The sergeant quietly unclipped the leash from the dog's collar and pushed on the canine's head to signal for the animal to attack the nearest Afghani soldier. The well-trained animal made a short run into the room and then lunged at the unsuspecting individual from behind. The Afghani man almost lost his footing, but hastily regained his balance, turned with gun in hand to swing the muzzle at the angry canine in an effort to ward off the attack. The next thing Walker heard was the distressed soldier howling in pain as he fell backward from the impact of the dog teeth sinking deep into his flesh. Jake knew he didn't have to worry about that fallen militant as he concentrated on the other men positioned by the open window.

Within seconds of releasing his canine partner to attack the one militant, Walker slid low onto the wooden floor as he aimed his weapon. Jake fired a shot at the man crouched near the window and since the unsuspecting Afghani was facing away from the Americans, he wasn't able to turn in time to fire back at the Marines. The man's rifle went off as his finger pressed down on the trigger mechanism sending random bullets into the floor boards. Then he slumped down onto the hard floor in a motionless heap. Next, Sgt. Walker aimed at the other upright Taliban soldier just as he was turning around to fire back at him. Walker's shots hit the man in the torso and a second bullet tore into the man's head sending his weapon crashing to the floor.

Nick Rhyker moved around the door frame with his rifle aimed towards the right side of the room where two other militant were located. The Marine pulled the trigger of his M16 twice and scored a successful hit. The one Afghani man wearing a dirty, grey turban and linen clothing jerked twice from the bullets slamming into his chest area and then his body fell backwards into the wall. His lifeless body slid slowly down onto the floor and lay there not moving. The second Afghani man quickly overturned the table and crouched down behind it. He stuck his AK-47 weapon around the end of the table and managed to get off a shot which hit Rhyker who had stepped inside the room. The insurgent's bullet hit Rhyker squarely in his upper chest area sending him spinning around and backwards through the same doorway. The insurgent's bullet had entered and exited his flesh leaving a hole the size of a golf ball in his back shoulder muscle. Walker could hear his team member cursing loudly as he tried to kick his boots against the wooden floor for traction in an effort to slide backwards into the hallway and out of the line of fire.

At the very exact moment that Rhyker's rifle blasted the first individual sitting at the table, Walker was aiming and firing his weapon at the other Afghani man kneeling down in front of a second open window. At exactly that same instance, the Afghani man had pulled the trigger mechanism on the rocket launcher positioned over his right shoulder. Walker's shot must've made a direct shot to his heart because the man died instantly, but he could hear the small rocket leaving the thick metal tubing of the elongated weapon and he could see the fiery evidence of the blast as the missile shot forth from the thick barrel of the sinister weapon. Jake's brain knew that the trajectory of the intended missile was headed for the stalled vehicle situated down below on the dirt road. Turning his attention and his M-16 weapon quickly in the direction of the final insurgent who was attempting to pick up and load the rocket launcher to aim it at the doorway, Sgt. Walker fired twice killing that insurgent before he could fire the heavy weapon resting on his shoulder. The rocket launcher crashed to the floor with a resounding thud; now the only sound in that room was the moans of pain coming from the injured Afghani man being held down by the dog. The other Afghani fighter was still hiding behind the overturned table as he waited for the right moment to stand up and fire his weapon.

Within seconds of taking out the two militants by the open windows, Walker had been able to slide to the right and squeezed the rifle's trigger three times sending multiple slugs through the wooden table barrier. One of his bullets had luckily struck the man crouched down hiding behind the table and in that next instant he heard a loud groan of pain emit from the wounded militant. The room was quiet except for the Afghani man who could be heard uttering a few choice words in another language. Walker ignored this individual as he scanned the room for any more movements, but the room was quiet now.

The man who'd shot Rhyker was slightly visible since his one leg was now protruding from the end of the table. Jake held his M16 pointed towards this still breathing individual as he approached the overturned table barrier. Then he kicked the man's weapon across the floor as his finger still held onto the trigger of his rifle. The Marine was contemplating finishing the job, but then he eased up on the trigger and instead he reached into his backpack for a zip tie to secure the injured man's wrists. The sergeant figured they could transport the guy as a prisoner back to base camp for questioning. If this guy survived the jostling in the back of the truck and the newest intern, Dr. Pelham, in the O.R. then they could force him to tell the location of his leader. He turned and crossed the room until he faced the Afghani militant being held in submission by the growling canine. He tied this militant's wrist behind his back and put a cloth gag in the man's mouth to keep him from shouting out belligerent words they couldn't understand. Then he turned back to step out into the hallway to check on the injured Marine.

"How bad is it, Rhyker?" he questioned the Marine.

"I've been hit in the upper chest area, but I'll live. I just need some morphine and fast. I can't move without a sharp pain throbbing in my chest! Dang, this pain is nasty. So this is what it feels like to be shot." Rhyker admitted.

"I'll radio in for some assistance here. In the meantime, I have a compress cloth to help staunch the blood flow. Hold on, buddy." Walker added as he reached into his front pocket of his jacket and pulled out some clean gauze pad. He ripped open the packet and placed the gauze directly over the open wound and then laid the extra thick compress pad on top of the gauze. Taking the injured man's hand, he placed it on top of the compress with some instructions.

"Keep the pressure on your wound until the medic gets here with more first-aid stuff." Sgt. Walker said.

"Okay, but tell them to hurry with the pain killer!"

"I need to check outside the window to see exactly where that blasted RPG missile landed a few minutes ago. The Afghani got off his shot before I could stop him."

He strode over to the open window and glanced outside and down towards the road some thirty yards away. He could see the damaged done by the RPG hit. The Humvee was incased with flames and smoke. It didn't look good.

"Well, they hit another one of our vehicles and its disabled. Son of a gun! I want all these weapons and this missile launcher carried back to our base camp. I'd like to blow up their hideout as soon as we figure out where these blasted militants are located in the hills. I'm going to title our next plan of attack, 'Shock and Awe' from the good ole USA!" He said." Then clicking the button on his hand-held radio, he called through to the man in charge of the transport vehicle as he moved closer to the open window.

"This is Sgt. Walker; I need you to send a medic and another soldier up here where you see me standing by the second-floor window. Can you see my arm waving? Let me know if you have located my position?" He said.

"Yes, Sir, we can see you up their now. I'm sending two men to help assist you promptly."

"Great, I appreciate your help." Walker replied.

When the medic and the soldier carrying a stretcher showed up in the hallway, they approached the fallen soldier. The medic assessed the Marine's wound and began working on him while giving him some morphine for the pain. Then he moved over to work on the injured Afghani in order to stop the bleeding long enough for them to get him ready to move downstairs.

"What's your name, soldier?" Jake asked the young Marine standing nearby.

"Private Jamieson, sir."

"Okay, Private Jamieson, stay put here and hand me your water canteen." He demanded.

Jake set his M16 against the wall and took a swig of water from the young soldier's canteen. Then he clicked on the radio set again and made a second request.

"This is Sgt. Walker again. I need you to send another Marine up her with a second stretcher for a wounded Afghani prisoner." He clicked the radio off and went back to check on the injured Marine again.

Once the wounded Rhyker had been laid on the first stretcher, Sgt. Walker barked out an order to Private Jamieson and the medic to be sure and walk slowly down the stairs to not jar this soldier until the reached ground level. Next, he called his dog to his side and jerked the one remaining Afghani man to his feet and dragged him towards the end of the hall where he met two more soldiers heading up the stairs. Walker shoved the last Afghan onto the floor while he talked with the Marines waiting for instructions.

"Private Anderson, I need you to secure this entire building and report back to me immediately."

"Yes, sir!" The Marine hustled off with his rifle held securely in his arms and ready for action in case there were any other militants hiding in the building.

What's your name, young man?" Jake asked the Marine standing in the hallway.

"Private Michael Jeffreys, Sir." He responded.

"Private, I need you to go into the second room on the right behind us and gather up all of the weapons to take them down to our truck. Then I want you to handle moving this last prisoner into a jeep to be hauled back to camp for interrogation as soon as you men check his restraints." He said.

"Sgt. Walker took a deep breath and smiled for the first time since engaging with the enemy. Taking one more deep breath into his lungs, he bent down to pat his well-trained canine animal on the head. The dog responded with a few wags of its tail. Sgt. Walker bent down to grab hold of the one remaining insurgent individual slumped down on the floor. The man's arm was bleeding from the dog's sharp teeth bite, but that injury was of no real concern to him. He merely double -checked the Afghani soldier's wrist to make sure they were still secured tight enough. Jake waited while the other Marine picked up the discarded rifles and rocket launcher and together they marched the insolent prisoner downstairs and shoved him into a military jeep.

"Good boy, good dog! I wouldn't have sent you into that mess of vipers normally, but this time, there were too many of them and I needed your help. Maybe next time, Blue', you'll get a chance to sink your canine teeth into one of the Taliban's meaty, hairy legs!"

The dog barked in response and wagged his tail as if the animal was happy to be of service. Jake rubbed the dog's head and backside in an effort to show his appreciation to the canine. Then he held the animal's leather leash in his left hand as he went in search of bottled water hoping someone had thought to pack them in the second transport truck which had been untouched by the attack. He was thankful there were still a couple of workable vehicles available to transport everyone back to the camp. While the soldiers loaded the insurgents' weapons into the back of the truck, Sgt. Walker poured what was left of someone's water bottle into his hand and splashed the liquid in his face to clean the sweat and grime away.

Once everyone, as well as the wounded prisoner, had been loaded into the back of the truck, then the driver turned the vehicle around and headed back to the base camp. Jake caught a ride in the jeep after making sure everyone was accounted for first. He turned around to remind Private Jamieson to keep his handgun pointed on the other sullen prisoner in the back of the jeep to prevent the man from jumping out of the vehicle. This prisoner only had a few puncture wounds from the dog's teeth so he could certainly answer questions from the interrogator. That night Walker ate a quick meal and went over to his commander's tent to give a full report of the day's operation and his unit's losses.

CHAPTER
Eight

I t was now October of 2008, and Jake Walker had just celebrated another birthday. He was having mixed emotions about becoming a civilian again and if he should work in his Dad's small business once he reached Illinois. His father had called him on his birthday to say hi and to tell him that official paperwork had just arrived at the house with an envelope containing his honorable discharge from the US military. His six years in the Marines were finished. The following evening as he sat in Fort Jackson's main lounge room watching an NFL game on the big screen, he found himself distracted by thoughts of the time when he was playing football as a senior at Riverton High School. He wondered what his high school teammates were doing now. His father had mentioned over the phone that five of his classmates had gone into the Army two weeks after he had enlisted. His father had kept tabs on two of the guys and had been informed that they both had been killed while fighting overseas. He'd felt sorry for the loss for those two families and then he forced his mind off of the sad news and back onto the football game as he checked the recent score. He needed to keep a positive outlook on his own future. Within two days he'd be sitting in one of his favorite pub hangouts in his hometown after getting picked up from the airport by his father.

* * *

The weather had been slightly chilly the next morning as he'd went for a jog around the base. Returning to his barracks, he changed into civilian clothes and stuffed his gear into a duffle bag. Two hours later, he had smiled with joy as he walked out of the provincial office of the Marines for the last time with his few belongings and a large envelope stuffed with his stipend monies from the military. Walker took a breath of fresh air into his lungs and felt a sense of freedom. He was heading to his Dad's place for a ten day visit before flying out the northwest region to take time for a fishing trip and to check out his Uncle Henry's cabin to see what repairs were needed there. Jake Walker noticed the time on his watch which read twelve fifteen and he realized that he had just enough time to get to the airport. He called for a taxi and gave them the address. When the taxi driver showed up he climbed into the back seat with his duffle bag and instructed the driver to take him to the airport and to hurry.

As he rested his head on the back seat of the taxi, he closed his eyes for a moment and visualized the last scene of his goodbyes to the members of his Marine Corps division. Strangely, Jake recalled thinking he'd seen his dead friend's (Josh Harrison) lanky figure standing to the left of the group of men. It appeared as if the figure of his fallen friend was saluting Jake and saying his goodbyes as well. That day Jake had saluted the few remaining buddies he'd felt a close connection while stationed in Afghanistan. Then before getting into the jeep to leave, Jake Walker had decided to give another honorary salute to the fallen heroes who would never walk on American soil again in this lifetime. He rubbed his hand over his eyes and closed them again wondering if he'd imagine seeing Josh standing there among the group. The image of his fallen buddy had disappeared and he felt another wave of sadness sweep over him. Then he eyes fell on his faithful companion, Blue Boy', sitting on his haunches there in the dirt next to the Marines. It seemed to Jake as if the canine was looking at him with a resolute intensity as if to say why are you leaving me here?

This memory of Blue Boy watching him leave the base camp while remaining behind had truly managed to pierce his emotional detachment. He had felt tears welling up in his eyes which threatened to cloud his vision as he'd travelled down the dusty dirt road for the last time. That one image of his faithful canine partner barking and straining at the leash was a lasting memory for him. It was as if the animal was trying to communicate something like, 'I'm coming with you sergeant so wait for me!' That image of the forlorn canine was the main reason that Jake was determined to make one last request to his commander in the hopes of adopting this particular military dog.

* * *

Once Jake was back in the states, he'd petitioned the higher ups with his request to adopt Blue Boy' again and surprisingly some high official had signed off on this request with a YES. He smiled at the memory of the phone call days later where Captain Reynolds had informed him that they'd be sending his faithful companion, Blue Boy,' back to the states to be picked up in ten days. After he'd petitioned the military to release this particular canine, his captain had shared that he'd made a recommendation in favor of Jake. Walker believed the only reason his name had been placed on the top of the list for the opportunity to adopt this particular Blue Heeler dog was because of this captain's influence and assistance in this matter. To actually own this brilliant animal for good after the ten days were up was remarkable. The dog seemed to be healthy and active with no physical issues the last time he'd seen Blue Boy' and so he saw no reason why they'd detained this animal. He was looking forward to taking his favorite canine on a few hunting and fishing excursions in the outdoors this coming season.

He'd called his father with the time of his arrival into his hometown of Dayton and he could tell from his father's voice that the man was extremely excited to spend time with him. Walker closed his eyes for a short rest before reaching his destination. After two hours of flying, he was finally disembarking from United Airlines aircraft and heading down the terminal to grab his luggage. He could smell the freshly brewed coffee as he strode past the food court and he almost stopped to grab a drink, but hesitated. Then he decided he would wait and get his favorite brew in town. He had a hunch his dad would be waiting impatiently in the no parking zone or departure lanes which could be extremely crowded at this time of day and he needed to keep moving. Jake knew his father would be listening to popular jazz music while he sat waiting in his truck. Spotting his dad's silver truck at last, he waved and then headed towards the vehicle to throw his gear into the bed of his Chevy pickup. Climbing into the rig, he smiled and gave his father a hug and buckled his seat belt.

"It's great to see you again, son! I am grateful the military finally let you go. I thought they'd tried to encourage you to sign up for another fourteen years as an incentive to receive their pension plan." His father smiled and winked at him.

"Well, they did try to tempt me with this idea, but I chose not to stay on in case they tried to deploy me again if the war on terrorism escalated. I don't need any more stress in my life like that. I've seen enough trouble over there in Afghanistan this year. Guys lost body parts and went home broken in body and spirit. No thanks, I plan to sit around and do nothing for a couple of months and take it easy. I'm still having nightmares and insomnia at times and it feels as if I have been through the worst experience of my life!"

"I understand, son. You've been through a living hell and it can do awful things to a man. Most men who served in WWII and in the Vietnam War never wanted to talk about their experiences it seems. I've learned about some of this info from watching a documentary on returning war vets." Matt Walker stated.

"Well, war can be extremely difficult on a person and I had my fill of killing the enemy and watching my own buddies get killed in action. When our first dog, Tank' died, I saw how this loss affected the men in our unit. The guys moped around the compound for days without talking much at all. To some of the guys it was like losing a member of their own family. I think it's because they really enjoyed having the mutt around. I really got attached to the next dog named Blue Boy." Jake shared.

"Well, I can understand how they the men felt. Nobody likes to lose a companion or close buddy, especially during war times. What did you find out about your efforts to adopt the last dog you worked with in Afghanistan?" I hope you have good news to share with me." Matt remarked.

"Yes Dad, I do have some news. The military decided that Blue Boy' had served his country well and deserved to be sent home and be in my care for good. Blue had suffered some minor burns on his body from the last conflict and so he is getting his final treatment before they ship him to my new residence address in Grandview, Washington. That's a city close to Uncle Henry's place."

"Oh, that reminds me I have all the documents and the title deed to my brother's property which is situated only a mile north of the town of Randall. You need to sign some paperwork for me to leave with his lawyer, Mr. Markham, and then the cabin and land will be deeded in your name officially and will belong to you."

"Did Mr. Markham mention anything about Uncle Henry's fishing boat and trailer or his 1969' Chevy truck? I am hoping to take a few days to go fishing and I'd like to use the truck to tow his fifteen foot boat to the lake. I always feel better when I'm on the lake."

"Everything you just mentioned is still there. You might have to check the boat motor and add oil to it and then winterize the motor after your finish using it. I imagine the old truck still runs, but there again, you will have to start the engine up and let it run for a period of time, since he hasn't used it for months as well. I expect you should check the oil level on the truck too." I'm happy that you have your own place now, son, even though I wish you'd consider staying here for awhile. You could help me out by working on Wednesdays and Fridays at the self-defense business. Ever since I retired from the construction job and bought this Tai Kwando shop, I'm busier than I'd like to be. I need to either sell it or hire some young guy to run it for me. You know, with you working part-time at the business, it would add a lot more life to the team. And who knows, the younger guys might join just to see an ex-military guy like you."

"I know, Dad, but I need to spend some time alone and sort things out for myself. I think the cabin and the lake will help me get over some of the difficult stuff I had to endure while overseas."

"Sure, I understand. I'm just saying that you might think about waiting another week or so before heading to the west coast. Just to make sure that everything goes as planned in the adoption of your military dog and his papers. By the way, son, do you remember Betsy McConnell?"

"Do you mean Sara, her younger sister?"

"Yes, that's the one. Well, she asked about you the other day and I mentioned that you'd be coming here for a visit. Why don't you think about stopping in at her father's store on Main Street and take her out for chocolate swirl ice cream cone or a hot fudge sundae? It might do you some good to get back in touch with the locals and a few of your high school friends from Riverton High."

"Dad, I lost touch with Sara McConnell after I attended community college. Besides, she was always a big flirt as I recall. I heard from Mark that Betsey got married to James Harper."

"Well, I remember your mother was a flirt in high school too, but she captured my heart and I managed to eventually sweep her off her feet regardless of the other guys who were hoping to pursue her. She only had eyes for me once I'd proposed to her. I had given her a dozen red roses and an engagement ring the following year. So think about getting back into the real world again and into the dating game sometime soon. Who knows you may find a sweetheart of a gal like I did in your hometown, son."

"Okay, Dad, I'm going to meet up with Brad Harkens tonight. I asked him to meet me at Benny's Bar & Grill so we could catch up. I also was hoping to learn more about my old girlfriend Briana at the same time. In the meantime, I'll keep my eyes open for a pretty gal who can cook and balance the checkbook. Isn't that something mom used to say to me?"

"Well, yes I believe she said that to you more than once for sure. Yes, these were her exact words. Jacob Walker, you be sure and look for a woman who knows how to cook your favorite dinner and one who can balance the checkbook for the family."

"Right, I loved the fact that Mom liked to remind me that it's not just about how a gal looks, but it's also about if she is capable of doing some important things which will contribute to a great partnership too. I plan to keep this in mind when I actually find someone I might consider marrying."

"Let's stop in here at Burger Boy and grab some a quick cheese burger, I'm famished from a long day of travel."

"A hamburger Deluxe with sweet potato fries sounds good to me. I'm buying tonight, son!"

The two men finished off the meal and drinks and climbed back into the truck to head down Main Street and once his Dad had gone through the light at the intersection of Weston Avenue and Fifth Street they pulled into the driveway of three bedroom one-level home. His parent's house still held its coat of paint well. The distinct purple flowers of the lilac bush out front were a sharp contrast to the light bluish tone of their home. The shutters next to the two main windows were painted a charcoal grey while the window trim had a white accent color that caught one's eye immediately upon driving up the street. The white birch trees closer to the place acted like stately sentinel soldiers guarding this house. This house spoke to Jake of a more tranquil time in his life and he had definitely missed this.

CHAPTER
Nine

It was two weeks into his stay with his father and Jake rolled out of bed early that morning to grab his running shoes. He'd decided to go for a long run across Main Street and up the hill to Harris Street. He continued on his jog until he'd ran up the hill overlooking his old high school and the football field as he'd done while attending community college. When Jake had turned fourteen, his folks had relocated to nearby city. Dayton was a much larger place than the town of Handley. Plus, it had a larger high school and a better pick of the athletes for their football team. He'd been thrilled to attend this newer high school where he'd made a few friends and became acquainted with the football coach who influenced his life considerably. Pausing to catch his breath, he gazed down at the familiar sight of his high school. A flood of memories hit him as he scanned the horizon and then looked down again to observe a large group of students moving from one building to the next. Then he sat down on the grassy hill to reflect for a moment beneath the blue sky. Watching with interest as the wispy, thin clouds shifted and changed against the darker background, it seemed to him as if a master designer had taken a brush, dipped it into the white oil paint, and then pulled the thick artist brush across the dark blue sky in an elaborate sweeping motion. Pondering this natural creativity and its sublime beauty caused Jake Walker to consider his plans for the future. It was time for him to head to the west coast and his new property. Even though he loved spending time with his father, he really needed to get settled and find his own way.

Later in the day, he'd planned to call his high school buddy, Mark Andrews, to set up a time to get together and shoot some pool. He was hoping to spend two evenings with Mark before leaving his hometown. As he glanced overhead at the clouds spreading out and changing shapes, he recalled another day just like this one where he'd hung out with his buddies in the summer months. They'd gone swimming at the ole water hole called Moulton Falls with the plan to meet girls at the same time. This river spot had a fifty foot high bridge that crossed over their favorite swimming spot. Once they'd reached the top of the trail leading to the wooden bridge they'd challenged each other to jump off into the deep pool of icy cold water below. Large rock formations jutted out from the hillside and overlooked the flowing river below. On the smaller boulders teenagers would lay out in the hot summer sun for a bit before jumping back into the cool, refreshing river. It was one of his best memories and he figured by this time his friends had probably changed considerably and might not be interesting in heading to the river to swim again. Mark had gone off to a four year college while Jake had chosen to enlist in the military instead. As he headed back to his parent's house, he wondered what Mark was doing for work here in the city of Dayton. He was looking forward to catching up with his friend when they did get together again.

The following day, he was out back cleaning up the cluttered garage and tool shed for his father while he listened to the country western radio station playing in the background.

Thirty minutes later he father appeared in the doorway of the shed with a drink in hand.

"Jacob, here is a glass of Pepsi to drink. I thought you might be thirsty after working so much." His father said.

"Thanks, I could use something to quench my thirst about now." He unbuttoned his flannel shirt and rolled up his sleeves and then he reached over to retrieve the chilled glass of soda. "Hey Dad, why don't you get rid of these old rusty tools and that push mower you don't use anymore?"

"Well, I suppose I should haul some junk off to the dump, but I want to keep the old push mower for the front yard since I don't need to buy gasoline or oil to keep it running properly. It just requires man power to cut our small yard. Besides, I need the exercise. That was your mother's favorite thing to watch on a sunny day, her husband pushing an ancient mower around as she planted flowers because it didn't make a lot of noise like other lawn mowers. Say, son will you take a break from helping around the place and drive the Chevy truck to Walgreens to get my medication."

"Sure thing, how much do your pills cost?" Jake asked.

"I can get you some cash as soon as you are ready to go." His Dad answered.

"I've got this; I still have plenty of cash to cover these kinds of incidentals." He said.

Jake finished stacking some boards next to the shed and then he went inside to clean up before taking his father's truck to the store. Within fifteen minutes of driving towards Main Street, he was at his destination. He climbed out of the truck and headed inside Walton pharmacy. To his surprise, Betsey's younger sister, Sara McConnell, was working behind the counter. She smiled upon recognizing him and he returned the acknowledgment and smile with one of his own.

"Hi Jake, I'd heard that you were back in town. What are your plans? She asked.

"How did you know that I was back?" Jake asked.

"Oh, your father bumped into me at the football game last night and mentioned you were staying in town for awhile." Sarah remarked.

"Okay, cool. Yeah, I needed to see my Dad and get reacquainted with some friends. It's nice to see you. How's your sister doing?"

"Betsey is great. She loves being a homemaker and taking care of her young son who's just turning one this next week. You should come over and visit her. The birthday party is on Friday night and Mark will be there too. I loved to have you come. I'm sure her husband would like to meet you."

"Alright, I'll see. I'm here to pick up my father's prescription refills. Are they ready for me? I'm paying for his medication this time."

"Sure, no problem, it's so good to see you. I hope to see you more, Jake." She said.

"Thanks for your help, have a great day." Jake replied with a smile. Picking up the pharmacy bag, he stuffed the receipt and doctor's instructions into the pocket of his jacket and turned to walk away.

"Oh by the way, do you want my sister's phone number and directions to her house?" Sarah asked.

"No, I'll catch a ride with my friend, Mark; he knows how to get there. Bye now."

When Jake got home he headed into the kitchen to give the pills to his father.

"Okay, Dad, you sent me on a mission with an ulterior motive didn't you?"

"What do you mean, son? I wanted to take a rest before going to the bingo night later on this evening. I appreciate your help around the house and for going to the store for me." He answered with a look of innocence on his face.

"Dad, you knew that Sarah works at Walgreens now and you set me up!"

"Well now, I thought you might need a slight nudge in her direction. And never mind that she a pretty young woman and you are a healthy all-American boy who needs a social life."

"Good try, Dad. By the way, I need to talk to you about something. Do you have a minute?" Jake asked.

"Sure, what do you need, son?"

"Well, I'm travelling to Washington State to check out my inheritance from Uncle Henry. I want to get there while the fishing is still good and the weather is decent. Before I leave Dayton, I'd like to take you to dinner tonight at Boswell's diner on Powell Street. Are you up for some ribs or buffalo wings and sweet potato fries?"

"Of course, I'm up for a good meal. You know I don't care to cook much since your mother has been gone for two years now. It just isn't as much fun cooking dinners without her expertise and her good humor! Of course, I hate to see you leave, but it has been great having you here." His father said.

"Yeah, I know what you mean. I was glad the military let me come home for her memorial service. It sure was a shocker to get that bad news while I was fighting overseas. I wish that I could've spent more time with you and mom before she passed. I have this one regret that I didn't stay longer after graduating from boot camp."

"You know something, son, we all have regrets in life. Your mother wouldn't want you to spend one day wishing she was alive or berating yourself for not being around more."

"I suppose you're right, but I sure miss her, Dad." Jake replied.

"Yes, your mother was proud of you and your dedication to our country in a time of war and there was nothing you could do about your deployment orders. she wouldn't want you to grieve forever. You have your own life to live now and she would want you to follow your dreams and do what you love most. Too bad I can't convince you to stay here and work in my business. What do you plan to do now that you're no longer in the Marines?"

"I want to take some time to relax and write about my overseas experiences and do some fishing at the lake near Randall. I don't want to jump into a job until I feel like I'm back to my old self again. I'm still having trouble with getting proper sleep at night." Jake remarked.

"Alright, I get it. You know that Boswell's cafe is one of my favorite spot to meet Frank and Ernie for lunch or coffee on a weekly basis. Occasionally, we come back to my place to play poker or twenty-one, so let's go there tonight." His father stood up and stretched and then walked towards the garage doorway and stopped momentarily. He was going to go to the house and into the kitchen area to get some food. He turned around to look at his son again. "Do you want some lunch since I'm going in to make myself a chicken salad sandwich?" He asked.

"That would be great. Thanks. Hey, Dad, I'd like it if you could come and visit me in Washington once I get the cabin place cleaned up and presentable in a few months. It's always warmer in July, August, or September at your brother's cabin. I mean my new place in the woods."

"I'd like that, Jacob. Let me know when the time comes, like the end of July maybe and I've hired another employee. I'll get Jillian's help to book a flight to the west coast a month before then."

"I'm going to go upstairs and pack some of my gear. I plan to store my military clothing and a few miscellaneous things here in my room since I won't need everything on this trip out

West. I also need to put a call into my captain to see if there is any news about my canine partner, ole Blue." Jake remarked.

"Tell me again about this dog. Why do you call him Blue?" He asked his son.

"We got this particular dog after our first canine was killed during an IED bomb went off by our vehicle. Then the staff officer contacted the military corps and sent us this dog. He's a pure bred Blue Heeler dog. They raised these pups in Tennessee hill country. Originally this breed of dogs came from Australia. I did some reading up on the history about this breed of dog while I was waiting to come back to the states. This is what I learned about the Blue Heeler." Jake smiled at his father and motioned for him to sit down at the kitchen table for this educational information.

"Good idea, my knee is bothering me today and I shouldn't stand on it for too long according to Doc Simmons."

"While I was sitting in the hotel room last week I decided to do some research. What I learned was this: the first person to cross breed the dog was a man named Thomas Hall. In 1840, he imported two blue Merle pups from the state of New South Wales to Australia. He had to mix a dingo dog with the sheepherder animal to produce a dog breed that would nipped at the heels of a cow in order to herd the cattle properly. This cross-breed animal did not bark at the cattle which turned out to be a great benefit to the ranchers. Plus, this Australian Heeler dog is said to be a hard working animal which also benefits a cattle owner." Jake walked over to his Dad's computer and pulled up an image of this breed of dogs to show him. "Take a look at these dogs."

"They look intelligent for an animal. What color of fur does your dog have?" He questioned his son.

"Blue Boy is a mixture of different colors. He has a blackish coat with a blue mottled blend of fur. There is some white fur in the front of his chest and head area. He's a beauty!"

"Nice. Will I get to see a picture of your dog before you leave town to fly back to Washington State?"

"Sure, I have a few pictures of him on my phone I could show you. Right now my phone is charging so remind me later to show you. I also need to place a call to Simmons Pet Care to get the paperwork I need. Remind me to do that before we leave for dinner. I want to get a copy of the medical report from the veterinarian who examined Blue Boy. I don't recall my new address and so I was thinking to have it sent to this address. Can you watch the mail box for me? I'll probably be back in the northwest by the time it comes?" Jake asked.

"I can keep an eye out for any mail coming here with your name on it." His father replied.

"When it arrives just put it in a folder and leave it in my room upstairs." Jake replied.

"No problem, I can handle this for you, son."

CHAPTER
Ten

The Soulee River drifted along peacefully as the winds began to steadily increase in the northern part of this border state. It was the year 2006, and the United States was still at war with Afghanistan over in the Middle East. The only time folks thought about that region was when the nightly news showed a young soldier who'd been killed in action overseas. The Johnson family had felt their own deep loss a few years back when Lisa's husband, Morgan, had died suddenly from a heart attack which caused an aneurysm while he was at work. Lisa Johnson was now a single mom who had to work at a bank in town to support her and her son.

This particular weekday she'd decided to take a short trip with her son, Max, to visit the Soulee Dam as a part of a field trip to help him get a better feel for his school project on water power. Looking at her clock on the dash she knew they were getting closer to their destination. Lisa moved her head slightly to stretch her neck muscles that seemed to be getting tight. As she turned her head to the left, she noticed a lone fishing vessel lying anchored just a mile off the shore of the river. The bow of the craft had a taut line strung from its bow which extended outward and down beneath the murky waters surface. The boat was a picture of a peaceful calm on the river's surface as it rocked back and forth against the waves. She wished she could stop and spend the afternoon relaxing on a boat like this one. She thought about the idea of coming to the river for a summer day in July as she wondered about the cost of renting a motor boat at the local marina.

The cloud cover of an early morning haze had gradually evolved into thinner ribbons of white stratus clouds which now lay against a powder blue sky. In the distance, a lazy eagle circled the skies like it was a royal monarch of this vast wilderness region. Slowly and gracefully, the eagle disappeared and then reappeared from behind the towering Evergreen tree on this day. Then the eagle flew above the orchard where two men were busily picking ripe fruit off the tree branches. There were a few men loading the crates of fruit into the bed of an old Ford truck. One of the migrant workers standing near the road had stopped briefly to look up and watch the majestic bird as it flew overhead in search of prey. Turning back around, he continued loading the fruit basket while wiping sweat from his sun-tanned brow.

Moments later, Lisa Johnson's vehicle was fast approaching those same migrant workers who were straining to finish their seasonal task before noon time. As her car came closer to where an older woman was holding a basket of fruit, she noticed a fruit stand with a large attractive sign closer to the highway. The farmer's brightly painted sign with the word PEACHES seemed to beckon her to pull over and purchase some fresh peaches. Wondering if she'd make it in time for the tour, she eyed the clock on her car dashboard. She decided to resist the temptation to stop. Reluctantly, she continued driving towards her destination all the while thinking about her need for fresh fruit. She longed to have ripe peaches and Bing cherries to eat again. She could almost smell the succulent peach juices as she recalled another memorable time when her family had driven to find a local orchard just a few miles outside of town. They'd spent the afternoon picking peaches and enjoying the fresh air and countryside experience. Once they'd made it back home, she froze some of the fruit and left some in the wooden crate and a handful of fruit in a large bowl so they could eat them later that evening. She loved a bowl of sliced peaches smothered in milk or whipping cream. Right now her mouth was watering at the thought of eating freshly picked fruit from the roadside stand they'd past.

Maybe she would stop at the fruit stand on the way home to purchase some fruit she thought to herself. Glancing over at her son who was fiddling with his tablet, she was glad he was entertained during their drive, and yet, she wished he'd shut down the handheld device so she could engage him in conversation about school or his friends. Driving down the road in silence for another mile, Lisa decided to encourage her son to chat with her. Lately, it seemed like such an effort to engage her son in a decent conversation.

"Frankie, hand me one of those croissants we packed earlier. I'm starting to get hungry and this tour could take a couple of hours before it's over today," Lisa requested as she brushed her wavy, brown curls off her forehead. Her dark brown eyes sparkled as she smiled at her son. Not wanting to miss her exit, she focused more closely on the road ahead so she'd take the turn needed to reach the thriving city of Grandview where the water resource center and dam were located.

"Mom, are we almost there?" Are you sure this is the right way?"Her son asked.

"Yes, I'm pretty sure our exit is coming up in about a mile." Lisa replied with confidence she didn't feel just then. I need you to keep an eye out for Exit 69 A."

"I wish we could've brought my friend, Kevin Braden or Chad Boswell on this excursion."

"You need to understand why I said no this time. Some parents don't want their kid missing the last few days of school to go with a friend on a tour." She replied in an irritated tone.

"I'll bet Mrs. Braden would've let him come on our field trip today since we're going to the second largest water reservoirs and its dam facility." He scratched his head and glared at her as he munched on a cheese croissant. "Besides, you told me this was an educational experience!"

"Well, yes, that's right it's a tour to explore the facility and to learn more about water energy sources." However, young man, I was concerned we'd have to pay for your friends and then you'd beg me to let them stay for dinner and a sleepover as well. I was hoping we could spend some quality together since I took the day off work." Lisa remarked. Then she reached over and swept his hair back away from his eyebrow. Her son pushed his hair back down to cause it to fall back over his brow. This action made her miss the little boy stage when her son loved her touch and welcomed an embrace from his mother. She wondered if the stress of being a single mom for the last few years had created a distance between them.

"Ah, Mom, I get that, but can one of my buddies come over for a couple of hours tomorrow? I told Anthony we might go over to the Braden's house this week. His Dad just made a cool zip line in the big field behind their backyard."

"I'll think about it. Maybe if you help me around the house, clean your room, and bring in some wood for the fireplace I'd be more inclined to say yes."

"Oh, I promise I will help you with the chores and even clean up after dinner. That would be cool, Mom, thanks." Max replied.

"Here's the deal. Once you've finished everything we've talked about then you can call your friend and see. Make sure you let his parents know about the plan to do a zip line. Some parents prefer to know about this kind of activity." Lisa remarked.

"Sure thing and thanks Mom." Max replied.

As they ended the conversation, she noticed the traffic starting to slow down to a crawl as they approached the intersection of Hillman and 56th street. It looked like there was paving crew and she could see a flagger person had stopped some cars up ahead. Annoyed and not wanting to miss the shuttle bus, she chose to turn down a different street before getting stuck in the traffic delay. The cloud formations looming on the horizon gave her doubts about her earlier decision to tour the largest dam facility in this region. An unusual sense of foreboding hung over her as she continued driving. What if it started pouring rain while they were outside today? She finally saw the groups of people and cars in a parking lot one block ahead and she momentarily forgot her concerns about the weather.

There was a crowd milling about in front of the ticket booth bearing a sign which read, "Water Facility Tour, seven dollars for adults and five dollars for children." After finally locating a parking spot, she locked the car and walked with her son towards the ticket booth. Overhead the air was enveloped with a scent of coming rain. Lisa fumbled in her purse for the cash and tugged on her son's shirtsleeve to move him closer to join the line of people waiting to purchase a ticket. She wondered about the lives of these eager tourists waiting to get on the bus. Glancing towards the group she observed that most of the couples were older, however, there was one young couple with two kids up further in line. She did not want to be turned away because of a packed bus so she glanced around to check if the bus was filling up to its capacity. She wanted this trip to turn out memorable for her eleven -year old son who was growing up too fast. Hoping her son would enjoy this tour, she gave a sigh of relief when the man in the booth handed her two tickets, told her there was still room and to head over to board the tour bus. Being a single mom this past year had put a lot of stress and pressure on her life lately. She'd even considered taking on a second job on the weekends. Lisa was worried about being away from home that much though. By taking a day off, she was hoping that this time together might bring the two of them closer. Reaching for her son's shoulder, she gave him a slight squeeze.

"Thanks for coming with me today. I didn't want to make this trip by myself. I miss doing things with you, son. I really miss your father being here too." Lisa said.

"Yeah, I miss Dad too." Max looked away in an effort to hide his feelings from her. He didn't want to cry again about the loss of his father. "Hey, Mom, do you think it might rains today? Gosh, we didn't even bring an umbrella."

"Frankie, according to the meteorologists' report it's not suppose to rain until four o'clock this afternoon. So let's hope for the best!" Lisa replied.

"Geez, Mom, all the kids at school call me, Max', so how about you use my middle name, Maxwell too! Besides, I'm too old to be called Frankie."

"Alright then, if that's what you want." She replied kindly. Not wanting to belabor the point today she turned away to watch some pedestrians waiting at an intersection light. Her attention shifted to another person across the way from them. A well- built, handsome man wearing a black leather jacket had parked his motorcycle at the curb, crossed the busy street, and then stopped to read the tour sign information. As he came closer she saw him reach into his backpack for something and she figured that he was also purchasing a ticket. She noticed his dark, intense eyes as he glanced her way. It felt as if they'd had a brief connection at that moment. She thought he didn't look like the average tourist interested in this particular site. Maybe, like most men, he was interested in the hydro-electric generators that sat just below the 550 foot high concrete barrier standing in the way of the mighty Soulee River's path. She noticed that this individual standing in line wasn't holding a camera like everyone else. In her estimation, he didn't seem like the usual American tourist.

As they made their way towards the bus, Lisa overheard the dark-haired man talking to someone on his cell phone in French. She surmised that maybe he'd travelled down from Quebec or Montreal to visit this famous America waterway. She needed to stop wondering about this interesting individual since she was mainly here for her son. Soon the line of people began to board the shuttle to find their seats. The last person to climb into the bus was this same tall, olive-skinned man. She smiled at the man as he approached the middle section. He hesitated for a moment as if looking for an empty seat in the back and then sat down in the vacant seat right across the aisle from her. She wondered again what his story might be and why he'd chosen this particular tour site.

Turning his head slightly he engaged in a conversation with her. "Hello, it's a good day to take the tour it seems." The man smiled slightly as he studied her face. "Do you live around here?" He asked.

"Well, not exactly, we live in a rural area just twenty minutes away from here," She replied as she wondered if he was just making polite conversation or actually interested in her as a single woman. "This is my first time taking a tour of this structure. I'm here because my son asked me a few questions recently about how a dam operates and why they chose to build it here. " His teacher had shown the class a short video of this well-known site and since we've never been to this facility, I thought it would be an ideal excursion. This is my son, Max. My name is Lisa. What's yours?"

"I'm Michael Belangey. He spelled his last name for her and then he noticed her obvious questioning expression. It's pronounce be' lon'jaay. My father was a Frenchman and my mother was Canadian. Glad to meet you both. Does your husband's work not allow him to take off a day to join you on this excursion?" His gaze lingered on her face as he waited for her reply.

A look of sadness crossed her attractive face as she wondered how much to share with this passenger since she wasn't quite sure of his reason for asking. She disliked the inevitable looks of pity she'd receive from people once they learned that she was a young widow. She drew a deep breath and proceeded to answer his question.

"Ah, well, not exactly, my husband passed away unexpectedly of a heart attack two year ago. It's been a difficult adjustment for us. I was able to find a job at the bank and my son is doing much better at school now. I've wanted to take a site-seeing trip like this one for some time now. Once I've worked at the bank a full year, the bank will give me a week off. I'm hoping to take a longer trip then. I'm grateful my boss let me take off from work today and we are planning to have a good experience. Aren't we, son?" Lisa asked her son.

Turning his head to look across the aisle of the bus, Max stared unflinchingly at the man as if to imply to this stranger, "Hands Off, Mister" then he spoke boldly to the man. "Yeah, we like going places together a lot and I can watch out for her." Max replied importantly.

"I see, well you certainly look big enough to protect your mother. It's a good plan to visit this well-known site so you can learn firsthand how it all works. I think folks learn more about their world by actually going there rather than just reading about it at school. That's why I'm on this tour too."

"Where else have you visited so far?" Lisa asked since she was curious as to why he wasn't at his job today.

"I've seen Whistler's mountain and I stayed in Edmonton, Alberta for a weekend recently. I've also travelled to Victoria Island as well." The man replied.

"So when did you move to the states?"

"I'm originally from Quebec, Canada, but now I'm living with a friend here in Washington. I'm looking for a better job and so in the meantime I've decided to do some sightseeing this week."

"I hope you enjoy the tour." She replied as she glanced out the window at the tall building looming skyward." Why did you choose this place to do some sightseeing?"

The man looked away for a moment as if he wasn't sure about what else to divulge about his plans. "This is my first time going on a tour of a water facility. My boss asked me to come here in person and see how this place operates." The man in the black jacket replied.

"Oh, I see. So does your job involve energy of some type?"

"Yes, the company I work for deals with repairing equipment as well as maintaining certain generators in our power plants. My job involves knowing how to fix certain problems that occur in generators. I plan to take accurate notes to relay back to my superiors after this tour." He said.

"I'm hoping this excursion will sparks more interest in my son to want to learn as much as possible about our country's natural resources and the need for sufficient energy sources. Maybe he is too young to grasp the importance of this facility, but I think this tour will show him first-hand how a river can produce enough electricity to maintain a region and that might be a learning moment for him." She added with a shy smile spreading slowly across her face.

"You're correct; this is a good experience for people of any age. Can you recommend a good place to eat later after the tour ends today?" He asked as he studied her pleasant features.

"Sorry, we've only moved to Randall and this is our first time visiting the city of Grandview. So I'm not able to recommend any of the local restaurants. My son likes to eat at fast-food places mostly." Lisa was intrigued by this handsome individual's dark, piercing eyes and she quickly looked away.

Her newly made acquaintance made a quick reference to the cloudy weather as he pointed past her to the window on her left. She could tell the man was finished making light conversation as she observed the way in which he settled back into his seat to stare silently out the other window at the passing scenery. She almost hoped they'd get a chance to chat again during the tour. This new thought caused her to wonder what it might be like to get involved with someone again. She caught herself thinking about how nice it'd be to go out on a date again. She sat quietly for the remainder of the ride lost in her own thoughts.

The lumbering shuttle bus pulled into the facility's parking lot and stopped with a lurch. Slowly and steadily people jostled about in the aisle of the bus until everyone had managed to depart. As Lisa and her son followed the group, their tour guide aptly explained how this well-designed gravity dam is the main source of electricity and irrigation for the entire region. As they continued walking and listening to the guide's conversation, a few people took photos of the structure while others just stood and watched in awe while the water flowed powerfully over the side of the cement structure.

Twenty minutes later, Lisa turned in time to observe that same individual she'd met on the bus drifting away from the group to disappear behind the generator housing section. She wondered why he'd decided to stray from their group. Maybe he'd grown tired of the tour guides presentation like her son had. Presently, the French-Canadian man came back into view as she watched him climb quickly down the small metal ladder and then rejoin the tourists without drawing much attention to his actions. She was curious as to the reason for his brief departure from the group. Well, maybe he wanted to get a closer look at the equipment and check out the generators for himself. Dismissing the incident, she turned her attention back to the guide's conversation. By the end of the hour, everyone had learned a great deal about this gigantic cement structure and its three powerful generators.

As they all followed the guide up a number of steps in order to reach the top of the structure's walkway, Max decided to go ahead of his mother in order to catch a better sight of the powerful force of water crashing down below. He took hold of the metal guard rail and leaned over the railing to shout into the noisy water flow. Max gave a loud gasp and then turned around to look at his parent standing some distance away. "Hey Mom, come here and look at this crazy sight!" He yelled in an effort to be heard over the roar of the water.

"Franklin Maxwell Johnson, you get back here right this minute." She cried anxiously as she envisioned him leaning a bit too far over the metal guardrail. Lisa was worried about her son's safety and of the extremely dangerous height of the dam structure. As Max made his way slowly back to her side, she chastised him angrily.

"Don't you realize how high we are right now? If you'd leaned over too far or slipped because of the wet railing, it would've been horrible thing for me to watch. I don't want to see anything bad happen to you, son. Please stay close by me for the rest of the trip." Lisa commanded.

After taking a calming breath, she hugged her son and asked him a question in order to smooth things over after chiding him so harshly.

"Frankie, I mean, Max' what was your favorite part of today's experience?"

"I liked walking on the top section of the Dam while the winds were blowing massively hard in our direction. It was kind of freaky, but exciting at the same time." Max declared.

"Well that wasn't my best part for me, but I'm glad that we made it safely across the windy section of the walkway. As a parent, I worry about your safety. I was worried when I saw a girl leaning over the thin metal railing today." Lisa recalled how she'd felt apprehensive during the return crossing. When the strong winds were blowing behind them, it had felt like the wind was attacking them like a group of angry, black crows trying to prevent her from reaching her destination safely. At one point during her return walk across the high structure, a strong gust of wind had caught hold of her and she stumbled too close to the guard rails. She recalled how the tall, dark stranger had quickly reached over to steady her and she'd thanked him for his help. The deafening noise of the water and generators had prevented them from hearing each other and so she hoped that they could resume their conversation again on the shuttle bus. By tomorrow she'd be busy at her bank job and have forgotten about this intriguingly handsome stranger and his motorcycle.

It was nearly one-thirty and both of them were beginning to feel hungry. Max reminded her of his reason for getting back home. Lisa thanked the tour guide for everything and then they hurriedly crossed the parking lot to climb into the shuttle bus. Once they'd been settled into seats closer to the front section this time, Lisa watched for the tall, dark-haired man to enter the bus. She waited expecting him to choose the same vacant seat again. This time however, he headed for the back of the bus after an older woman plopped down in the vacant seat first. Lisa felt a slight disappointment as she was hoping to learn more about this mysterious individual. Pulling his New York Yankee's baseball cap down over his forehead, her young son leaned in closer to whisper in her ear.

"Hey Mom, remember that guy who was talking to you on the bus ride to the site?"

"Yes, I remember him, why do you ask?

"Because he's no longer carrying his backpack," Max spoke in a quiet voice.

"You're right."

"Isn't that weird? I thought adults don't forget stuff like kids do!"

"I suppose he laid it down while checking out the generators. Once he realizes he's missing his backpack with some valuables inside, he will return to retrieve it. It's not our problem." She dismissed the man and his missing backpack from her mind as she dug through her purse in search of her car keys. She was more concerned about getting on the road before those ominous rain clouds made the drive more difficult for her.

CHAPTER
Eleven

Since moving to Randall, Washington, Lisa had hoped to one day travel up north, cross the border, and spend a day of sight-seeing in the city of Vancouver, B.C. Canada. From where they lived, it was only a two hour drive to the border. Lisa Johnson had moved to Randall nearly two years ago and with the help of a kindhearted realtor gal she'd been fortunate to find a nice house to rent which conveniently fit into her budget. It was an ideal place for them since the house was situated on the outskirts of the town and there was a forest that lay a short distance from their backyard. They were close enough to drive to the bigger city of Grandview if they needed more culture and shopping opportunities. The closest house to her place belonged to a friendly couple named Jeff and Helen Braden. They had a thirteen year old girl named Alyson and a son the same age as her son. Max Johnson and his friend, Kevin Braden, had developed a friendship soon after he enrolled at the same school. They both played on the school basketball team and Max could get a ride home with Mrs. Braden and Kevin. It was an ideal arrangement for a single working mom.

The two boys liked to do the same things such as; camping in the backyard, riding bikes, and going swimming in the nearby river. These two families were situated just outside of the city limits and thus, these boys spent hours traipsing through the forest nearby their homes. They had plenty of acreage between the two families to make dirt hills and bike jumps to have fun on as well. The two boys loved sports and exploring the woods. They liked to have adventures and they couldn't wait until school was out to spend more time in the outdoors together. Kevin Braden's father worked for the county as a surveyor. His uncle Zachary was stationed at Fort Bragg for his first month of boot camp. His uncle wanted to be trained as a special ops person like in the movie, "Blackhawk Down". Kevin(nicknamed Crash' by his dad) Braden and his family lived close to the Canadian border in a rural community of Randall, Washington. When he first made the acquaintance of Max and his mother two summer's ago, he'd informed the new neighbors of his preference to the nickname.

"Hey Kevin, why do your folks call you 'Crash' instead of your actual name?"

"My dad used to think it was hilarious how often I fell off of my tricycle.alot. Plus, he said that I would usually crash into people whenever I ran around the house as a four year old kid. He jokingly called me Crasher' one Thanksgiving Day with the relatives all sitting around the table after they learned that I'd accidently ran my bike into the family car. My classmates think the name is cool so I've stayed with it at school. Another reason why I liked having the name of Crash' is because of the boy in the movie, "Home Alone". Remember he was called Kevin and his siblings usually yelled at him a lot. I really didn't like how the family members made fun of that kid and I really didn't like being called Kevin after watching the sequel to the first movie." He stated.

"Oh yeah, I can see why you don't want to be called Kevin." Max retorted.

"So does your older sister, Alyson, have a nickname too?" He asked his friend.

"She is just plain ole Allyson. She didn't want to be called Allie either. She's thirteen years old and loves to read books and spend time with her best friend, Amanda. She had no time for me and my goofy antics as she calls them. She's always saying that I'm simply an annoying pest." Crash Braden stated. "One time, I asked my folks if they would consider adopting a kid from the foster care program since I really wanted a brother. Heck, it's no fun doing things alone all the time."

"Yeah, I always wanted to have a brother too. Life is boring when you're the only kid in the family." Max stated.

"Six months ago I asked my folks if we could adopt this foster kid I saw on television and my mom said no. She doesn't understand how I feel. They just keep saying it costs too much to have another kid in the home." He said.

"My mom is the same way about this idea. Of course, now that she has to work every day at her job at the bank it's impossible for her to even consider taking in a foster kid." Max scratched his head and heaved a big sigh. "So that's why she let me invite you over to our house for the sleepover and pizza." Max said.

"Well, that worked out well for the both of us. I like having a friend that can do the same things I like to do. We can ride bikes and make jumps in the dirt field and go swimming in the river without having to worry about a younger brother tagging along." Crash remarked.

"Hey, you're right!"

The Braden boy had recently told his parents how he wanted to join a military unit like his uncle Zach when he grew up. But in the meantime, he and his eleven year old friend, Max, acted as if they were a younger version of a Special

Forces unit. They tried to build a small fort in his backyard one week and they'd run out of plywood boards to finish the roof. They'd discussed the lack of plywood and decided it would serve as a temporary military site. They were intent on finding a better hideout in the woods on the weekend which could become their real base camp.

* * *

It was now June 29th and Crash' Braden was bored since school had let out for the summer. He noticed how muggy it felt as he raced out the front door to locate his bike and ride over to Max's place to share his plans with his friend. After reaching the neighbor's yard, he jumped off of his bike, climbed the porch steps, and knocked on his friend's front door. Inside the house, Max could hear the knocking and so he strode over to the front door and opened it to see his good friend standing there with his baseball cap on backwards. He smiled and invited him inside.

"Hey, what do you think about heading into the forest to look for Indian burial grounds and a better spot to hang out?" He asked.

"Sure, I'll bet we can discover some old hidden treasure or maybe an old Indian artifact. Have you ever looked in the field beyond your house for things like arrowheads, knives, or maybe an old discarded native Indian hatchet?" Max asked his friend.

"No I haven't tried looking for any old Indian stuff in the fields."

"Well, I'm hoping to find some cool relics like my teacher, Mrs. Morris was talking about in our history class. Of course, I'd rather find some cool things like a pocket knife or an old rifle that the people living here before us may've left behind." His friend replied.

"Do you have a handy shovel we can use in our digging?" Max stood and went into the kitchen for a drink. "And another thing, do you own a pocketknife?" Max questioned.

"Yeah, if we locate a spot we want to dig up, I can go back to the shed and grab one. As far a a knife, no such luck, but my dad has a cool four inch pocket knife he keeps in the shed. I wish he'd give it to me for my next birthday. My mom thinks I should wait until I am twelve years old before I get a sharp knife like his."

"Yeah, my mom doesn't want me to have a knife or a BB gun. She thinks I might hurt myself or someone else by accident." Max stated woefully.

"Well, I can handle a dumb ole pocket knife for cripes sake!" Crash Braden exclaimed.

"Let's go for a bike ride and see what we find down the old mill road and then we can come back for the tool."

"Okay, I'm with you. I could use some excitement for a change. School is over now and I want to celebrate not having to go sit in a boring classroom. I like exploring the woods with you."

* * *

The Braden family lived just outside of the city limits of the town of Randall. They all thoroughly enjoyed the beautiful scenic countryside with its wooded forest, clear streams, and the backdrop of the Cascade Mountains. They were also fairly close to the larger city of Grandview and the famous Grand Soulee Dam site which they'd taken their son to visit since it was a spectacular sight. When they weren't on a camping trip to the mountains, their son had dirt hills and bike trails to race and jump over in their back field that was the envy of his school age friends. Mr. Braden had made the move from town to the country area because he hoped that his only son would be happier growing up on acreage. Out in this rural area there were more places to explore and less traffic to avoid while riding his bicycle. Occasionally, they would invite one of their son's classmates to stay overnight on a Friday so the boys could play video games or ride bikes on a Saturday.

It was Sunday morning at the Braden home. Jeff was reading the paper while Alyson chatted with her friend on the phone and Mrs. Braden did the laundry. Crash Braden was bored with playing his Xbox games so he went in search of his mother in the laundry room. Upon finding her folding clean clothes into neat piles, he sat down on a wooden stool to talk to her.

"Mom, I really want to have my own knife to use whenever I need to. Can you talk to Dad again about letting me use his pocketknife, you know, the one Grandpa Evans gave him?"

"Ah, kiddo, I know you've been wishing for your own knife, but like your father said, a knife is like a weapon. We normally use a weapon to defend ourselves from predators living in this area."

"You mean because cougars and bears live in our woods and they're dangerous predators?"

"Yes, that's what I'm referring to when I say we need guns and knives to protect us from certain animals."

"But what if I just want to use it to sharpen a stick for roasting hot dogs by the campfire? "And maybe I want to have a knife in case I need to protect myself sometime!"

"Maybe we'll consider getting you a pocketknife for your next birthday present."

"Jeepers, Mom that's almost another whole year away. Why can't I have a knife now? I won't hurt myself using it, I promise." He pleaded with her.

"We'll see, son." Mom replied with an annoyed tired voice. "I know what you're up to young man. You think if you pester me enough I'll give into you. Well, think again. And besides, what if you lost your father's knife? It was a gift from Grandpa Evans to your father. You don't need to carry around a knife unless you and your Dad are out hiking a trail." She stated. She stated.

But Mom, I'm not a little kid anymore. I hate that you don't trust me to have a dumb ole knife."

"You are not even twelve yet and so you can wait. Now go to your room and think about showing me some respect!"

"I wish grandpa was still alive, he'd let me use his knife. Dad doesn't even have time to teach me how to use a knife or shoot a rifle. I wish I had an older brother."

"Oh stop feeling sorry for yourself. Go get some wood for the fireplace and change your attitude young man or I will ground you to your bedroom for the day."

He stomped outside to be alone with his thoughts. Angrily he loaded the wheelbarrow with the wood from the woodpile and pushed it over by the back porch. He'd stack the kindling and split wood later once he cooled off. As he shuffled down the gravel driveway muttering his frustrations, he kicked a stone with his shoe. A noisy blue jay made shrieking sounds at him from a pine tree. He scowled right back at the angry bird. Yelling in a loud voice, he wished he had a 22 rifle to shoot the annoying bird out of its perch in the tree branch. His thoughts turned to how to obtain a knife without waiting for his parents to relent or for another long year to pass. Like most young boys his age, he could figure out how to get that knife.

Walking towards the back yard, he went past his fathers' outbuildings and into the tool shed. He dug around in the musty, old shed for what he needed for his hike in the woods. After scrounging through the pile of boxes and tools he finally located his father's pocketknife. *This is just the weapon I need to defend myself from predators or aliens. Grandpa Evans would want me to have his knife since he's not around anymore to use it and I'm sure Dad would understand how important it is for me.*

The excited youngster folded the knife back up after admiring its sharp four-inch blade. Then he tucked it securely inside a pocket of his khaki pants. He went back inside to his room to get his favorite baseball cap. Slapping it onto his tousled thick brown head, he scampered down the stairs and into the kitchen area. Next he devoured a peanut butter sandwich that his mother had left out on the counter for him to eat. He needed to bring some water on his hike so he raced back to the shed to look for his water bottle container.

Then after filling the plastic container with cold water, he hollered goodbye to his mother who was digging in her vegetable garden. With a plan to locate a perfect spot for his mock- military HQ, he headed towards the main trail leading into the woods. The further in he travelled the less light was able to penetrate through the towering trees and thick foliage overhead. As he walked along the old path, he saw lots of silky, green mossy substance hanging from tree branches everywhere. It gave the forest an eerie, mystical appearance. Feeling spooked by the darkened forest all around him, he was wishing that Max had come with him. He pulled out his pocketknife in case a gruesome, snarly creature sprung out from behind the alien-looking trees. It was as if some industrious little elves had spent arduous hours draping this silky material onto the branches to shroud the interior and ward off unwanted visitors. He picked up a broken tree branch and began to swing it at the tangled tall grass and ferns around his feet. It felt like he had a powerful sword in his hand to hack away at the brambles and brush. The force of his swinging stick caused the foliage and branches to snap as he made headway through the woods. Then because of the gloominess of the forest, he began to hurry along the widening path. To the left of the trail, he could hear sounds of a flowing stream as it tumbled over large rocks in its forward movement.

CHAPTER
Twelve

I t was July 2nd and the town of Randall was getting ready for the coming celebration of the Fourth of July. Firework stands had been put up all around the bigger city of Grandview and two weeks ago another firework stand had gone up on the outskirts of Randall. Crash Braden's father had promised to take him to buy some cool fireworks on Friday, but being swamped with his work load he'd forgotten about it. He'd felt disappointed and had stayed in his room for most of the next morning feeling sorry for himself. He hated the fact that his father was too busy to spend time with him. When his father said he was sorry it didn't seem to help much or take away the pain which flooded his heart. He resented his parent for using the same old excuse of too much work and too little time for him. Maybe he'd go do something exciting on his own.

Maybe he'd go back soon and check to see if Max wanted to go exploring this stream. He'd been annoyed that his friend hadn't listened to his mom's instructions to clean up his messy room and was stuck cleaning up his house and bedroom. While stopping to get a quick drink from the stream, Kevin (Crash') Braden heard a pounding sound like a hammer striking metal.

Staying on the familiar, wide trail, he listened closely for the source of the sound coming from the forested area. As he drew closer to the noise, he could see a big cabin with a battered-looking truck and an old car parked nearby.

The one-story cabin nestled in the open clearing showed signs of neglect. It had peeling paint, two broken shutters, and a dirty plastic piece that had been tacked over a window opening instead of the usual glass pane. There were a few signs of life however. He noticed a fine-looking dog sprawled on the front porch. There were three damp shirts hanging from a thin rope strung between two small birch trees to the right of the rather rustic, yet appealing homestead. In the front yard there was a shovel stuck in the dirt next to a hydrangea bush and pair of man's boots left on the steps leading to the porch. Creeping closer to the rusted, faded blue truck, Crash' Braden was able to crouch down next to the vehicle's back bumper to observe the old weather-beaten sheds standing to the back of the property. He wondered what the smaller building contained. Maybe it was an old pump house. The pounding noise had stopped. He contemplated going around to the back so as to not wake up the dog or announce his presence, when he saw some movement through a second window facing the front yard. Wondering if he should run or stay put, he started to approach the yard thinking that he should give a shout out to alert the occupant.

Realizing that the sleeping animal on the front porch might be a watch dog, he turned to leave when a tall individual came out onto the porch with a tin bowl containing dog food in his hand. Crash Braden noticed the man was working on a day old scruff of a beard and he was wearing tan cargo pants and a rather shabby looking blue- gray flannel shirt partially tucked in his waistband. On further observation, he could see that the man had a fairly muscular physic, a stock of black, wavy hair, and brilliant blue eyes that captured your attention immediately. The boy watched as the man placed the bowl down on the porch and stood back up. Noticing the young boy in his yard, the man hollered as if he was a grizzly bear needing to protect his territory.

"What are you doing trespassing on my land?"

"Ah, nothing really, mister. I was hiking in the woods and when I found this stream I decided to follow it. That's when I came upon this place. I thought that nobody lived here."

"Oh, so you thought you might come inside to see if there was anything of value you could take if no one was around?" He said.

"No, I just wanted to say howdy, mister. I reckon we are kind of neighbors since my folks live about a mile from here. I guess I should be getting back home now." He replied with a quivering voice as he backed away from the old Chevy' truck.

Suddenly, the multi-colored dog bounded off the porch and raced over to sniff at his pant leg. Not knowing what else to do, the boy stuck out his hand for the dog to smell. Luckily the dog didn't nip at his hand. Instead, the canine sniffed the boy's shirt sleeve and then began to lick his hand in a friendly manner. Crash' couldn't resist the temptation to bend over and stroke his thick fur. He was thankful the dog had not acted in a more aggressive manner with him.

"Blue Boy, come here, dog. Stop trying to smell his entire body." Sit and stop jumping up on the kid! Mostly, he's gentle unless you rile him or step on his tail. He won't hurt you in the least bit, as long as I'm around. I guess you're a kid just looking for something new and exciting to do during your summer break. I suppose you could come over occasionally and toss a ball to him. This dog used to be in the military and he is well-trained animal. You can call him Blue."

"Thanks mister, I'd like that. I don't have a dog, but I always wanted one. My mom doesn't like dog hair in the house or dirty paw marks on her sofa. She says it's one of her pet peeves!" He exclaimed.

"Well, that's a shame, but I understand how most folks feel about wet dog fur or dirty paw prints in the house. It can be just plain annoying to clean up after certain dogs especially if they're meant to be outside pets." Jake Walker announced.

"Say mister, what was the banging noise I heard while I was coming onto your property just now?"

"Oh that sound, I was using my hammer to repair a missing board in the back room of my cabin."

"Well, I have to be going now. Maybe I will see you in a couple of days. Say, can I bring my friend, Max, here to play with your dog too?"

"I suppose that wouldn't be a problem as long as you don't touch any of my tools and equipment. So long, kid. By the way, what's your name?"

"My name is Kevin Braden, but I like to be called Crash'. My folks started calling me this because I had a lot of crashes on my bike and scooter from the time I was four years old. My Dad nicknamed me Crasher' when I broke my wrist the last time and it's stuck ever since."

"So how did you break your wrist?" Jake asked.

"Ah, well you see, I was riding my bike up and down our long driveway one morning. On the way back up the driveway I accidently crashed into the backend of our car. I was looking at this strange animal that had run across our yard at the time and I forgot to watch out for the car. When I put my hand out to stop from hitting the car I broke my wrist."

"Oh I see. I had a bad crash one time when I was eight years old too. As a boy I used to ride my bicycle really fast too. There was another time when I was older when I broke my arm after falling from a tree. I slipped and grabbed a branch which broke and I landed in a heap on the ground. That day the doctor put a cast on my arm so it would heal properly."

"Yeah, wearing a cast on your wrist is no fun at all. I couldn't do much for almost two months. It was a real bummer."

So which is it then, Crasher or just Crash'?" Jake questioned the young lad as he studied him.

"Well, either one works. My Dad and my sister, Alyson, call me Crasher' mostly, but my friends usually call me Crash'. Hey mister, what did your dog do in the army?"

"He was a bomb sniffing dog and he was trained to smell IED bombs that the enemy had hidden beneath the dirt roads in that area. He also was capable of attacking any of the Afghani Taliban soldiers at my command. He is a very smart animal."

"Wow, that's really neat. He won't bite me or my friend, Max, will he?"

"The only time my dog might attack someone is to defend me or our property. So like I said young man, when you come over here make sure you don't bother things on my property or do something to alarm Blue Boy'. Do you understand?"

"Yes, sir. Well, I best be getting back to my house now, so have a good day. See you around."

Without glancing over his shoulder to see the man's expression, he ran through the forest anxious to tell his mother about the new neighbor he'd just met. Bounding into the front door with a loud 'hello', the disheveled boy looked for his mother who was normally in the kitchen making some food or cleaning the counters. Not seeing her anywhere, he raced out back to find her hanging up his father's shirts on the backyard clothes line.

"Mom, guess where I've been today?"

"Son, I'm not playing this guessing game with you. Just tell me or else start handing me the wet shirts to hang up on the clothesline." Helen Braden retorted impatiently.

"I met this man who lives in a run-down, old place near the edge of the forest. It must be a mile or so from our property. He has a cool dog named Blue Boy'; he said I could come by again if it's okay with you guys to play with his dog. So can I Mom? Can I, huh?" He asked.

"That must be the newcomer I heard about from Mr. Phelps while I was shopping at his store. She turned from her duties to look at her excited son. "Mr. Phelps said he was an ex- military man who was looking for some peace and quiet. In other words, he might not want to be bothered by a snoopy young boy. Maybe, I need to talk with your father about him first. Did you get this man's name?"

"Gosh, I forgot to ask him." He answered.

"That certainly wasn't very friendly of you, son. The next time you wander over to his place to see his dog and chat, you need to find out who you are talking to. I might call Mr. Phelps to ask a few more questions about this new neighbor."

"Okay. So then can I go over to see if Max can ride bikes? If it gets hot later today we might head to the bridge since it's the best place to go swimming."

"That would be fine, just be home by four thirty to help me set the table and take down the laundry before dinner." She said with a smile as she gave him a hug.

Racing into the house to grab his shorts and throwing a towel around his neck, Crash' Braden skipped back out the front door and hopped onto his BMX bike. He'd wanted to go see if his buddy could get away to swim with him today. Within ten minutes he was on the front porch pounding at Max's front door while waiting for a response.

When Max finally stopped what he was doing and came to the front door to see who was knocking, he heard his friend yelling for him.

"Hey, Max, do you want to ride bikes on the dirt hills for awhile and then go for a swim?"

Opening the door he smiled at his good friend and gave him a high five.

"Yeah sure, Crash', come on inside while I write my mom a note saying where I've gone!"

After scribbling a hasty note to his mother, he joined his friend outside on the front lawn. The two youths raced excitedly to their bikes and headed towards the dirt trails just past Blanton Road. They spent a good hour riding and jumping over the mounds of dirt they'd made months before. There was a larger circular dirt path which contained three good jumps and a better challenge for these boys.

At one point Crash Braden yelled at Max to race him around the dirt track to see who could finish first. As Crash' neared the last curve in the loop, his front wheel slid causing him to lose control of his bike. He landed in a heap after crashing on top of his handle bars. Feeling embarrassed and extremely hot by this time, he decided to stop racing for the day. They agreed instead to ride over to the river's edge and wade into the cold water. After ten minutes of splashing one another, the two swam across to the other side. Three older boys were climbing over some boulders to reach a rope swing tied onto a sturdy branch hanging above the deepest part of the river. Waiting for their turn, the boys laughed and joked as they watched the teens doing flips into that section of the river. Then when it was the younger boy's turn at the rope swing they gave a holler of jubilation as they sailed through the air and sunk beneath the water's surface. Not wanting to wait in line anymore, Crash' gave a challenge to his friend to see who could make it across the river first. Naturally, he won this swimming contest. Once they reached Max's house, they dropped their bikes in the grass and headed inside to grab a snack and relax.

"Hey, let's play your video games for a while before my mom gets home from work."

"Okay, I made it to level ten with the Mario Brothers Sega game yesterday. Do you want to play a different game? I have Warlords as well as a Minecraft game." he said.

"Hey, bro' that sounds good to me. Maybe tomorrow we can go spy on this new neighbor guy who moved into the area recently?" Crash' jumped up off the sofa to grab an orange juice drink from the refrigerator. "My mom wants my Dad to talk with this guy first before I can visit him again. I've decided to call him "Mr. Nobody" since I don't know his actual name."

"Why do you have to get your folks to check him out?" Max asked his friend.

"I don't know exactly, I guess they want to check him out. If my Dad thinks he's a good guy then I can go over there to play with his awesome dog." Crash Braden replied.

"Oh, I get it. I wish we could get a dog. My friend from school has one and he's always talking about teaching the dog new tricks." Max said.

"He calls his dog, Big Blue'. It's a cool looking dog. His coat is bluish-black and brown coloring. There's a small white marking on his forehead and on his front chest area. I wish I could have a cool dog like that." Crash Braden exclaimed.

"So is this guy's dog friendly?" Max asked.

"Oh, are you asking if his dog unpredictable? I'm not sure. At least the man didn't mention this to me. I think it's a friendly type of animal. We could ask my Dad about Australian cattle dogs. He's pretty smart about stuff like this."

"What was the dog's owner like?" Max questioned.

"Well, he's a big, husky dude and he seems kind of mysterious! He acted grumpy at first when he discovered me on his property. My mom said he is an ex-military dude and supposedly he needs some time alone. She mentioned that he might be writing about his war experiences." He said.

"So, then let's go check him out. Maybe we should bring my dad's binoculars so we can spy from a safe distance. Did you say his dog could be a watch dog type?" Max asked.

"His dog was friendly enough with me so we should be okay. Crash' took his baseball cap, turned it backwards onto his head, and hopped onto his bike with one fluid motion. "Go grab your backpack and stuff it with things we might need today."

"Yeah, like a pocketknife, a water bottle, and some chocolate bars!"

"That's a great idea."

They peddled their bikes down the driveway as if they were heading on a daring new mission. Then they both stopped at once realizing they'd forgotten to grab the gear. Turning back around they raced to Max's house to see who'd reach his front porch first. Crash Braden arrived there first and gloated triumphantly. Then he waited for his friend to get the binoculars, pocket knife, and a rope. Discovering a lightweight flashlight lying on the shelf, Max grabbed it along with his old sweatshirt. Next, the two eager youth headed into Max's bedroom to retrieve his backpack and water bottle.

"You fill up the water bottle while I leave a note for my mom. She won't be home until six o'clock tonight." Max said.

"Don't forget to grab some snack food to go with the chocolate bars since I don't want to have low blood sugar. My mom says I need more protein in my diet because I'm a growing boy!" Crash commented to his buddy.

"Well sure, buddy-o, I've noticed your head getting a little too big for your ears lately!" Max said.

"Hah, it's growing larger to fit my brain size! The doctor said I must be extra smart since my head is bigger than most eleven years old. So eat my dust, grasshopper." Crash Braden replied.

"Hah yourself, Cheese head. If you're not careful your brain might just grow huge and explode since there's no more room inside your puny, little head." Max exclaimed.

"Okay lame brain, for that remark you have to carry the backpack full of stuff." Crash Braden announced triumphantly.

CHAPTER
Thirteen

I t was the morning of July third and the two neighbor boys were making plans to go exploring again in a different area of the woods. Max had suggested they hike over to see the new guy and his dog, but his friend wanted to travel on a different path which should lead them to an old logging road just west of that section of the forest. Crash Braden had been interested in checking out an old mine entrance he and his father had seen once during their hike together.

"Since my dad hasn't made it over to meet the new neighbor yet, we need to do something else today. Let's take a longer hike until we reach the logging road that leads to a spot I saw last month. I didn't want to go exploring there until you were with me." Crash Braden announced as he stuffed the last bit of spicy bean burrito into his mouth. "Besides, we need to make sure the guy is actually at home before we go over to see about playing with his dog."

"Why?" Max asked.

"My Mom says he's a recluse which means he's a loner and so I don't want to wear out my welcome with this guy we are calling Mister Nobody'. We need to wait a few more days before asking about his dog." Crash said.

"I thought your dad was going to find out his name when he goes to visit him at his place. What happen to that plan?" Max questioned.

"Ah, well, my dad's been really busy lately. He hasn't even taken me to buy fireworks yet. Hey, if your mom goes to get some fireworks maybe I could tag along!" He remarked.

"Sure, I'll talk to her and see if we can't go tonight after she's finished working." Max replied. He scratched his head and picked up a rock and then threw it towards a tree. The well-aimed stone hit the trunk of the alder tree with a resounding clinking sound and he hollered out with a loud cry. "Wahoo, now what do you want to do Lt. Braden?"

"Well, I found a stream that runs through our woods and maybe we could find some crawdads there." Crash' remarked.

"Good idea, do we need to have a plastic bag to carry the critters in for the trip back to the house?"

"Yeah, a bag would probably be smart if we want to use their meat for bait when we go fishing next Saturday.

Grabbing two bags, they raced out the front door, jumped onto their bikes to ride until they came to a clearing in the woods and the start of the trail that Max was anxious to explore. The sun overhead was beginning to blaze hot in mid-afternoon and so the shelter of the tall pine trees that blanketed the forest area held a welcomed respite from the warm temperatures.

"See there's the stream over there!" Max shouted with glee.

"Yeah and it even has a deeper section to swim in if we can't find any creatures lurking beneath the shallow area!" His friend gave out a whoop of delight as he kicked off his tennis shoes. "I wish we'd worn our swimsuits under our pants." Crash Braden exclaimed as he dusted off his shirt from the underbrush they'd just walked through. "Oh well, I'm so hot that I might jump into the deeper water with my pants on today!"

"I'd jump into the water with just my underclothes to stay cool." Max shouted as he took off his shoes in order to wade into the stream. Scanning the stream for crawdads, he inched his way carefully over the rocks in the stream bed. "Hey, look I found one. Don't they look like small lobsters?"

"Yep, I'm going to catch more of those critters than you!" His friend shouted jubilantly.

"Hah, we'll see about that Maxwell!"

Crash Braden raced over to the water's edge eager to begin the competition. Sitting down on the grass, he tossed off shoes and socks and walked gingerly across the larger rocks until he was standing barefoot in the swirling, cold water. Max had rolled his pant legs up pass his knees in an effort to stay dry. A lazy egret bird floated and glided in the wind above the forest trees watching the escapades of the two boy's intent on capturing their crustacean prize. Max let out a holler sound as he captured a salamander crawling near the edge of the stream which he quickly stuffed into the front pocket of his pants. He scrambled out of the water to place a crawdad into his plastic bag lying on the grassy slope. Then he returned to wading slowly over the slippery rocks in search of another crustacean. Within moments of splashing and trying to not fall in, both boys had looks of glee on their faces as they displayed two more squirming crawdad. Next thing, the circling bird witnessed was the two excited boys heading downstream over the slippery wet rocks until suddenly one of them fell backwards into the cold water.

"Hah, I still have a tight grip on my slippery crawdad." Crash Braden whooped with glee as he lifted the squirming creature up in the air. This poor water creature was trying desperately to get back into his safe watery environment.

Meanwhile, the other crawdads had escaped the bag and were making their way down the grassy embankment to crawl rapidly into the shimmering stream like thirsty puppy dogs rushing to drink from a tantalizing river's edge.

"Hey cheese head! Hey, look over there. Our critters are getting back into the stream. Darn it. All that work for nothing and my clothes are soaking wet!" Max growled at the disappearing crustaceans while struggling to regain his balance and footing.

"Well, you should've tied off the bag. Hey, let's head across the stream to jump into the deeper water. I think there is an easier spot to climb up onto the fallen tree log. Come on let's check it out. Last one there is a rotten egg!" His friend shouted as he scrambled out of the water to search for his tennis shoes.

"Ah, you're on, baloney head'. I'll make it to the other side before you because I'm faster at everything!"

"We shall see about that, you braggart."

The boys forgot about catching crawdads as their competitive side emerged. Barefoot and anxious to win this race, Max forged ahead looking for a better spot to cross over the widening stream. Watching his friend getting a head start, he yelled for Max to wait for him.

"Hey, dummy, that's not playing fair!"

"Ah, come on you know it's my turn to win a race!" Max shouted.

"See that log way over there? It's is the perfect spot to jump from." Crash yelled.

After reaching the other side of the stream, the two managed to climb onto the fallen tree that lay close to the deeper section of the water. After jumping a few times off the log, they had a splash war and then decided to rest on a large flat boulder to dry off in the hot sun. Eventually, their clothing dried enough for them to get up and talk about hiking further into the woods.

"I think we should go this way and blaze our own trail this time," Crash remarked with a knowing smile on his face.

"Hey, wait a sec', I need to put my shoes back on for this hike." Max declared.

"Okay, but hurry up! I think we need to find a couple of solid sticks to be able to hack away at this crummy vegetation." Crash mentioned.

Forty minutes later they found themselves facing a new terrain. Their trailblazing adventure had brought them to a slight barrier in their hiking plans.

"Well, we can't climb down this ravine. So let's head to the right instead."

"Yeah, you're probably right. Besides, even though it'd be loads of fun to run down this slope, it'd be much harder to climb back up this ravine." Max retorted wisely.

Continuing onward, they hacked away at the underbrush to make their new path wider. As he thrashed away at the brambles and ferns in his way, Crash' asked his friend about the other night.

"So who was that guy who came over to your house? Is he a relative?"

"No, he's not related to us. His name is Blaine Wilson and he came by to check on us or so he says. My mom was just talking to him on the front porch for awhile. He works at the fire station in town and he seems like an okay guy. She said he talked to her earlier in the week at the bank about checking out the fireplace and chimney to make sure it's safe enough to use." Max answered.

"What does this guy mean by safe? Isn't it just a plain old fireplace?" Crash' turned around to look inquisitively at his good friend. Scratching his brow with his other hand, he poked

Max in the ribs with his stout branch and smirked at him. "Are you telling me this guy is worried about your fireplace? Don't people just throw wood in there to keep the house warm?" He bent over to retie his shoe lace and then stood back up. "I think this is just a ploy to get closer to your mom and maybe ask her out on a date. You just wait and see, buddy." Crash remarked.

"Ah, what do you know? My mom didn't invite him inside our house the first time he came by. Maybe this guy was on the level about fire safety since he works for the fire department." Max exclaimed to his friend. "My mom is just fine without a guy in her life. She told me that I'm her main man. Besides, she doesn't have time to date men she told me recently. So be quiet, wise guy!"

"Okay, Mr. Grouch, geez; I was just making an observation."

"Yeah, yeah, well, you have a piece of mush for a brain, dork-head!" Max exclaimed.

"Ha, ha, same to you, knuckle head!" Crash Braden shouted.

* * *

Turning northeast to continue on their journey, the boys kept hacking and chopping at the underbrush which had become a bigger problem along this part of the woods. The stickers and brambles were scratching and pulling on their pant legs and yet, the boys seemed to enjoy this challenge. Another fifteen minutes had passed when suddenly Max looked up from his task to see a small clearing at the edge of the forest. As they drew closer to the spot, they could see a huge oak tree situated near the end of the forest area.

"Whoa, do you see what I'm seeing?" Max asked his friend as he stood transfixed.

"Wow, that's the coolest looking tree house I've ever seen in my life!" Crash Braden exclaimed.

"Let's go explore this spot." Max whispered to his friend as he stared at the sight of a well-built tree house in the distance.

"Yeah, there must be a way to climb up that tree. Maybe we'll discover that it's not being used now." Crash' replied.

Both boys raced over to the base of the large tree and looked up. The thicker branches of this tall tree had spread outward in a perfect manner to be able to hold a tree house. They both shouted exuberantly as they spied six small pieces of wood which someone had nailed to the trunk of this tree. The makeshift ladder pieces led up the tree and stopped below the platform of the wooden structure. Crash began his ascent by placing his shoes on each small piece of wood until he could grab onto the boards of the structure above him. Once he'd clamored onto the small deck which someone had built onto the tree house he looked back down over the railing to yell at his buddy to climb up. Max made his ascent cautiously until he reached the safety of the tree house platform.

"Heck, this tree house is awesome! Don't you think? I wish my Dad could see this place." Crash exclaimed excitedly."

"Yep, I can't believe this beauty is for real. No one builds a cool tree house like this and then leaves it abandoned in the woods to rot. Look over here; they even put in a window space. The framework and the floorboards seem sturdy enough. Gosh, the owner of that old house in the distance must've hired someone to build this fort for his kid. I wonder if they mind us trespassing." As he inspected the strength of the railing, he noticed something interesting. "Take a look at that house across the field; I see a few of the windows are broken. I bet the place is deserted. Maybe the people moved away and left this tree fort." Next, he glanced inside the small framed opening of the tree house and gave out a whoop of excitement.

"Come here and see this."

"Wait, maybe we need to head over to the old house and see if it's actually abandoned first." Max remarked.

"We can head over that way later. I want to check out the inside of this place first." His friend demanded. He was eager to see what someone may've left behind. As he entered the small wooden structure, he yelped with excitement. "We could use this place as a lookout!" He exclaimed as he peeked out the window. "Guess what else is here!" He grabbed his friend's shirtsleeve to drag him over to the end of the deck attached to the tree house structure.

"Are you kidding me? Max grabbed his friends' shoulders and punched him playfully. The wooden slide was partially hidden by branches and overgrowth from below.

Not waiting for an invitation, Max hurled his slender form down the wooden slide. He landed on the ground after his fast ride down. His arms and face were now scratched and blotchy from the branches and brambles that had grown over the sides of the slide. Looking back up at his friend he smiled and shouted jubilantly.

"Come on down, that was great fun!"

"Boy, it's a good thing this slide is firmly attached to the tree or you'd be in a heap of hurt right now." Crash yelled back down to his friend. "Okay, here I come move so out of the way."

Once he'd made it to the bottom of the wooden slide, he stood and holler back up to his friend.

"Darn it, we need to chop at these sticker brushes!" He shouted. "What do you say we call this place, Fort Wilderness?" He declared with boyish enthusiasm.

Working his way slowly back up the makeshift ladder, Crash' finally made it to the wooden deck. Once he'd reached the decking of the tree fort, he was able to look again towards the house in the distance.

"Yep, I declare this tree house to be our new lookout station. Since that house in the meadow looks abandoned, I don't think it's a problem for us to be up here." He declared.

That was when he turned around to discover a rope draped over one of the thicker tree branches. Eager to use the rope swing, he hoisted his body up onto the railing and tried to reach the end of the rope, but to no avail. He yelled for his friend to grab a broken tree branch to assist him in pulling the rope closer. He finally was able to hook the rope with the broken branch, grab it with one hand, and move back down to the open portion of the decking area. Placing his hands right above the thick knot tied in the rope, he was able to hang on and swing out away from the tree and land on the ground below with a thump.

"Go ahead, give it a try. It's worth taking the leap!" he hollered back up to his waiting friend who was looked nervously at the rope and then down at the hard ground below.

"Maybe we should tie another smaller thin rope to the end piece of this rope swing. Then it will be easier to catch hold of each time." Max said.

Searching around in the tree house, Max found a long piece of old twine from inside of an old box container that could be used to tie onto the end of the longer rope. He hooked the slender piece of rope around the thicker rope and pulled it closer in to him. "Now we will be able to grab the rope each time without any trouble."

After three more swings the two boys settled down to relax inside the tree fort. Crash wiped the sweat and dust off of his face as he tried to take in his good fortune at finding this abandoned tree house. Max leaned back further to rest his body against the wall of the wooden structure.

"This is a fantastic find! I just hope we don't get in trouble for trespassing here." Max said.

"Ah, don't worry about that. No one lives on this property anymore. Hey, I'm glad we decided to explore this part of the woods. Can you imagine getting to spend the night here sometime?" His friend asked.

"That's an idea. We should come back here tomorrow. He pulled out a blue bandana from his pocket and draped it over the window sill of the tree house. If it's gone when we come back then we'll know the owner still comes here. Let's head for home now."

"Smart thinking, and that's why we call you Lt. Braden!" Max replied.

CHAPTER

Fourteen

The following day, Max sat at the kitchen table eating sliced peaches and piping hot pancakes smothered in syrup when his mom turned to talk to him.

"Max, I have to head to work in a few minutes, so I need you to pitch in and help me clean up the house before you leave to hang out with your friend." She stated half expecting him to balk at her request.

"Okay, Mom."

"Max, do you remember Mr. Wilson, who stopped by two weeks ago? He'd asked me about checking the chimney to see if it needed to be cleaned. He is coming here later so I need you to pick up the living room for me. Make sure there is none of your video games or nerf guns along with the soft bullets lying around on the floor please."

"Okay, Mom. How do you know this guy anyway?"

"He was in our bank just last week asking if his fire department could post some flyers about the auction event happening next month. I gave one to my boss and then he asked me if he could leave some on the front counter for people to grab. He was just making pleasant conversation and then he asked me about our fireplace." Lisa replied.

"What do you mean he asked about our place?" Max queried."

"I mean that he wanted to know if we had an old fireplace that was in need of an inspection."

"So why does he care about inspecting our fireplace? It looks fine to me." Max asked her.

"Well, sometimes an older home needs a professional to inspect the wiring and the interior of the chimney that lets out the smoke from the fireplace. He thinks the house is due for an inspection. I mean, we need to make sure there is no potential trouble which could cause a house fire, especially at night while we are sleeping. As a homeowner I need to take precautions to make sure we are safe here. Does that make sense, Max?"

"I suppose so. I just don't understand why he is taking an interest in our house."

"I think he is just doing the responsible thing in looking out for folks who have a fireplace. I appreciate his help and his expertise in this matter. Normally, he said this type of inspection would cost a homeowner roughly $450 to $500. I don't have that extra money to hire a professional." Lisa placed her finger on her ring finger and rubbed the spot where her diamond ring used to sit. At that very moment, she felt a twinge of regret that she'd taken her ring off months before. *What if he was interested in her because she wasn't married? She didn't need that kind of complication right now.*

"Mr. Wilson will be stopping by tonight to check out our fireplace so make sure you are back from the neighbors by six o'clock for dinner. I want you here while he is here. Maybe you can learn something from Mr. Wilson if you watch him inspect the fireplace with me. I don't want to have to go looking for you or call Mrs. Braden to get you home. Do you understand me, young man?" Lisa asked.

"Fine, I'll be home by six to keep an eye on this guy since you said I'm the man around our place now that Dad's gone." Max stated.

Lisa went into her bedroom to get ready for work. She was glad that Max had someone nice to spend the day with during the week days. She was very grateful to have a friend like Helen Braden in her life. Her neighbor was always willing to have Max over anytime or to feed him lunch while Lisa was away at work during the summertime.

After the dinner meal, Lisa hurriedly finished cleaning up the dishes. Then she went to her room to stand in front of her closet looking for something presentable to wear. After pulling out three different outfits, she finally decided on a pair of grey slacks and a burgundy sweater along with a pair of silver ear rings to match her silver necklace. She wanted to look presentable.

She was thankful that Blaine Wilson was concerned about her safety and well-being. When he'd made this offer to check her fireplace she hadn't considered that he might be interested in her until this conversation with her eleven year old son. Max seemed to be stepping into the role of her protector now. Then while she was brushing her hair, she remembered the good-looking Canadian individual who'd rode on the tour bus two months ago. Her son had been very standoffish with this man during the bus ride. She wondered what exactly was going through her son's mind today. She imagined that he was not interested in having a replacement father. Whatever his concerns might be, she wasn't going to rush into any kind of serious relationship with a man unless her son was open to the idea. Would she have to wait until he was much older before she could date someone she really liked? She hoped not, but then life can throw you a curve ball when you least expect it.

She certainly hadn't expected to be a widow and living in a totally different city at this time in her life.

Twenty minutes later, she heard the doorbell ring and she went to answer the door. Blaine Wilson was standing there on her porch smiling and holding a bag in one hand. She invited him in and noticed he wasn't wearing his fireman uniform this time. She caught her breath as she noticed how his dark brown eyes seemed to sparkle as he studied her expression. She glanced away momentarily and then she invited him into the foyer where she took his jacket and grayish- black scarf from his hands and hung them up on the metal hooks by the door. He followed her into the living room area where the fireplace was located. After fifteen minutes of a thorough inspection of the chimney and the flume mechanism, he rose up to his six foot three height and smiled broadly at her.

"Mrs. Johnson, your chimney looks clean enough for the time being. A year from now you may need to hire someone to clean it properly. It really depends on how often you actually use this fireplace to burn wood. The creosote starts to build up when you burn wood on a weekly basis in order to stay comfortable during the winter months." Blaine Wilson stated.

"That's certainly good to know. I haven't had a chance to locate someone who sells treated wood in this area. I suppose I could also buy those small presto logs to start the fire and then add a few bigger chunks of wood on a chilly night. Thank you for coming by to check on this situation. I really didn't want to ignore something that could potentially become a fire hazard." Lisa mentioned.

"You are welcome, Lisa. May I call you Lisa?" He asked.

"I suppose." She paused for one anxious moment as she waited to see if he wanted to say anything else. She didn't want to hurry him out the door and yet, she was wishing that Max would hear their voices and come out to meet Blaine Wilson and change his opinion about this man.

"I am glad I could come by since it gave me a chance to talk with you again." Blaine said.

"Well, you said you have an account at our branch and so naturally I assumed I'd see you when you come into the bank, Mr. Wilson."

"By the way, I don't mind if you call me Blaine. I was hoping you might be interested in going with me to the local Beef and Brew for dinner this next weekend." He said with a broad smile on his face.

"I'd have to ask Alisha Williams if she would be available to watch my son, Max."

"Oh, how old is you boy?"

"He's eleven, but I still don't like to leave him here by himself for too long. Maybe I can check with our next door neighbors, the Braden's, to see if he could stay with them. Can you check back with me in a few days to see if I can arrange this?" Lisa asked him.

"Definitely, I am looking forward to finding out if you find a sitter. How about if I leave my phone number with you today so you can call me before Friday night?" He smiled charmingly as he asked her this question.

"That would be fine. Once again thank you Mr. Wilson, I mean, Blaine, for coming over. I feel so much better knowing that our house is safe. Good bye." Lisa said.

"You're entirely welcome. I'm counting on seeing you this weekend, Lisa. Goodnight."

Blaine Wilson strode off the porch and over to his Jeep Cherokee with a lilt in his step. Opening the driver's door with ease, he climbed in behind the wheel and looked back to see her standing on the front porch so he waved goodbye. That was when he noticed the dark-haired boy peering out of the front window as he drove around the circular driveway to leave. He wondered if her son would try to throw a monkey-wrench in his plans to date Lisa. He would have to turn on the charm with her son as well if he wanted to make any real headway in this new friendship with Lisa Johnson. He was definitely attracted to this woman and he was willing to make a real effort to win her son over. He was willing to bet money on them becoming more than just mere acquaintances. In fact, Blaine would spend plenty of money on making sure she'd go on a second date with him. He was used to women falling for him because of his good looks and his disarming manner.

CHAPTER
Fifteen

It was a Monday and Jake Walker had decided to drive into the town of Randall to set up a bank account. He found a parking spot a block away from the only bank in town. Locking his car door, he strolled down the street and went inside the building situated on the corner of fifth and Broadway Street. Once inside he had to stand in line to wait his turn. The busy bank teller referred him to her bank manager who could help him set up a new account. As he was finishing up the new account transaction, Jake saw a dark haired, attractive woman enter the front door and pass by and head to a back office in the bank. For some odd reason, he thought he had seen her somewhere before this, but that was highly doubtful since he'd just moved to this area. He figured she must be an employee coming back from a lunch break since she was wearing a name plate and had a login key card in her hand. Jake watched her disappear into the back room and then he waited to see if she would reappear. *Hands off, Walker, she's probably married with a couple of kids to boot!*

Then he turned back to conclude his business with the manager. Thanking the man for his help, Jake gathered up his bank paperwork and walked outside. Feeling the warmth of the sun on his face, he smiled and thought about going to the lake one afternoon this week. He needed to grab a few groceries at the local supermarket and then he would head back to his cabin in the woods. His thoughts turned to wondering about the attractive woman he'd seen in the bank as he meandered down the street in search of a store. He was perplexed as to why she'd captured his attention in such a brief passing. What was going on in her world and why did he feel so drawn to her? He was definitely attracted to her, but not ready to go back inside the bank and ask for her phone number. Maybe he'd wait until they bumped into each other in the grocery store one day.

Jake remembered that he wanted to go to the local post office and see if Blue Boy's paperwork had arrived yet. He was waiting for one more authorization from the vet in order to sign his pet up to become a service dog in the future. His new pet was adjusting to life in country and the freedom to roam about. Life was good again. He was walking south on Broadway when all of a sudden an old car back-fired making a loud noise which caused an immediate reaction from him. Jake instinctively dove for cover as if he was back in the middle of a war zone with a RPG attack coming in his direction. He scrapped his hands and one arm on the hard pavement when he landed so abruptly. After a few seconds of being on the ground, he lifted his head up to scan the area around him. That was when he heard an old vehicle make a loud backfire noise for the second time. Realizing there was no real danger, he jumped back to his feet feeling quite foolish and awkward. An older lady heading his way glanced over at him with an odd expression and then passed on by without asking if he was hurt. He tried to shake off the feelings of bewilderment and anguish from this recent frightening experience, but he knew that if he'd reacted like this once it could probably happen to him again. Would this type of unchecked response ever go away he wondered? He didn't want to have to keep going into hiding in his own home for the next few years. He didn't mind the nasty abrasion on his hand and arm, but he abhorred the intrusion upon his peace of mind. He just wanted to get on with his life and feel half-way normal again.

As he was driving back to the cabin, he recalled his unusual vision of a dark-haired woman who seemed to be in desperate need of help. As he pondered that brief image, he recalled the part in the vision where it could've been him reaching out to catch the woman falling through the air. As he sat there in the quiet car waiting for the traffic light to turn green, he was almost sure that the woman's face in his brief dream was similar to the woman he'd just encountered in the local bank. He wondered if this particular bank employee was dealing with some major trouble in her life and how could he reach out to her without being too forward.

When he arrived back at the cabin, he dismissed the thoughts about the woman in the bank and proceeded to work on small repairs on the inside of his place. The next thing on the check list was to see if there was an adequate water hose connection for the old pump house. Living in his newly acquired cabin for the last two weeks had shown him the things needing to be fixed before spending a day on the lake fishing for trout or bass. He had been looking forward to a day of relaxation ever since he'd arrived here. He had an affinity for spending time in a boat on a lake ever since he'd gone on a few fishing trip with his Uncle Henry as a youth. He usually felt totally centered when he was in the outdoors and near a river or lake water; it seemed to bring him closer to the author of this natural beauty and quiet serenity. Jake knew that he was in need of a calm, peaceful life after being stationed in the middle of the conflict in Afghanistan.

He was confident that this relocation to Randall, Washington with its surrounding rivers, lakes and mountain scenery could be the perfect place for him to live. His plan was to relax more and to make time for writing about his experiences in Afghanistan. Surely, since he had firsthand experience of what it took to survive the dangers and hardship over there maybe folks would see him as a credible witness to the realities of war. He wanted to write about his experiences from a soldier's perspective on what it was like to deal with the ruthless Taliban. He wondered if anyone had written a book about their tour of duty after coming back to live as a civilian. He had a second reason for wanting to journal about his experiences overseas. He was hoping this writing endeavor would help him shake off the flashbacks and the constant reminders of his losses which seemed to have followed him. It was as if the horrors of war and the tragedies were burnt into his mind and soul. He thought about the idea of locating Anthony Rizzo to see if he'd made it back safely to the states. Over in Afghanistan, he could usually talk freely with Rizzo. Plus, they had a few things in common such as hunting and fishing. The man could usually make him laugh at life especially if they had just finished a tough day of dealing with new recruits.

* * *

The next morning after gulping down his coffee, Jake Walker headed outside to put more water in the dog's bowl. He'd decided to check the trail that went deeper into the woods instead of heading to the nearby lake like he wanted to do. He was curious as to what might be going on just north of his property. He seen a man on a motorcycle ride by twice in one week and it had peaked his interest. He strode briskly along the path looking for signs of broken branches or trampled ferns incase that same person had turned off the beaten path. He followed the trail until he saw an old logging road that veered to the left of the well-worn path. He made his way over to the dirt road and hiked on it for another mile. Eventually, he stumbled onto a clearing in the woods. He walked on over to the cleared area. Upon reaching it, he noticed something odd about the place. There in the midst of the clearing he saw two sets of wooden pallets stacked together and nailed firmly in place. On top of each wooden base it looked as if there was an extra section of metal lying on top of the platform.

Upon reaching the two stacks of wood pallets, he could see that indeed there was a thicker metal section bolted into the thin layer of metal which had been first attached to the wood pallets. On top of that second platform piece there was something strange which didn't normally belong with a logging business. Plus, it seemed odd to Jake for timber men in a logging enterprise to leave certain equipment such as hammers, thick cables, and high quality tools lying on the ground next to these two four foot high grouping of pallets. As he searched the area further he discovered a black gear bag next to a cedar tree and a few empty water bottles on the ground. There were candy bar wrappers strewn in the dirt which looked as if they had been discarded recently. Jake thought this was odd that loggers would leave equipment out in the air to rust or be stolen. As he walked around the clearing spot more, he saw a box which was labeled Ammunition Shells. Trying to pick it up or move the box was difficult since it was quite heavy. So he left the wooden box on the ground. He figured he'd come back the next day with a crowbar in order to pry the lid open. All in all what he'd seen here made him even more suspicious about what was actually going on in these woods only a few hours from the Canadian border. It was time to return to his cabin to call Major Holt to share these new details.

Jake jogged back to his cabin and put a call into Major John Holt, who was still connected with the military as well as the Homeland Security department in Washington, D.C.

"Hello, Sir. This is Jake Walker again. Yes, Sir, I need to report about some unusual activity going on in one area of the woods. I've discovered an old logging site and I suspect someone is using this particular location for their own gain. When I came upon the site things didn't quite jive. The area in question is situated nearly four miles north of the town of Randall, Washington."

"What is going on there, Jake?" John Holt asked.

"There has been some more unusual activity happening a few miles past my property. I have a funny hunch that I need to keep a close eye on a certain person who's been coming and going past my cabin and possibly meeting with some unsavory people at this location. I hiked on further today and checked out an old logging road and I don't like what I'm seeing there. I know the Fourth of July holiday is coming up soon and you might be out of the office so I'd like to get your personal phone number in case I need to contact you again." Jake stated.

"Yes, I see what you are saying. I will send my cell phone number in a text message. Call me if something comes up and you need clearance. I'll make sure to keep my phone on me. I trust your judgment in this matter, Walker. It's good to have eyes on the ground there." John Holt replied.

* * *

It was Saturday morning and the two boys were planning to go on another adventure in the forest. They'd agreed earlier to do all their house chores promptly in order to have the rest of the day to play. Making each prospective parent happy would help them to not have to back home until dinner time and so they hustled to carry out their individual tasks. As soon as young Crash Braden was finished cleaning up his messy bedroom, putting away his clean laundry, and stacking the firewood neatly on the back porch, he told his mother goodbye and informed her that he was heading over to hang out with Max.

Grabbing a backpack, Max was busy filling it with water bottles, plates, P & J sandwiches, and a bag of chips to eat while hanging out together. After meeting at the entrance to the forest, they set off to retrace their steps in order to locate the same tree. Once they'd arrived at Fort Wilderness' or their new secret hide out, they stowed the items in an old wooden crate in the tree house. They saw no sign of inhabitants at the two-story house nearby and the bandana was still where they'd left it draped over the window sill. So they proceeded to enjoy a time of sliding down the wooden slide and taking turns on the rope swing like happy chimpanzees until they decided to stop to eat a late lunch of chips and sandwiches. Then they left the same bandana along with an old shirt of Max's draped over the railing of the tree house structure since they wanted to see if the owner of the property returned or noticed the clothing during their absence.

"Let's plan to meet at the entrance to the forest by eleven o'clock tomorrow and jog back here to see if anyone noticed our clothing or took the food items we left in this old box." Crash Braden said.

"Right and I will tell my mom we're going for another bike ride on the dirt hills." Max chided in.

"Yeah, I think we should keep this place our little secret. We don't want them telling us we are trespassing on someone's property. Then we wouldn't be able to come here anymore." Crash' said.

As they hiked back home, they talked about the tree house.

"This fort is an ideal place to sneak away to whenever we like!" Crash Braden stated. "Let's meet here every Saturday after doing our chores throughout the summer."

"Do you like the name I gave this fort?" Max asked his friend.

"Well, I prefer this military type name of, 'Covert Command Center'. Or better yet we should call our new place, CHQ."

What does CHQ stand for?" Max queried as he scratched his head in wonderment.

Covert Headquarters, the military often uses abbreviations for actual words. You know like our own secret Intel abbreviations of BRB or BFA." Crash replied with a smile and his usual know-it-all attitude. "I have another great idea. How about we planned to come here if there's ever a natural disaster in our region? You know like a terrorist attack! We can use this tree fort like a safe place to hide out in?"

"Okay, I like your thinking. Maybe we should store some water bottles and candy bars here in case we may need supplies or we have to spend the night here. Do you have an old sleeping bag to leave here that your folks won't miss and even some blankets for cold nights." Max asked.

"I will have to check in the shed behind our house! On the way back let's stop to say hi to the neighbor guy and his cool dog before we keep going home." Crash Braden mentioned.

"Yeah, it's been a few days since we saw the tall man or his animal. I think we need to keep an eye on this guy don't you?" Max queried.

Stashing their walking sticks in the undergrowth of the forest, the two eager boys hurried along the well-beaten path until they spied the clearing and the house belonging to the ex-military guy. Moving slowly and cautiously the two boys used sign language until they'd reached the tool shed situated a few feet past the main building. Then they hunkered down to watch for any sign of life inside. Crash' pulled out his small binoculars and adjusted the sights until he had a good view of the front porch and the sleeping dog. Hoping to catch a glimpse of some activity inside the place, Crash Braden positioned his elbows on the soft, green grass with his binoculars propped securely in front of his eyes to wait and see if the man was inside. He lay prone for a good ten minutes watching the front porch of the cabin.

He rummaged about in his backpack for the four-inch knife and handed it to his friend. Max found a young tree which contained the exact size of branch he needed. After cutting one branch off, Max began to whittle one end to a sharp point in case he needed a spear-like weapon. Finishing his whittling project, he came back to lay down next to his friend, and whispered in his ear.

"Any sign that the guy is home, Lt. Braden?" Max asked.

"Nothing yet, maybe we ought to sneak up and look through a window around back. If there's no one home then check to see if a door is open. I want to can go inside, look around for any evidence showing that he is really an ex-military dude."

"Sounds like a good idea; I'll sneak over there to peak in through one of the side windows first before heading around back. You stay here in case I need you to go for help if I'm caught trespassing." Max stated.

His friend nodded his head and adjusted his binoculars to better catch sight of the mystery man. Then Max left his backpack hooked over a tree branch, signaled his plan to his friend, and slowly inched his way closer to the newcomer's shack in order to peek into a side window that had been left half open. While standing by the same window, he heard a loud voice coming from inside the man's cabin.

"Early this morning about 6 am, I was outside working on my car when I was surprised to see a man on a motorcycle going past my property. I think this dude might be connected to some activity that might be going on deeper in the woods. I'm planning to go for a hike into the forest in order to see where this motorcyclist is going and why. Yesterday I spotted a civilian copter drop something odd in the same area while I was out jogging with my canine pet. I'm getting more and more suspicious about their reason for being in that location. Just two days ago the guy on the motorcycle got off his bike and walk on foot into the interior of the woods. So I'm planning to take the same trail he did in order to see what he's up to. It's no longer just about an individual visiting the woods or wanting to enjoy a campout there. So check your emails and wait for my next phone call. I'm wondering if this guy is involved with something illegal and shady. Alright, thanks for the agents contact number; I will be sure and update you both by the weekend." The man inside the house spoke clearly this time. Then there was silence.

Moments later, the front door of the house creaked nosily and then abruptly swung open. Crash' picked up his binoculars again and glanced towards the porch area. Adjusting the lens control more, he could now see the husky, sun-tanned man who stood on the front porch staring into the forest. He thought this guy looked like his mom's favorite movie actor, Tyler Haines. As the stalwart man bent down to put on his boots, the boy noticed the man's muscles bulging beneath his grey Henley shirt. Then, with quick, determined strides this man headed across the front yard, grabbed a blue flannel shirt out of his truck and pulled it on over his long sleeved Henley. Next, Crash heard this man whistled for his dog to come with him. Not noticing the boy crouched down by a large shrub next to the house, the tall individual strode purposefully towards the same path which he'd taken a day earlier, past a dilapidated, old pump house, and then he disappeared into the dense forest.

Back in the stand of birch trees, Crash' jumped up from his hiding spot and waved at his friend to join him in following their mysterious neighbor. The two boys moved as quietly as possible in the same direction that their suspicious acting neighbor had taken. The boys talked in a low whisper as to where this new neighbor, Mr. Nobody', might be going and what might lie ahead as they entered a darker, more secluded section of the forest. Neither of them gave any thoughts to the possibility of encountering some inexplicable events in their near future. And yet, this was exactly what would transpire for these two unsuspecting youngsters.

Moving at a quick pace, the two boys gradually began to close the gap while maintaining a safe distance so as to not be discovered. Keeping the tall, dark haired man in sight was easy enough, but it was getting harder to keep from talking the entire hike. It felt like they'd been walking for some time when the tall individual stopped and looked around as if he was listening for something. They'd actually been traveling for nearly forty minutes and almost two miles from his property. Relieved to be standing in one spot, the two boys started whispering again.

"Hey, I'm not sure it's worth following this guy. I think he's just out for a nice hike with his dog." Max retorted glibly to his friend.

"Well, I'm the leader of this scouting expedition and I say we keep tailing him to see if he maybe stashed a rifle or something important in the woods. So I vote to continue following him. And be quieter so he doesn't hear us, Private Max Johnson."

"What, you're still Lieutenant Braden of the 7th special ops and I'm now demoted to a measly first- whatever private! What the heck. What kind of military group is this anyway?" Max demanded in a hushed, but grumpy voice.

"On come on buddy. I'm just trying to get your attention and make you realize that this mission requires more stealth on our part. So you need to whisper at all times and stay on task! Otherwise, I may have to demote you from Private Johnson to Private first-nothing in this army, ha hah." He retorted in a joking manner as he pushed his friend's shoulder playfully.

"So did you learn anything while you were standing by his window?"

"Ah, yeah I did hear him talking to somebody on a phone. I could tell he was on the phone because there was only one voice in the entire conversation. I recall he said something about trying to discover what a guy on the motorcycle was doing out in these woods and if it had to do with folks sneaking into our country illegally."

Not seeing any sign of the man they were following, the two boys got worried and began to hustle faster along the trail. Finally, they almost ran into the man who'd stopped in order to peruse the landscape one more time. It seemed to the boys that he was trying to locate something or someone in the woods nearby. Their neighbor continued climbing upward on the trail for another fifteen minutes. The two boys had begun to get overheated and sweaty with the exercise and wishing they had more water to drink. Suddenly, the neighbor they called 'Mr. Nobody' stopped to sit down on a fallen log and appeared to be resting for a bit.

At that moment Crash' turned to his buddy, Max, and spoke in a hushed voice. "Sgt. Johnson, stop here. We need a better view so let's sneak up further on this slope. See that boulder over there to our right? That's where we should hang out until he moves again."

"Fine, but what if he's an ex-military guy as we've heard and he's carrying a gun?" Maybe one of us should head back to tell your Dad or call the police." Max said.

"Yeah, I thought of that earlier, but first we need to learn whether or not this guy is involved in some type of criminal activity before we tell our folks!" his friend responded.

"Shush, you're talking too loud. I don't want him to hear us."

After reaching the outcropping of large boulders, they hoisted themselves up on the granite rock and proceeded to get comfortable. They began conversing in hushed voices so as to not be heard by the man sitting some thirty yards below.

"What's he doing now? If he is just taking a long rest, maybe we should circle back and look around in his cabin to see if we can find anything interesting about this guy. He could have some cool military weapons at his place." Max remarked enthusiastically. They both lay there thinking about what to do next.

Suddenly, they heard an unusual sound coming from the trail below. As they waited in anticipation, a man on a motorcycle could be seen approaching closer to the spot where the tall stranger had stopped to rest. The two boys watched in amazement as this new neighbor quickly stood up. They could see he was holding a thick stick next to the right side of his body. Next thing the boys saw was the motorcyclist veered his bike closer towards this solitary figure standing in its path. Then as the motorbike was almost upon the man, the boys saw the tall man neatly sidestep the front wheel of the bike and yell loudly as he swung the wooden club directly into the motorcyclist's torso. Swinging with such force, he'd managed to send the surprised rider back off his motorcycle. The man landed on the road with such momentum that his helmet flew off and his inert body lay there in a crumpled heap.

"Gosh dang it, we'd better get out of here before the guy attacks us too!" Max spoke in a shaky voice.

"No, let's watch to see what he's planning to do with the guy. If we stay out of sight and keep quiet he might not be aware that we are around to witness what happens next." He spoke in a hushed tone.

Heck, maybe we should tell someone what we just saw him do?"

"Sure, after we're sure he didn't kill the guy. Let's sit tight and be quiet!" Crash spoke in a hushed tone.

The boys watched the tall stranger turn off the motorcycle engine. Then he pushed the bike over into the underbrush to cover it up. Without any hesitation, he reached down to pick up the unconscious person and lifted him up onto his shoulders. He turned back towards the path and began trudging in the direction of his large, well-built cabin. The two astonished boys slid off of the boulder and traipsed down the hillside to follow him at a safe distance until he reached his property. Hiding behind a large fir tree, they could watch unnoticed as the neighbor man eased the unconscious individual off his shoulder and onto the ground. Next, he strode purposefully into the old shed and then returned minutes later with three items in his hand. With the first item, a car key, he opened the trunk of the vehicle. Secondly, he stuffed a cloth rag into the limp man's mouth. Then he slid plastic zip ties around the guy's wrists making sure they were tight and secure. Lastly, he lifted the unconscious man onto the back bumper and shoved his body into the car trunk. The boys watched as this tall stranger slammed the trunk lid down. They peered from behind the brush and saw him turn to jog back along the same trail which the boys knew runs through the forest and eventually connects with the old logging road.

Intrigued by all of this, the boys agreed to continue following this newcomer. They stayed far enough back on the trail to not be noticed. Finally, after another thirty minutes of travel, the dark-haired man stopped to sit down on a tree stump. The two wary boys hid behind some brush waiting to see what he'd do next.

"Well, at least we packed some candy bars to eat if he stays here awhile. I'm curious as to why this guy comes this far into woods only to stop in this spot. Maybe it's a meeting place. Do you think he could be involved in smuggling? You know, like folks who live in Canada trying to bring illegal drugs across the border into our state." Crash Braden remarked.

"Yeah, he's acting like he could be involved in something not so good." Max retorted.

"Yeah, this logging road actually branches off soon and heads in two different directions. My Dad says if you take a left turn the road will takes you north to the Canadian border. If a person continues down this way, it eventually will go past the Parker's place. My Dad also said the Parkers were forced out of business by the recession two years ago. Mr. Parker used to work for the military in Blevins County delivering old restored military jeeps and Humvee trucks. Then he'd decided to sell them to people who want to buy them. Mr. Parker had told my Dad that a used, restored WWII jeep cost $24,000. Can you believe that?"

"Heck no, that's crazy amount of money. It would be cool to own a jeep though. Hey, maybe we should take a hike over to the Parker place to see if we could use his place as a hideout." Max replied.

"Sure, we can do that later." Crash Braden said.

The two boys were getting bored with following their neighbor. Five minutes later, two noisy, angry crows flew overhead making noisy, squawking sounds which alerted the boys. Looking ahead of them, they saw the man they'd been following heading towards the old logging road they remembered was some distance away. The afternoon sun was beginning its descent behind the tree tops and within another hour or so it would be hard to follow their neighbor. The boys were in the middle of a discussion about their next move. Neither of them wanted to lose sight of the guy in the woods. They both admitted to being curious about the neighbor man whom they'd referred to as the 'tall stranger'. Max was thinking that they should tell their parents about this situation with the unconscious motorcyclist person and yet, they were too intrigued by his recent activity to want to leave now. They both agreed to continue following him for a bit longer to see what he'd do next.

CHAPTER
Sixteen

Within minutes of deciding to follow this tall stranger further into the woods, Max could hear his stomach growling. Crash on the other hand was still intent on watching the tall stranger' as he crossed a small stream and then up an embankment to reach the gravel road.

"I'm starting to get hungry, why don't we head back to the house and see what's for dinner!"

"I want to see where this guy is going, don't you? I mean what if he's mixed up with some drug dealers in this area and he is meeting someone to get a package. They could make a hand off without the local authorities even knowing about it right here in these woods." Crash stated. Suddenly they both heard a whirring noise coming from somewhere above the tree tops.

"Do you hear that?"

"Yeah, it sounds like rotating blades of a helicopter."

Craning their necks the boys searched the skies overhead to determine which direction the aircraft was going. As they listened intently, a helicopter eventually came into view. What appeared to be a small civilian copter was heading towards a location some yards away from them. As the aircraft got closer and began to hover in the air, they could read the white lettering on a background of dark blue paint. It read, KWX News. Suddenly, through the craft's open doorway, three men could be seen sliding down black nylon ropes. Both boys watched this bizarre occurrence unfolding. They held their breath in astonishment and anticipation. There was a wider clearing just north of the old logging road and they wondered if the aircraft might try to land there afterwards. It was like they were seeing a movie scenario taking place right before their eyes. Max quickly reached into his backpack for his small binoculars to get a better look at the activity. The men were wearing black outfits and caps which gave them the appearance of black ominous nighthawks floating through the air. Within minutes these men had landed on the same logging road where they'd seen tall stranger' go. Next, they watched as the copter move away until it was hovering over a cleared area some yards away from the gravel road. Then they observed a large oblong object in a large black bag being lowered to the ground. Max whispered at the same time, "What in the heck is that thing coming down from the chopper?" Then he yanked on his friend's shirt to pull him down lower in attempt to hide behind some large ferns. Breathing heavily, the two lay in the dirt. They were hoping to not be discovered by these ominous looking men.

Two of the men converged to join a third individual wearing black clothing and they all managed to quickly gather up their gear to stash it in the bushes. When one man turned to scan the entire landscape, the boys noticed he was wearing a small backpack and an Uzi- looking weapon strapped to his back. The sight of his black military style garb and the nasty looking weapon caused the boys to both gasp in unison. The boys watched as the men loosened the straps around this large black bag to expose pieces of equipment. The men began to drag the machinery items over to a platform site. The boys crept away from their hiding spot to get a better view of this strange scene unfolding at what was an old abandoned logging site. Once they'd reached the logging road, Max stopped to adjust his backpack. They began to argue about whether to stay there or leave.

"I think we should wait here to see if the tall neighbor guy meets up with these guys." Crash' remarked.

"I say we should leave before they discover us here!" Max remarked.

"We need to find out what they planned to do with the stuff that was inside of the black tarp."

"Then you stay here and I'll go home." Max stated petulantly.

"Fine, since you're so hungry then head home!" Crash Braden exclaimed in a huffy tone of voice. He wanted to stay and spy on the strange men, but not all by himself.

"I'm making this final decision; we'll head back to tell my dad or Uncle Zach about what we've just seen."

"This was my plan originally! Why do you have to have the final say in this plan?"

"Because I'm the leader of this team, that's why. I wish we had a camera along to take some photo of what we've seen here today because our parents won't believe us!"

Just at that very moment, without any warning and from behind them, rough hands reached out and clamped down over each boy's mouth. The two frightened boys found themselves down in the dirt unable to move or scream. Max's eyes were bugging out as he tried to focus and turn his head to get a glimpse of his attacker. Crash was trying to fight his way out of the tight hold by kicking and punching. It seemed as if they'd been apprehended by the guys they'd seen drop from the helicopter earlier. Just as quickly though, everything changed when the boy's would- be attacker spoke in a firm, but hushed voice.

"I need you boys to listen carefully for a minute while I talk. Stop squirming kid. Once you agree with my request, then and only then will I remove my hands from your mouth. I'm not here to harm you boys. Do you understand me?" He waited for them to nod their heads in agreement. Once they complied with his demand, Jake Walker released his hold on them both. Allowing the boys to turn over to stare at him, he questioned them brusquely. "Now why are you following me? and don't even think about lying to me."

"We were just hiking on the same trail as you, mister. We were looking for squirrels to hunt, he whispered in an attempt to dissuade their attacker from tightening his grip on their arms.

"Then where is your BB gun, kid? Are you planning to catch them with bare hands or trap them with pieces of dry bread somehow? Who are you and where are your folks?"

"I'm the neighbor kid you met the other day and this here is Max'," he replied with a quiver in his voice. "Remember me? I came over to your place a while ago, we talked briefly, and we were curious enough to follow you today." Crash took a breath and felt somewhat calmer after seeing who the man was.

"I need to stay here to observe the men who just dropped out of the sky since I figure they might be up to no good. You kids head for home and I'll consider letting you use my dog to hunt squirrels tomorrow. Now get going." He said gruffly as he turned to leave them.

"Well, can we play with your dog later after you get back to your cabin? We'll be careful with him and use a leash if we take him for a walk over to our house and show my mom?" Crash Braden persisted in his attempt to persuade his neighbor to relent. The disgruntled neighbor gave a stony glare at the annoying youngster and started to argue his point.

Suddenly, from out behind the thick cedar trees, two men in black clothing jumped on Jake from behind. These two muscular men finally overpowered him and managed to wrestle him to the ground. Then one of the attackers hit him in the head with the butt of his gun and he went unconscious. Crash Braden jumped up and ran as fast as he could from the chaotic scene. Max, who was startled by this second attack, was not as quick to respond and thus, he was snatched up by the third individual before he could escape the man's strong grasp.

Desperate to not get captured, Crash ran as fast as his legs would go until he had to stop and catch his breath. Meanwhile, Jake's dog who'd been instructed to stay put some distance away turned to go after the boy, but then the animal hunkered down in the brush waiting for a command from his master. When Crash Braden turned to look behind him there was no one chasing him. He decided to leave the main trail and search for a better hiding place. At last, he found what seemed to be a good spot and he hunkered down behind a fallen tree. Breathing heavily with dirt in his face as he hugged the ground, he waited and listened for any sounds of being followed. Feeling frightened and alone, he stayed hidden there for nearly forty minutes in an effort to stay safe. Suddenly, he heard twigs snapping closeby and he froze. Then he saw the shrubs and fern leafs moving slightly. Watching the thickets anxiously, he was surprised to see his new neighbor's dog emerge from the bush and slowly approach him. The kid figured the Blue Heeler dog must've wandered away from his owner and followed him to this spot. The dog was obviously excited to see the boy as his tail was wagging furiously.

"Good doggie. Stay here boy and be quiet. We need to wait right here to see how we can help your owner and my friend, Max." The dog remained by his side as if he was now the boy's newly appointed protector. At one point, the dog made a whining sound so the kid tried to console the canine by rubbing its head and back. The evening shadows were slowly turning into darkness around the boy and his new pal. Fortunately for him, he still had the backpack containing a rope, his friend's candy bars, matches, and a small flashlight. Feeling tired and worried about his friend, he struggled to get comfortable while waiting for Max to show up.

"Come here Blue or whatever your owner calls you. Maybe it's Blue dog'. Come over here, fella' and lay down next to me." Crash shivered and tried to huddle closer to the warm fur of the dog as it scooted next to him on the ground.

* * *

Meanwhile, nearly a half of a mile away from this location his friend, Max, had been half-carried, half-dragged in the dirt by the men in black clothing. They pushed him roughly onto the ground next to what looked to him like some army gear and supplies. One man placed a tie band roughly around the boy's wrists to keep him still for a the rest of the day. Worried that he would be hurt, Max chose to stay put and do exactly what the man said. He watched as the two other individuals shoved their other hostage on the ground next to a large, cedar tree. It looked to Max as if the man was either dead or unconscious, but he couldn't tell since the tall stranger' was nearly four feet away from him. He hoped it was the latter since he'd never seen a dead person before. As he watched the men in black clothing secure the neighbor man's hands and then his ankles, Max realized the guy must still be alive.

Two of the men pulled their Ak-47's out of their packs and loaded them with ammo. Then they moved a few yards away to converse in low voices. The third guy walked over to go inspect the missile launcher and occasionally turned back to watch Max to make sure he did not try to escape. It looked to Max as if this was their second trip to the area since most of the large military-looking weaponry was already here. As he strained to listen, it sounded like one of the men spoke Russian or Slavic dialect. The second man spoke in what the boy assumed must be French. He'd learned about mercenaries from his school history book. Since it appeared that this group had managed to sneak past the security agents at the northern border, he wondered what they plans were now.

Meanwhile, closer to home, but still hiding in the woods, Crash Braden had fallen asleep on the ground while lying next to Jake Walker's dog. During the night he had a bad dream. In his horrible dream, he was being chased by dangerous men with guns trying to harm him. Wanting desperately to escape, he'd opened his mouth to scream for help but his words were caught up in large bubbles and drifted away into nothingness. Then his dream changed and he found himself running inside a huge space craft with a huge fire- breathing dragon chasing him. Looking over to the wall panel of the spacecraft he'd discovered a large button by doorway of the aircraft which he pressed on to cause an opening. Next, the scene changed to where he jumped out into the black night while the huge space ship was still soaring through the sky. Freefalling downward into nothing but black space, he started to feel as if he might plunge to his certain death since he wasn't wearing a parachute. A feeling of terror gripped his soul. Once again, he tried to scream for help and the words got swallowed up in a mirage of wispy bubble-like shapes which slowly floated away into the night air. Thus, his cries merely drifted off into a gloomy universe of oblivion and silence.

He felt all alone. Would he die without saying goodbye to his family? Would anyone miss him or mourn for his absence? Then without any warning the fire-breathing animal flew closer and closer to him. This monstrous creature sent forth a blast of its fiery breath at his figure which sent him reeling backwards and spinning through empty air until suddenly, it felt as if he'd fallen headfirst into a cold pool of water. He struggled to catch his breath and a chill ran through his entire body. Then the strange dream ended abruptly. What had just happened and where was he really? For some strange reason he was no longer stuck in his awful nightmare. He could feel his arms and legs as well as the chill of the night air around him. Waking up more fully, he gradually realized that it was only a frightening dream.

Feeling cold and afraid, he was having trouble seeing in the dark. He rubbed his eyes and slowly he was able to adjust to the darkness around him. Lying underneath the forest's darkened canopy of thick branches, lit by only moonlight shinning through the tall trees, he could see shafts of light. That's when he realized where he was. He was not in a body of water; instead he was lying on the cold ground next to a patch of ferns. At first, his cold body shivered once and then he stood on his feet. For some unknown reason he turned around to look overhead, and that's when he noticed a big star shinning above the tall trees. The man's dog had roused from its sleep when he moved. Marveling at the nighttime brilliance, Crash Braden found a new sense of comfort as he gazed up at the glowing star. Then in the next instant, the light from the night star began to glow brighter until suddenly it blazed downward and shone its light beam all around him. Then it stopped as quickly as it had begun. He felt as if this star light had enveloped his entire being. Strangely, he felt an undeniable sense of peace and confidence infusing his being after that brief experience. What had just happened to him? Marveling at the brilliance of this unique light star, he found himself wondering what this intensely unusual experience meant. Even though he was still unsure of what lay ahead for him in the dark forest, Crash had the strangest feeling as if he was going to survive whatever it was that he might face in the future.

Then he suddenly remembered his backpack still hanging over his shoulders. Grabbing the pack he unzipped the front pocket, rummaged through the contents, and at last found something to eat. He noticed the dog watching him intently and so he surrendered a piece of his peanut butter bar to the hungry dog. Feeling safe enough by this time, Crash relaxed momentarily and stroked the dog's fur and rubbed his ears affectionately.

"Wow, pooch, are you hungry for more food like me?" The dog looked over at the boy with questioning eyes as if waiting for the boy to do something or give him more treats. Then the animal moved closer and laid his head on the boy's thigh. This movement pushed on the metal object in his pocket. He was reminded of his grandfather's knife which he'd stuffed in his pants earlier that morning.

"Hey fella, maybe this knife could be some help to the neighbor guy who owns you. I can try to send it with you, Blue Boy!" He exclaimed excitedly.

Then Crash thoughts turned to a new worry about what had occurred back in the woods. What if this tall stranger they'd nicknamed, Mister Nobody' had been injured by their attackers. An anxious, but determined Crash' pulled the animal closer to him and stroked its fur gently. Believing the man's dog had been trained to follow a few commands, the kid showed the dog his pocketknife. He gently stroked the thick fur of his new companion and spoke some soothing words to help the canine pooch feel safe and to bond with him.

"Come here, dog, see this knife here. I need you to take this and deliver it to your master back there further in the woods. Maybe this knife could be used by your master to help him escape from those bad guys. Take this knife I'm putting in your mouth! Take this pocketknife to your master. The dog made a soft whining noise as he looked quizzically back at the boy. "Dog, I mean, Blue', I need you to listen to me. Pay attention pooch, this is important! You have to help your master! Get going and don't bark. You can do this. I only hope that man and Max are still alive. You must take this knife to your master now! It's very important! Go Blue Boy', go find your owner." Then he affectionately rubbed the dog's fur and pointed into the woods. Then he said goodbye to the dog and turned to head back to his house. He needed to tell his mom to call the authorities for help. However, the dog began to whine and act like it wanted to follow him instead. Seeing the animal's apparent dilemma, Crash made a sharp command once more for the animal to go find his owner. Finally, the neighbor dog turned and disappeared into the gloominess of the forest.

CHAPTER
Seventeen

I t was July third now and Jeff Braden was sitting in his front room at four o'clock watching CNN channel when the monitor flashed a news alert banner which scrolled across the TV screen. This banner caught his attention and his eyes stayed glued to the television even while he was hearing his wife in the background trying to talk to him.

"Helen, wait a minute. There something happening in the bigger city of Seneca right now. Shush! I want to hear what the newscaster is saying." Jeff barked out his request.

"What are you saying, dear?"

"Come here and sit down with me and listen for yourself."

The news media stated that a missile or apparently some type of military grade device had ripped through the structural support system of a well-known office building causing the seventeen story high building along with the high rise restaurant on the top floor to collapse and people were being reported as dead from the aftermath of this recent attack. A news reporter was explaining to the audience that the number of lives lost in this strange explosion or terrorist attack were yet to be determined. First responders and police could be seen working to search for victims in the scene right behind this reporter. Jeff and his wife could hardly believe their eyes and ears. The banner continued to scroll beneath the video of the scene in downtown Seneca, Washington. This major city was only one hundred and fifty miles from where they lived and this gave Jeff some concern. They continued to watch the news that evening and on into the following day which was the Fourth of July.

* * *

Back at her house, Max's mother, Lisa Johnson, had just arrived from her bank job. She placed some leftover food in the microwave oven and then she sat at the kitchen table wondering where her son was. Hurrying through her meal, she went into the garage to call for him. Checking in his tent in the backyard and not discovering him, she yelled loudly for him. At last, she decided to head over to the Braden's place to check with the neighbors. It was almost seven o'clock in the evening and she was tired, and perturbed with her son's absence. Upon arriving at their two-story country home, she made her way up the steps to the porch where she knocked and waited anxiously. Within a few minutes she heard footsteps approaching. The front door swung open and a petite, blonde haired Mrs. Braden stepped out onto the porch to welcome her visitor. Lisa gave her a weak, slightly forced smile and stated the reason for the visit.

"I am looking for my son. He left a note saying he was playing with your boy which I don't mind ever. And yet, it's late and I'm concerned he is not home yet."

"Well, I was just coming out to call the boys in for spaghetti dinner." Are you sure they're not on the swings outback? Let me go check. Oh, I recall him saying they planned to go for a swim over by Crandon's saw mill which is close to Braxton Bridge. I can check to see if their bikes are here."

Within minutes, Helen Braden had come back inside her house to call her husband, Jeff. A deep wrenching knot began to form in her abdomen. A feeling of apprehension settled in her heart as she realized the late hour and what the absence of these two boys could mean. Since she had not located them by the zip line someone needed to drive over to the bridge to look for the two boys.

Overhearing Mrs. Braden's agitated tone on the phone gave Lisa cause to worry even more about the boys.

"Jeff, I need you to come home now. Our son and Max are not here and it's getting late. I don't allow him to be off somewhere in the dark like this. Their bikes are gone and I have a bad feeling about this. Hurry home and go look for the boys. I'm going to drive over to Braxton Bridge area where he often goes swimming. " She hung up the phone and went in the next room to ask Lisa some more questions and to try to dispel any fears she might be having about her son.

"If I find the boys, then I'll call you at your house with the news." Helen said.

"Okay, thanks. "I told Max to be home by six- thirty for dinner. A man is coming over to our house to take a look at the fireplace. His name is Blaine Wilson. Do you know anything about him?

"Oh, yes, my husband knows Blaine. He works at the fire station and he inspected our fireplace last year. We had to hire someone to come and clean it. But it is totally worth the money to keep our home safe from chimney fires." Mrs. Braden remarked.

"Well, I need to get back to my house to meet him. If Max doesn't show up within another forty minutes, I'll have to call and cancel our plans for tonight. I appreciate your help in locating the boys. I will have to take away his video privileges again if he doesn't get here soon."

* * *

Meanwhile back in the woods an unconscious Jake Walker had been left on the ground by his assailant. Max was sitting on the ground watching and hoping the man they called Mister Nobody' would regain consciousness soon. It was another ten minutes before Jake raised his head, groaned in pain, and then shook his head as if to clear the fog away. He vaguely recalled being hit on his head and falling to the ground before everything blacked out. Now that he was conscious he waited a few minutes before attempting to sit up and lean his back against the tree since his head ached from the blow he'd received earlier. As he sat on the ground contemplating his situation, Jake overheard one of the men speaking in broken English. This gist of their conversation contained facts about getting their weapon finished in time to launch a ground to air attack He listened intently as the main guy mentioned the targeted facility, a dam structure situated on the Soulee River.

From what Jake could decipher when the man continued talking was that he was referring to a heat seeking missile that could locate its intended target. If they were able to fire that large weapon it had the potential of causing damage to the structure. Realizing what it would take to prevent them from accomplishing their mission, he tried to formulate a plan in his head. He needed to get free from his restraints and stop these culprits. Now that he'd confirmed his suspicions about their actual intent, it might be too late to warn the men operating that facility. Jake was smart enough to know this: If they were successful in launching a small rocket from this spot, the damage would result in shutting down phone lines and other electrical power systems in this area. Plus, a second attack elsewhere would be catastrophic. He had to do something to stop them.

As he struggled to get a better view from his position behind the fir tree, he noticed the young boy sitting a few feet away. Making a soft whistling sound, he finally managed to attract the boy's attention. Speaking in a hushed tone, Jake proceeded to ask the kid a few pertinent questions.

"Hey, kid what happened to your friend?"

"I'm not sure. After they grabbed me and shoved me down in the dirt, I dozed off. Right now I'm starving and uncomfortable. What can we do? My mom will be very worried since I didn't make it home. Do you think those guys will hurt us?" Max questioned him anxiously.

"Listen, kid, these guys don't care about a youngster like you. They know you can't cause them any trouble. They won't harm you." even though he had no way of knowing for sure what the intruders' plans were, he wanted to keep the kid from getting too upset.

"I heard one of the guys talking earlier about hauling you across the border into Canada and disposing of your body."

"Well they can try to get rid of me but they don't know who they're dealing with. So don't worry about me kid."

Do you think they will take me to Canada too?" Max asked.

"No they'll just leave you here since you're no threat to their mission." Jake replied.

"You really think so? I've never been so scared. How are you going to get free when neither of us can chew through our ties?" Max questioned.

"Stay calm, okay? We'll get out of this mess. I need you to do whatever I tell you to do from here on out." Jake tried to flex his arm muscles as if his physical strength would be enough to get free of his restraints. "What's your name, kid?"

"I go by Max."

"Okay, Max, I need you to work on scooting closer to me. I need you to try to untie the thin rope wrapped around my wrist. Then I'll be able to undo the restraints on my ankles myself."

"Alright, but how can I help you when my wrist are tied too?"

"Simple, your hands are in front of your body. You can work at loosening these ties just a bit. It's worth a try, right?"

"Gosh, I wish I had the pocketknife we brought on our hike right now to cut through the ties. It'd be much faster."

While Max was working his way across the distance between them, they both heard a crackling noise in the brush which startled them. As they glanced over to the area where the sound was coming from, suddenly a familiar sight appeared in the bush. Blue Boy' cautiously sniffed the air, hesitated briefly, and then after hearing Jake's whispers beckoning him nearer, the dog came closer and dropped the knife onto Jake's lap. The dog began sniffing the boy as he wagged his tail in a friendly manner.

"That's a good dog. Now sit here by me." The dog looked intently at his master and then it tilted its head to one side as if to say what's wrong with everyone here? Fortunately for the two captives, the dog didn't whine or bark, but instead the canine settled down next to his master.

"Hey, kid, scoot closer to me and be as quiet as possible." Jake commanded. "Okay, do you know how to open up that blade?"

Max reached down to retrieve the pocket knife and then he looked intently over at Jake. Then the boy managed to release the four-inch blade.

"I've changed my mind. I want you to cut the ties around my ankles first. That way you will have a chance to practice using this sharp knife before you attempt to work on my restraints on my wrists. I need you to place the open knife blade under the ties with the sharp blade pointing away from my skin. Then keep cutting until I'm free. Can you do that?" Jake held his breath while keeping a watchful eye on their captors as Max slowly and cautiously made the sawing motions.

"Yes, I think so." Max said with a slight quiver in his voice.

"Good! You're doing fine, kid." After the twine-like rope material was fully removed, Jake moved his legs and then bent his knee a couple of times to allow the circulation to flow better in his legs. "Listen to me; I'm really glad you are here to help me get free of the rope restraints."

"Okay, great job, now I need you to work on these ties around my wrists the same way. I'll hold very still while you do the slicing. Just make sure to cut away from my wrists each time you use the knife! Go ahead, kid. No one is watching us right now. Their backs are turned away from us while they try to solve a problem with the weapon!" Jake whispered.

He could hear the men arguing about a problem with the firing mechanism on the equipment. It was just enough of a distraction for the kid to continue his efforts to free Jake's hands.

"Why did you stop? Keep going." He whispered in an urgent tone.

Max continued working on the restraints again. "What are these guys doing here?" The boy asked him.

"I have a theory that they are plotting some kind of terrorists attack on our energy supply. Since it is the third of July, there will be plenty of fireworks going off tonight and tomorrow. I have a hunch they plan to hit a local dam facility during our holiday celebration. You know, people like to shoot off loud fireworks like the noisy M-80s. The Fourth of July weekend is a perfect cover for this kind of subversive activity. I've been aware of their presence in the woods since last week when I heard a helicopter make a run over the woods and then disappear back up north. While I was hiking through the forest three days ago I discovered this crude makeshift platform sitting behind us; it looked strong enough to hold heavy equipment. I became curious as to why someone would go to this kind of trouble to position heavy metal platforms on the wood pallets. Apparently, they are getting close to being ready to use this new piece of weaponry they recently flew into this area. I needed to come here today to confirm my suspicions before I made a call to warn the proper authorities." Jake whispered again.

"Why would any criminals want to come here to this particular forested area, mister?" Max spoke in hushed tones as he scratched his head and turned to watch for any change in their captor's actions. He observed the men still involved in working on the ominous weapon.

"I'm convinced these want- to- be military guys are planning to wreck havoc on our country's energy infrastructure. This spot in the woods might be a landing area for their operation. They probably figured that they could do this without being detected by someone. I realized now that I should've brought my handgun on this trip to handle any potential trouble. I didn't know which day they'd return to the woods. I was going back to the house to contact Homeland Security when I heard you boys talking and that's when they jumped me from behind. So now I need you to leave here and head for home. Don't stop for anything. Do you understand me?" Jake spoke with an earnest expression on his face as he felt his hand come free of the tight bindings.

"Aren't you coming with me, mister?" Max questioned.

"No, I need to stay here and somehow prevent them from using that weapon."

"But you don't have anything to defend yourself. What if they shoot you first?" Max asked him.

"My plan is to overpower one of the men and grab a rifle from one guy. I want you to get going before they notice you leaving. Do you think you can do an army crawl on your belly until you reach that cluster of trees and underbrush?" Jake questioned the boy.

"Yeah, I can do an army crawl in the dirt!" Max whispered to the man they referred to as Mr. Nobody.

"Come here Blue', I want you to go with this boy. Here shake his paw, Max. He needs to be more familiar with you. Blue, go straight home and stay there with the boy!"He said as he took the knife from the kid's hand.

Don't stop for anything and stay with my dog, Blue Boy', do you understand me? He's your best bet of making it home safely. That's an order, kid." He said in a stern voice.

"Yes sir. I will not look back. Tell me your name before I leave."

"My name is Jake Walker."

"Okay."

Max looked with a new respect at the man in front of him as nodded his head. Then Max slid to the ground and onto his belly as he moved away and disappeared from sight. Jake felt better about his dog going with the kid. After running for some time, Max came upon his young friend who was still hunkered down behind a log and afraid to move. The two boys both hugged each other and then jumped up to head home. Running frantically to avoid anymore encounters with the culprits, Crash didn't notice they'd taken the wrong direction to reach home. Unknowingly, they'd been running away from their houses. Jake's dog began whining as if it knew something was wrong. Suddenly, the Blue Heeler dog stopped and refused to move on ahead in the direction the boys were going. Realizing the dog was no longer following along behind them, the boys turned around to glare at the canine. The two of them began to argue about whether or not to leave the animal there and go on further. Finally Max sat down on a fallen log to recover his strength and catch his breath and that was when he recalled the man's instructions to him.

"I believe we need to follow the dog. I'm pretty sure he knows the right way back to his owner's place. Once we get there then we're home free. You'll have to trust me this time." Max stated.

"Alright, Private Johnson, I'll let you make the important decision this time.

"What, seriously, now I'm just a puny private soldier in your military regiment! You know I'm only doing what our neighbor guy told me to do before he sent me away!" Max remarked.

"Ah, I'm just giving you a bad time for the fun of it. Sgt. Maxwell Johnson." Crash replied.

The two boys affectionately rubbed Blue Boy' on the head and then they told the dog to go home and they'd follow him. It would take another forty-five minutes to discover that they'd gone in the wrong direction again and in the meantime . . .

CHAPTER
Eighteen

As Jake Walker rubbed his sore, bruised wrist and arms and warily contemplated his next move, he watched the youngster and his dog make headway through the underbrush and then the two of them disappeared from sight. He gave a deep sigh of relief since now he'd be able to plan his attack without having to keep the youngster safe too. He started flexing his leg and arm muscles until he could finally move them without numbness and tightness from being tied up so long. At last, he was able to gradually stand up without feeling weak. Next, he bent down low so he could move across the short distance in order to reach a larger tree trunk that allowed him to stay hidden from his captors. Cautiously, he looked around the tree to observe the three men working to ready the ground to air- missile weaponry. He overheard the men speaking in broken English phrases and he had a better idea of their next move when the one man mentioned words such as, 'rocket launcher should work' and 'got the necessary firing pin into the proper location'.

"I think it is safe to use now!" The heavier set man exclaimed.

"You better know what you're doing Jacko because we don't have much time to execute this plan."

"Stop talking you two and get this launcher ready to fire. I will contact Marco Bateman and let him know what's going on here. We still have to break camp and head to the next assignment by July fourth to reach the dam located on the Columbia River once this job is accomplished. The boss said the name of Blanville Dam which is a long ways further south from this first location."

"Right, we won't get our payment if we don't succeed in hitting our target. So let's get moving along and finish our two assignments so we can reconnect with Slatermen."

The taller man dressed in black garb and acting as if he was the leader of this team pulled out his cell phone and texted their boss about the current situation on the ground. Then he went over to check on the ammunition pile over by the pallets.

Next, two of the men grabbed thick, steel cable wires leading from the weapon platform. They ran the cable lines over and attached them to the large hooks which they'd previously managed to screw into two different trees. Once they'd secured the menacing looking weaponry, they moved away to grab water bottles and guzzle down the fluid. Seeing the two men heading for cover and the third man preparing to fire the weapon, he knew he was too late. Next thing he heard was a loud deafening noise coming from the large piece of military-grade equipment. The blast shook the earth around the weapon's solid looking platform. Jake hugged the tree trunk as he wondered exactly where this deadly shell would land and how much devastation would result for an unsuspecting community lying within the target area.

Since they'd already fired the weapon at their main objective, Jake realized he needed to stop these men from using the rocket launcher again. He figured they might have a truck stashed somewhere in the wooded area. He also contemplated the idea that this bizarre para- military group could have a plan to haul the launching weapon to a second destination. such as another power source or dam facility elsewhere and so he needed to act fast. Looking around the tree, Jake saw one man who'd been knocked backwards and was still holding his ears as if they'd been damaged from the deafening booming noise of the military grade weapon. Jake could see that this same man's face was covered with black gunpowder soot and he seemed disoriented because in the next instance the guy stumbled again and then he fell over a tree root and went down. His head must've hit a rock since he didn't move after landing on the hard ground.

Luckily for Jake, he could now focus his attention on the other two individuals closer to him. He knew he'd have to act fast if he was to overpower them. Having only the kid's pocketknife, his brute strength, and a strong desire to survive, his plan was to rush them and use the act of surprise to his advantage. As he moved stealthily like a wary panther stalking its prey, he visualized in his head the strategic moves he would make. First he'd kick the one man closest to him since he was crouched down low and then he'd make a swift frontal attack with his knife towards the second intruder's torso. As an experienced ex-military person, Jake didn't plan to lose this fight today.

Without any hesitation, Jake kicked the closest attacker right in the head. He heard a cracking sound as if it was a watermelon breaking open as his heavy military boot drove into the man's cranium. The powerful hit ripped open a portion of the surprised man's scalp causing blood to pour forth and momentarily knocking the man unconscious. The second man, no longer caught off guard, reached for his weapon which was slung over his shoulder. As this dangerous individual swung a sinister looking gun around in the direction of his oncoming opponent, Jake only recourse was to grab the gun barrel with his free hand. Then he shoved the gun away just as the man was beginning to squeeze the trigger of his weapon. The bullet flew past Jake shoulder hitting a tree behind him. Jake's made a slicing motion into the man's forearm with his knife. The man grimaced in pain as he grabbed his bleeding arm in an attempt to staunch the bleeding wound. Next thing Jake saw coming at him was the butt of this man's rifle stock. Jake managed to turn sideways and with a swift upward swing, he was able to lift his arm to block the attack. However, the blow from his opponent knocked the knife out of his hand. With a menacing growl of anger and hatred, the foreigner flung his head into Jake's forehead with a swift, crushing force that nearly took Jake out of the fight. As stars flashed before Jake's eyes and shooting pain coursed through his cranium, he stumbled backward and gasped in agony. Before he could regain his footing, the angry attacker rushed at him lowering his shoulder into Jake's chest and shoved him backwards into a tree. Jake was now pinned to the tree by his attacker's brute force and the raging determination to kill him.

Jake no longer had a weapon to defend himself with as he grimaced from the stabbing pain which was causing his head to throb; the knife had been knocked away during the fight and lay a few feet away from his grasp. His primary objective was to get free of the tight hold from his assailant. He could smell the man's sweat mixed with blood oozing down onto his shirt. Instinct kicked in as Jake reached over and grabbed the man's injured arm. Next, he used his other fist to punch his attacker's wound two times with a vengeance until he felt the man's grip on him start to loosen slightly. With one swift movement, Jake managed to jab his fingers into his assailant's eye thus, causing the man more pain. The stunned man quickly released his tight grip around Jake's chest as he immediately reached up to hold his injured throbbing eye socket. The belligerent opponent stumbled backward in agony and confusion as he let out a loud cry of pain. Not waiting for the man to attempt another tight grip on him, Jake sent the man reeling onto his backside with one hard swift blow to his nose with his right fist. Then he kicked the prone man in the solar plexus. Using his boot again as a weapon, Jake delivered a powerful hit to the groggy man's head and temple area which sent the man reeling backwards as he lapsed into unconsciousness. Jake searched around in the dirt for his knife. Seeing this knife at last, he bent over to retrieve the only useful weapon available to him. That was when he heard a twig snap behind him and as he whirled around to see what had made that noise, he found himself facing another vicious, angry looking opponent.

This first individual who'd been knocked down earlier by the missile blast had regained consciousness and was now posing a very real threat. This man's face was covered with gunpowder residue and it gave him a sinister, menacing appearance. This individual had managed to find a metal object left on the ground next to their supply stash. Apparently, this attacker had every intention of retaliating with his newly acquired metal object. Jake's newest opponent took one step closer and then decided to hurl the metal pipe thing forcibly at Jake. Fortunately, the metal pipe rod missed Jake's head, but instead landed squarely against his chest and left shoulder causing him stumbling to one knee. He nearly fell backwards from the impact at close range, but he managed to brace his leg and one foot to maintain his balance. Without any hesitation, the black garbed assailant quickly retrieved the strange weapon, gripped it in his right hand, and swung it towards Jake's head with all his might. Jake reached out instinctively to grab the metal pipe weapon. and remembering his tactical training skills he grabbed hold of the metal pipe with both hands and then used his assailant's forward momentum to hurl him headlong into the dirt. In one swift motion, Jake leaped over onto the man's back in order to contain him. His intention was to twist this huge man's arms behind his back until he'd subdued the guy. However, before he was able to accomplish this goal, the strong individual maneuvered his body with such force that he knocked Jake sideways. Then the enraged man turned around and began hitting Jake relentlessly on the side of his head. The next thing Jake knew was he was in a strong choke hold and the assailant was starting to squeeze his throat in a determined effort to end his life.

Unable to get enough air after two minutes of struggling, Jake realized that he was going to die soon if he didn't escape his attackers' monstrous grip on his neck. It would be over in seconds since his thorax felt as if it might get crushed by the man's tightening pressure on his throat. Was this the way he would die? Suddenly, Jake felt a surge of an undeniable and intense burst of adrenaline start to flow throughout his body and muscles. Whatever it was or wherever its source came from, Jake didn't know the answer, but this powerful life force was absolutely electrifying his body and upper thigh muscles. With a renewed vigor, he braced his legs and threw his head back into the man's forehead. This sudden forceful blow caused his enemy's grip to lessen just enough for Jake to gasp some air. Feeling revived, Jake was now able to turn his head and break free of the man's hands. Stepping back enough to give him room, Jake extended his right leg and placed a well-aimed kick into the man's knee joint in an effort to disable this madman. He'd succeeded because the man quickly bent down to grab his injured knee joint, thus making him more vulnerable for another hit from Jake.

Upon hearing the popping sound which can result from a side -sweeping kick like Jake had just delivered, he realized that the man's knee ligament may've torn. Jake's training had taught him that a serious injury to the knee could prevent an opponent from finishing the fight. But just to be sure, Jake reached down to retrieve the metal rod piece and he used it to slam into the attacker's head thus, sending the stunned man to the ground in a crumpled heap. Jake stood there holding the unusual, but deadly new weapon in his hand while his chest heaved in and out as he tried to pull in more oxygen into his lungs. He wiped his face with his other hand to rid his brow of the grime and sweat that was beginning to sting his eyes.

Without any warning, Jake was hit from behind by another opponent who'd managed to stay down on the ground while waiting for the right moment to spring into action. Jake had made a mistake in thinking that he'd knocked the man down sufficiently enough to put him out of commission, but apparently not enough. This mistake could cost him his life. Having seen the knife fall to the ground moments before, this last assailant edged closer to the two men fighting until he was able to grab the loose pocket knife. Then while Jake was regaining his composure and balance, the individual carefully crept up from behind him. In one swift motion, his attacker thrust the four–inch knife blade into Jake's back shoulder ligament. Jake felt the stabbing, sharp pain pulsating throughout his shoulder region as he gasped for air. The knife now lodged in his back was causing an excruciating amount of pain whenever he tried to move. Since he couldn't reach around to pull the four inch blade out from his back, he just left it there as he grimaced in pain and turned hastily around to face this new enemy.

Fortunately, Jake Walker still had the use of his right arm. Steeling his mind against the nausea and pain of the knife wound, he let out a deafening cry and rushed the man. It was as if he had become like an enraged bull trying to defeat a deadly opponent. And who would finally win the deadly battle between these two angry men?

Jake saw a huge fist coming at him and at the last second; he deftly dodged to one side to avoid this onslaught. Swinging his right fist with all his might, he gave the attacker a smashing hit to the chin which sent the stunned man reeling backwards against a tree. Jake didn't hesitate as he sent another powerful blow to the assailant's abdomen. Then Jake grabbed the man's hair with his good fist and brought his right knee up and under his opponent's chin with such force that it sent the man crashing down to the ground. This third attacker was rendered unconscious momentarily. Not wanting to risk another attack, Jake chose to silence him for good. Jake torn off a large piece of his dirty shirt material, wadded it into a ball, and stuffed it into the unconscious man's mouth. Placing his knee on the fallen man's chest, he held the nostrils closed tight until there was no longer any sign of life coming from the body beneath him. Breathing in huge gulps of fresh air, Jake slumped to the ground while his chest heaved and shuddered. He started to relax for the first time since the fighting had begun.

Pulling his tired body up off the ground, Jake moved over to check on the other two individuals lying in the dirt by the recently abandoned rocket launcher. That's when he noticed something sticking out of the bushes behind the wood pallets and the machinery. Jake walked over to examine the shiny object that he'd seen in the reflection of the moonlit night. As he pushed aside the branches and leaves of the shrubbery, he could see the outline of a military grade transport vehicle which carried a second weapon called a S-75 Dvina missile.

Not wanting to leave the men unattended for too long, he turned around and retraced his steps until he was staring down at the man who seemed to be disoriented and unsure of his surroundings at the moment.

This man dressed in black clothing was in a crumpled heap on the forest soil still bleeding from his head wound. He continued to lie there making weak, pathetic groans. Jake headed over to their military gear to rummage around until he found some twine to use as a restraint. He grabbed a few of these slender rope ties and strode back to the site where the injured men lay in the dirt. He secured the disabled mans' wrists behind his back as he ignored the man's bleeding head wound. Next, he walked over to examine the other individual lying in the dirt a few yards away. This man had a busted knee and wouldn't be able to stand up or fight again. He proceeded to tie his wrist behind his back as well. Jake then worked on disabling the Russian made missile launcher until he was confident it wouldn't fire again. His objective was to disarm the weapon by destroying the firing pin mechanism with some vicious blows from the metal pipe rod that had almost put him out of commission during the earlier fight. Each time he dealt a blow to the missile weaponry, his knife wound throbbed, but he kept on hammering away at the mechanism.

Satisfied at last that the firing pin was damaged and worthless, he attempted to reach behind his back shoulder area in order to grab at the handle of the knife. After a few moments of intense pain, he was able to dislodge the blade from his shoulder. Tearing off another portion of his ragged shirt material, he was able to lay the material over the knife wound and then hold it in place until the oozing blood matter could keep the small cloth from falling away. Next, he strode over to the vehicle which the para-military guys had hidden behind a pile of branches and shrubbery until they needed to move to the next location. Jake climbed up onto the back of this vehicle and did the same thing to this weapon's firing pin mechanism. Trusting that the intruders were tied up securely and none of the missile weaponry could be fired by anyone else intent on harming US citizens, he worked at putting one foot in front of the other in an attempt to make it back to his cabin. At one point, his knees buckled and so he stayed down there resting and gathering his strength for the last part of his hike. After a few minutes, Jake staggered to his feet again. Wearily he made his way home on unsteady feet. He was determined to get to a phone to contact the local authorities in case Max hadn't been able to accomplish this task for him.

After walking for an hour, extremely exhausted and thirsty, Jake finally reached his uncle's cabin porch. He stumbled through the front doorway and found his way over to the water faucet. Turning the handle, he put his hands under the flowing water and splashed it all over his grimy, dirt laden face. Next, he leaned over and guzzled the refreshing cold water into his mouth. Feeling like he could finally stand on his feet without collapsing, Jake splashed his face and hair again with the cold water until he finally felt invigorated and refreshed. Grabbing a hand towel by the sink, he dried his face and hands. Then he picked up the house phone and dialed the number of his CO.

"Is this Major John Holt?" Jake asked.

"No, this is his staff secretary, Hannah. He is in a staff meeting at the moment." She replied.

"Tell him I have an urgent message to relay to him. This is of vital importance, so I need to hear back ASAP. This is concerning national security. Do you get my drift, Hannah?" Jake demanded.

"Yes, I will get a message to the commander immediately. Do you want to hold while I direct this call into the meeting?"

"Yes, that would be in your best interest, Hannah, if you want to keep your job!"

Jake waited while the phone was being rerouted to his former commanding officer. Two minutes later Major John Holt came on the phone.

"Hello, Jake, what do you have for me?"

"Sir, I request your immediate response to a serious threat which occurred here in the state of Washington. I had a major run-in with some militants recently. I believe they were able to launch one missile towards a landmark site or maybe a power plant somewhere nearby. I'd like to get a confirmation of a possible missile strike, Sir." Jake insisted.

"Tell me your exact location and I'll send some men in to secure the area. I will put in a call to the local authorities if you give me your address, name of the closest city, and any other helpful information regarding the region in question." Major Holt replied.

"I'm situated about twenty-five miles northeast of the town of Randall which is close to the city of Grandview, Washington. These para-military type individuals were dropped from an aircraft and they landed in the wooded area some miles east of my place. They shot off a rocket launcher mounted on a humvee before I could stop them, Sir." He stated.

"How many men infiltrated the area?" Major John Holt queried.

"I dealt with three men who were dropped from a helicopter. It seems that they'd made the aircraft to appear as if it was a news helicopter. I believe that it was used as a cleverly disguised aircraft and not simply a harmless civilian helicopter. One man is dead and two are tied up where I left them at their weapon launching site. They'd established an accessible trail leading to the exact spot and that's how I was able to find them. You'll find a rocket launcher clamped to a platform along with miscellaneous gear lying behind a large fir tree. There's also a partially hidden vehicle and its weaponry which I managed to disable so it shouldn't be a threat now." Jake said.

"And there was no sign of any other men in the vicinity?"

"There was one other individual I'd encountered riding his motorcycle right before I ran into the other three guys. I managed to subdue this rider without much trouble. He is still tied up and stuffed inside the trunk of an old car located on my property." Both men laughed at this point. "He shouldn't give your men any trouble! However, we still have one potential threat from a different individual."

"What do you mean?" The commander asked.

"Well, I overheard the military looking guys talking about getting a message to their leader about this particular mission. So I believe there is another command post somewhere in this region. Or it could be located somewhere in Canada just across the border from here."

"That doesn't sound good. Just yesterday there was an explosion that is being investigated by the FBI and the local authorities in the major city of Seneca, Washington which took out a tall landmark building. There were a lot of casualties and some fatalities which resulted from that attack. This is not looking good for our country. In other words, what we are looking at is a threat to our national security." Major Holt declared.

"I have done my best to contain these extremists in this locale and I will keep you informed about any follow up needed here, Sir."

"Well done, I commend you on your expert handling of this breech in our northern borders and in your area, Jacob."

"Thank you, sir, just my way of doing my duty. By the way I'd appreciate it if you would contact the right security personnel in this northwest region to determine if an important energy facility near here may've been damaged today by the rocket launcher that was fired from that site. I was told that the man to contact is Howard Jenkins in Bellingham, WA."

"I will keep you posted once I've learned of any relevant information." Major Holt responded.

Lying down on his bed with every muscles aching after his weary journey back home, Jake drifted off in a restless sleep.

CHAPTER
Nineteen

J ake was jarred out of a sound sleep by a loud ringing sound emitting from his phone. Stumbling from his bedroom to the living room of his cabin, he located the clamoring phone and managed to push the right button to respond.

"Jacob Walker?

"Hello. Yes, sir. Commander Holt, it's good to hear from you again.

"Can you talk right now?" asked Major Holt.

"Yes, I've had some adequate sleep and I took some Advil for my head pain and the shoulder injury so I'm good, Sir."

"We found out some more information on those intruders you tangled with in Washington State yesterday. They are from Quebec, Canada and their interest in our country was to procure a launching site for their recent missile attack. The one individual, a French-Canadian man you had tied up and stuffed into the trunk of your vehicle was taken into custody late last night and he told us everything in order to garner a plea deal. He revealed that their plan was to take out the first of two major water and energy sources like you suspected."

"Did he say who's behind this act of terrorism?" Jake asked his prior commanding officer.

"He admitted that it was not his own government, but instead he pointed the finger at the Russians. He was part of a terrorist group which we were told has originated out of Moscow; this terrorist group called El Jihad is behind this attack on the U.S."

"It would appear these crazies are in every major country now! They almost succeeded in disrupting our power/energy sources and the water supply facility in your state as well as the lives of some American citizens residing in two major cities at this time." Major Holt paused for a moment to let this all sink in. "Well, I just wanted to keep you updated on how the interrogations are going. The other men are not talking. They will spend a long time in prison for their involvement in this attack. Oh, by the way, the department of Homeland Security is sending someone over to get your statement. They will bring in a crew to dismantle that rocket launcher and move it."

"That's good news. I'll keep an eye out for him. I hope his credentials are up to date because I don't want any one traipsing around here who's not a government agent, if you know what I mean! If I find out the person is not who he says he is, then he might end up in the trunk of my old car for a few days." Jake retorted humorously.

"Hah ha. I'm sure you mean this warning and therefore I will give this particular agent a heads up. Maybe you should post a No Trespassing Sign on your front lawn signed by Uncle Sam." Major Holt remarked glibly.

"Yes Sir, I just might do that. But you remember I'm no longer in the military now. Not that they haven't asked me to reenlist to help train new recruits in certain self defense tactics. I'd consider their offer if it was a part time job. I like the peace and quiet out here now since those criminals have been apprehended and locked up." Jake said.

"Well, don't get too comfortable in your isolated rustic place, I have a proposition to make to you in the future. I like you to consider working for the government on a new assignment."

"I'm not sure what you mean by the word assignment, Sir. Whatever you might be hinting at I'd be willing to consider it if I don't have to sign up for another tour in Afghanistan." Jake replied.

"No, it's nothing like that. I'll get that information you asked for and call you back shortly. In the meantime gets some well-deserved rest."

Thirty minutes later, Jake received a phone call from Major Holt. His suspicions were confirmed by his commanders' answer.

"Jacob, we've identified the damage inflicted on the area you asked about. An energy facility called Soulee Dam was hit yesterday evening around six-thirty. A military investigator, Will Benton, and his team determined that it was a heat seeking missile they fired towards the dam. There was a night watchman who had turned on his portable heater in his tower station located at the east end of the structure. The rocket missile blasted into his sector and blew away that small shack building where he normally sits at night. Fortunately for us, the impact didn't destroy the main cement structure as was their intent." He stated.

"What became of the worker from that exact station hut?" Jake asked.

"Apparently he'd left his tower station just moments before the hit to relieve himself. He was heading back across the top runway to get back to his station when the blast sent him reeling to the ground. He's in county hospital at the moment being assessed by a medical team. He's in critical condition, but still alive. The collateral damage could've been far worst if the heater had not been turned on prior to the attack. They found a grey backpack which contained a heat sensor device that had been lodged behind a generator unit situated near the top section of the dam. Hundreds of lives were spared because of the unusual fact that this night watchman had turned on his portable heater to stay warm an hour or so before the missile strike occurred. We've notified the White House and they are grateful, but alarmed that these men were able to slip past the northern boundary of Canada and the U.S."

"I'm glad to hear this, sir."

"All right then, I request you get back to me when you can to give me a full report."

"Yes sir, I'll try to report back to you in three or four days."

"Goodbye and thank you again for your fine efforts at spotting the enemies' encroachment on American soil. You may well have thwarted a deadly plot to destroy our energy sources in that region."

"Oh, I just remembered there were two boys involved in this event as well. Can you try to find out any information of their whereabouts? I hope they made it safely home. I'd sent my dog with the one boy named Max Johnson. His mother's name is Lisa Johnson and I believe she works for a city bank in the town of Randall." Jake shared.

"I can get my man on the ground there working on this matter. Do you know the name of the other boy?"

"Hmm, I believe Max said his name is Crash or something similar. His last name I don't recall at this time. Maybe Mrs. Johnson can help you out there. Max told me that his friend's family lives nearby. That's all I know." He remarked.

"Fine, we'll work on locating these boys and make sure they are safe."

"Thank you, sir." Jake replied.

"Yes, fine work. Oh, and thanks for making sure the trunk of your car was left open so our men could grab the hostage and take him in for questioning." Get in touch with me if you need anything, Jacob."

"I will, sir. Thanks for looking into this for me." He said goodbye and hung up the phone.

* * *

After getting off the phone, Jake went into the bathroom to splash water on his face in order to wake up. Then minutes later, Jake heard a banging on his front door. He strode over to turn the door knob to see who was intruding on his quiet morning. He hadn't even started his coffee maker yet and already someone was annoying him. Could it be the homeland security officer he'd been told was coming to question him about the recent event? Well, whoever it was they needed to stop pounding on his front door so rudely.

"What do you want and who are you?" Jake demanded from the harried and anxious looking individual standing on his front porch.

"My name is Jeff Braden and I'm looking for my son and his friend, Max, They told my wife they'd wanted to come to your cabin and play with your dog." He shifted nervously from one foot to the next as he observed his new neighbor. "Have you seen any sign of two boys? They're both eleven years old. One has light brown hair and the other boy has dark brown hair." Jeff asked.

"Yes, they had come by here to talk for a bit and asked if they could play with my dog. The day before, I'd mentioned that the kid could toss a ball around with my dog sometime. The interesting thing about these two kids is that instead of waiting to talk to me here at my cabin, they followed me into the forest and then they managed to get involved in some criminal activity which has occurred about four miles from here ."

"What do you mean by criminal activity? Did something bad happen to my son? Where are the boys?"

"Calm down Mr. Braden. The boys were alright when I last saw them. You son ran off immediately and once Max was able to get free, he ran off into the woods with my dog. So since he's not at your place then we need to look in my outbuildings to see if he's hiding in this vicinity."

"You said Max, but what of my son, Crash?" Wasn't he with Max? What aren't you telling me and what is your name? How did you get involved in this situation? Maybe I should call the police right now!" Jeff remarked.

"Like I said, mister, Max was safe the last time I saw him. Your son had run off as soon as the men started attacking me. Unfortunately, the thugs managed to apprehend me since it was two against one and they'd come from behind me while I was telling your son to stop following me." Jake wiped his brow with his shirt sleeve and then he held his palm up to signify that the discussion was over. Turning away in apparent indifference, he went into his kitchen to pour hot water into the coffee maker.

"Hey, wait a second mister; I'm sorry if I misjudged you. It's just that I'm really worried about my son who didn't come home last night." Jeff Braden exclaimed.

"I just got off the phone with the proper authorities and this official is now looking into this matter. He promised me he'd contact the local authorities to check on the two boys involved in this rather unusual activity. In the meantime, I'm making myself some hot coffee and you're welcome to come inside to wait while I get ready to traipse around in the forest in search of my dog or you can go and hunt for the boys by yourself. It's your decision."

"Fine, I guess you're on the up and up. What did you say your name was again?"

"My name is Jacob Walker. I recently took ownership of this property from my uncle. He used to spend the summer here and then he passed it onto me in his will. I was hoping to recoup from my tour of duty overseas and do some fishing in Trout Lake. I was planning to just relax for a few weeks and then attempt to write about my experience while in the military. This trouble in the woods recently has kept me otherwise occupied. Now I'm waiting to hear back from a certain official. Once I've learned that the national security team has captured every one of the criminals in this operation then I can truly relax."

"Oh, I see. Well, then if you don't mind, I would like to wait here. I'd like to enlist your help trying to find my missing son and his friend." Jeff Braden mentioned.

"Fine, I'm sure your kid is safe, but I don't know that for a fact. What I do know for sure is that I believe the kid named, Max, is bound to be alright since I told him to stay with my well trained dog. And per your question, I don't mind you tagging along with me when I do head out to look for my Blue Heeler dog." Jake replied.

"I appreciate your generosity. I just need to make a phone call and let my wife know of this latest development so she can call our neighbor friend, Lisa Johnson."

"Go ahead and use my phone then." He said.

"Thank you."

"Hi, it's Jeff. I've been talking with our new neighbor, a guy named Jake about the boys. He said he thinks our son is okay but he doesn't know where he is right now. However, there is some good news and bad news. Here's the bad news first. He said that he had stumbled into a very difficult situation with some men who'd come into Washington State illegally. I guess the boys had decided to follow this ex-military guy on his hike deep into the forest and they'd gotten into some trouble with a few bad men. He just told me that Max had managed to help him escape from being tied up by these same intruders. Then this ex-military guy was able to release Max and he mentioned just now that he'd sent Max away with his dog. The two of them were supposed to head back to get help." Jeff expounded.

"So then did Max get back safely to the man's cabin like this neighbor guy mentioned?" Helen demanded.

"Ah well, he isn't here on the porch and the dog isn't in sight either so we are going to go check out the man's pump house and his shed to see if Max might be hiding inside one of the shed buildings on his property ." Jeff retorted.

"Are you telling me this is the good news? How is Max not being at the man's place now actually good news? And why would he be hiding in some shed on this guy's property? Helen questioned.

"You're right this is a little complicated. Let me explain further before you go wild on me. He said that Max was with his Blue Heeler dog and it's a very safe, well trained military dog. At least, our son was alright the last time this man saw him. So the good news is that this ex-military guy has decided to join me in a search for the two boys. You might want to inform Lisa about this so she can relax a bit. I promise you I'll get back to you as soon as we find them." Jeff hung up the phone and sat back down on the hardback chair next to the aged, pine wood table in Jake's small kitchen. He watched the ex-military man with great interest as he set down his coffee cup and gathered up some necessary gear. Then ten minutes later the two men left the cabin to search the outbuildings for the dog and Max. There was no sign of either the boy or his new companion.

"Do you have any idea where your son and this Max kid might have gone to hide besides my place after encountering those para-military attackers?" Jake asked his neighbor.

"Well, I'm very surprised they didn't return home to inform us of the trouble. That's what has me worried." Jeff Braden replied. He wiped the sweat from his brow and frowned considerably. "What if there is another person involved in the group you had a run-in with and they've apprehended my son?"

"You need to stop thinking the worst and concentrate on anywhere your son or Max might go to feel safe." Jake said. Walking around to the back of his property, Jake hollered for the missing boy. When there was no response he turned to talk with his neighbour, Mr. Braden.

"Do you know of another place or hideout where the two boys may've gone after their frightening experience with the attackers?"

"Ah, okay give me a minute to think about this. Actually, I don't have a clue Mister Jake, but my wife will have a better idea since she deals with my son and his friend, Max more during the day than I do. Let's head over to our place and ask her or even Lisa Johnson if they can steer us in the right direction. It's going to get dark in another hour and we need to find them before then."

So the men continued on towards the Braden's home. Jake questioned Jeff about the boys in an attempt to keep the man's mind off of the possibility that the kids may've been abducted.

"So what do the boy's like to do mostly?" Jake asked.

"Besides playing video games a lot they like to ride bikes on the dirt hills. They also love to go for a crazy ride on the new zip line I put up in the very back section of our ten acre property."

"Okay, are there any tree forts or abandoned cabins in this vicinity the boys might want to use as a hideout place? Jake asked the neighbor man.

"Not that I'm aware of. My son had asked me to build him a fort a few weeks ago but, I've been too busy with my job to do anything like that. Plus, my wife had asked me to take care of some house repairs. My wife did mention that she'd overheard the two planning to gather old boards, some plywood, and a handful of nails to try to build their own fort over at Max's place. Maybe Lisa will have some idea of where we should go after we talk to her."

"Sound good. Hey, Jeff, do you mind if I call you Jeff?" Jake watched Mr. Braden's facial expression to see what his reaction would be.

"Ah, sure, no problem and say, I really appreciate all your help so far. It's great to have someone like you helping us civilian in a scary situation like this. By the way, why did these men want to gain illegal access into this region? I mean we don't have anything they'd want, do we?"

"I'd become curious about some rather unusual activity which seemed to be transpiring in the forested area. I'd become aware of this one individual travelling on a motorcycle past my property. I was curious as to why he was coming and going in this area. It just seemed a little unusual to me. My gut kept telling me to follow him. So later on I took the same trail he'd used and that's when I discovered a large platform which resembled a launching pad setup. Then there was no activity for the next three days and so I waited.

It just struck me as bizarre that this setup was on the same site as to what appeared to be an abandoned logging development. I decided to contact my friend, Major John Holt, who has connections with someone at Homeland Security office in Washington D.C. He encouraged me to keep an eye on the unusual activity and report back to him. Yesterday when I was attempting to persuade your kids to leave the woods, a group of men attacked me and knocked me senseless. Then they tied me up, along with the kid named Max. That's when I learned about their intention to destroy some important facility within a twenty or thirty miles radius from here. According to my contact person, this first hit was directed at a large water facility and the connecting dam structure just outside of a larger city in this region. My CO also mentioned they could've succeeded in sending a second RPG to destroy the water facility structure situated on the Columbia River if we hadn't stumbled onto their operation. Fortunately, I was able to disable that particular military-grade weaponry."

"Wow, that's intense. I hadn't been listening to the news the last couple of days. Are you saying that they already hit the first dam/ energy structure?" Jeff asked in disbelief.

"Well, according to the FBI and homeland Security people, the local dam was superficially damaged by that small hit on July third and one worker was seriously injured. When there is only one wounded civilian and a relative minor hit then it's called minimal collateral damage. No attack on American soil is minimal in my mind." Jake responded.

They had reached the front steps of Jeff's home by this time. During their short time of chatting, Jeff was feeling a new kinship with this neighbor. After introducing his new friend to his wife and Lisa Johnson, Jeff went to grab a warmer coat and find some bandages for Jake's wound. He asked his wife to apply the astringent and some Neosporin ointment to the open knife wound on the man's back while he worked at getting the gauze ready. Next, he asked Lisa to cut strips of adhesive tape to secure the thick gauze in place. Once Jake's wound was tended to properly, he proceeded to ask them if they had any idea where the boys might have gone to hide. Mrs. Braden was the first to respond.

"I've already searched at their favorite swimming hole. Sometimes the boys go to the dirt hills and ride their bikes. We could go look there." Helen stated.

"Then let's get moving before we lose any advantage of daylight." Jake replied.

The small group continued walking in order to reach the well-used trails the boy's often went to for bike jumps. Max's mother spoke up for the first time as she addressed Jake.

"Why did our boys end up with your dog?" Lisa queried.

"As I've told Jeff, I had to send Max away from an unsavory situation we'd stumbled upon in the woods. And the only way I could count on your boy being safe was for him to take off with Blue Boy. I figured Max would be safer if he wasn't alone in the woods." Jake said.

"Who in the world is Blue Boy? It sounds like a character in a kid's movie." Lisa asked.

"This is the name I chose to call my pet because of his breeding. He's a blue Heeler dog with a slight mix of German shepherd. The military picked this breed because of its temperament. The Blue Heeler is known for being cautious, protective, brave, and obedient animal. The military discovered they were able to train these dogs to locate IEDs better than we could. This particular dog had been stationed with my unit in Afghanistan before being shipped stateside. Luckily, I was able to adopt him." Jake replied.

"I see, well then do you think Max and your Blue Heeler dog might be with Jeff Braden's son?"

"That's a question I'm hoping your son has the answer to Mrs. Johnson." Jake replied as he noticed how nice Max's mother looked. He liked her beautiful smile and wondered about her husband and why he wasn't home to help her in this ordeal.

CHAPTER
Twenty

During the walk, Jeff hollered out for his son hoping to get a verbal response while Jake and Lisa paused for a moment to discuss the idea of going in different directions if the boys were not at the dirt hills. There was no sign of the boys or their discarded bikes at this jump site so they moved on to scour the outlying fields. Finding no signs of the two boys they met again to discuss their next plan.

"I wonder if they maybe decided to go to their favorite spot. You know where I'm talking about? I'm referring to the bridge where they go to swim often. You know how boys like to play under bridge coverings and throw rocks. I may've missed them the first time I went there?" Helen Braden asked.

Fine, why don't we have the Braden's go to the bridge area again while Mrs. Johnson and I head in a different direction. We need to limit our searches and the time it takes to explore those possible options. We're starting to get less and less daylight and thus, I think we need to spread out more in this search." Jake declared.

He took Jeff Bronson aside momentarily to speak quietly to him. "Listen, if we don't find the boys by tonight, then when you return to your house, you need to call the police and report them missing. I plan to head back in a bit to leave Mrs. Johnson at her home and head back to my place to see if my dog returned home. Tomorrow I plan to get up at first light and follow a hunch. I'm thinking about heading into the woods again. There are two different trails that loop around from my place to the other side of the ravine and I want to follow the second trail to see where it goes. If we can't get them to respond to our shouts during our walks tonight, then something might have prevented them from reaching your place." Jake Walker said.

Meanwhile Lisa Johnson had stepped closer to the men and she overheard that last remark.

"What are you saying? What would've prevented the boys from getting back here?" Lisa questioned him.

"I'm not actually saying something bad happened. I'm just referring to the likelihood that one of the boys may've had an accident. You need to look at this possibility. What if one of them fell somehow, He could've twisted an ankle. If that's the case, he'd be limping which could hinder him from getting home by nightfall. It is also possible that they took a wrong path. If that's the case then they could be lost. We need to get some more people out here to help to cover a lot of ground. The forest can be deceptive and difficult to transverse on foot. So let's hope for the best, but plan for the worst case scenario. That's the Marine's motto and I think we need to have a working plan." Jake remarked.

"Sure, I understand what you're saying now. I'll try to stay in touch and maybe check in with you tomorrow to see if your dog returned. Thanks for spending your time helping us in this hunt. See you later." Jeff replied.

The two groups split off to cover a wider perimeter. Jake and Lisa made their way back to the road leading to her place. Once they'd arrived at her home, she ran inside to call out for her son. Jake checked the backyard and her tool shed with no sign of the boy. Lisa could hear him calling for Max as he edged into a grove of birch trees just beyond her boundary line. The sound of a male voice hollering for her young son brought tears to her eyes as she realized just how much she missed having a strong man in her life to care for them. She glanced over on the dresser at a photograph of her young son standing next to her. She had her arm around his shoulder and they were both smiling as if everything was wonderful. It had been taken at the county fair and she recalled that day had been filled with fun rides, much laughter, and sharing stories together with her boy. Memories she would cherish and now more so if something awful where to happened to her young son. She wished desperately her husband, Morgan, was here to comfort her. She had struggle for the last two years in not having a husband to shield her from worries and fears. What would she do if something awful happened to her child? She couldn't imagine life without her dynamic, energetic son. Max gave her so much to live for and she needed him. Hearing the sound of the door shutting jarred her from her reverie and deep thoughts. She turned away from the photograph with its memories and went to talk with her new neighbor who stood waiting on the front porch.

"I searched everywhere he might have gone to hide. No sign of him, sorry. He's probably still traumatized by the recent events. He could be hiding somewhere or with my dog like I instructed him. We will find your boy, I promise you."

"I am getting more and more concerned as the time goes by. This is not like Max to not check in with me, especially after dark. I just hope he's safe and with the Braden's' son too. The idea of him being hurt and lying somewhere all alone and scared is too much for me to bear. He isn't wearing warm clothing to get through the chilly night temperatures. I just want him to be here safe at home with me."

Lisa started crying. She couldn't believe she was getting so emotional in front of this neighbor. She hardly knew the man and here she was sobbing like a child who'd just lost their favorite, snuggly-soft teddy bear. Jake stood there unsure of what he should do next. He'd fought against insurgents, taken out snipers with total accuracy, and trained men to survive in hand to hand combat, but a woman crying was beyond his capabilities or training in self-defense. Hesitantly and awkwardly, he reached out to hold her hand in an attempt to console her.

"I will get up early in the morning to go hike the other trail and search for your boy. I'm confident I can find my dog, Blue Boy' who always responds to my voice and hopefully your son will be there with him. I'm confident that I will find them. I don't believe there were any more attackers in the area, so the boys may've decided to hide out and wait until they felt it was safe. After all it was a frightening experience for the two youngsters. It's going to turn out alright. Will you trust me? I will do my best to locate them."

"Yes, you're right. If they stayed with your dog then it will make it easier for people to locate them." Lisa smiled at him and he was drawn into the depths of her beautiful chocolate-brown eyes.

Jake became suddenly aware of a heat rising within him that could only be from their closeness. He found himself desiring to hold more of her than just her hand. When she withdrew her hand, he sensed a new, strange feeling of loss; he needed to be close to this desirable woman. It was as if some age old ancient cry to be with one's true soul mate had taken over his responses at that moment. *Get a grip, buddy, you need to calm down and focus on the missing boy right now.* Taking a step back Jake looked at the wall clock and realized the importance of getting home.

"I need to get back and get my gear ready for the early morning trek back into the forest. You need to get some sleep so try not to worry; we'll find your boy. I am confident that my dog will protect your son because that he's nature. Blue Heeler dogs are known to be friendly and also good companions. I'm confident that my dog will defend your son if provoked by a strange person. Max is in good hands or paws. In fact, if I know anything about boys, they will probably steal my dog's heart away. I'll probably have trouble keeping him at my place from now on. So I'll say goodnight to you, Lisa Johnson. I will stay in touch with you after I return from my next jaunt in the woods."

Lisa thanked him profusely and made a feeble attempt to wipe away her tears and clean her face with her sleeve. She gave him one more tentative smile and then bid him a safe journey in the morning. She felt an unusual connection with this larger than life man. She wondered if it was merely his caring mannerism and helpfulness or was there something more between them. While he was holding her hand she had felt a definite pull towards him. It was almost as if she'd been a candle held in his hand waiting to be lit by a match that would ignite her heart's fire. Lisa wasn't sure how to handle this strange new attraction she was feeling. As she walked to her room to change out of her work clothes she wondered what he was doing in these parts and how long he might stay. Then she recalled he'd said something about his friend who was a fellow soldier so maybe he'd chosen to stay in the military for his career. He was probably home on an extended furlough and then he'd leave to go back to his other world and out of their lives for good. She needed to push away any thoughts of him being more than a helpful neighbor.

It had been nice though having a man to relate to on a personal basis for one night. Lisa gave a deep sigh. Lying down on her bed, she wrapped the soft comforter around her slim figure. Heartsick at the thought of her son alone in the woods, she began to weep as she felt her emotions taking over again. She missed holding her son. Suddenly it dawned on her she was also missing the comfort she needed from a strong man's embrace. She lay in bed thinking about her time spent with this handsome individual.

Lisa tossed and turned until she finally fell into a fitful sleep; towards the early morning hours she had a strange but very vivid dream. In this unusual dream, she was being held securely in the arms of a tall, muscular man. This person was smiling down on her and it felt as if he was intent on capturing her heart and soul along with her physical body. Then she woke up to the noise of coyotes howling in the distance. This sound from the wild animals brought her back to the reality of her missing son somewhere in the same woods and in danger of the likelihood of certain predators roaming through this wilderness region during the night time. Shivering slightly in darkened bedroom, she couldn't help but image her husband still alive and feeling his warm body lying close beside her. He'd be the first person go looking right away and somehow he'd know just where to find their son. She could almost imagine him carrying a lantern in one hand as he tromped around in the forest for most of the night searching desperately in spite of the darkness and not stopping until he found Max.

CHAPTER
Twenty-One

The clock on the living room wall said ten-thirty at night and still no sign of the two boys so Jeff Braden picked up the phone to place a call into the police station. When a male voice came on the other end Jeff spoke into the receiver piece to make a request for the officer to take down the information about his son.

"Hello, yes, I'm Jeff Braden and I need to report a missing child."

"What? Oh he's eleven years old and has light sandy colored hair and blue eyes. His name, ah it's Crasher', oh I mean his real name is Kevin Braden, but we call him Crash' as a nickname because he's been crashing into things since he was four. Well, anyway, he's been gone for an entire day and part of the night and so far we haven't been able to locate him. He's also possibly with a neighbor boy, Max Johnson who's also missing. His mother is frantic with worry."

"I understand your concern, Mr. Braden, but your son hasn't been gone long enough for me to do a search of the area where you folks live. Also our captain has been away from the station on another serious matter." The police officer replied.

"Well, can't you take down our information and give us a call when your captain returns? Where is he that you can't or won't get a hold of him to enlist his help in this matter?" Jeff questioned the officer in an agitated voice.

"Mr. Braden, he was called away to help in an explosion over at the Soulee Dam facility. One person was reported seriously injured and they are investigating the incident. I will have him or someone else contact you in the morning." The officer said.

"No, I want you to tell me that an officer will be sent to my home in the morning to help us search for the two boys. This is a matter of grave importance. I believe my son was involved with those dangerous criminals who tried to blow up that same water structure." Jeff stated emphatically.

"Your son is only eleven years old and you think he was involved with these men? Can you explain yourself, sir? Better yet, I'm sending an officer over to your place shortly. What is your address, Mr. Braden." The officer replied.

"Twenty two hundred Northeast Menlo Road. We are two miles south of the Carlton Road turnoff. I will leave my porch light on and meet the officer on my front lawn. And thank you for sending someone over here."

"You're welcome and rest assured we will check into this matter, Mr. Braden."

Jeff hung up the phone and shared this news with his agitated wife. They both hugged and sat down for the first time in hours to talk about their son's situation. He tried to reassure his worried wife that their son would be found safe and sound. He didn't share with her any of his anxious thoughts, but instead he asked her if she'd like some hot peppermint tea with honey. She replied with a yes.

* * *

Meanwhile, deep in the forest the two exhausted boys and their new canine companion were trying to get comfortable on the hard ground beneath the large oak tree.

"I don't think I be able to get to sleep. This ground is way too hard. Look I've found another couple of rocks. Help me move them out of our way. My ankle hurts too much to get up." Max informed his friend.

"Okay, and then I'll climb up the tree and grab the other snacks from our tree fort. Plus, we still have one food item in the backpack. You can have the oatmeal bar if you like. I'll eat the protein bar."

"I wish we could sleep in the tree house instead of down Max stated.

"Well, those wooden floorboards of the tree house will be hard and uncomfortable, but since you went and slipped off the makeshift ladder we are now stuck down here. If you hadn't been in such a hurry to get your hands on the stash of food we'd left in the tree house, we'd be on our way home right now and sleeping in our own comfortable beds tonight." He quipped.

"Oh, piped down, Captain Braden. You are such a smart mouth. Save your breath, we would be in a heck of lot more trouble if we'd both been grabbed by those men in the woods!" Max retorted disgustedly.

"I wish we'd brought some bottled water in our backpack. The neighbor guys' dog ate part of the protein bar and now my stomach is growling." I wish we had a way to let my parents know where we are." He remarked.

"Maybe we should send Mr. Jake's dog away to get help. Do you think he'd be able to find his way back here to the tree fort?" Max asked his friend.

Well, I suppose the dog wouldn't come back to our exact location." Crash Braden answered. And that would leave us completely on our own in the woods."

"Hey, did you find out that neighbor's name? I'm talking about the guy we were following in the woods?" he asked.

"Yeah, he told me his name is Jake and he was in the Marines before this. He's a pretty cool guy. Max stated. I hope those bad guys didn't capture him again. Gosh, what if they actually took him to Canada? I overheard them talking about getting rid of him?"

"We can't be sure of anything. We just need to stay put. We're safe here and they won't find us in this part of the forest." Crash Braden insisted.

"I'm just glad I was able to escape before they took me into Canada as well." Max exclaimed.

"Yeah me too, however, we could still starve to death here in these woods."

"Yeah, you're lucky you didn't fall over a tree root and damage your brain or maybe even break your measly, ole nose!"

"Watch out buddy! I can still whip you and teach you something about what pain feels like." He punched his friend playfully on the shoulder and smiled in an effort to make light of their situation. "Maybe I should leave before it gets dark. I think I can find my way home and get my Dad to come here and carry you back. I can leave my backpack here with you if you'd like."

"Yeah, that sounds like a great idea. However, I don't like the part about me staying here all by my lonesome in the woods. There might be cougars or coyotes prowling around here at night." Max stated nervously.

"I'll be back before any serious predator discovers you're here. Just keep quiet. Cougars won't even know you're here if you don't snore too loud."

"Hah, you're so not hilarious! Just don't forget me here."

"It might take me awhile to return so I can leave this stick for you. You can use it as a club to fight off coyotes and possums. I hear possums really growl and hiss when a person bothers them."

"Gee, thanks for nothing."

Crash grabbed a different branch to use as he headed through the brush to look for the same path they'd created earlier. The dog stayed beside the injured boy as if to guard him from any harm. Max scooted over to look inside the discarded backpack lying in the dirt. He found a half of a peanut butter sandwich lodged in the bottom of the front pocket. Not minding that it was partially squished, he hungrily wolfed it down. Wishing he had a quart of chocolate milk to wash his food down, he settled back to wait next to his furry new companion, 'Blue Boy'.

Crash' Braden continued on walking through the woods wondering as the time went by if he might've gone in the wrong direction. Things can look different in the woods as the light was fading. Finally, he noticed the gloom of night starting to engulf him and he began to actually worry. Taking more tentative steps in the dim lighting, he soon realized he was coming to an area that wasn't as thick with trees as before. Now he could plunge on ahead with more ease. His steps began to quicken and he hoped he'd found the right way again. Suddenly, he felt the soft dirt and rocks break loose beneath his tennis shoes. His first reaction was to grab hold of a nearby small sapling for support. Next thing that happened was the thin branch he'd grabbed suddenly snapped causing him to lose his balance. His long sleeved shirt material tore loose and stuck on some brambles as he lurched forward. This momentum and the law of gravity sent him flailing and stumbling rapidly down the incline. His body tumbled and flipped over a number of times until he landed heavily against a good size rock. He cried out in excruciating pain. His wrist and right knee felt like they were both injured seriously from the impact. He lay there in the dirt trying to not move his injured limbs. His head felt as if it would explode. Eventually that part of his body stopped throbbing so intensely, so he pushed himself up with the one good hand until he could stand. Thinking he'd just climb back up the slope, he began to move forward. His body felt weak and his head began to hurt from the initial impact when he'd landed so abruptly. Unable to take more steps up the slope, he collapsed into the dirt. Sitting there all alone in the dark, he started to bemoan his predicament. With the chill of the night air all around him, he decided to scoot backwards until he was able to prop himself up against a rock formation lodged in the side of the ravine. Leaning his back and head against the solid rock, he wished he'd never ventured out on this evening journey. In spite of the dull pain and discomfort he was feeling, he closed his eyes and eventually fell asleep from sheer exhaustion.

* * *

Daylight came streaming through the window at six a.m. waking up a slumbering Jake. He groaned and shoved the pillow over his face to block out the intrusion. Every muscle in his back and arms felt as if someone had pounded on them with a hammer. Wishing for a massage, but realizing where he was right then, he opened his eyes and then quickly closed them shut. He recalled having a horrific nightmare. Once again the night terrors had invaded his subconscious and threatened to rob him of the deep ream sleep he desperately needed for today's search for the missing boys. In this reoccurring dream, he was teamed up with two Iraqi soldiers who were canvassing the town of Kabul. Suddenly, a female with two small boys ran into the street trying to find shelter from gunfire from the insurgents. Jake had tried to warn the two soldiers while he fought off a militant who had fired his rifle in the fleeing woman's direction. He watched helplessly as the woman and one of the boys were knocked to the ground. Then he raced over to scoop the second child in his arms and ran. In his dream he was still running away from the mayhem yelling for return fire from his unit. He'd jerked awake that night in a cold sweat and then he had collapsed immediately onto his bed again.

Pushing away the memories of the horrific dream, Jake thought about calling a physician and requesting some Ambient pills for the following night's sleep. Then shaking himself roughly, he turned his thoughts to a more pleasant image, that of the beautiful neighbor woman from last night and the desire she'd awaken within him. Suddenly, his weary brain remembered the immediate problem of two missing boys and his dog. He climbed slowly out of bed and walked over to the sink. Turning the faucet handle to the right, Jake stuck his hands underneath and quickly splashed cold water on his face and then he donned a clean shirt. Over this he added a long sleeved, army fatigue jacket. He gingerly pulled on his hiking boots, turned on the coffee pot, and grabbed a mug from the cupboard. This time around, he decided to bring a handgun. He shoved the weapon and some ammo into a lightweight pack and secured the shoulder straps tight before leaving. He worried that there might be more dangerous people lurking in the area and he certainly did not want to be without a weapon this time. Finishing a piece of buttered toast he wiped the crumbs from his mouth and strode resolutely out the door and disappeared into the thick forest.

Jake headed northwest in the hopes of locating his dog along with the two boys. He wanted to believe that they were just scared and not wanting to be found by their attackers. He wished he had a two-way radio on him so he could get a hold of Jeff Braden, who had apparently been detained or had forgotten to stop by his place last night to make a plan. Regardless, he was capable of searching on his own. If those boys were in these woods he'd find them. Besides, he'd promised Max's mother he'd locate the boy so now he had to do everything in his power to make this happen. Alone with his thoughts he plunged onward and deeper into the forest.

An hour had gone by when he thought that he heard a weak response to his hollering out the names of the boys.

"Max! Blue Boy'!! Not remembering the other boy's name he hollered out the words, 'hello anybody'. The next time, he yelled at the top of his lungs, 'Max' where are you? This time he distinctly heard a youthful voice in the distance.

"Help, here I am, mister." Max replied.

"Woof, Woof."

Jake recognized the barking of his dog. He picked up the pace until he was running and leaping over the brush in his way. However, the massive overgrowth of ferns, bushes, and prickly plants threatened to impede his forward motion at one point. He stopped to catch his breath and then he searched around in the forested landscape. Locating a fallen tree branch lying in the thicket he began attacking the thick, troublesome brambles. At last, after another twenty minutes of hacking his way through the overgrowth of plants and bushes, he saw a small clearing and what appeared to be a large, tall oak tree in the distance. He followed the freshly made path leading him closer to the boy and his excited dog. Upon reaching the clearing, he knelt down to check on the boy sitting there on the ground. His dog jumped on him enthusiastically and began to whine.

"Calm down, Blue'. Good dog, come here boy." Jake bent down and hugged his dog and stroked the dog's head briefly. Then he turned his attention back to the boy. "So how are you, kid?"

"Gosh, am I glad to see you. I'm hungry and cold. I slipped and fell off the makeshift ladder someone had nailed to this tree trunk when I was climbing up to the tree fort. My ankle feels as if it's swollen and hurts like the dickens!"

"That's not good. Do you need some water to drink?" Jake asked the boy.

"Yes, I could use some water. I'm really thirsty, thanks mister."

As Jake was giving the boy a drink he noticed the old house a few yards away. There was a dark blue helicopter sitting in the field just beyond the old home. He climbed up the tree to reach the wooden fort's decking to get a better view. From this vantage point he could make out the lettering on the side of the craft. It read KWX NEWS. That had to be the same copter that had dropped off the weapon parts and the men dressed in black garb. Jake noticed the thick rope draped loosely over the railing and so he grabbed it and dropped back down to sit next to the boy.

Leaning in closer to whisper in the boy's ear, Jake said this. "Remember when that dark blue helicopter dropped off those men and the piece of equipment attached to a small parachute? I thought I saw the lettering on its side which read News. It had some white letters like KGW or KXW or something similar. I'm not sure why a news chopper is sitting over by that house, but I think I need to investigate."

"Why do you have to check out a news helicopter, mister?" Max asked.

"Well, they had probably repainted this small helicopter and then transposed new lettering on the sides to depict a harmless news copter. What people would see in the sky was simply a news crew flying over the city and its surrounding rural area on an assignment. This seemingly innocent type of aircraft would garner no suspicions from people on the ground. It was a clever ruse to allow intruders to sneak undetected into our country. It was the helicopters presence flying to and fro in our area that caused me to wonder why they were in our area and what they were looking for." Jake said.

"Is that why you decided to hike through the forest the other day and then stay around to watch if they returned?" Max questioned the man they'd jokingly named Mr. Nobody.

"Yes, I was able to see clearly the lettering on the side of the copter. I began to question why a local news channel would want to send a copter to fly over this old logging road. There had to be an important reason." Jake stated.

"What do you mean?" Jake questioned him.

"It takes money to fuel a helicopter. It takes a valid reason for a local news channel to spend money doing a story for the nightly news on the television and they'd have to pay their news people to cover a legitimate assignment. Plus, they'd also have to pay a pilot to fly the aircraft. Do you recall anyone mentioning a news story about any hikers being lost in the woods or other noteworthy coverage in this area?"

"Oh, I see what you are saying. Ah, no there has been no such news like that." Max replied.

"Have your parents heard anything on the nightly news about cougars attacking people in this area?" Jake asked.

"There was a story last year about a cougar attacking this hunter just north of here in the woods. Our neighbor friend, Mr. Braden said the authorities went out searching for the predator but didn't catch it. Do you think the local news helicopter is out here again trying to look for any cougar activity?"

"Probably not right now, it seems to me that the police unit with trained canines would be out here in the woods first searching for the cougars or coyotes on the prowl before the news copter would come here." Jake paused momentarily to stretch his muscles in his back and neck. "I was trained to think like a military person. So therefore, my mind went to the fact that Washington State borders the neighboring country of Canada." Jake stated.

"What does the fact that our state borders Canada have to do with anything around here in our woods?" Max asked.

"I deduced that it is possible these intruders are involved with smuggling in drugs which is against the law in both countries." Jake Walker stated.

"Now I understand. You believe that these men are doing something illegal and that's why they attacked you. Do you think they'd try to hurt any of our families?" Max asked.

"Well, it just depends on whether or not they feel threatened by the locals around here. I think they are just up to no good and they will leave this area real soon without any more trouble." Jake declared in an effort to comfort this young boy.

"Max, from here on out I will only talk in a whisper voice to be safe. I need you to stay right here for a few minutes while I check out that old house in the distance. If anything happens to me I want you to scoot a ways back into the bushes and hide until it's completely safe. Do you understand me?"

"Yes, sir."

"Good, I'll be right back after I make sure there is no one lurking around those premises. I need your help in keeping my dog, Blue Boy quiet. You can do this by stroking his fur and talking quietly to him. I don't want him barking and alerting the bad men of your hiding place. Do you understand the importance of being quiet, kid?" Jake asked.

"Yes sir. I will stay here with the dog and be quiet until you return."

Max watched as his new friend moved slowly and cautiously among the trees until he was forced to run across the open land. Within another ten feet, Jake was able to hug the siding of the old house and he crept further along until he came upon a stack of lumber. Climbing up on this pile he was able to look through a cracked window pane.

Jake peered into the dimly lit room of the two story structure. He had to wipe off grime from the window pane to be able to see more clearly. He noticed some boxes piled on the floor and a bed that looked messy. Some clothing was draped over the bed and a pair of pants lay on the floor. Then he saw a dark figure walk past the open doorway. The man had a rifle in his hand and a dark ski mask covering his head. Jake didn't wait around to see how many guys were inside. Instead he hopped back down and ran quickly back to the tree house. This could present a huge problem for him considering the complication of having to carry an injured kid as he made his retreat. Once he reached the boy's side, he spoke in a calm voice so as to not alarm him.

"Your mom is going to be elated to have you safely back home again. She's been rather frantic since you disappeared. How about I lift you up and carry you on my back, Junior?"

As he was lifting Max up off the ground they both heard the whirring sound of helicopter blades rotating in the air high above the fir trees.

"Hey, I hope that's not the same bad guys coming back again." Max exclaimed.

"I'm ready for them this time. I'd managed to disarm the other bad guys in the woods and so it could be that there is only one more culprit in that copter to deal with. Just the same, I'm setting you back down and climbing up this tree to get a better look." Jake replied.

Jake climbed up the makeshift ladder nailed into the tree trunk until he'd reached the tree fort's decking. Then he pulled out his army binoculars from his backpack to wait for the next flyby. Within minutes of the first sighting, he heard the rotator blades humming loudly and coming closer to where he was located. Through the lens he could read the familiar lettering of the word 'KXW NEWS' on the side of the aircraft. Not knowing whether this craft was authentic news team or if it truly belonged to the sabotage team, he unsheathed his gun and held his breath.

"Come on you filthy dirt bags; drop the copter down more so I can send you my own method of retaliation!"

"What's going on, mister?" Max strained his neck looking upward as he hugged the dog and wondered what to do next.

"Hey kid, try to get my animal to relax. Stroke his fur to calm him down. I think we have some unwelcomed company heading this way. I want you to move around behind the trunk of this tree and stay there until I tell you it's safe. Do you understand?" Jake asked.

"Ah yeah sure and I'll bring the dog with me."

"I wish I knew if that was our local news channel coming to cover the search for you or not. I don't want to shoot at this aircraft without provocation."

"Hey mister"

"Yeah, what do you need?"

"You don't think those bad men have a grenade launcher on that helicopter, do you?"

"Geez, kid, I'm not sure of anything right now. Just stay down and don't move away from behind the tree like I told you."

"Okay, but I'm scared they might grab me. I don't want to be a hostage again." Max cried.

At that very moment, Jake realized that if it was a search and rescue or a police helicopter, it would either have the police logo on the side or it'd have the lettering of Search n Rescue. As the aircraft came closer, he cocked his handgun and aimed it at the copter's fuselage section.

CHAPTER
Twenty-Two

Jeff Braden strode out of his house at the sound of police vehicles arriving onto his property. It was nearly nine o'clock the next morning and he hadn't slept much for worrying about his son. He felt extremely relieved to have this police presence in his front yard.

"Good morning, Mr. Braden, it's Officer Brad Colton here. What other information do you have for me before we start gathering a search team?"

"Thanks for coming officer." Jeff finished telling the police officer everything he knew about the disappearance of his son and the few details he'd learned from his new neighbor, Jake Walker. "Can we get a search team together as soon as possible? My son and Max Johnson have both been gone for two days now."

"Well, seeing how your boy is not old enough to have gotten involved in any criminal activity on his own, it does appear to be suspicious that he's not home yet. I need to relay this information back to my department. Once I get the okay from our captain, I can request a search team and maybe even a helicopter since the area we are talking about is quite expansive if you are talking about Bandier Road where the logging company use to run their big trucks in and out of the woods."

"Then let's hurry up. The only thing I really know about the attack is what the ex-military guy, Walker, told me last night. He mentioned trying to warn the boys to return home when three men dressed in black garb and carrying weapons grabbed him and Max. They were tied up and left alone while the men worked on a military piece of equipment I believe he said."

"What size was the weapon, do you recall him saying?" the deputy interrupted.

"He mentioned that it was similar to a rocket launcher. He believed they wanted to knock out something of extreme value in our area. He'd sent Max away and he attacked them with only a knife and his physical strength. I'm guessing that since he's ex-military that he was trained in self-defense because he survived the fight. He also mentioned his plan to head out to look for his dog and the boys." Jeff Braden replied.

"This recent activity he was referring to could have been the same discharge which occurred two days ago. It's possible these guys were trying to shut down the dam just south of here. I'm going to contact my superior with this information. We will get a team in here promptly once I get the go ahead from my department. I will need you to take me in the direction of where your son and the other boy might have gone so I can radio in the estimated location for our GPS tracking device."

"I think we should start at the guy's place since that's where he sent Max and his dog. I want to go with your searchers when they get here." Jeff exclaimed.

"It will take me half an hour to gather a team and we'll be back here shortly. Did your neighbor say what had happened to your son after they apprehended him? The officer asked.

"He told me that he believed my son had managed to escape and he doesn't know anything else about his whereabouts."

"I'm heading back into town to gather some volunteers to help us in the search. You have my cell number now so call our dispatcher if anything further develops, like if you hear from that neighbor guy again."

"I will call you." Jeff replied.

Forty-five minutes later two squad cars of police and a van with volunteer group of men arrived onto Jeff's property. The eager volunteers all piled out of the vehicle and then stood waiting for instructions. The police officer called Jeff over for a brief conference with Blaine Wilson, the lead man for the second search team.

"I'm sending one team in the northeast section of the forest. I can send you with the second crew. The head man of this second group is Isaac Watson. He's well versed in this type of search and rescue so follow his instructions. He has a two-way radio to get me if they find the boys. The other team leader of four men is Blaine here. So everyone get ready to go in ten minutes." Officer Colton explained.

"Sounds good, I need to go inside to grab a jacket and my hiking boots. I'll let my wife know what's going on and be back outside waiting with the rest. We should start at the cabin located at the south entrance to the forest's since that's our best bet for following the right trail our kids may've taken recently." Jeff said.

"I want everyone here to grab a bottle of water for the trip. Isaac, make sure you get my first aid kit out of the van and put it in your backpack. Officer Colton, I want you to man this hand-held radio in case we need to contact you. We'll report back here in no less than three hours to debrief and decide our next step." Blaine Wilson explained to the gathering of volunteers.

Three hours later, the search parties were back at Jeff Braden's place and they all heard gunshots echoing off of the nearby hills causing everyone to feel a renewed sense of urgency. The officer in charge immediately turned on his phone and called in a request for a police helicopter to be sent into that specified area.

"Officer Colton here, I need immediate backup. I will wait here for support before going any further into the woods to check this out."

"I have a rifle back in my shed. Should I go get it? My son could be hurt or in grave danger. I can't just sit here and wait."

"Sir, it would be smart for you to go back home and stay with your wife. I will contact you as soon as we know more. Trust me; this is going to take more men power and even a helicopter to handle this problem since we don't know exactly where the boys are located and what's actually happening. Maybe that was a hunter shooting at coyotes or something else. Please relax and let us handle this. I have your phone number and I will get back to you, I promise." Officer Colton insisted.

Jeff Braden turned and headed inside of his home. He was certain his wife would be more anxious and worried after hearing the gunshots. After informing his wife of the police's decision, he decided to call Lisa Johnson and invite her to join them at their house until the police could give them more information.

* * *

Meanwhile a few miles deeper in the forest, Jake was positioned inside the doorway of the tree fort waiting with his gun aimed directly at the copter twenty-five yards away. At that moment he was wishing he'd brought more fire power with him. He felt like a sitting duck as he stood there trying to determine if this activity warranted his return fire on the civilian aircraft. He needed to be absolutely positive this was the same group and the same copter he'd seen before near that old logging site. Suddenly, as if in response to his very thoughts, the helicopter's side panel slid open and a man appeared with a rifle in his hands. The assailant fired two rounds towards the tree fort where Jake was located. Jake retaliated by firing back at the aircraft as it hovered in the air. His bullets dug deep into the metal siding of the copter.

He knew he could not defend himself from a sniper, but he'd hoped to disable the copter by hitting the fuselage section. Then a few bullets ripped through the thin plywood section of the tree fort where he was hiding. The third bullet from the sniper's rifle hit its mark. Suddenly, it felt like his left bicep muscle and shoulder area were burning hot. It was as if someone had plunged a hot branding iron into his flesh. Jake knew he'd been hit as he fell to the wooden planks with a heavy thump. As he was trying to access his injury another bullet tore through his left leg that was protruding out of the doorway of the tree house structure. He lay still hoping they'd assume he was dead and then leave. Jake cursed his foolishness at not bringing a more powerful rifle with him instead of handgun. He needed to staunch his leg wound before he lost more blood. He'd be no good to the kid below needing his protection if he couldn't get off an accurate shot off in the next few seconds. He placed his right hand over the seeping wound, press tightly, and tried to mentally shut out the intense pain. Aware that his strength was slowly waning, he made a feeble attempt to rise up on his good arm. Aiming his gun in the approximate vicinity where the gunman and the copter were located, he fired off his last bullet. Then he grimaced in agony and tried to shake off the queasy feeling assailing his stomach. As he felt his consciousness drifting in and out, a strange tiredness began to overwhelm him. Then mysteriously, a woman's pleasant face appeared before him. What was her name again? How would he be able to keep his promise to her? Where in the heck were his army buddies, Nickolas Rhyker or Private Rizzo, when he needed them?

"Mr. Jake, are you okay? I'm scared. What should I do now?" Max called up to him.

There was no answer coming from the man who lay prone and silent above him.

Then the boy heard the sound of another helicopter coming closer. As the police helicopter approached the clearing, Max heard more shots ring out and the assailant, who moments before had been shooting at them from the smaller news copter, tumbled out of the small civilian aircraft. He simply dropped out of sight behind some large fir trees. Then Max watched as the news copter started to move away. The next thing he heard was a bullhorn blaring out these words to the pilot of the retreating copter.

"This is the police! Cease firing or we'll blast you and your puny aircraft out of the sky. Put down your weapons and land the craft. If you refuse to obey our orders we won't hesitate to shoot you down." The Swat team leader yelled through the megaphone device.

The small civilian aircraft was forced to comply with the police. Once the pilot had landed his helicopter down in a small field behind the abandoned house everything grew quiet. It was too quiet for Max. He was beginning to worry about the man in the tree fort. The dog started whining and barking again as if to arouse his owner. Max didn't know whether to shout for help or try to hide deeper into the woods in case one of the assailants came for him. He finally decided to stay behind the tree as Jake had told him to do.

Two of the Swat team members had skillfully repelled out of the copter to take the remaining persons into custody. Then one of officers ran towards the area where they heard the dog barking loudly. Discovering the dog and the boy partially hidden behind the large tree trunk, the officer picked up the boy and carried him over to the newly created landing site. Next thing he did was to wave for the pilot of the police craft to hold steady. Then he radioed to the team to lower the carrier basket onto the ground. Once the long basket was on the ground, he carefully placed the boy into the metal carrier and wrapped a blanket around his slender form.

"You'll be okay now, son. This copter will take you to the hospital and they will fix your injured ankle. We'll also contact your mother who is anxiously waiting for news about you. See you later, kid."

"Don't forget about my friends, Mister Jake. He might be hurt bad. I think they shot him before you guys arrived. You've got to go find him." Max said quickly.

"Take it easy, buddy. I'll go check on this for you. If someone is alive back there, I'll take care of him. You're in good hands now so just relax and I see you soon."

"Thanks for rescuing me. Did my good friend, Crash' Braden, make it back home yet? He was trying to get back to his house to get someone to return here and help me."

"We check on this for sure. We had sent out a crew of men to search the forest and if he's in this area, we'll find him."

The man on the ground signaled up to the pilot to bring the boy up in the air and into the aircraft. After he saw the boy had been placed safely within the aircraft, he radioed his counterparts about the successful operation. He ran back to investigate the same area where he found the injured boy. The dog continued barking incessantly while it remained by the large tree. The agent bent down to pet the fur of the anxious dog and spoke calming words to comfort the animal. That's when he noticed the blood on the animal's coat. He turned his attention upward to the tree house where he spied a man's leg protruding from the tree fort. He holstered his gun and began his ascent up the tree. Upon finding an injured male in the tree fort, he quickly radioed his superiors with the new information calling for a medical evacuate copter to land in the clearing site by the abandoned house. He gave them his coordinates and did his best to staunch the bleeding leg wound. Once he stopped the bleeding sufficiently, he checked on the other bullet wound. It looked as if the second bullet had entered the man's upper shoulder area and then exited out his back. Next, the officer applied pressure with his shirt material on the prone man's second wound. He tried speaking a few reassuring words of comfort to the dog below. Then he sat down on the floorboards and waited for reinforcements since he could not lower the injured man down from the tree on his own.

CHAPTER
Twenty-Three

During the next twenty minutes of waiting in the well-constructed tree house, the officer heard a commotion in the forest nearby. Suddenly, a group of men along with Officer Colton appeared from the thick underbrush. The search team had heard the gunfire and the police loudspeaker minutes before coming to the edge of the forest. Thus, they were able to follow the sounds of the dog barking which eventually had led them to this clearing spot.

"What happened here and do you know anything about the missing boys?" Officer Colton asked the Swat team member sitting up on the small deck of the tree house structure.

"One youngster was flown to a hospital in town. He's going to be fine. I believe he'd suffered a twisted ankle and couldn't walk on it. As for this individual up here lying on the floor of this structure, he's been shot twice. Once in the leg with a clean shot and another bullet hit him in the shoulder area. My team was able to force the rogue helicopter to land on the ground. Actually the sniper guy we shot while in midair fell to his death. So we are securing this area now. You need to radio back to your base to keep all civilians away from the woods and especially this property and the abandoned house.

This is now a crime scene and there is evidence inside the house that needs to be investigated by the FBI."

"Alright, I will radio the police chief this information. When I get back to my vehicle I'll let the folks in this area know about your instructions." Officer Colton replied.

"We just need to lower this injured man to the ground and then get him to the medical team ASAP." The officer sat down on the decking of the tree house and waited to hear the other officer's response.

"Alright, what do you want us to do to help facilitate this?" Officer Colton questioned the Swat team member. He pulled his radio handset off his belt and held it in his hand as he listened.

"I'd like to have a rope and pulley system to lower this guy down from this height. Did anyone bring a rope with them today?"

"There's one back in our van, but that will take us an hour or more to get it and then head back here."

"Look up there at the backside of the tree fort. There's a rope swing. If you can grab it then we can try to cut it down and use it to extract him from the tree fort." Isaac hollered to the officer.

"That might work! Did anyone bring a pocketknife along?"

The searchers dug into their backpacks in the hopes of finding a sharp object. Finally, one of the men hollered excitedly to the team that he'd found a small, but sharp knife. He tossed the handy pocket knife to one man who was eager to climb the tree. They all stood there watching as the officer cut away at the long rope connected to a tree limb above. It wasn't nearly long enough by the time he finished cutting it, but it would have to do. The officer and the volunteer person wrapped the hemp rope around Jake's torso and slid him closer to the edge of the deck. Then he tied the other end of the rope to a wooden post connected to the structure and the two men began to ready Jake's inert body over to the side of the deck. Jake groaned in extreme pain and this made the worker stop his efforts.

"I have another idea." He yelled down to the men waiting below. "I'm going to positioned him onto the slide and then lower his body on down the slide to you guys below. I think placing his body on the slide and then slowly easing him downward will alleviate the extreme movement and possibly lessen the pressure on his open wounds." The officer stated.

"Okay, sounds like a good plan. Move over to the back of the tree, men." Officer Colton yelled.

Then he turned to radio his headquarters and give them an update of the rescue.

Three men stood waiting with hands extended outward. Slowly, the man at the top let out the rope as he managed to lower Jake's body down on the slide until he could be grabbed by the waiting volunteer's outstretched hands.

"Toss us down the knife so we can cut him free. The knot is too tight now." Officer Colton exclaimed. He caught the folded up knife and handed it to Blaine.

"I'm going to slice through the thick rope and it may take a bit so I need three men standing close by to handle his movements. Keep your hands on his body. Michael, I want you to put your hands under his armpits to support him while I sliced away at this rope. This blade is rather dull.

"Did anyone bring a first aid kit with them?" The Swat member still standing up in the tree called out.

"Yes, there's one in Blaine's pack. We can do our best to attend to his wounds right here until they send a transport copter."

One of the men below opened the first aid kit and began applying iodine to Jake's wounds. Next he placed some gauze over the two wounds and then strips of adhesive tape over that. The others standing around could be heard discussing the day's events and the fact that there was still one more boy to be found. Jeff Braden became agitated about this and anxious to head back into the forest to resume the search.

As soon as they'd treated Jake's injuries and discussed their next move, Officer Colton turned to the small group of weary men with instructions.

"A medical evacuation copter has been authorized to fly out here for this injured man so I will stay here and wait for it. The rest of you men go with Blaine. He will be the lead man for this next search. It will be getting dark in about one more hour so if you don't find the Braden kid soon, then head back to the Braden's place and regroup. Wait for further instructions at that point."

"What is this next kid's name again?"

"His actual name is Kevin; however, he goes by the nickname we gave him of Crash'." Jeff remarked.

"Watch for any signs of someone maybe going off the obvious trail. This youngster might've wandered off the main trail in the dark and lost his bearings. So stay alert." Officer Colton explained.

The group of volunteers with Jeff Braden headed off back into the dense forest area following Blaine Wilson's lead. After a fruitless hour of searching in vain, Blaine glanced at his watch and realized he needed to stop the search and head back to the van to debrief the team.

We need to stop and go back gentlemen." Blaine said.

The team as a whole began to voice their resolve to continue looking for the missing boy. "We all think we should keep looking for him since we still have some daylight left."

"Well, as much as I'd like to keep searching for the boy, we need more water and there's no sense in us getting lost as well. If we get some sleep tonight and start out real early in the morning, we might have a better chance of finding the missing kid." Blaine Wilson declared.

"What about the fact that he's been without food and water for nearly seventy-two hours so far. By tomorrow he could be dehydrated and very chilled from having no warm clothes. I don't mind continuing on with the search for as long as we have enough light. If it was your kid, Blaine wouldn't you want to keep going on."

"Certainly I would want to keep searching for the kid; however, I am making the final decision. We stop looking now and go back to the base headquarters. Everyone get a good night sleep and meet back at the same place by the first sign of daylight. Common sense dictates we make sure there are no more people lost in this immensely forested area."

"Okay, he's the new boss, so let's head back. We can only hope the kid is still alive and safe tomorrow. If he is, we'll find him. Maybe by then, there'll be more volunteers to cover more area."

"Good thought, does anyone have some water left, I'm hot and thirsty?" Issac asked the team.

"Nope, we all drank ours long ago."

The team of men followed Blaine back in the southern direction in the hopes of finding the original trail to the Braden's property. After they'd reached Jake's property one of the men pointed to the porch of the cabin and mentioned that they should leave the dog there with a fresh bowl of water. This same individual bent over to pat the dog on the head before turning to leave the porch area. Noticing the animal's doggie dish still had some food left in it he placed it next to the animal and stood there as the dog hungrily devour the remaining dog food. He secured the leash to the canine's collar and jumped off the porch to run and catch up with the others. He decided he'd try to locate the owner's bag of dog food somewhere in his cabin to make sure the dog was properly fed before they headed out in search of the second missing kid the following morning.

* * *

Within minutes of the search team's return, Lisa Johnson was informed of the good news once Blaine Wilson had stopped by her place before heading into town. He was hoping she'd invite him inside again. After sharing his good news with Max's mother, he decided to make up an excuse in order to spend more time with her.

"Lisa, would you mind if I got a drink of water? I'm dry as a bone and it would be nice to quench my thirst." Blaine inquired.

"Certainly, Mr. Wilson. I'll be right back with a cold drink of water. Would you prefer orange juice or water?"

"Well, coffee would be great if it's already made." Blaine remarked with a smile.

I am so thrilled to hear about your successful search efforts in finding my son. I'm sorry to say there is no hot coffee made. You could probably get some over at Helen Braden's house though. If you'd like I can get you some ice water."

"Thanks, it's been a long day and I'm thirsty. I could really use something cold and refreshing." Blaine Wilson remarked.

Lisa went into her home and quickly grabbed the glass and poured water and ice into it. Then she returned to the front lawn to ask him some questions as she handed him the drink.

"Mr. Blaine, where did your team finally locate my son?"

"He was hiding behind a tree at the edge of the woods which was close to the old Simpson's abandoned house and property. He was dehydrated and it looked as though he may've sprained an ankle. He was shivering and cold, but alive.'

"Did you mention that he'd suffered an injury to his foot?"

"Ah, yes, your son fell from the tree ladder and sprained his ankle. It appeared to be swollen and so we sent him in the copter to the hospital. I'm sure they are attending to his needs as we speak. He will be glad to be reunited with you. Would you like to catch a ride into town with me?" Blaine asked.

"I would be very grateful if you drove me. I'm feeling a bit overwhelmed with everything that has happened recently. It would be better if you did the driving tonight. Let me go inside and get a coat, I'll just be a moment." Lisa stated hurriedly.

When she returned with her warm coat and scarf she asked another question. "Mr. Wilson, I was wondering"

"Just call me Blaine."

"Well Blaine, as I was going to retrieve my coat, it made me wonder since I need to wear a coat tonight, then how did my son manage with this chilly climate the night before."

"When we found your son, he was okay because he'd managed to stay close to a man's dog. The fact that the dog stayed with Max throughout the night probably kept him warm enough. That canine was amazing. It was remarkable that the dog stayed there and didn't run off or decide to chase after a squirrel."

"I guess I do have plenty to be thankful for. What about the Braden boy did they locate him as well? Lisa Johnson asked. "He must be very cold and dehydrated after this length of time."

"No sign of that other boy yet. I believe we will locate him tomorrow now that we have some idea of where he was heading after he left the tree fort and your son, Max."

They walked together across her front yard towards his vehicle and she climbed into the front seat. Blaine put the car into gear and drove the few miles back into town. Once he'd dropped Lisa off at the hospital entrance, he headed to a burger joint to grab some hot food. Blaine was definitely interested in getting to know this woman better, but he figured it might be smart to wait until her son was fully recuperated from his injury before asking her out.

CHAPTER
Twenty-Four

Lisa Johnson called her friend, Helen Braden, as soon as she'd arrived at the hospital. She'd shared the recent good news about Max and then asked Helen to come to the hospital to keep her company. She mentioned that since she didn't have family close by she could use the support. Helen put the phone down and relayed Lisa's message to her husband and then asked if he minded her going to stay with Lisa overnight. He thought it'd help his wife keep her mind off of their missing son so he agreed wholeheartedly. She went into the hallway to grab an overnight bag, her purse, and her jacket and car keys from off of the wall hook. Giving her husband a quick hug, she ran out to the mini-van and started up the motor. Once she reached the hospital and parked the van, she went up to the main desk to ask about Max Johnson. The receptionist informed her of his room number and which floor the children's ward was on. Hurrying into the open elevator she rode it to the fourth floor. Stepping out of the elevator brought her into a world of nurses, assistants, and medical staff that were busily monitoring the different patient's needs and doing paperwork. She wasn't sure which turn to take or where the correct hospital room was located and so when one of the nurses looked up briefly from her station, Lisa asked where to go.

"Can I help you?"

"Yes, I'm here to visit with Lisa Johnson and her young son, Max."

"What room number did the desk give you?"

"I was told he was in room 414, but I must've headed down the wrong corridor."

"Yes, that's easy to do in our hospital. Just go past our station and down this hall and go left at the end of this hallway. The numbers get bigger as you follow that way."

"Thank you."

Helen Braden continued on her way looking for the correct room. Finding the appropriate door with number 414 on the wall, she knocked to let the occupants know of her presence.

"Come in."

"Hi, Lisa, it's me, Helen. How is Max doing?"

"He is getting some more meds for the swelling and pain in his ankle. The doctor says it will heal in two weeks to three weeks. In the meantime, Max needs to ice it for two more days and then he can use these crutches they brought in to help him walk. He has to stay off his foot and keep it elevated today so they can determine if the injury is minor. Tomorrow they will do an x-ray of the area just to make sure nothing is broken or to see if he tore a ligament."

"These doctors know their stuff. It's good he is resting and taking ibuprofen for the swelling then." Helen remarked.

"Yes, I'm just so thankful to have him safe and with me. Let's go out to the waiting area and chat for awhile. Max will fall asleep as soon as his pain meds kick in." Lisa stated.

They chatted casually as they walked to the area where there were two large bay windows and a television monitor which hung on the wall. Helen reached over to hook her arm into Lisa's in a show of comfort and kinship. Lisa reciprocated with a smile and a gentle hug. The two women sat side by side in the chairs as they gazed out the enormous windows of the hospital.

"Lisa, how was your son's experience out in the woods?"

"He told Officer Colton that they were following our new neighbor, the ex-military guy into the forest just for fun. Then they watched him attack a man riding on his motorcycle who was heading straight at him as if the guy intended to run him over. The next thing Max told the police officer is that our neighbor carried the unconscious individual back to his property. Whereupon, he stuffs the guy into his trunk of the vehicle and then goes back hiking further into the forest. Our boys felt like they were on an adventure and so they continued to follow him to see what else he was planning to do. Suddenly, he backtracks and come around to catch them both by surprise. Max told me that this ex-military guy grabbed a hold of them and shoved them to the ground. Next thing that happens is he clamps his rough hands over their mouths to keep them quiet. Can you believe this?"

"Why did he push our boys to the ground?" I don't understand this at all. Did he harm my son?" Helen questioned.

"No, not really, Max said that he only put his hands over their mouth to keep them quiet while he demanded why they were in the forest." Lisa replied.

"Was he angry because the boys had been following him or maybe because he didn't want them seeing what he was up to that day?" Helen questioned.

"I wish I knew exactly what his intentions were. I was shocked to hear about this strange incident too." Lisa retorted.

"Yes, me too and I'd heard from Mr. Dennison that our newcomer was an ex-military man who had moved here to Randall recently. Supposedly he was purchasing the old Parker home that sets at the beginning of the forested area. Our friend said that this man had been in town last week to purchase more lumber and sheetrock to repair parts of the old place. He seemed harmless to us and we figured that he'd planned to stay around and fit into our thriving community. I even heard some speculation that he might be writing a book about his war experiences. Who would have thought he'd turn out to be a person involved in roughing up a man on a motorcycle riding in the direction of that old logging site?"

"I want to go talk to this neighbor guy. Surely he shouldn't have involved our boys in his crazy activities. Max seems to think of him a hero of sorts and I don't want him idolizing a person who uses a gun to handle his troubles. I'm still not convinced this neighbor man is totally innocent. What if he is part of this terrorist plot and he sold weapons to the enemy? Have the police even considered the idea that this newcomer might have been planted here in Randall so he could show the intruders where to hide their drugs or gun stash? He might even be helping these bad guys." Lisa remarked

"What do you plan to talk to this guy about anyway? He was the one who caused the entire ruckus and brought this retaliation upon himself. It's just sad that our kids were dragged into the middle of this conflict with bad people." Helen retorted. "I hope we will be able to learn the real story behind this recent trouble and the recent shootings that Jeff told me about."

"Well, yes, he seems to be a hothead of sorts. I just think I should probably thank him for trying to help Max until the police could get there. I don't believe he is all bad. You see, he did tell me in the beginning he'd do his best to locate the boys while he was out in the woods searching for his dog. After all we were not there in the woods when he started shooting at the helicopter so I'd like to hear his side of the story before I judge him too harshly." Lisa retorted.

"Tell me about the helicopter. I thought your son just fell down while climbing a tree. Did someone shoot at Max?" Lisa could hear the alarm in her friend's voice right then. "Did Max say my son was around during this shooting incident? Do you know if Officer Colton has any news about my son?"

"Max told the policeman that your son had left the night before to hike back to your house in order to get help. He realized that he couldn't help Max hobble home to get medical help. It was too far to travel on his injured foot." Lisa said.

"I'm really getting worried now about my son's safety. There was gunfire. Someone was shot twice and almost died. The gunman in the helicopter... what became of him?" Helen asked.

"Max said the assailant was shot and he fell out of the copter's open door. I think Max mentioned that the bad guy or sniper individual was shot by this ex-Marine guy who lives near us."

"Our new neighbor appears to be an excellent marksman if he can hit a guy up high in a helicopter. This man seems to be capable of hurting people. I'm not sure we need someone like him living close to where we are raising our boys.

"I wonder what he is really doing here in this rural part of Randall. What if he's not really someone who'd been in the military? I mean he could be spinning lies about his true motives for coming to stay here. What if he is only staying in that old cabin near the woods just long enough to sell contraband to people living in Canada? What if he is involved with drug smugglers or connected to some individuals who are here illegally from Canada. I'm rather concerned about this man's true identity and purpose here, aren't you, Helen."

"I suppose our local police chief, Nathan Barrows, should look into this matter in the future." Helen remarked.

"After Max told them what had happened during the shootings, the officer who was questioning my son also mentioned to me he would definitely inform his chief about these new details. I don't like the fact our neighbor managed to allow my son to be right in the middle of a terrifying shooting spree. I've a good mind to go find him to let him know just how unsafe his actions have been so far. What if Max had been seriously wounded by the gunfire?" Lisa queried.

"I have to agree with you." Helen replied.

"In fact, if you don't mind sitting with Max while he's resting, I might head over to learn just where he is located in this hospital and tell him exactly what I think of his unsafe actions."

"I can stay a while longer since there is no reason to rush home. All I will do if I'm at home is stay up and fret about Kevin. I can stay here and worry about what might be possibly happening to him alone in the woods. Jeff said he was going to bed soon in order to get up real early in the morning. He plans to head out again with the search team to look for our son."

"Okay, thanks, Helen. I'll be back shortly. By the way do you know this man's name?"

"Well, one time I'd heard the boys refer to him as mister nobody and then recently they referred to him as Mr. Jake."

Lisa left the room and went to ask where the man who'd been shot recently was located. The nurse on duty referred her to the main desk downstairs in the lobby. The receptionist had this kind of information. She also stated that his room would be the one with a police officer standing by the door entrance to his room. Within minutes of getting the information she needed, Lisa headed up the stairs to the fifth floor where the wall plaque stated the words of "recovery after surgery". Apparently the man had survived his injury, but she wasn't so sure he'd be so carefree about telling people about his audacious tales once she expressed how she felt about his unsafe heroics with her son.

Lisa chatted with the police officer stationed outside of the room and told him she was here with her son who'd been involved with this wounded man and that she just wanted to thank him for finding her boy. He nodded and motioned for her to proceed. She knocked once and then decided to enter his room without waiting for a reply.

"Mr. Jake' I would like a few minutes of your time if you don't mind." Lisa requested as she attempted to control her emotions.

"You can call me Jake Walker. I have plenty of time on my hands to chat. I'm not going anywhere soon it seems. What can I do for you Mrs. Johnson?"

"I was told this afternoon by the police and my son, Max, that you were involved in a shooting in the woods. Is this correct?"

"I was definitely a part of that event. Would you like to examine my wounds more closely?" Jake managed to sit up enough to allow her to view his injuries as he adjusted the IV tubing away from his chest. "That way you could confirm that I was indeed involved in the conflict since the last dose of Vicodin has not been able to stop the extreme pain and discomfort I'm feeling right now." He gave her one of his disarming smile in hopes of getting her to relax and sit down. Instead, she seemed oblivious to his charms. She just stood near the doorway of his hospital room watching him. Jake thought back to the other day when they were together searching for her son and he recalled how difficult it had been to keep his eyes off of her. He was hoping to see her smile back at him, but that didn't seem to be happening yet.

"What did you say, Mrs. Johnson?"

"I'd rather not inspect your injuries, but I'm sure your nurse will help you out."

"Yes, these nurses have a way of pushing and prodding their patients in this facility."

"I am grateful that you made an effort to search for my son, but you should have left this problem to the police and their excellent efforts'." Lisa replied testily

"Just what have I done to offend you Mrs. Johnson?"

"Did you or did you not place my young son in harm's way two days ago when you began shooting at a helicopter with him close by you?"

"Well, yes I suppose so if you're implying that I made a big mistake by firing my gun while your boy was in the same place as I was." Jake replied.

"So you do agree with me that your recent action could have potentially placed my son in harm's way?" She said with a definite look of exasperation on her face. "What if my son might've been shot at like you were?" Lisa took a big breath as she stared intently at the wounded man lying in the bed across the way from her. "He's all I have left in my family and I don't know what I would do without him." Lisa stated.

"I told your son to crawl around to the back of the large tree in order to have better protection if the shooting began. Max listened and did as I'd requested. He's a smart kid and he obeyed my command to stay put until the shooting stopped. I had your son's life in mind when I made an effort to defend myself against the sniper determined to kill me. Fortunately for the both of us, the police copter arrived on the scene to deal with the criminals before things got more serious."

"Well, I'm truly grateful for the police intervention. However, Mr. Walker, that does not absolve you from almost getting killed and my son being shot or maybe kidnapped by these men. What if a stray bullet had hit him in the lungs or one of his arteries? What would you have told me to keep me from wanting to harm you myself? That you're sorry, Mrs. Johnson?" I think you should have put aside your desire to be a hero by shooting down that helicopter yourself. If you'd just tried to grab Max and carry him back into the forest and hide from these attackers then you would have been doing your civic duty by caring for a youngster's safety. Now that would be the kind of answer I'd like to have heard from you." Lisa exclaimed as she finished her tirade. Even as she stood there wanting to shake some sense into this handsome individual, she also sensed a rising heat in her body. Was this an obvious attraction she was experiencing or just her imagination as she looked at this seemingly arrogant individual sitting there smiling at her. She needed to leave his room before her flushed face gave her away.

"I guess coming from a mother's viewpoint the absolute safety of her son would be her priority. I do regret the fact that Max was directly involved in this incident and that he could have been wounded in the gunfire. I only had a split second to decide whether to return fire and protect us both. Since you don't agree with me then I guess that the only thing for me to say is that I'm sorry it went this way. I regret causing you any undue grief and concern about your boy. Unfortunately, I cannot redo what occurred and therefore, I hope you'll now let me get back to my sleep. My head is beginning to throb and the nurse told me to not get too excited or agitated. I plan to give my statement to the police tomorrow. I imagine they will determine if I was guilty of negligence with your boy at that time. Good bye Mrs. Johnson." Jake lay back down on his pillow and closed his eyes as if to end any further conflict.

Lisa turned around and walked out of his hospital room determined to finish this conversation later when he was more alert. She couldn't seem to shake the feeling that this man was not just annoying, but that he made her feel more than anyone else had done for years. She wasn't quite sure how she would be able to talk to him without being affected by the strange attraction she seemed to experience whenever she got too close to this infuriating man.

* * *

Later that day after some of the excitement had died down and the news media team had departed, Jeff headed back inside his house to get ready for bed. His alarm would go off by six a.m. and he needed to be fresh for the early morning search team's arrival. He was happy to know that the potential kidnappers of the two boys had been apprehended by the police. Now all he needed was to find his missing son. He'd tossed and turned half the night and then he awakened after having a bad dream. He'd barely heard his alarm clock going off an hour later around five thirty in the morning. As he swung his legs out of the bed and planted them on the cold floor, he recalled a news story from last September. A hunter had been hiking through the forest hoping to find some deer to shoot. Jeff remembered how the newscaster had mentioned that the hunter had been unaware that the predator was tracking him as he continued looking for signs of deer in the forest. The hunter had actually managed to swing his rifle around just in time to kill the male cougar. During the reporter's interview with this hunter, he had mentioned that the man was startled and yet, he managed to kill the animal. He told the news reporter that he escaped with his life since he'd only been standing about three feet away from this vicious animal when it attacked him. Jeff wished he hadn't recalled this awful story because now his young son was out there in the forest alone and at the mercy of these wild predators.

Jeff experienced a grave sense of apprehension and then fear gripped him. He tried to shake off this newest concern for his son as he walked into the bathroom. He stood in front of the wall mirror trying to wet down his tousled hair and he felt as if his stomach muscles were beginning to clench in a tight knot as if he was sick to his stomach. He tried to shake off the sense of impending danger for anyone lost in the vast expanse of wooded forest area just a few miles away. In his haste to get ready, he turned on the wrong faucet and hot water poured out and onto his hand. He quickly splashed cold water onto his face with both hands in an effort to get relief from the burning sensation and to also to help him wake up and get a grip on his emotions. After drying his hair and his hands, he hurriedly threw on a flannel shirt and a pair of jeans and his hiking boots.

Grabbing a coat and a woolen cap from the hallway hook before leaving, he ignored the idea of taking extra time to make hot coffee and pack it for the journey. Jeff stopped at the threshold to lock the front door behind him and then strode briskly down the path until he had left his property. He headed over to the base camp site since he didn't want to miss being a part of this next crew's efforts. He was determined to continue to search for his missing son regardless if others needed to quit. As he walked along the worn pathway, he started berating himself for not spending enough time with his son this past year. If they found him alive he'd made a promise while getting dressed earlier that he would change his ways and make more time for his young son. He was prepared to convince his boss of the necessity to change his hours in order to be home more for his family in the future. His wife had been telling him of the importance of being there for his son as he was about to enter the pre-teen years and would need a good role model. He realized that she was right and he had been foolish to ignore her suggestions.

Six a.m. rolled around and the search teams arrived on schedule. This time, Blaine was the main leader of the operation since the police chief and his deputy were both occupied with their investigation of the recent incident and damage done to the Coulee Dam structure. He was hauling his gear and radio out of the cabinet of the van when someone outside called his name. Stepping out of the command vehicle to check on the disturbance, he noticed two men in suits talking with Mr. Braden and so he took a cup of hot coffee from his aide and strolled over to ask what they were doing here.

"Are you men part of this search team? I don't recall seeing you here yesterday. We are in a hurry to get going and we don't need the news media here right now!" Blaine stated emphatically.

"We are from Homeland Security. We were sent here to locate the man and his property where this trouble may have originated from. Is there a person here by the name of Jacob involved with this search team or assigned to go with your men today?" The one tall man in a dress suit and overcoat asked. Blaine turned to ask his crew about the newcomer who was living in Henry's old cabin place.

"Anyone know about a person new to this community, with a name of Jacob?" Blaine asked his crew members.

One of the volunteers named Sam responded. "As far as I know, mister, he didn't sign up for this search and rescue team yesterday." Then a rather husky, muscular individual came forward and spoke up as well.

"Wait a minute; I recall something the officer mentioned when they found him in the forest. I heard him referred to the injured man by the name of Jack or maybe it was Jake. Could he be the guy you are looking for?"

"Yeah, that's right." A second man standing over by the back of the vehicles replied. "There was a man who'd been injured while helping the Johnson kid yesterday. Right before the boy was air lifted in the medical evacuation kind of copter, he had told the lead officer to take care of his friend, Mr. Jake."

"Well, does anyone here know where we can find this Jake individual or where he lives?"

"He was seriously wounded by the attackers and he was flown to county hospital. You could call them and get more information about this guy probably."

"Thanks for your help folks. We'll get out of your way. You have a successful day gentlemen."

Everyone watched them leave in their black SUV. The team wondered what the two dignified looking strangers wanted with this man. What had this newcomer Jake done to cause the team from Homeland Security to come here asking questions, Blaine thought to himself. He stopped worrying about this Jake Walker guy and turned to holler orders to the group of men standing around to grab water bottles and extra protein bars for the day's all important search efforts.

CHAPTER
Twenty-Five

It was a foggy morning as the search team gathered to discuss the day's plan. The group of three men waited for Jeff Braden to join them as they sipped on a cup of hot coffee. One volunteer reached into the van and grabbed a handful of protein bars to stuff into his backpack just as Jeff came walking down his front steps so they could leave the base site. Within ten minutes, the team had hiked over to Jake's cabin area. As they passed closer to the cabin, the same man who'd stopped the day before to feed the newcomer's dog told Blaine he wanted to make sure and feed the dog again and he'd catch up in a few minutes. Finding the dog food bag in the man's kitchen, he scooped up a cup full and patted the dog on the head. The dog stood up on all fours and began wagging his tail as if to insist on going with the team of men leaving his owners property. The longer the dog barked at the retreating backs of the group, the more agitated the dog became. The man named Sam quickly undid the leash from the dog's collar and the excited canine bounded off the front porch and raced after the men. Sam raced after the dog and caught up with the team. Jeff felt the dog brush pass his pant leg and then it turned back to walk beside him. Without thinking much about his decision, he chose to include the frisky dog in their efforts to locate his lost son. Maybe, just maybe this dog could be some help today. His gut told him that it was worth the effort to advocate the help of this man's dog in their new search.

"What's that dog doing here?" Blaine Wilson asked.

"He just decided to join our team all of a sudden."

"We don't need an extra problem here today. Besides, we didn't bring any water for this animal." Blaine remarked.

"I would like to have the dog's help. I believe that most dogs have a keen sense of smell and he might be able to locate the boys where we couldn't. I'd like to keep the dog with me."

"Fine, then he's your responsibility, Mr. Braden. You will have to share your water with the mutt."

"I don't mind giving the dog some water if he needs it."

After a brief discussion with the men standing in a circle, Blaine finally agreed to allow the dog to join in their search. Just before the group of men continued hiking, one of the men mentioned that maybe they should have gone back to the kids' room and retrieved a shirt with his scent on it. He'd seen a show where a dog had been able to locate a missing child this way. Five minutes later, a guy named Michael started talking with Jeff Braden about the lack of any tracks or any evidence of the boys being on this particular trail.

"What if the kid isn't in this general vicinity? We'd be wasting a lot of time following this trail. Maybe we need to send one man back to Jeff's place to get the kid's clothing like Michael said." A second person stated to the leader.

"Fine, who wants to volunteer to go back?" Blaine exclaimed.

"I will, Blaine. Mr. Braden is your house open or is anyone there to let me inside?" Michael asked.

"Ah, well I believe that back door is unlocked. If not then there is a spare key over the ledge of that doorway. After you enter the kitchen then go upstairs where you'll find my son's bedroom. He should have something we can use. Don't grab one of his shirts from his dresser though. Grab one of his shirts he may've left on the floor. Any of those items should have his body scent still on them. Bring a couple of those for the dog to sniff. I think you're right about this, the dog would be able to track my son if he had his scent to go on."

"Sure thing, Jeff. I should take a radio with me so I can make sure I reconnect with you guys if you head in another direction entirely." Michael retorted.

"My plan is to head east towards where the encounter with the intruders started and then if need be we'll circle back around to this same spot. If we don't see any sign of him then we'll have to increase our radius in this search. Some more volunteers will be joining in this search tomorrow. So let's head out." Blaine turned back to his team and slapped one member on the back and spoke some encouraging words to the group as they forged on through the dense brackets and bushes.

Twenty minutes had passed when the group heard a holler from behind them. Then Michael, who'd been running the entire way back, appeared through the trees and brush holding a blue t-shirt in his hand. He waved and began jogging to catch up with the team. The dog smelled the boy's shirt and headed off in a direction leading to the right of the other path. The men followed behind the animal feeling hopeful of finding the missing boy.

Another thirty minutes passed as the men prodded on. A few of the volunteers had asked to stop to rest their aching limbs or hot, tired feet and to get some water to quench their thirst. By this time Jeff had become more worried about his son. He couldn't imagine not finding his child at all or the thought of finally discovering his lifeless frail body days later and having to give this horrible news to his wife, Helen. He tried to push these ugly, negative thoughts out of his mind as he concentrated on the trail ahead. At one point, he missed seeing a tree root in the ground. Jeff Braden tripped over the root and nearly stumbled headlong into the person walking in front of him. Luckily another member close by caught him and kept him upright.

Weariness was starting to settle into his body and leg muscles. Maybe he needed more fluids. It was beginning to look as if they might need a search helicopter to fly over the area. However, the lead person in charge of this search team had informed them that because of the density of the forest and with such a large area to search, it might be impossible for the helicopter crew to spot a lone boy in this wilderness area. The idea of never finding his son was beginning to overtake his mind. He was starting to feel helpless and frustrated. He recalled hearing about a cougar tracks which had been found in the forest just four months back by a hunter. This idea gave him great concern for the well-being of his boy. How could he protect Kevin from a dangerous predator if he wasn't there in time?

What was it that his father always said to him? When mere man has exhausted all their mortal strength and abilities, then God is still able to step in and lend a powerful hand. Maybe it was time to turn to this God his father had often spoke about.

"Hey, Jensen, I need to rest for ten minutes. Jeff remarked.

"Hey, I understand Mr. Braden. Sure thing, I could use a breather too. I'm thirsty and maybe some of the other guys want to take a short break as well." He replied.

This same person went up ahead to inform their leader to wait for ten minutes before proceeding further. Jeff sat down on a nearby log and laid his head down into his hands. He hardly noticed that the Blue Heeler dog had followed him and sat on its haunches nearby where he was sitting. Jeff began to utter a foxhole kind of prayer to God for his son's life. It had been years of being distant from God and now here he was asking for help from the one he'd ignored for too long. Would God answer his plea for guidance since he'd been so wrapped up in his own world he wondered? "If you're who my dad always told me that you are, then I'm asking you to show up. We need a miracle and help to find Kevin. I promise to spend more time with my son and even tell him about you. I need your help to find my son in time. Please God don't let him die alone in the woods. " The canine lying in the brush nearby began to whine and bark as if to motivate him to get moving. Forcing himself to let go of his anxious thoughts and to continue on the journey, Jeff gave the dog a quick hug and hurried over to join the other men.

CHAPTER
Twenty-Six

Back in the hospital bed, Jake woke up to experience pain radiating in his shoulder muscle and his thigh. He noticed the medical equipment by his bed and remembered where he was. The morphine was wearing off since he couldn't ignore the pain any longer. If he tried to move his extremities, he regretted it. The nurse came into his room at the same time he was moaning and making strong expletives. She acted as if she hadn't heard his outburst and proceeded to manage his IV fluids. Out of the corner of his eye he watched the petite nurse finish flushing his IV tubing. Then he watched in fascination as she produced another bag of liquid which she hooked up to the metal stand. Then she deftly moved a clip on the tubing connected to his IV bag. This action allowed the necessary fluids to begin to flow through the tubing and into his weakened body.

"Hi there, miss. I hope that clear fluid you're putting in my IV line is what folks call 'the fountain of youth water.'"

"Well if you believe that our doctors have somehow located the fountain of eternal youth then it'll cost you plenty of money to take advantage of the new miraculous discovery. Of course, I'd be in line to receive that kind of miracle life source way before you." She chuckled in amusement.

"I need something more than electrolyte fluid since my muscles have taken quite a beating recently." Jake retorted glibly.

"Trust me; you'll not be receiving any special medicine while I'm on duty! You might as well get some sleep because Dr. Nelson will be coming in to access your progress around nine o'clock. Shall I tell him about your request for this special miracle water instead of regular fluids?" She quipped.

"No, I'll live with what you're giving me I suppose. Just skip the next vitals check though, nurse!" Tell the doc' I'm recovering amazingly well and I want to recover back at my own place!"

As she was leaving he muttered his dislike for being woken from a deep sleep every hour to receive his meds. The next time he woke there were two tall, well-dressed men standing in his room and they were both staring intently in his direction. Who could they be and what did they want with him, Jake wondered sleepily? They must have gotten the wrong room number. He turned away and closed his eyes as if to rudely ignore them. They were still in his room when he opened his eyes again. They appeared to be either businessmen with a remarkable job offer or someone from IRS hoping to question him about money he owed. He decided to call his nurse and have them removed since he wasn't in the mood to talk to anyone, especially men dressed in dark, tailored suits with rather unpleasant faces. As he reached for the nurses call button, one of the two spoke up first.

"Is your name Jacob Walker like your nurse mentioned?

"Yes, that's me. What do you want? He asked.

"We are here to ask you a few questions. Do you mind?"

"What's this about?"

"We need to know the facts about what happened on your property recently. Did you stuffed a man inside the trunk of a rental car two days ago and then leave him there with a piece of material shoved in his mouth?"

"Yes, I put him out of commission. He almost ran me down with his motorcycle while I was walking on an old logging road. I decided to contain him until the two kids who had unknowingly followed me could be sent back to their respective homes. You fellows wouldn't have wanted me to deal with this assailant or any other men in the area while two boys were close by; I'm assuming?" He answered succinctly.

"We didn't know there were kids in your vicinity at that time." The taller of the two men remarked.

"We were sent here from Homeland Security office to get some more facts from you. Glad to see you're recovering enough to talk with us." Pulling out a pad of small tablet and an ink pen from the pocket of his suit jacket, the other man proceeded to write down Jake's answers to the next question.

"So tell us about your military background."

"As a new recruit I needed to use some self-defense moves during a fight with another soldier. The sarge in our unit relayed this fact to his superiors. Next thing I knew, I was told I'd be instructing the men in a few of these tactics before they were deployed overseas. I was placed in a team that searched for IEDs in the area around Kandahar in Afghanistan. Our company was ambushed while on one such mission and my friend was killed in that action. Why do you need to know my history in the Marine Corps?"

"We want to get some knowledge of your background and expertise. Our supervisor needed to get some basic facts about who you really are." The suit replied.

"Can you tell us what happened when you confronted the men in the woods?" The other man in a dark suit asked.

"Like I told Major Holt, I'd been following these guys' strange activity for nearly two weeks and I was getting more evidence about this suspicious activity before putting a call into the person connected with Homeland Security."

"How do we know whether you are telling us the whole story? How do we know you weren't in cahoots with these men? Maybe you were planted in the area to help them find the perfect location in order to hide a lethal weapon such as a missile launcher?" The man with the ink pen queried.

"The man you knocked unconscious and stuffed into the trunk of your car says he's innocent of any criminal activity. He was just out joyriding on his motorcycle that afternoon. In fact, he mentioned that he's planning to sue you for defamation of character and assault with a metal pipe." The second man in the fancy suit remarked in a matter of fact tone.

"Well, you guys have some crazy notions. I used a broken tree branch to knock the guy off his motorcycle and not a metal pipe like he said." Jake replied. I did not know these foreign militants nor did I have any knowledge of their plans to destroy a valuable site in this region. As to the dummie on the motorcycle, trust me, he's up to his neck in this criminal activity! I refuse to defend my actions in this matter with you guys since you've barged into my hospital room without any authority to do so." Jake managed to lift his upper body off the bed pillows and point his index finger in their direction. "Get out of my room before I yell for a nurse to bring the security personnel and physically remove you both. I don't like your insinuations. So from here on out take this matter up with my lawyer. When you come back again I'll have his card and number for you guys." Jake was fuming by this time as he punched the button to call his day nurse.

"Nurse I need your assistance here. There are some guys harassing me right now! They are not welcome here. I'd like you to remove them from the premises as soon as possible!" He heard her voice responding to his high pitched voice with a "just one moment, Mr. Walker, I'll be there shortly. Do I need to call security to come to your room?"

Jake looked up in the men's direction to see if they were planning to leave or not. After a brief interlude of silence, he saw the taller man nod his head in acquisition so he replied. "They appear to be going now so thanks. I guess there's no need to call security after all. I'll be fine now. However, I could definitely use a thick, rare steak with garlic roasted red potatoes. It seems my appetite is returning." Jake said.

"Dinner will be coming to your room in forty minutes. Until then keep resting and let us know if you need more pain pills." The stoic nurse retorted.

Two hours passed uneventfully for Jake that morning in the hospital. He was annoyed with the constant medical attention. He simply wanted to be left alone and to be able to find a good football game on the TV channel. He began to ponder the idea of calling around to get a few names of good lawyers in the city of Grandview. He knew what could transpire if a person didn't have sufficient evidence or a reliable witness to co borate their story, especially if it had to do with a fight. However, his record was clean of any misdemeanors and this would certainly benefit him if this matter went to court. Plus, he had two material witnesses who'd seen the man on the motorcycle try to run him down that day so he could talk with their parents to get permission to get the boy's testimony on tape if he went to court. He wished he could get out of this hospital bed and take a walk to the pediatric ward to visit with Max. The kid could probably use some company as well.

Two hours later, another visitor entered his room. This time Jake was delighted to be woken by a female not wearing a crisp, white nurse's uniform. He watched the woman walk over to stand against the wall and it seemed as if she was nervous or hesitant to speak. As he studied her face, he found himself wishing that this attractive, dark-haired woman could be his personal nurse.

"Hello there. I just wanted to come back here to apologize for my huffy attitude and to thank you for helping my son. The police chief stopped by today to explain everything that happened in the incident with the criminals. It seems the police agree that you did your best to maintain your position and to keep Max safe from the attackers. Please accept my apology. After talking with my son it seems he thinks the world of you and apparently he has fallen in love with your dog too." Lisa remarked.

"I am glad he is safe and they were able to fly him out. I just didn't plan on being carried out of the woods in a copter myself. He's a great kid and brave too. I'm just glad I was close enough to hear my dog barking or this might have taken another day of searching to locate your son." Jake replied.

"Well, my son calls you a hero. The fact that you risked your own life to protect him means an awful lot to me, Mr. Walker. How can I ever thank you enough?" Lisa smiled at Jake and he totally forgot about his misery and pain for the moment.

"I do need something from you Mrs. Johnson. I'd like it if you simply called me Jake instead of Mr. Walker and maybe you could help me with something important."

"I'd be glad to help you with anything within reason." Lisa replied.

"Well, there is this problem with my animal. I'm hoping my dog, Blue Boy, is back at my place by now and he might need to be fed. Would you mind stopping by my place tonight and check on him." Jake remarked.

"I'll be glad to take care of this for you. Where do you keep his food?"

"You'll find his sack of food in a cupboard next to the kitchen sink. For now give him two scoops full since I'm not sure when they'll let me leave the hospital yet. Oh and he goes by the name, Blue' too."

"Okay, I'll be sure and call him Blue'. Will your front door be locked?"

"No I don't lock my house. There's a rental car in the driveway, but it should be locked. I'm worried that someone might try to take him while I'm stuck here. I suppose there are a ton of curious folks tramping about your place and mine by now."

"Yes, there has been a news channel vehicle camped on the Braden's property since this morning. I learned from Helen that they had tried to park on my front lawn first, but since I'm not home they moved to the gravel road leading to your place now. I doubt that they will be able to get in here to pester you however. From what I can tell the hospital staff has kept reporters away from both of us so far."

"That's one small consolation I guess. How are you doing?"

"Much better now that my son is safe and being taken care of. The doctor said he can go home tomorrow and use his crutches to get around. He wants to stop in to see you before we leave. Would you mind if we keep your dog at our place for a few days? It would be just until you get back home." Lisa mentioned.

"Uh, I suppose this would be fine. Maybe, you could tell your son to brush his fur for me. Of course, he'll need to ice his ankle and wait for it to heal up before he tries to take on anymore responsibility like taking the dog for a walk."

"I'm sure he will be glad to have a pet around." Lisa smiled back at Jake.

"By the way, when Max was sharing his recollection of the past few days, he mentioned seeing you man-handle a person on a motorcycle. Then he said you stuffed this unconscious individual into the trunk of a car. Did this really happen and why did you have to take such extreme measures with the guy? I mean, what did this person do to get you so angry?"

"I had been noticing him driving past my property one day while I was working on my uncle's old truck. Then I became rather suspicious of him when I was hiking one day and I watched him on his motorcycle riding deeper into the woods. I thought it was out of the ordinary for him to be traveling off the regular roads, I guess. Maybe you could say I had a gut feeling he was up to no good. The second time I saw him he tried to run me over with his motorbike, but I managed to knock him down. I wanted to head back into the woods to check on some other strange activity. However, before I could return and contact the police, I encountered some rather unfriendly individuals who managed to overtake me and that's when my plans went awry.

"Now that you are talking about this, I do remember a dark haired man on a motorcycle who'd joined our tour group in Grandview just three days before for the Fourth of July holiday. He'd forgotten his backpack while we were on the dam structure near some huge generators. Could this man have been the same one who tried to run you over with his motorbike?" Lisa questioned.

"He could very well be the same guy. Do you think you could identify him if you went into the police station and talk to the chief? If the chief of police let you view the man from behind a two-way glass you'd be safe enough and you'd be doing your civic duty. Plus, with your statement and my account we might be able to solve the mystery about why he was really in the woods that day. And why he tried to run me down with his motorcycle. Right now, it's my word against his. I certainly don't want him to get away with attempted murder. Do you?"

"Certainly not, if he is a part of this militant group and guilty of a crime then he definitely needs to be sent to prison.

Did you pay attention to ther color of this man's hair when you tossed him inside the trunk of the car?" Lisa asked.

"Ah, yeah, he had black hair and day old stubble growth on his face." Jake replied.

"The man I met on the shuttle bus had dark hair. I suppose it might make it easier for me to determine if he was the same person I met on the tour." Lisa remarked.

"I'd like to see justice served in this particular matter. Did he talk to you on that tour?" Jake asked.

"Well, yes, we chatted briefly while on the shuttle bus. During our brief conversation, he said he was from Montreal, Canada. He also mentioned he was visiting this well-known energy site to give his boss more information about the way these large generators worked." She said.

"He probably was scoping out the entire facility, hoping to plant a heat-sensor device for their surface to air missile is my guess. I believe your information could help the FBI and police in their investigation of the minor blast that occurred recently. It's important that you inform the police chief what you saw that day at the water facility." Jake stated.

"I will try to go in on Thursday before I come to the hospital to sit with my son. He keeps asking about you and now I can let him know that you are receiving visitors. And again I'm very grateful that you found my son. Thank you for putting yourself in harm's way to save a kid you barely knew."

"It was worth it, Lisa Johnson. I'm looking forward to seeing the both of you soon."

Lisa left his hospital room with a spring in her step and a smile spreading across her lovely face. She was starting to feel more at ease around this ex-military person. In fact, as she left his room that afternoon, she was wondering if he was thinking about her too.

CHAPTER
Twenty-Seven

The darkness was falling all around eleven year old Crash' Braden as he sat next to the slightly warm boulder wishing for some huckleberries to satisfy his hunger cravings. His lips were dry and cracked while his tongue and throat felt terribly parched and he was beyond thirsty. He wondered if he should make a second attempt to climb the hill. He remembered the cool, refreshing stream he and Max had played in the other day and he felt a strange lump in his throat. He tried yelling and hollering for help again. No one answered his cries for help. Why wasn't anyone coming to find him? How could he survive more days of this kind of hunger? As he sat in the dirt, he began to wonder if he might die before he was discovered. *What happens to a person after they die? Does a person just go and live on another planet or galaxy and wait forever until the next person shows up?* He wished he could talk with his grandpa right now. His Dad's father always spoke of a place called heaven and that he was going there after he died. What was it like to be in heaven and how did you get there he wondered. Not having any good answer to this question, he turned his thoughts as to what may've happened to his friend Max back at the oak tree. Right now he wished he'd stayed with his friend instead of traipsing around in the woods on his own. What a mess he'd made of things.

Crash Braden had tried to remain confident of being rescued up until this very moment. With another cold lonely night approaching and his courage dissipating with each terrifying howl of those wild coyotes, he felt more and more like crying. He needed to stop this dull aching in his stomach. He was feeling lightheaded and he hoped he wouldn't have another bad dream or wake up in the middle of the night again. Feelings of helplessness and fear were only heightened as he sat there all alone in the middle of a dark forest in the gloomy night hours. He fell asleep finally. Hours later when he rolled over in his sleep, he managed to hit his injured wrist and the pain woke him up. He tried lying on his back with the hope of preventing this from occurring again. There were a myriad of brilliant glowing stars meshed together in the coal-black night sky above him. He lay there for a long time gazing at the immense number of stars and not caring about the dampness of the ground beneath him. The splendor of this natural lighting overhead gave him a sense of security and calm. He waited in anticipation to see if a falling star would ever appear in the night sky. When one star did finally appear in all its blazing glory he forgot about his troubles and eventually drifted off into a deep sleep.

The third morning of being lost in the woods had found him once again hungry and desperate to get home. He heard a grumbling sound inside his aching stomach region and he wished he was back home safe and warm in his own house. He could almost imagine the smell of bacon cooking in his kitchen as his mother prepared another breakfast of eggs, waffles, and hot bacon strips. He wished someone would find him before he wasted away from hunger and thirst. This wasn't going to happen anytime soon and so he decided to make an effort to stand up and walk. He tried bracing his feet on the dirt and pine needles. Next, he pressed his back against the granite boulder. Then he slowly worked his body upward until he was completely upright. Leaning his body on the hard wall of stone, he pondered his next move. So far, he'd been careful to not jar his injured wrist, but his bruised, knotted thigh muscles caused a sharp pain up from his leg to his chest area. His right knee still ached from when he hit the hard ground. Moving away from his support rock, he managed to move a few feet until he had to stop and rest.

As he studied the steep incline of the ravine facing him, he thought of using a walking stick to support his efforts. This seemed like a good idea so he looked around for a sturdy branch or stick. A few feet to his right he spied a thicker stick which might work and so he made his way over and bent down to secure the loose branch. As he hobbled rather slowly across the distance leading to the sloping hillside, he stopped for awhile to observe the incline. Finally, he decided he would have to try and reach the top of the ravine in order for people to find him. He labored up the slope for five minutes and then he collapsed onto the dirt. What had happened to his energy he wondered? *Am I too weak from lack of food to even climb a stinking hill? 'Come on Captain Braden of the 7th Army Rangers. You can make it up this lousy hill.*

"I can't stay here any longer in these woods. I'll expire from lack of food and water." He shouted to the emptiness around him.

There was no answer to his cry only the whisper of a light wind brushing the tree leaves and bushes nearby. Then a crow squawked annoyingly from its perch in a fir tree above as if it was laughing at his distress and predicament. Right then he experienced an overwhelming sense of discouragement and grief. He glanced around at the emptiness of the forest and he felt all alone and scared for the first time as the reality of his desperate situation hit him. Wiping the sweat from his brow, he placed one good hand over his eyes to stop the tears spilling out and from falling onto his cheeks. He had to get back up and keep trying in order to get back home. He just needed to move to his right and work his way to that section of the ravine. As he studied that top portion of the ravine further away from his location, he noticed a couple of exposed tree roots. If he could manage to reach that spot, maybe he could grab that particular root sticking out of the earth and then pull himself up and over the embankment. If his knee didn't hurt each time he put weight on it he'd be able to maneuver his body upward without so much pain. He decided that his best option was to get on his knees at this point. His plan was to crawl the next few feet to avoid stumbling on the loose dirt and rocks.

His muscles were hurting more and he needed to stop climbing. He was wishing he had a proper sling to rest his injured arm in. A sling for his injured wrist would definitely help him. As he drew closer to top of the ravine, he tried to stand up again. Bracing himself with both feet in the loose dirt, he reached for the exposed small root hanging slightly away from the embankment. He gripped the root with his one good hand and then to his dismay, this thin means of support snapped and broke loose from the attached tree growth just above his head. Unfortunately, he found himself tumbling down the slope until he landed on the bottom. He'd fallen awkwardly on his injured wrist. He emitted a loud cry of agony as the pain intensified up his arm. He realized that he was stuck in the worst way and he wouldn't get out on his own. Would he die here in this lonely forest with no one to help him? "Oh God, are you real? Can you hear me? I need your help to get out of this awful mess. What do I need to say to get your attention?" He began to sob and finally he stopped and rubbed his eyes with his one good hand.

Maybe he should try one more time to get back up to climb the slope again. He figured if he could just reach the top of the ravine then maybe some hikers or a hunter would find him. He needed some food soon or he'd probably expire. He'd taken a class on biology and he knew that the human body could only last for seven days without water. He certainly couldn't stay out here in the forest much longer. He was imagining the possibility of dehydration and starvation if no one came for him. He attempted to stand up again. However, his body began to shake and he fell over into the dirt. Was his mind playing tricks on him because he thought he saw someone at the top of the ravine? In this person's hand was a thick hamburger and then his vision became blurry and he dismissed this crazy idea from his mind. Wondering if he was hallucinating he tried to ignore the grumbling noise in his stomach which only reminded him of an intense hunger and need for real food. He pushed his leg muscles to continue moving up the incline. However, this time as he took two more steps everything went black and he fainted. He lay there unconscious and unaware of anything around him.

* * *

Miles away Kevin Braden's father had managed to catch up with the team of searchers. The leader asked him if he was alright or if he needed to return to his house for the remainder of this trek.

"No, I'm fine now. I just needed a few minutes to gather my thoughts. He was determined to insist that the lead man listen to his idea. He grabbed the dirty shirt belonging to his son and held it for the dog to sniff.

"I want the dog to lead our group forward for the remainder of the search!"

"We've had the dog with us this entire time and it hasn't found anything so far to keep us in the woods this late in the day. I think we should return to the house and get some water and more supplies. It's too dense in the forest to spread out and widen the search." Blaine remarked.

"But we've kept the dog close to us and you've been leading the team. I have a feeling we've been going in the opposite way of where my son may be located. Remember it was turning dark at one point in my son's hike that night. He must have gotten turned around and lost his sense of direction. It's possible that he was heading in the opposite direction of our home." Jeff implored.

"Fine, what do we have to lose? We have to find your boy today or I fear for the worst." Blaine responded grimly. "Send the dog and we'll follow him."

Jeff knelt down beside the canine with his son's dirty shirt and gave the dog a longer time to smell the missing boy's garment. The excited dog danced around for a brief second and then eagerly ran in a different direction.

As the team forged on ahead making a new trail away from the old existing path, the dog ran faster and then stopped to make sure Jeff was still in sight. Another twenty minutes had passed as they followed behind the sounds of the Blue Heeler dog as it made progress through the underbrush. Suddenly, the men heard the dog in the distance whining louder now. When Jeff finally reached the dog and caught his breath, he noticed a torn piece of a shirt material that was hooked on a slender branch of a young sapling tree. Just beyond this spot, the ground dropped away to nothing but air. As he edged closer to where the dog stood expectantly, he glanced down and saw the miracle he had cried out for. At the bottom of the steep ravine lay a body. The prone figure wasn't moving. Scrambling down the slope, Jeff Braden nearly tripped over some loose rocks. He forced himself to go slower as he proceeded downward. Reaching the bottom of the ravine, he bent over and wrapped his arms around his son's inert form. He started shaking and crying as an unexplainable emotional relief began to over take him. Slowly and gently, this father brushed the dirt from Crash's face and swept the boy's matted hair away from his forehead. Then Jeff checked for a pulse on his son's wrist and he noticed Crash's chest moving slightly and so he anxiously spoke his son's name.

"Kevin, wake up! Crash', can you hear me. Speak to me, son." Jeff pleaded.

His son moaned once and then was silent. Being awoken by the sounds caused Crash to become aware of his injuries and the ensuing pain. He appeared to be disoriented and confused.

"We found him" a volunteer shouted near the top of the ravine.

Blaine reached the excited dog and then he looked down the ravine to where Jeff Braden was sitting and holding his boy. "Is he alive?"

"He has a pulse, but we need to get him to a hospital. I don't think he recognizes me right now. I need some men to help me carry him back up the hill. I almost fell once on the way down here."

When two men reached the spot where Jeff was now standing they grinned broadly at him. And they thumped Jeff on the back and exclaimed enthusiastically how glad they were to locate the missing boy. They then stood on either side of the pair to support their bodies as they all began the slow process of moving forward to climb back up the steep slope. At one point, Crash' groaned as if in pain and his father stopped climbing to check on him.

"What's the matter, son?"

"My body hurts. Don't touch my wrist or my knee." He spoke in barely a whisper of a voice since his throat was parched and hoarse by this time. "We'll be more careful. I wish we had a splint or something to protect his injured wrist." Jeff exclaimed.

"I can create a temporary splint with the adhesive tape from my first aid kit in my backpack," one man offered. All I need first is a couple of semi-flat sticks or slender branches along with an extra shirt material. I'll roll the material around his arm and then the sticks won't hurt as much when I taped them to his arm."

"That will work for now." Blaine replied. Everyone worked together to assist him and one man offered his own bottled water to the thirsty lad. When they'd finished applying the temporary splint to the injured wrist area then they continued climbing up the steep ravine to reach the top.

"Ow, my wrist hurts when you guys move too much! Crash exclaimed.

"Son, we're trying to be careful, but we need to reach the top of this steep incline. So hang in there and once we make it up, then we'll figure out a better way to help you." Jeff promised.

After the men had reached the top of the hill, they positioned the boy in Jeff's lap while they discussed a plan to transport him. Isaac offered the exhausted kid more sips of water while another volunteer mentioned using his flannel shirt as a makeshift sling in order to protect the wrist and arm from being bumped during the journey back. Blaine agreed with this plan and so the man carefully placed the cloth material around the boy's injured arm and draped the sleeves of the shirt around the kid's neck to be tied in a knot. The young Braden lad gave a weak smile as he looked up at the man and then he closed his eyes once more. Everyone in the group began to smile too. One man walked over and placed his hand on Jeff's shoulder as a way of expressing his joy at finding the man's boy alive.

"Congratulations, Mr. Braden. This day turned out to be a great success! Brad Jones stated.

"I am truly grateful to have found my son. I want to thank all of you men for your efforts and for not giving up on this grueling search." Jeff said. Trying to contain his emotions, he brushed the tears from his eyes and gave a huge sigh of relief mixed with joy.

"Yeah, we are all thrilled to have found your son. Now we need to talk about using a fireman's carry to hike back to civilization." Isaac stated.

"I'd like Isaac and Brad to take the first leg of this journey and then Walt and Jason will carry Jeff's son on the next part until we reach his house." Blaine Wilson said.

Once his son was situated in the arms of the two men, Jeff walked over and stroked the dog's head and back as a way of showing his appreciation. Then the eager dog made its way over to the youngster and began to lick the boy's face affectionately. This brought a faint smile to the face of young Crash' Braden. The lad tried to say the dog's name but his voice only gave out a slight squeaking noise which sounded more like the word, Bluh. The entire crew laughed excitedly and a few men clapped each other's backs enthusiastically. Blaine commended his team of volunteers for their work together in the recovery efforts.

"Okay, men, this was a fine job by all. Now let's get this boy back to civilization and to his mother who is anxiously waiting to hear from us. I am glad we can give them such good news."

"Blaine, here's my shirt to cover up the kid. He's shivering and this might help. I don't need it right now anyway."

"Good idea, Michael. I'm sure the boy appreciates your clothing."

The men were eager to take their turn at carrying the injured lad until they finally reached Jake's cabin. They took a few minutes to rest and take a couple of deep breaths and then they moved on ahead until they reached the Braden's property. A news reporter was the first to see the group staggering in to view and she turned and headed back to the news crew to set up a microphone and cameras to film the rescue team as they drew nearer. People were milling around on the front lawn and when they saw the group along with Mr. Braden smiling they gave out a cheer.

Someone went up the steps to knock on the front door. Hearing no immediate response, the excited individual decided to crack open the door and holler for Mrs. Braden to come outside. By the time the group had made their way to the searchers' van, the news team had their camera crew ready and rolling. The weary travelers were being filmed as lights flashed around them. None of the searchers looked clean shaven or anxious to have their faces splashed over the nightly news. Helen emerged from her house, headed down the steps, and ran over to greet her husband. Pressing her way through the crowd of onlookers, she saw her young son being held in the arms of two men with day-old stubble on their tired faces. She noticed Blaine Wilson standing to the right of her boy and talking to one of the reporters from the Daily news paper. She'd known Blaine Wilson for a number of years so she went over to give him a hug as she thanked him profusely for leading the crew of men on the search and rescue efforts. The two men made their way over to the house and gently placed the boy down on the front porch so his mother could sit close by him. Helen Braden was elated to have her boy home safe and yet, she couldn't seem to stop crying. He was clearly awake at this time and trying to speak in a low, weak voice.

"Hi, Mom, it's okay, I'm here now and I'm starving. I've been dreaming of having a cheese burger the entire time I was stuck in the woods."

"Of course, I'll cook you up your favorite meal when all of this commotion stops and people leave our place." She cried. "I will wait to give you a proper hug. I don't want to cause you any more pain or discomfort." Helen Braden said.

"We are a family again. I'm sure he'd appreciate a kiss on the head before they take him to the hospital. And by the way, I'm starving too!" Jeff exclaimed joyfully. "I'm going to head inside and get some water for our thirsty boy to drink."

Everyone around them started laughing and another cheer went up from the crowd of spectators lining the driveway of the Braden home. Even though this weary lad could barely speak he could formulate thoughts in his head and they went like this, *I didn't die out in the wilderness. I'm home and safe at last and I'll never go on an adventure in the woods without that awesome dog named Blue Boy.*"

From outside of the Braden's home a commotion was going on and someone ran over to inform Mrs. Braden that the transport vehicle had arrived. Most of the men were gathered around the main truck waiting for hot coffee and food after a grueling day in the woods.

"The EMT guys are here now and they're waiting to check on the Braden's son. Someone needs to go tell Mr. Braden to come outside." Michael announced loudly.

"I'll let them know." Isaac replied. He headed up the front porch to inform Jeff of the medical team's arrival. "Mr. Braden, the paramedics are here to take your son to the hospital."

Once the Braden's son had been placed securely in the back of the EMT, the driver went over to confer with his parents. The paramedics informed the parents about the need for a doctor to check their son for dehydration and possible hypothermia problems. Of course, the doctor would take care of his injured wrist and knee after the initial examination. The Braden's didn't want to be away from their son for even a short ride to the ER so Jeff asked the driver if they could ride in the back with their son. He replied by telling him that only one person could be in the back and so they would have to follow in their own vehicle. The couple understood and then they spoke with their son briefly as he was being loaded into the back end of the EMT vehicle.

Their missing son was alive and that was all they needed to know at that moment. Smiling through her tears, Helen Braden made an effort to acknowledge the many remarks and words of congratulations from those around her. She tried to dismiss the thoughts of what her son must've endured while alone in the woods for days as they drove to the hospital. Arriving at the entrance which led into the hospital parking area, Jeff finally found a spot to park his car, and they hurried into the building together. The nightmare of a missing son was finally over and there was only joy and a sense of relief now coursing through Jeff's mind and emotions. While standing in front of the hospital's coffee machine dispenser, Jeff Braden took a moment to thank God for rescuing his son from a possible death in the wilderness. It was certainly divine providence which had enabled the search team to finally locate their only son. Jeff went back over to the chairs of the waiting room to sit down next to his wife.

"Sweetheart, I was thinking that we owe our new neighbor a debt of gratitude for all of his help. He didn't have to join in this search or allow us to take his dog on the hike. Maybe we could offer to buy a year's worth of doggie treats and food as a way to thank this man." Jeff said.

"Of course, that's a good idea and I also want to have him over for dinner once Kevin is home from the hospital." Helen mentioned. "Do you know his first and last name? I'd like to call him something besides what the boys have nicknamed him." She said.

"Well, I recall him saying that his name was Jake, but I don't think he mentioned his last name to me. I can find out by asking Mrs. Johnson if she knows his full name. Why, do you want to write him a thank you card?"

"Yes, that would be appropriate. I just really want to refer to him in a proper manner instead of calling him, 'the neighbor guy'."

CHAPTER
Twenty-Eight

wo days after the holiday, Jake was getting a new dressing on his wounds by Nurse Watkins. She frowned as she noticed her patient had not taken his last pill and medication needed to prevent an infection happening in his two wounds.

"You have to finish this prescription we gave you. If you don't follow doctor's orders then we can't release you at the end of this week."

"I'm feeling better now. However, nurse I'm growing weary of taking pills, ingesting medicine daily, and having stuff called TSP pumping into my veins. It's time to fish or cut bait, you know what I mean?" He smiled charmingly at the young nurse. "I was wondering if the lunch room had my favorite food items like deli roast beef sandwiches or sweet potato fries. I will show you my appreciation by being more cooperative, I promise." Jake stated.

The nurse only smiled at him in a patronizing way as she walked out of his room to check on her next patient. Ten minutes after the nurse had left his room, an unexpected visitor walked into his hospital room.

"I checked with the nurses at the station and I mentioned that I was here to visit their local hero. I'm not the kind to bring folks flowers when they in the hospital so you're out of luck with something colorful to decorate your room from me.

"No worries, I'm fine without a bunch of flowers in my room. They are fine in a person's yard, but I have no need of them here. What can I do for you, mister?"

"My name is Blaine Wilson and I have a special interest in this youngster named Max and his Mom, Lisa Johnson. Do you recall this woman?"

"Yes, I'm acquainted with the boy and his mother, why do you ask?"

"Well, I've taken a liking to this woman and she's had me over a couple of times. So I'd appreciate it if you just stay away from her in the future. I'm planning on taking up all of her free time and she doesn't need another temporary distraction right now, especially from a guy who might be leaving this area in six months or so. Aren't you thinking of fixing up the old cabin and then selling it for profit like I heard from someone in the town's mercantile store?" Blaine demanded.

"I had considered the idea of turning this property over for a resale value if the opportunity arose. However, what I do with my uncles' old house and property is no business of yours, Mr. Benson."

"The name's Wilson and it concerns me since it involves a certain acquaintance of mine. Lisa Johnson needs a man who is settled, responsible, and willing to be around indefinitely. In other words, mister, she doesn't need to have her heart broken by a guy whose intentions might not be what she really needs in her life. And besides, seeing how you're probably thinking of leaving this area for a better job prospect or a fancier bigger house, I'm thinking that you should stay away from my girlfriend. From what I hear, you're a man on the move ever since you left the military. May the best man win in this affair of the heart and sadly for you, Mr. Walker, I am confident it will be me that she decides to stick with and not you! So with that being said, I'll be on my way. And mister ex-military/drifter, you need to be smart and stay away from Lisa Johnson."

"Oh, so you're dating Lisa Johnson. Well, for the record, the best man will win this challenge because... as of today, I've decided to throw my hat into the ring, if you get my drift. I'm not sure where you learned your manners, but from where I come from this is a free country and I can spend time with any woman I choose to. I expect she is capable of making up her own mind about who she will or will not go on a date with. So yes, you will be seeing me in your near future and way more than you might care to."Jake insisted in a matter of fact tone.

To his relief, Blaine Wilson marched out of the hospital room in a huff leaving Jake to lie back on his pillow and reflect on this new situation. Whereupon he closed his eyes and contemplated the idea of actually spending more time with Lisa. Of course, he wanted to spend time with her son and teach him a few things about hiking responsibly and taking care of a dog. Jake fumbled around for his bedside attachment and finally, he was able to retrieve the object and punch the red call button for the nurse on the day shift.

"Nurse Isabelle, I don't want any more visitors coming today or the next day. In fact, keep everyone out until I say differently." Jake growled into the intercom.

Within ten minutes, he heard a loud commotion in the hallway by his door and in burst another person who was followed closely by a nurse. Jake rolled over and sat up in a bad mood at being disturbed so soon after issuing his warning to the hospital staff. The fiery words of angry and disgust were quickly forming in his head when he spied the culprit making all the hoopala and noise outside in the hallway and now presently in his room. He simply stared at the two women approaching his side of the room and then his face broke out in an enormous grin and he gave out a loud whoop of pure delight. The nurse left his room after she saw that Jake was fine with the next visitor.

"C. J. Walker, what have you gotten into this time? I thought going into the Marines was enough excitement for my favorite nephew! And just why have you cloistered yourself in this room as if you never plan to leave? Give me a hug, young man."

"Aunt Cabbie, you're here. It's great to have you here. I've missed your humor, your stories, and your creative genius which you so willingly bestow upon our normally unpleasant world."

"So Jacob, oh I mean to say Jake, tell me what's been happening to you since I've been in Europe for the last three months and why there's a 'no visitors allowed' sign on your hospital door."

"Well, plenty has been happening in my neck of the woods. I inherited a small piece of property with a comfortable, but rather small house in this area. Before that I'd travelled through three southwestern states and stopped off at Yosemite National Park for a guided tour. Then I stayed three nights at Lake Shasta Resort on the way to Washington State where Uncle Henry once lived. I decided to step away from the military life and see how the normal folks live."

"And how has that experience been so far?" His aunt asked him playfully as a big smile spread across her sun-tanned face. Her eyes seemed to sparkle as she studied her favorite nephew. He had grown into a confident man she observed as she listened to him speak. Hearing him say he no longer wanted to stay in the military as a career gave her a renewed sense of anticipation for his future.

"Well, as you can see I ran into a couple of snags recently. Now I'm recuperating here and wishing I could go home and rest up. A person doesn't get any decent sleep with nurses interrupting you and intercom sounds going on day and night. Say, you wouldn't want to stay at my place as my nurse so that the doctor would release me from this place early would you?"

"You mean you'd trust me to nurse your wounds and administer your meds?" Aunt Cathy asked.

"Yes, exactly, if you were there with me to satisfy the doctors' orders then I could stay at home and get more rest and enjoy better food. Maybe even get a home cooked meal for a change. I'd pay you for your time and trouble. You'd like being here in this somewhat quiet community." He displayed his charming, roguish grin to her in the hopes of winning her over to his idea. "The two families I've already met are friendly and hospitable. They just might need a lovable, grand lady like you to help keep an experienced eye on their two youngsters and teach the energetic boys how to do cool jumps with their bikes. Besides, Aunt Cabbie, you know you really miss spending time with your active, rowdy nephew ever since I graduated from high school and went off to join the Marine Corps. I recall how most kids love spending time with you; these two families both have a boy around eleven years of age. You're so much fun and most kids seem to sense as I do that you truly care about them. So what do you say?"

"Oh, you're still as charming and amiable as ever, young man. I guess the time spent here with you would be a treat after tromping around Italy and the south of France. I soon tired of certain individuals in France trying to sell me a piece of land or a villa for the price of half of my retirement funds and my IRA savings."

"You're the best, Aunt Cabbie; I'll call you to let you know when they will send me home. Where are you staying so I can get a hold of you later today?"

"I'm at the Holiday Inn on South Hampton Street. How about I call you around five thirty? Then you can let me know if they're releasing you from the hospital tonight or tomorrow. Is there anything you need me to buy for your place before I settle in?"

"Well, yes there is a huge need for groceries since I've been so busy chasing bad guys and getting shot up. Oh and by the way, will you look in on my dog, Blue Boy'? See if he needs more food. He's being cared for by a woman named Lisa Johnson for the last two days.

"Who is Lisa Johnson and why is she taking care of your dog?"

Just then Jake's room phone buzzed and he winked at his aunt and picked up the receiver. She heard her nephew respond to the person on the other line. As he continued to answer their questions, she realized this was an important call so she found a stuffed chair to sit in and wait.

"Yes sir, I did. No, sir, I wasn't aware of these boys at the time. I inadvertently met Mrs. Johnson's young son, Max, when I was caught up in an unsavory confrontation with some bad guys who were up to no good. I'd been watching some suspicious comings and goings around my part of the woods. I had phoned your office and left the information with your secretary, a gal named Hannah. I told her to give your office staff the facts about the problems I'd discovered in this area. As you recall, sir, we'd established a plan for me to report back to your two contacts when I had absolute evidence of any illegal activity."

"Yes, that's correct. I do recall saying for you to get back to me or the other contact person." Commander Holt remarked over the phone.

"So the day I inadvertently decided to venture further into the woods to check things out, these two boys chose to follow me as a lark. I didn't know they were tracking me until it was too late to insist that they turn around and go home. Unfortunately, for them it turned out to be on the wrong day and the wrong time. They found themselves caught in the middle of an extremely difficult mess when three intruders jumped out of a helicopter and chose to fire off a large weapon towards one of our nearby facilities. I managed to extract just one boy, Max, from the dangerous situation only to have them both go missing afterwards. You know me, sir; I couldn't live with myself if I left those youngsters alone and unprotected from those criminals."

"Let me guess, you decided to be your own search and rescue team. I do know you, and I can envision you taking on those illegals single handedly as you did once in Iraq. Your Rambo reputation precedes you once again." John Holt proclaimed.

"Let me explain, Sir. Max's mother, Lisa is on her own since her husband died nearly two years ago. She was frantic or may I say she was really desperate to get her son back alive. Max is all she has in this area. Her other two relatives, an aunt and a brother, live in California. I was just doing my part to facilitate this rescue effort when things got out of hand. I ended up in a gunfight with a rogue helicopter crew that almost ended badly for me. So when the contact in Homeland Security office that you just mentioned sends an agent over to my cabin in a few days, tell your man to go past Lisa Johnson place, then keep heading due northeast past the next house where Jeff Braden's lives. Once you see the Braden's two-story white country home which is located on Bremer Road, I think. Anyway, then my cabin is just a short hike from their place. After going pass the Braden's house head to the right on the gravel road, go past the large oak tree, and then you'll see an old weather-beaten wooden fence line. If you have trouble locating my house, you can ask one of my neighbor folks there to give you better directions."

"Just text your physical address and we'll figure out your exact location. Get some more rest and do what the doctor orders. Then report to my office so we can discuss this further. Call my secretary, Hannah, to set up a meeting. I have a proposition for you, Jake and I hope you will say yes to this idea. I want to commend you for your involvement in apprehending these criminals/terrorists. Good work! We'll finish up the job there and shut down their entire operation ASAP. So get back to us when you're recovered."

"I will, sir, goodbye."

Once Jake had replaced the receiver back onto the phone set, Aunt Cathy proceeded to ply him with her own questions.

"Who was that? It sounded very official. Why was the person asking you these things?"

"That was my old commanding officer from Fort Jackson. We have a longstanding relationship and I still stay in contact with him even though I'm not in the military per se."

"Are you planning to still work for the military after this little vacation time, Jacob?"

"Well, not exactly."

"What does well, not exactly really mean young man?"

"I stumbled onto some crazy plot to destroy a huge water resource facility and I just couldn't help myself. I had to get involved and try to stop these terrorists."

"So you put yourself directly in front of a gunman whose objective was to kill you. This sounds a little extreme. Why didn't you call in the national guard to handle this matter?"

"I hadn't figured on meeting these people head on that day. It was merely a scouting trip until they brought the fight to me. And as far as calling in the right authorities, I was going to get back to my house and relay my findings into Homeland Security, but things got out of hand before I could do that."

"I see, so we can safely say that we are very fortunate to have you around with us still." She said.

"Yes, I'm going to live to fight another day against foreign terrorists and haters of America. These types of criminals need to be stopped. I am considering applying for the police academy or maybe something involving Homeland Security work in the future."

This last comment brought a smile and a burst of laughter from his aunt. Her next question was not so serious in nature.

"What kind of animal were you referring to when you say the word, pet?" His aunt queried.

"He's a Blue Heeler dog. He's actually a bit more blackish in color than most of his breed. He's lovable and well trained so you shouldn't have any trouble with him. His name is Blue Boy'. He will respond to the name of Blue too. Thanks for choosing to take care of him for me. I imagine Mrs. Johnson might be tired of this new responsibility I put on her."

"I'll be glad to stop by her place and relieve her of this dog caring job. She works a job outside of the home as you mentioned before and she doesn't need to be feeding a dog or cleaning up after him." She got up from her chair and walked over to massage his neck and back being careful to avoid contact with his wound. "Oh, by the way, I received a phone call from your sister, Jillian. She is anxious to talk with you after she found out about your gunshot injuries. She would've come with me today except that the twins don't do very well driving in a car for six and half hours. I'd rather not have them in my car either if they become fussy or crying for long periods of time. So give her a call. Here, use my phone if you don't want to use the hospitals phone. I believe she mentioned that she is planning to fly here to see you for a couple of days if her husband can watch the boys." She reached into her leather purse and pulled out her extra cell phone to give him. "Also, your Father and my brother, Wilbur, were away the past ten days on a white-water rafting excursion in Colorado. They didn't know anything about your injuries until Jillian called them. Your dad is flying here to meet us in a couple of days."

"Thanks for the heads up. I will call Dad after I take a short rest. I need you to check on whether or not Blue Boy' needs more dog food. Find out if he's being a bother to the Johnsons. If that's the case, you can grab the dog and take him for a walk. When you are done then take him back to my place. He'll be fine on my front porch." Jake insisted.

"I won't forget to check on your dog. I'd like you to consider doing a favor for me in return. I have this small project I could use your assistant with."

"Okay, I will have a few weeks until I need to start looking for a job if I'm going to stay here permanently. So what's this brainstorm idea of yours? If I remember, you love helping children and giving them encouragement to develop their creative side, right?"

"Never mind my idea. You need to rest and get your strength back. Then we'll discuss the matter. She replied with a big smile. I have just enough time to shop for dog food and a few miscellaneous items and check with your friend, Lisa. I should also call Aunt Debbie and Uncle Doug to let them know you're still alive and kicking. They told me about how much they'd enjoyed the last Thanksgiving weekend you spent with them at their mountain home. Alright, Jacob, make sure you take those pain pills lying over there on the tray, get some rest, and try not to flirt so much with the younger nurses!"

As she strode over to place her hand on the door knob, she turned back to him.

"So why did I get stopped from visiting you by the nurses today? I almost left without seeing my favorite nephew when they tried to block my attempt to enter into your room."

"Oh the reason for that was because I've had several annoying people come here and either threaten me or bully me around and I just got fed up with the lot of them. I'm glad you were persistent. I need you in my life and Aunt Cabbie I plan to share some more details with you when you and I are together at my cabin."

She gave him another big hug and promptly tousled his dark, wavy hair as she'd done so many times before in his youth. After Cathy Harper left his room, Jake had sat in his quiet room gazing out the window. He was remembering the many hours his aunt had stayed with him in the hospital when he was eight years of age. He recalled vividly the amazing story she'd made up just to entertain him and help to push away the lonely, depressing days while he had undergone medical treatment. He was glad this delightful woman had driven all this way to see him. He closed his tired eyes for a moment and wondered what would be the next adventure in his life journey and would it include this beautiful woman named Lisa Johnson. Jake also wondered what his father and his adorable aunt would think of Lisa and Max. Looking out the expansive windows again he noticed how the sunlight seemed to warm up his world as it filtered through the glass panes.

There were shafts of glimmering light rays that had been graciously warming the interior of his hospital room as he'd sat and chatted with his aunt. This moment reminded him of the portion of his aunt's first fiction story that included the brilliant 'light star experience' for the young hero named Destin Morgan. He wished for the light beam with its magical powers to visit him as well and transform his body and soul to health quickly. He needed another miracle to get totally free from the night terrors that gripped his being and his sleep troubles. The warmth of these rays had mysteriously been warming up the inside of his soul at the same time as he'd conversed with his aunt today. Maybe it was the magic of his awesome aunt and her infectious humor that he needed to help him recover. In the past, she'd imparted encouragement into his life and here she was again just when he needed some inspiration and answers for his plans for the future.

There was also something else drawing him to stay in this area as well. What if he could actually belong here? What was his aunt secretive idea she wanted to share with him? Was she sent here by his heavenly angel messenger to impart her wisdom and infectious joy into his life once again? He'd just have to give her a chance to tell him this new idea and then he'd see. Could this town and its inhabitants have the capacity to heal the deep wounds and grief he'd experienced while serving overseas in Afghanistan?

When his friend, Josh, had died overseas during that awful deadly conflict it had left him feeling crushed by the loss. At times, he'd felt an intense anger well up inside of him and then he wanted to kick something. It felt like he was a time bomb waiting to explode. One time he'd had the temptation to hurl his fist into a wall to release his pent up frustrations and anger. He had been told by the chaplain that he was dealing with survivor's guilt and PTSD and he needed to talk it out with a professional for stretch of time to get healing. Watching an army ranger in his unit lose a leg from IED explosion had definitely left an indelible mark on his soul. He'd had another nightmare last night while in the hospital and he wished there was a pain pill to take as a remedy to stop this dark, sinister PTSD which threatened to eliminate his sleep patterns and his well-being again. Gradually, his eyelids became heavier and the exhaustion of the weary day caused him to fall into a restless sleep.

CHAPTER
Twenty-Nine

T he next day, his aunt returned with clean clothes and a pair of his cleanest boots stuffed into a satchel. In another tote bag slung over her shoulder was something that smelled delicious and tasty. He was feeling much better after a good night sleep without any night terrors and he was more relaxed.

"What do you have inside that canvas bag besides some Starbucks Coffee for me?"

"Oh, I bought you a hot sandwich with all the trimmings. She sat the bag down on the chair next to his bed and crossed the room to close his door. Then she edged over to his bed and bent down to whisper in his ear.

"I discovered a delightful deli shop two blocks away. I hope you like roast beef and pepper jack cheese? You don't have to eat the chips or the pickle."

"Terrific, let me see. Reaching into the bag, he produced a loosely wrapped sandwich and hungrily took a bite of the delectable food. Jake savored the tender cut of meat smothered in mushrooms and a delectable sauce and responded with this. "Um, good stuff, much better than the food here. Hey, Aunt Cathy, what's the little project you want me to do for you?

I've been wondering about it ever since you drop the thought on me."

Simmer down, boy! After you've eaten, showered and comb your hair, I'll be back for a short visit. Your family is arriving at the airport around five-thirty this evening and I have to grab a few more items first before we all invade your peaceful hospital room. Here, take these clothes I brought in this bag from your place. They are for you in case the doctor releases you tomorrow."

"Swell, I'll take a shower and watch the news while I wait for them. It's great to have you here, Aunt Cathy. I've missed your humor and your joy. You bring a party wherever you go!"

"Ah, thank you, I feel the same about you. From what I've learned from the youngster you helped save called Max, folks now call you Big Jake'. I guess I can call you Jake too. Say I talked with your friend, Lisa Johnson, and she's letting me barrow her big crock pot to cook a roast for the family on Thursday. You don't mind this do you big guy? She's a lovely woman and her son is very entertaining."

"Well, I can definitely agree that she is a smart, interesting woman. And this is for your ears only, Aunt Cabbie. I am attracted to her. She's an amazing and intriguing woman. She is a single mom trying to work and take care of her son and I admire that about her as well. Remember, auntie, what I'm admitting to you right now is strictly between you and me. Besides, seeing how my last meeting with her did not go that well, I doubt if she'd want to see me on a more personal basis. I think she could be dating a guy named Blaine Wilson and if so then its hands off for me. I won't encroach on another man's territory."

"Be it as it may, she is still a terrific gal and she'd called me an hour ago and said the Braden family wanted to do something special to show their appreciation for you, Jacob, I mean Jake."

"What do you mean they want to show their appreciation? I thought you were just barrowing a crock pot to make dinner for my father and my sister, Jillian."

"Yes, but these two families are also offering for us to use their home if we need a bigger place than your tiny house."

"That's fine since I spent the last two weeks repairing my place and didn't have time to go buy certain household items for cooking." Jake wiped his greasy lips with the colorful cloth napkin from her basket.

"Say, whose house are we having this family dinner at anyway? My place is not presentable. Maybe we should go to a local restaurant this time."

"Well, since Lisa Johnson and I've been talking recently, she's become aware of your situation more. She offered her home for the upcoming dinner party as a way of thanking you for your efforts in saving her son from those dangerous criminals. She said if it hadn't been for your heroic rescue and standoff with the bad guys, her son might have been kidnapped. Apparently, she has changed her opinion of your actions in that recent minor skirmish. I'm sure it wasn't your illustrious charm and good manners that brought this reverse in her attitude towards you! Hah ha. But if you'd rather not impose upon this gentle woman and her home, fine. What kind of answer should I be giving to Mrs. Johnson and Max then? I suppose we could have the dinner meal at the Braden's place instead. They offered their home and the use of their smaller kitchen as well." She remarked.

"Are you sure this wasn't your idea and you are finagling this party? Maybe Lisa Johnson is too polite to refuse an elderly aunt's request." He said.

"To tell the truth, Jake, I think she is rather thrilled to be entertaining folks again. Her life has been quite lonely since her husband passed away. It might be a good change for her son too. It's settled then. I have to hurry to go pick up your folks. Relax and enjoy a hot shower." She winked and turned to leave his room before he could argue further. Truth be told, he didn't want to disagree with the plan. He was anxious to spend some time with this woman and find out if what he was sensing might be real and worth pursuing.

The following day, Lisa and Max were busy getting the place ready for their company. Helen Braden had called earlier in the day saying she would bring dinner rolls, dessert, and the drinks for the gathering. She thanked her neighbor and proceeded to cut up the raw vegetables as a side dish for people to enjoy. There was also an artichoke dip for the veggies. She would make a blend of beef gravy and a thickener of rice flour which would be added to the stew when she arrived home from her job. The slow cooker with meat and vegetables would be simmering in the pot in her kitchen all day long and its rich, savory aroma would also be drifting throughout the home making the house smell even more inviting for visitors. Max was practicing his new idea of applying hair gel to his unruly mass of thick hair. He taken his ace bandage off of his ankle the day before so now he was walking without much discomfort. He'd taken plenty of Tylenol for the pain the first two weeks as he foot and ankle were healing. He was glad he didn't have to wear a walking boot like his friend Crash' Braden had to a year before when he broke a bone in his foot. As he was hobbling back to the sofa he heard someone walking onto their front porch. Seconds later, the doorbell rang and he hollered for his mother to answer it.

"Who is it?" Lisa asked.

"It's Blaine Wilson. Can I come in to talk with you?"

"Certainly Mr. Wilson." Lisa responded. She opened the door wider to welcome him inside. She quickly untied her apron and tried to brush the thick curls out of her face. She smiled at the handsome tall fireman standing in front of her. She eyed the nice bouquet of flowers in his outstretched hand. She was pleasantly surprised by his presence and the gift.

"Oh my, these are lovely. Thank you. To what do we owe the pleasure of this visit and these lovely spring flowers?"

"These are for you, Lisa. I wanted to give you something to match the beauty of your smile. You've been through a lot of turmoil and stress lately and I just wanted to cheer you up. Also I'd like to invite you to go to dinner with me next Friday if you're available."

"That would be nice. I'd need to find someone to watch Max while I'm out though. Maybe I will call you by Tuesday once I've made those arrangements." Lisa said.

"Great. The reason I didn't call you first is that I wanted to see your face when I handed you these flowers. It looks as if you are preparing to have company. The aroma coming from your kitchen smells terrific." Blaine exclaimed hoping to be invited for a home cooked meal.

"Yes, we are having company. We invited our neighbor and his family over for dinner. They heard of his injuries and flew in to visit him. His father, his sister, and an aunt are only here for four days and so I invited them to join us for this celebration dinner. It's my way of thanking this man for locating my missing son." She said.

"Well, just be careful how much time you spend with this newcomer. I'm not sure he is the trustworthy or dependable type. He just might up and leave this area for something better. I've heard talk from some folks in town that he tends to keep to himself. He strikes me as a loner or a recluse type." Blaine remarked.

"I will be cautious. Thank you for your advice, Blaine. My going out with you on a dinner date is a way to show my appreciation to you as well. It would be a little crowded if you were to come tonight what with the Braden family joining us. So I'll see you next Friday for dinner and I'll be sure to give a call to confirm our plans. You have a wonderful evening."

"Alright, and you too Lisa."

As soon as she had closed the front door, Max proceeded to share his thoughts about the fireman's visit.

"Mom, apparently, this guy doesn't just want to help you with the fireplace problem. It looks as if he's interested in dating you. You don't like him like that, do you? Oh and for the record, I don't need a babysitter. I'm almost twelve years old now. I can take care of myself for a few hours." Max exclaimed.

"You are growing up and showing me that you can take on more responsibilities lately. I've watched how you've done a fine job taking care of Jake's dog; I mean Mr. Walker. I really do appreciate the fact that you've been helping me with the housework. However, I just feel better if someone was here in the house at night with you."

"You didn't answer my question. Do you like this Blaine guy? Are you really going on a date with him?" Max questioned.

"Well, yes, I am considering going on one date with Mr. Wilson. After all, son, he did spend some time looking for you and Crash Braden. I want to thank him properly for helping in the search."

"Fine, what about Jake coming over to stay with me? If he can't come then maybe I can spend the night with the Bradens."

"I have no intention of allowing you to spend alone time with a neighbor man I barely know. So put that idea out of your mind, young man. Yes, I can ask Helen Braden if she doesn't mind you coming over for the evening, but don't' ask about spending the night there." Lisa remarked.

"Okay, but can you ask Mr. Jake first. I'd really like him to stay with me and tell me some of his war stories if he doesn't mind. He likes to play video games too. Please Mom, at least ask him." Max insisted.

"I said no and I meant no. I would rather pay someone like Alisha Williams to come here and stay so you could get to bed on time. Now stop pestering me about the neighbor man. We are going to let him take his dog home after tonight and you can check with his aunt or him about playing with his dog later on."

"Fine, I'm glad his aunt had to do some errands and let us keep the guy's dog for one more day. I like having a cool pet around the house."

CHAPTER
Thirty

L ater that same day, Max Johnson was in the bathroom attempting to get ready for their visitors.

"Mom, come here and help me with my thick, unruly hair." He yelled.

"I'm coming. What's the problem," she asked as she entered the bathroom to see her son grabbing another hunk of thick hair in his hand.

"I can't get this front part to look right and stand up like my friend, Anthony, does with his hair!" Max said exasperatedly.

"Let me give it a try." Lisa said.

Taking the tube of hair product from the counter top, his mother squeezed out a small amount into her hand. Then she placed the hair gel on his head, gathered a portion of his hair and styled it as he'd requested. Then she stood back to admire her work. Just then they heard a loud knocking on the front door. She hurried into the front room to answer it. Opening the door she was greeted by a well-dressed individual. He smiled broadly at Lisa and she couldn't help but notice the resemblance between this man and her handsome neighbor, Jake. Matthew Walker handed his hostess a bouquet of red and pink roses as he quickly introduced himself.

"This was my sister-in-law's idea. I asked her what she thought I should bring to this special occasion and she told me that every woman loves to get roses. She said that roses makes a woman feel special and appreciated. My daughter, Jillian, also agreed with her. I want to introduce you to Jillian Hansen; she's Jacob's older sister." Matthew said.

"Oh, how lovely, thank you and please come in both of you." Lisa replied.

Leading her company into the main room which consisted of a rich, dark brown leather sofa and two comfortable chairs, she told them to make themselves at home. The framed pictures on the wall displayed classic black and white photographs of either amazing scenery, or a sailboat on water or large, well-accented flowers. All in all, the room was perfectly fashionable and yet, comfortable to any visitor. Lisa went in to the kitchen to locate a large vase for the roses. Her son, Max, came bounding down the stairs and then entered the living room to greet his guests.

"Hello, are you Mr. Walker?" He asked.

"Yes, I am young man. I'm glad to be here. Thank you for inviting me into your fine home. My son has told me good things about you, Max."

"Yeah, Mister Jake is a cool guy. Would you two like a drink of ice water or lemonade?" He asked remembering his mother's instructions for their guests.

"I'll try your lemonade, how much does a glass of lemonade cost in these parts?" Matthew asked his young host.

"Lemonade doesn't cost anything at our house, mister." The adult humor apparently had gone over his young head completely. Matthew laughed as he observed Max's look of bewilderment.

"Let me explain myself. Usually when we see lemonade stand on the street, the sign reads fifty cents or a dollar for a cold glass of lemonade. So apparently, I just made a rather lame joke. I can see you haven't encountered a lemonade stands around your fair city. Therefore, you wouldn't understand my attempt to be humorous. Oh well." Matthew Walker made a sighing sound and the others laughed with him this time.

"Nope, I haven't seen one of those ever. Maybe my friend and I should set up a drink stand to make money. I think we'd have to put it up in town though because not many people come out this way."

"What did Mr. Jake tell you about me?"

"He said you were a brave boy when you had to deal with some bad dudes recently. He told us you helped him escape from a dangerous predicament in the woods. When he instructed you to do something important, you listened and took his advice and this probably saved your life and your friend. Jacob told us that he was proud of you, Max." Matthew replied.

"Cool, I like him a lot too." Max stated.

As they were conversing with one another, Max heard feet stomping on the porch and he went to answer the door. The Braden family was standing on the front porch, smiling, and holding a few food items in their hands. He welcomed them inside to join the others and introduced everyone like his mother had asked him to do earlier in the day. Then fifteen minutes later, another knock sounded on the door of their house and he knew immediately who was coming. He raced to the front door and opened it wide as Jake hobbled inside followed by his aunt. She was carrying a large bowl of salad fixings and a bottle of red wine. Jake made his way over to the chair with the footstool and gingerly placed his injured leg up on the ottoman. Setting his crutches aside, he grimaced at the pain the use of crutches still cause him. Where the bullet had entered through his upper chest and armpit area was still throbbing from his recent trip to do physical therapy. He took a deep breath and gave a meager smile to young Max. Then he turned to ask his family members how they liked this part of Washington State so far.

"Fine, we've enjoyed the town so far. We haven't seen much of this area yet, but we plan to drive up to see the gigantic structure called Soulee Dam and then travel across the border into B.C. Canada in a few days." Matt replied.

"Yes, I want to do some exploring of Victoria, B.C. and take a boat to Prince Edward Island if we have enough time for that." Matt Walker added. "When we talked on the phone Jacob said something about going fishing with me. The only way this could happen is if we fished from a dock and he sat in a chair. I wanted to take the motor boat out and troll about the lake and try our luck in fishing with my son on this trip, but it will have to wait until he's through using the crutches and his leg is all healed up."

Aunt Cathy nudged her niece, Jillian, and whispered to her that she was heading into the kitchen to check on their hostess.

"Lisa is there anything Jillian and I can do to assist you while the men talk?"

"I would love it if you could set the table for me. The flowers make a wonderful center piece. I haven't been given a bouquet of beautiful roses in ages. Actually it's been a few years since my late husband, Morgan, passed away and he usually brought me red roses on Valentine's Day. I miss getting flowers from a handsome man. Thank you for inspiring Mr. Walker to bring a gift for our celebration dinner."

"Your certainly are welcome, young lady. I know my brother-in-law quite well and I used to remind him to buy a gift for his wife on occasion. Men tend to get so involved in their jobs and they forget the little things which bring a woman joy such as flowers, pastries, or dark chocolate." Cathy Harper said.

"Where do you work, Mrs. Johnson?" Jillian asked.

"I have a job at the local bank in Randall. It's not what I want to do forever, but it pays the rent and utilities, etc. It is so nice that you were able to get away to come visit your brother." Lisa remarked.

"Well, I couldn't believe that he'd taken on some crazy militants and been shot twice. I wasn't able to visit him in Afghanistan and so I'm thrilled to be here to help him out during his recovery time. His new place has needed a woman to spruce it up a bit. Besides, he isn't much of a cook and I can certainly take care of this for him while he stays off of his leg for one more week." Jillian confided. "My husband is such a help to me. I really appreciate him taking care of our twin boys while I'm gone for six days. Of course, he will take them over to his folks' place often especially when he needs to get some work done at his office."

"How old are the twins?" Lisa asked.

"They are six years old and a handful if they have to stay indoors for too long." She smiled over at Lisa as she picked up the plates in her arms to follow her aunt to the living room. "I am glad to be here to see where Jake is living now and I needed a break from the boys and the laundry duties anyway."

Max raced past them and opened the pantry door to let Jake's dog free from his confine. With a bounce of energy, the canine made his way into the other room to nuzzle his nose on Jake's hand as he wagged his furry tail enthusiastically. He was happy to be with his owner and looked as if he was expecting a treat from Jake. He sat there waiting and then he barked once as if expecting to be rewarded for good behavior.

"Not this time, Blue boy. I forgot to bring your doggie treats with me tonight. Sorry boy, I couldn't manage to grab your treats and handle my crutches."

Blue boy' ambled over to sit by Max who was happy to pet the dog's fur and rub his ear gently. Matthew remembered the gift bag he'd set down when he first entered the home. He went to retrieve it from the small table by the doorway and handed it to the boy.

"Here's a small gift from our family to you, Max."

"Gosh, thanks Mr. Walker. But it's not my birthday until August 16th. What's the deal?"

"Oh, this is what I call a 'get to know you' kind of gift." He replied.

"I'd call it a grand gesture of thanks." Aunt Cathy responded.

"What did I do to get this thank you gift anyway?"

"You took care of my nephew, Cole Jacob's, pet and made sure he was watered and fed. That was an important job and besides, you've allowed us to come and relax and enjoy a meal in your home. I wanted to say thank you."

Max tore open the tissue paper and tossed the gift bag full of white tissue paper aside as he exclaimed with joy at the sight of a new video game he always wished for. He went over to the television monitor and hooked up his game boy to play the new video game.

"Wait a minute, young man. There's one more item in the bag you dropped on the floor. Go check what's still in the bottom of your gift bag." Matthew commented knowingly.

"Wow, it's a pocketknife likes my friends' Dad owns. Did you hear how his four inch pocketknife helped Jake get out of a very bad situation awhile back, Mr. Walker?"

"No I didn't, but I'd like to hear you tell the story."

"You see Mr. Jake and I were taken captive by these bad guys in the forest. They were trying to shoot off a rocket launcher thing to destroy the big water facility. Anyway, after those bad dudes captured us and tied us both up with these rope ties, the dog brought my friend's knife in his mouth. Then Jake told him to drop it in his lap. Then I managed to use the knife to slice through the ties on Mr. Walker's ankles and wrists so he could help me escape. He told me to leave with his dog. We had to maneuver like real soldiers do in an army crawl over the ground until we were hidden under the coverage of the brush so we could sneak away. He told me before I left him in the woods that he planned to fight those three men with just a measly knife and his fists. The fact that he was able to fight these guys and win, well it was simply remarkable." Max exclaimed.

"That sounds like something my son would do." Jake's father said.

"Yeah, he's awesome and I would like him to teach me a few self-defense holds someday. You know, incase I ever get into a fight with some bullies at school." Max replied.

"Of course, every kid should know how to protect themselves in a bad situation for sure."

"Dinner's almost ready everyone I just need a few more utensils like big serving spoons for the meal." Lisa called out to her company.

Reaching for his crutches lying on the floor next to his chair, Jake stood up slowly and awkwardly as he placed them underneath his armpits. He wished he was more independent and could present himself more capable as he came into Lisa's home. He almost tripped over the throw rug as he made his way towards the dining room table. Watching Lisa Johnson move about in her home brought him a new sense of satisfaction and excitement. He couldn't deny the increasing attraction he was feeling towards this beautiful, amazing woman. He wanted to spend more time with her and Max. He wanted to see where this new connection might take them. Would she reciprocate with the same interest he wondered?

CHAPTER
Thirty-One

Everyone was gathered around the table for the dinner meal. Laughter and small conversations could be heard as they passed the bowls of food around. Suddenly, Jake's aunt took a drinking glass in one hand and her spoon in the other and made a loud clinking noise to get everyone's attention.

"I was planning to tell Jake about my new idea and since this is as good as any time to share it, here goes." Cathy Harper stated.

Everyone stopped chatting and laid their serving spoons down to listen to Jake's aunt.

"I want to take some canvas tote bags and put my art design and logo on them. Then with Jake's help we can stuff the bags with simple art supplies and a teddy bear for the sick children at the local hospital here in town. I was even thinking about visiting the bigger hospital located in Grandview and maybe even one located in Bellingham as well. So what do you think?"

"Sure, I'd be glad to donate some money to purchase the supplies." Jake replied.

"I can purchase some stuffed animals to include in this gift for the children." Lisa answered with a big smile on her face. "Max and I will help you distribute the tote bags if you'd like."

"Aunt Cathy, I wish I could help out with this new venture, but I will need to fly back with Dad to take care of the twins. Keep me informed as to how your plan is doing and maybe we can send you some support money to buy more stuffed animals for the children." Jillian said as she smiled. "I remember you talking about doing something similar back when Cole was out of the hospital.

"I'll give you some money right now to buy plenty of those canvas tote bags you need. Don't you have to get special permission to bring items into the children's hospital? Are you talking about visiting kids who have cancer and other rare diseases?" Matthew asked.

"Yes, Matthew, that's my plan. I know it can be difficult to get this kind of permission, but I was thinking that since Cole Jacob was once in the hospital for cancer treatments as a boy, they might allow him to come with me and talk with the families of these children. It's worth calling the medical facilities and asking the supervisors of each hospital to see if they would be interested in our project. I can't imagine them not wanting to have someone like an ex-Marine come and visit their facility to encourage the patients there."

"So who is the person named Cole Jacob who was very ill that you are talking about?" Lisa questioned the aunt.

"Oh, you see, we use to all call him C.J. or Cole Jacob when he was young. In school the kids called him Jacob. Then when he was in high school the guys on the football team started calling him Jake and it stuck." She said with a radiant smile on her face. "He actually prefers being called Jake."Jillian replied.

"Aunt Cathy, you usually have very clever ideas even if they might be difficult to achieve. I have to admit I love your generous heart and your good intentions. So when do you want to get started on this new project?" Jake asked his aunt.

"I was thinking we'd meet by the end of the week and discuss who to contact. That way I'll be sure to have rounded up the tote bags, the supplies and the stuffed bears by then." Cathy replied.

"This sounds good to me. I should be more active by then as long as you come over and help me do a few things around my place this week. The doctor told me to get plenty of rest and stay off my leg as much as possible, remember? Therefore I might need some help cooking and tidying up my house and I think you are just the person to help me. What do you say, Aunt Cabbie?"

"Now that's Lady Catherine to you, young man! It seems that you are taking advantage of my good nature, as well as my valuable time!" She declared with a big laugh. This humorous, playful remark caused everyone at the table to laugh too.

"Okay then, Lady Catherine it is! I plan to take advantage of your time here with me. And yet, I feel as if I might become caught up in one of your mischievous, crazy plans if I commit to helping you." Jake replied glibly. He walked around the table and gave his favorite relative a big hug and smiled down at her. Then he made his way back to his own chair and sat down to fill his plate full of food. Soon everyone was partaking in the wonderful meal and the time of getting to know each other better. Soon the food began to disappear from some of the large bowls as people took seconds on the roast beef and garlic and herb flavored potatoes.

Lisa excused herself from the merriment and teasing for a moment in order to go to the kitchen to bring the coffee pot in for those who desired a hot drink. While she was there she looked for the remainder of extra napkins to bring back to the table. Jake followed her into the other room to help with this task. He hoped to ask her about her recent new relationship with Blaine Wilson. He didn't want to create any friction between the two of them especially now that they were on friendly terms. He liked being a part of her life as well as her son's.

"Lisa I'd like to ask you something in private." Jake mentioned.

"I've something that's been on my mind too, Mr. Walker." She sat her hot cup of tea down on the coffee table and moved the arm chair closer to where Jake was sitting. "What kind of cancer did you have and how did the doctor help you to be in remission at such a young age?" Lisa asked.

"How did you know about my battle with cancer?"

"I was with your aunt when she was talking on the phone to your other aunt. I believe her name is Debbie maybe. She mentioned how this time was much better than the first time you stayed in the hospital." Lisa said. She looked deeply into his clear blue eyes and saw the intensity with which he was observing her right then. "They were talking about that time you were in the hospital and your aunt referred to you as Cole Jacob."

"Ah, yes, that's my legal name. I've been going by the name, Jake, since I was in high school." He remarked as a smile appeared on his handsome face.

"Someday, I like to hear how you survive your battle with cancer."

"Someday maybe, in the meantime I'd like to ask you about a certain guy that seems interested in you. Are you two an item now?" Jake asked.

"Well, not exactly. He just wanted to help me around the house to make sure it was fireproof since he's a fireman by profession. He wants to take me out, but we are not a couple."

"So you are not dating? I wouldn't want to interfere if you are in a relationship with him." Jake responded.

"Actually, he did ask me out on a date this coming Friday evening and I said maybe if I could find a sitter to stay here with my son. I don't like to leave Max home alone for an entire evening." Lisa replied.

"So you are involved with this guy then?" Jake questioned.

"Well, we are not in a serious relationship exactly; we are just friends right now. I don't want to get involved with someone who isn't interested in being a part of my son's life and so I'm taking it slow."

"Okay, I understand. Then would you like to go have coffee with me this Saturday in town? I promise to share some more about my life story with you then."

"I'd like that Jake Walker." She smiled broadly and turned around to head back into the living room to serve her guests something hot besides tea.

"Does anyone prefer hot coffee? I made some decaffeinated coffee for those who don't want to stay up until midnight because of caffeine!" Lisa Johnson declared as she returned to the living room and joined in with the laughter and merriment.

"I would prefer some decaffeinated coffee please." Matthew replied.

"Could I have some more hot tea? I really enjoyed the flavor of tea that you chose for me." Aunt Cathy replied.

A new feeling of joyful anticipation and wonderment started seeping into her heart at the thought of spending more time with Jake and his family and especially his incorrigible, but totally adorable aunt. She felt more at home with this woman than she'd ever felt with anyone before. What did this new awareness of a definite attraction to Cathy Harper's nephew mean for her? Could she trust her heart to this handsome individual and believe that he was attracted to her as well? She wondered if spending more time with Jake or his remarkable aunt could affect her and Max in a good way. She felt very good about the idea of having a better friendship with this caring family. As she glanced over at Jake and felt drawn into the depths of his sparkling, intense blue eyes and ruggedly handsome features she wondered deep in her heart if it could be possible that he might become more than just a real-life hero who'd protected her young son recently.

Could her very interesting neighbor possibly be the answer to her deep longing to feel excited about the future again? Was he the type of individual she and her son could rely on and trust? Could she hope to dream again about finding a safe haven with a man, possibly someone like this tough, but caring and rather dynamic person? Or maybe she needed to keep her options open as far as her newest admirer, Blaine Wilson. Surely time would tell as would her heart. But could she trust her heart to make the proper assessment of this unusual individual, Jake Walker, who seemed on the surface to be merely a free spirit. She smiled graciously over at the man who she was beginning to feel a certain fondness and sense of compatibility with as the night wore on. Lisa glanced over at Jake Walker while he was engaged in a discussion with his sister, Jillian, and she couldn't help but notice his eyebrow arch upward as he reacted to his sister's response. Suddenly, he turned his gaze upon her in that same moment and she saw the glint in his eyes as he smiled in her direction. That one powerful exchange was enough to make her heart beat more wildly than it had for years.

For Jake, in that brief moment of seeing Lisa's gracious smile and her eyes looking back at him, he wondered if something amazing could be waiting for him if he chose to pursue this new friendship. Everything about her seemed to catch his eye; she had dark brown eyes, well-defined eyebrows that highlighted her other facial features well, and lips which were full and enticing. He was captivated by her dark brown curly hair style that flowed nicely about her attractive face. He liked what he saw of her physical appearance for sure, but he also noticed that her eyes held a caring quality that was very appealing to him as well. He could almost imagine what his sister might be thinking about Lisa as he turned his attention back to his sister's explanation of why they didn't have a dog for a pet at her house.

"Jake, not everyone is supposed to have an inside house pet. You have a well-trained animal that is use to taking care of itself and a group of Marines. You don't live in the middle of a suburb with your canine pet so he's free to roam about and be safe from traffic. What would we do if our new dog accidently ran out the front door and into the street to chase a car? He might get hit and suffer a broken leg or even possibly get killed by a motorist speeding by." Jillian replied.

"Okay, yes, Jilly, there is that problem when you live in the city and have a dog. But that's why people use leashes and they make sure the kids know how dangerous it is to leave the door open where the young dog could run outside."

"Besides, you live in the country now that you've moved in to Uncle Henry's cabin near the woods. You can let your dog roam about freely and not worry about traffic or someone hitting your pet by accident." Jillian remarked.

"Yes, you do have a valid point there. I just think the boys would love having a smaller dog that you could keep in the backyard. If you had a fenced in backyard, then your pet could be outside in the fresh air and chew on a good bone without you worrying. I'm just saying there are ways to have your pet and enjoy its company when the kids are growing up. I remember wanting a dog when I was six or seven years old and wishing my parents would get us one. It could've been a great watchdog too." Jake stated emphatically.

As he considered his sister's remarks about family life and the reasons why not to have a dog, he started to think about the reasons why he might not be the right person for a woman such as Lisa Johnson. She didn't have a pet and she hadn't ever been around a military man who'd served two tours of duty overseas. What if she couldn't handle some of the difficult combat troubles and his reoccurring flashbacks which he couldn't seem to shake yet? Not every woman would be able to handle a man who was still dealing with PTSD symptoms such as his. What would she think if he became irritable or distant and uncommunicative? As he studied her beautiful face across the table from him, he wondered if she was interested in more than a casual friendship or was she merely flirting with the idea of dating a handsome ex-military guy for a short period of time? Maybe she would be disappointed with him and return to a more stable kind of guy like Blaine Wilson.

Then in the next moment the conversation at the dinner table turned from humorous to serious with this next question.

"Mister Jake, will you tell us about one thing that happened to you and your buddies when you were overseas with the Marines." Max queried.

His mother reached over to place her hand on his arm as if to silence her son and then she gave him a warning look. Max moved his arm away from his mother's touch and looked back at his neighbor friend waiting to hear what the man would tell him.

CHAPTER
Thirty-Two

Taking a big breath and trying to think of something the entire family could hear, Jake began to share his experience with the now attentive group.

"Well, I don't have much to tell you about the war in Afghanistan except for this one true event. I suppose you are old enough to learn something about the conflict over there." Jake sighed and moved his crutches further under the table and took another drink of water before continuing his narrative.

"This happened to our platoon during the second month that I was in the town of Farquhar. Our team had been ordered to move some equipment and trucks to another town ten miles east of the original spot. This region was suppose to have a general election in their main city and we were ordered to maintain a presence in that locale and keep things safe for the people during that two days of voting for a new leader in the district. So we positioned five soldiers at the first checkpoint just outside of the city and six more guys closer in by the voting facility. We had also been assigned two medics who were to come along with us that same weekend. They were given the task of handing out medicine, astringents, and bandages to some poorer families in this province. My unit was guarding this section of town. I was glad to have my canine partner nearby to keep a watchful eye on the Afghani men who came and went near our site. We didn't want any surprises happening on those two specific days.

Towards the evening time of the second night there, we were getting ready to retire for the day, get some grub, and then spend the night just outside of the city limits when a noisy ruckus broke out in one of the local shops close to where the medics where handing out the last of the medicine. There were three women with children still waiting in line. I decided to take one Marine with me to investigate the trouble and left two men guarding the medics in the makeshift medical site." Jake took a deep breath and reached for his water glass to get a drink and then he proceeded to finish his narrative. "I headed over to check on the commotion with my weapon ready to defend myself if needed. As we entered the establishment, I could tell that a fight had broken out between two men. I ordered the men to stop arguing and to sit back down at the table. As I was talking in Farsi with the one belligerent man, the second individual started yelling and saying some curse words in his native language. I shouted to the bystanders to leave the building and I pointed my gun at the angry man. Next thing I did was order the two men outside where I could direct them to their own homes. Suddenly, a shot rang out from somewhere and my buddy was hit. The bullet shattered his leg bone and he was disabled. I dragged him behind a truck out of sight of the sniper's aim and called for a medic's help. I told the other soldier on the hand- held phone that I was pinned down by a sniper and I needed backup.

I was in a precarious position during this enemy attack and I couldn't get a proper bead on the man hiding on the second level of the building across the road from me. I managed to help my Marine buddy by making a compress from my shirt so he could apply adequate pressure to his leg wound. Then I fired my weapon in the direction where I'd seen movement and a flash of gunfire in a second-story window. I sat there on the ground waiting for backup and I felt a sense of helplessness as I realized my precarious situation. If I moved away from behind the truck shield, I'd be dead within minutes, for sure. I needed to get that sniper before he shot me. It felt like an eternity as I tried to fire back and keep the sniper distracted while I waited for assistance. During this exchange of gunfire, I came to realize that there was no help coming from the two men guarding that American position and the medics who'd been assigned to help Afghani women in this village. I had to do something soon or I would run out of ammunition and we'd both be shot.

Since I still had a working radio on my backpack, I grabbed it and called my team member again. I waited to hear a response from the two Marines who were still at the end of town and guarding the medic personnel there. There was only silence. Suddenly, two more shots rang out from the building directly across the dirt road and I held my breath. I was considering the idea of leaving my safe spot to hustle across the dirt road in order to reach the same building the sniper was hiding in and take this fight closer. I hunkered down close to the injured soldier and told him to stay still and I'd be back for him. Within moments of hearing those last two gunshots directed at my position, I noticed someone wearing the traditional Middle Eastern garb approaching the tall building where the gun fire had been coming from. This individual wearing the loose clothing and a turban wrapped around his head went inside of the building across the street from me. Then this man disappeared from sight. Within minutes of this Afghani person entering the building, I heard two more shots and then complete silence.

I waited for two more minutes and then suddenly, the same man person slipped out of door of the tall building. I watched as this individual waved his hand at me and then he took his turban off long enough for me to understand that he wasn't Middle Eastern at all. Putting the head covering back on, he ducked around the corner of the building in an effort to protect himself from more shots being fired from elsewhere on that same street. I could tell that this individual was an American by his facial coloring and I quickly recognized that he was one of the Marines who'd been ordered to guard the medical team earlier that same day. I learned after the fact that this particular soldier had come up with a plan to help me. By a plan, I mean he told me afterwards that he'd barrowed a friendly Afghani person's clothing and head gear to wear as a clever disguise so he could sneak down the streets in order to reach my location and not be captured. Once he returned to the medical team's site, a team member radioed me to let me know the sniper was dead. Apparently, this Marine in disguise had managed to get close enough to surprise the man who'd been shooting at us. His aim had been accurate that day and he kept two men from being killed by insurgents. Knowing that I'd be under heavy fire, that brave soldier came up with a perfect plan and I'm in his debt. I am hoping to look him up with the help of my commander who still has connections within the military. He might be able to give me this man's stateside address. With this information, I might be able to locate him and show my gratitude by taking the ex-Marine out for a steak dinner." Jake remarked.

In the next moment, Jake watched Max slide out of his chair and come over to stand next to him. When he reached up to give the boy a high-five slap with his hand, Max instead gave him a hug and in that split second he knew what he needed to do. His newest challenge would be to win the affections of this boy's mother too. Right then, Jake decided he'd talk to Lisa after dinner about going on a date with him soon. After everyone had pitched in and cleaned up the dinner table and thanked their lovely hostess, Jake said goodnight to Max and then he walked outside and stood on the front porch talking with Lisa for awhile. They were both enjoying the starry lit night as they waited for his aunt to finish chatting with his sister, Jillian, in the front room. While his father was warming up the car, Jake took Lisa's hand in his and told her how much he'd enjoyed spending the evening with her and Max. Having her small hand enclosed in his caused Jake to have a new sense of excitement and anticipation. This attractive woman had captured his interest very quickly. In fact, she took his breath away as he gazed longingly into her eyes. He wondered if she felt the same thing too.

He wanted to say so much at that moment, but he refrained from speaking his heart. He wasn't sure this was the right time to tell her how he felt. So he simply smiled down at her and wished her a good night. He wondered again as he turned to make his way carefully down the front porch steps with his crutches if she felt even a twinge of what he was feeling right now. Making his way cautiously to the car, he sensed a new awareness of the stars overhead and the quiet beauty of the country. Jake turned to waved goodbye to the woman who he now believed could possibly be the female in his long ago vision. Was he ready to explore the true meaning of this imagery of a woman falling through the air. As he recalled the unusual vision he remembered seeing a person reach a hand out to grab hold of the woman with dark brown hair before she hit the ground. As Jake settled properly in the passenger's side of the car, his thoughts were of when he would see her again. For the first time in his life, Jake wanted to have more than just a friendly acquaintance with a woman. However, there was something important that he needed to take care of before they went on an official date.

Jake made his way back out of the car. Then he moved around the vehicle to hobble closer to the front steps where he could see her clearly.

"Come here for a moment, Lisa, I have something I want to give to you before I leave."

"Alright, I hope you are going to tell me that you want to take me out for a fancy dinner in town soon." She stated with a whimsical look on her face. She walked down the path towards him wondering what small gift he'd forgotten to give her for being a good host.

"Oh, this small gift of appreciation might be better than a small bouquet of flowers or a coffee mug for your kitchen." Jake Walker replied with a slight smile on his lips.

As she came closer to him, he held the crutches in one hand and with the other he held her chin gently. Then he slowly bent down to brush her lips with his own. Jake had been longing to do this for awhile now and the urge to touch her had become stronger this evening. He felt a unique and amazing sensation cross his lips. Suddenly, he hungered for more of this woman and her warmth. Being so close to Lisa Johnson reminded him of summertime and the taste of sweet honey. He knew it was too soon and yet, he couldn't resist this impulse to keep her close within his arms. As he pressed his lips over her mouth hungrily, he felt like his world had suddenly been turned upside down. As he ended that longer kiss, he noticed that Lisa had her eyes closed as if she didn't want the moment to end either. As soon as she opened her eyes to look up into his, Jake smiled. Then he whispered in her ear.

"Lisa, you've captured my full attention."

Then moving his crutches back under his arms, he managed to turn and head carefully down towards his vehicle. As he opened the car door, he turned to thank her for a marvelous evening.

"You are very welcome, Jake Walker. I look forward to seeing you again." Lisa remarked.

CHAPTER
Thirty-Three

T he next day Jake secured the plastic bag from the hospital around his injured leg so he could take a hot shower. After cleaning up and putting on clean clothes, he turned on the hot coffee pot and ate a toasted bagel while he waited for it to brew. Then he placed a long distance phone call to his college friend. He'd made up his mind as he lay in bed the night before. He plan was to get professional help for his wartime traumas which had produced symptoms of PTSD. If he was going to have a healthy, long lasting relationship with Lisa Johnson and her son he knew this was necessary.

"Brad, I have a big favor to ask of you, man." Jake took another gulp of his coffee drink and settled back in his Uncle Henry's old, comfortable recliner chair. I'm thinking about flying back to spend a few weeks with my father and I need to talk with you about something important. I've been having a lot of trouble sleeping at night and I get flashbacks of things that I experienced during my tour of duty. All of this has been affecting my life and my normal habits. Can you spare a few days for me when I get there?" Jake asked.

"Sure buddy. How can I help?" Brad questioned his long time friend.

I'm still having those darn nightmares and feeling anxious at times like as if I need to carry a gun with me to protect myself from the enemy! I figured since you've received a degree in psychology a year ago and you are working in an internship program with another qualified professor, maybe you could put me in touch with someone who could help me with my sleep disorder problems. I have noticed that I get irritated more easily than before and I can't ignore these issues anymore."

"Sure, I'd be glad to listen to you share more details when you get here. I can definitely be a sounding board for you to bounce ideas off of as we sit together and you share your struggles with me. And after you've been here for awhile we can even go out on the town and have a drink with Mark and the hometown gang." Brad stated. "I also know of a therapist that my professor recommends as well. Her name is Amy Barton and she has an office over in Handley which is now a suburb of Dayton."

"Hey, thanks man. I will owe you big time. Don't mention any of this to Mark or the guys though."

"I hear you, Jake. Call me when you get into town so we can meet up. By then I should have the therapist's office phone number for you."

"Will do, Brad. See you soon. I have to make arrangements with my cousin, Daniel Hammond, to take care of my dog, Blue' while I'm gone. I plan to drive half way to Seattle to transfer Blue Boy into my Aunt Cathy's car and then she will take him the rest of the way back to my cousin's place. He doesn't mind having Blue there for a few weeks since they have a border collie around the same age, actually a year younger, I believe. My aunt is staying with my cousin and his wife in the city of Seneca for a week before flying back home and she said she could help out."

"Sounds good, Jake. So I'll wait to hear from you after you fly into Dayton." Brad remarked.

"Right, I'm heading to the lake later today for a little fun after spending some time in the hospital here. We had a little too much craziness and local excitement so I need to go fishing to relax. Thanks again Brad."

"You bet, buddy. And I want to hear about the reason why you've been in the hospital when you get here." Brad commented.

"Sure thing and thanks again."

* * *

The next day found Jake sitting on the old dock at the lake. He'd cast his line into the water and while he waited for a fish to bite, he turned his thoughts to his time with Lisa and their kiss.

He was becoming more and more aware of his actual, true feelings for Lisa Johnson. He found himself thinking about her when he woke up and when he laid his head on the pillow at night. He wondered what she was doing after work tonight. He wished he could tell her how he was feeling, but he realized that he needed to wait until he'd returned from visiting his father. He was hopeful that by spending time with a therapist, he could solve his immediate problems. He had to make sure he was ready for a serious, more intentional relationship with this woman before he confessed his affections to her. And then there was her son to consider as well. Was Max ready to have a man in his life or should he wait longer? These were all good questions needing an answer. He was also concerned about this other guy named Blaine Wilson who he was certain was also interested in capturing Lisa's attention. What would happen if he waited too long to share his serious feelings with Lisa?

He needed to talk this out with his aunt when they connected in a few days. She had always been there for him especially after his mother had passed away four years ago. He knew he could trust her advice and he needed to get a woman's point of view in this matter. He decided to share his recent unusual vision of a dark-haired woman with his aunt and get her take on this. He wondered what his aunt would think about his other dream too. He'd recalled his grandma Eunice telling him once as a young boy that she believed God actually gave certain people(who were open in their hearts) specific visions or warning dreams for a reason. Maybe he should share his concerns about these two dreams with his Aunt Cathy and see what she thought about this unusual phenomenon. He wrestled with this question for a few minutes and then he turned his concentration back to hooking a fish again. By one o'clock in the afternoon he'd had enough of sitting by the lake water in the hot sun; it was time to head home. Jake pulled up the small anchor, tossed it into the back of the boat, and headed back to shore. He was glad that he had decided to take the small rowboat that was tied up to the dock since he'd been able to catch three good size fish that afternoon. He needed to get back and cleaned the trout and cook it for dinner. Plus, he needed to secure the cabin and pack for his trip back east the following day.

* * *

Later on, Jake used the phone in his cabin to call his aunt and confirm their meeting place on highway 10. While they were talking, he mentioned his plans to stay in Dayton for awhile. The conversation with his aunt went like this.

"Jake, so what you're saying is you want to spend more than a week with your dad and a friend named Brad. Have you told anyone that you are leaving for maybe longer than a week?"

"Ah, well, no I haven't mentioned this to anyone other than you, Aunt Cathy."

"The reason I'm asking you this is because I thought you told me that you wanted to ask Lisa Johnson out on an a second date in the near future. Doesn't she deserve to know what you are planning to do and when you will be returning to the area?"

"I suppose so. I hadn't given it much thought. I've been so busy trying to get things situated with the dog and my cousin, Daniel, and his wife, Julie. You're right; I hadn't considered the importance of telling Lisa about my trip back to Illinois."

"Well, if you don't have her home phone number yet, then maybe you ought to write her a note and stick it in her mailbox or at her front door so she knows when to expect you back. You plan to leave tomorrow right?" His aunt inquired. "And be sure to include your phone number and that you are really interested in taking her out on a special date night to some fancy restaurant." She said.

"Yeah, I guess maybe I should stick the message in an envelope and slide it partially under her porch mat in the morning before I leave for the airport. I imagine her son, Max, will see it even if she is gone to work by then."

"Good idea, Jake. Alright then, I shall see you today around one o'clock at the rest stop on EXIT 49 just outside of Bremerton. That's a perfect place to transfer your pet into my vehicle so I can deliver him to your cousin's place. See you in a few hours."

They said goodbye and clicked off the phone receivers to go about their tasks. Jake grabbed a piece of paper and wrote down his new plan and his phone number for Lisa and then he added the date for his return to the cabin so she wouldn't wonder what had happened to him. Folding the paper in half, he inserted it into an envelope and wrote her name on the front. Next, he placed the envelope by his backpack and the travel bag so he wouldn't forget to run it over to the Johnson's house before leaving to the airport.

* * *

At six a.m. he retrieved his jacket and the envelope with Lisa Johnson's name on it and made his way over to her house. Crossing her lawn that was still wet with morning dew, he went up the porch steps and bent down to slide the note under the porch mat. He left a portion of the envelope partially exposed so Lisa would see it on the way to her car. He figured they would easily see his envelope and so he headed back to his cabin to wait for a taxi cab to come and take him to the airport since he'd already returned the rental car a week before this. He didn't count on Lisa hurrying out the door for work without spying the note. Unfortunately, for Jake her son, Max, left by the back door that same day.

Jake had no idea that Blaine Wilson would stop by Lisa's home later on that same day to visit her. It was late afternoon and Blaine had stopped by the florist shop first to purchase flowers as a gift for Lisa Johnson. He'd wanted an excuse to see her in person instead of calling to check on her and make sure she had a sitter for their coming date. As he turned off his car engine and strode to the front porch of the house, he couldn't help but notice a white envelope protruding from one side of her welcome mat. He reached down and retrieved the envelope thinking he would show this card to whoever came to the door. He supposed it might be from her only neighbor, Helen Braden. Noticing that the handwriting on the front of the envelope looked as if it was written in a man's scrawl, he became curious as to what was inside the note. He opened the envelope and quickly read the short message and saw that

Jake Walker's name was at the bottom of the paper. Feeling jealous of this other individual, Blaine decided to slip the note card back into the envelope and slide it further under the welcome mat so she wouldn't see it. His intention was to give him more time with Lisa Johnson without any interference from this newcomer. He didn't like having competition and he certainly didn't like this ex-military guy trying to vie for the same woman he was interested in dating.

Blaine Wilson stood back up and knocked twice on the front door. He waited with anticipation for someone to come. When no one came to open the door, he rang the doorbell this time. He quickly ran his fingers through his hair and then put a broad smile on his face. Within a few minutes, the door opened and young Max stood there eyeing him. By the look on the kid's face, Blaine could tell he was not the person the boy wanted to see on his front porch. So he put on the charm in the hopes of winning the young lad over to his side.

"Good evening, young man. Is your mother home? I have a gift for her since she works so hard at the bank. I thought maybe she could use a night out."

"My mom is in the kitchen fixing dinner. I can give her the flowers. Thanks for delivering this gift. Are you leaving now and if so, then I will let her know who sent these flowers."

"These flowers are from me to give to your mother. May I come in and talk with her?"

"Uh, I guess so. Is she expecting you, mister?" Max queried.

"Not exactly, it's a surprise visit. I wanted to come by and talk with her today."

"Okay, wait here and I will let her know you're asking to see her." Max replied.

"Mom, someone's here to see you." Max yelled from the front room.

Lisa took off her apron and dried her wet hands on the kitchen towel and proceeded to enter the living room to see who was there. She was surprised to see Blaine Wilson standing in the open doorway with a handful of colorful flowers and a sheepish grin on his handsome face.

"Hi, Blaine. What a pleasant surprise and what lovely flowers. Are those for me?" Lisa asked.

"Yes they are for you, beautiful lady." He said.

"Thank you, come on in. Tell me what brings you over here besides this flower delivery?"

"I just wanted to see you and make sure everything was still on for our date coming up."

"Yes, I was able to get someone to watch Max for that night, but you could've waited to give me the flowers on our date this weekend." Lisa remarked.

"I suppose I could've, but I didn't want to wait until then in case something came up for you and you may've post phoned our date." Blaine replied quickly.

"Well, that is always a possibility because I have a young son and sometimes things do come up that prevent me from getting a sitter."

The two stood there in the front foyer area and chatted for a bit about Max. Then when Lisa mentioned she needed to finish making dinner, he gave her brief hug and said goodbye.

CHAPTER
Thirty-Four

Jake spent the next three weeks in Dayton on his important mission. He stayed with his father and they talked about his struggles and the value of him seeing a therapist. His father soon came to understand his reason for making this trip and spending the time and money to see a professional counselor who had the required credentials to help veterans of war in their recovery from traumatic experiences. His friend, Brad, was supportive of Jake's efforts after he shared a few things he'd learned during the first two sessions. He was feeling more confident that his family would be more supportive once he shared everything with them. The following weekend, his sister, Jillian, dropped by to spend some time with him and to learn more about his reason for returning to his hometown.

"Hi little brother, so how has your visit with Mark and Brad been this time around?"

"Real good, we've hung out at the bar and grill for the last two Thursday nights and played some pool. I made a few bucks on our usual game of stars and stripes!"

"I want you to be honest with me, Jake." Jillian said. "Tell me about your PTSD symptoms. I overheard you and Dad talking as I was leaving to put the twins to bed last weekend. I thought I heard you mention your were having night terrors and flashbacks." Jillian said.

"Well, most war vets struggle with insomnia or nightmares. My therapist mentioned that some guys often get irritable for no reason or they might become hyper-vigilant and over react to normal circumstances like I've been doing. Being super aware of danger was necessary when I was fighting in the war, but it's not good to react like a soldier while being a civilian here in the states." Jake stated.

"I understand what you are saying. So you feel overwhelmed and unsure of your surroundings at times. Do you react to strange loud noises or certain crowded activities in the city?" She asked.

"Yes, and I don't want to struggle like this for the rest of my life. I want to get involved with the family that invited us all over for dinner when you came to visit me. Her name is Lisa Johnson and her son's name is Max."

"Yes, I thought she was a lovely person. I think you should go for it. She seemed to be interested in you as well." Jillian remarked.

"How can you tell something like that? Jillian, you only spent one evening in her home and we weren't alone for much time then either." Jake asked.

"We're siblings, dude. And I'm a very perceptive gal. I noticed the looks you two exchanged at the dinner table. On top of that, Dad told me that later that evening he waited patiently in the car, you two talked quite awhile. The fact that you were holding her hand showed him that you liked being with her. If you ask me, I'd say she's into you, darling brother.

"Awe, just because a woman let's a guy hold their hand doesn't mean it a done deal, Jillian." Jake replied petulantly.

"Well then, let me ask you this dear brother. Did she pull her hand back and step away to protect her personal space? By this I mean did she act as if she didn't care about being with you?" Jillian questioned.

"Ah, well, no she didn't pull away from me that night. And I did feel a real connection with her! I see what you're getting at now. She didn't seem to mind it when I held her hand in mine. I really want to take her out on a second date when I return from these sessions, however, she hasn't responded to my message or called me yet. So right now there is nothing that would lead me to believe I have a chance with her. Maybe I should've planned better and taken the time to go over and actually speak with Lisa before catching my plane. I thought the note with my phone number I'd left on her front porch would let her know how much I cared about her and that I wanted to continue seeing her." Jake said.

"Silly man, you left a note card on the front porch. A squirrel or a bird might've seen the envelope sticking out of the porch mat and quite possible carried it off. That wasn't a very smart idea, brother." Jillian remarked.

"I actually stuck the envelope with her name on it underneath the porch mat with enough of the white showing for anyone with good eyes to notice it. Someone must've taken it to cause trouble. Maybe her son saw it first and tossed it. Do you think Max doesn't care for a guy like me dating his mom?" He asked.

"It's hard to say, but some kids are very protective of their mothers in these kinds of situations. And I suppose you didn't think to get her home phone?" She replied.

"Well, no I didn't ask her for her phone number then. I was busy packing and taking care of my dog before I flew out early that morning and that's why I dropped off the note with my number."

"So Jake, how is the counselor helping you to process your difficult time overseas?" She asked.

"Well, the therapist had me talk about some of the details of the more troublesome times where we were under attack and she believes I suffered some definite trauma which has been the cause for my insomnia problems." Jake said as he looked away for a moment."In our second session, she had me talk about the attack four times in a row. Then my therapist told me it would be beneficial to listen to my voice which she'd recorded on tape. The hope was that once I'd heard this incident played back to me afterwards, it would dispel some of the harsh effects of the traumatic memory. This therapist says she has had significant success with other vets; she feels that the memory recall in this safe environment will hinder the subconscious memories from resurfacing so often. My therapist also said that psychologists in the last six years have been able to recreate this virtual war experience like I'm explaining to you and they have been able to make significant progress with people who've suffered from PTSD. Her success has given me great deal of hope. She is also giving me insight as to the truth that I don't have to accept the 'survivor's guilt' syndrome. You know, Jillian, I never told anyone how it affected me when Josh Harrison died while I was safe back at the camp base with a pounding headache. It's been really rough dealing with the grief and pain. Since I've had the opportunity to talk with the therapist, Amy Barton, about my troubles, I feel better about myself now. She even told me that it wasn't my fault that my team members died. I realize now that I'd been blaming myself for Josh's death. I plan to meet with this therapist one last time before heading back to the town of Randall." Jake said.

"I'm glad you shared all of this with me. I really had no clue as to how much you've suffered other than the little bits that Dad told me about your tour of duty and that two of you buddies died in Afghanistan. I'm so sorry. It might be a good thing if you forgive yourself and try to enjoy life." Jillian said.

"Okay, sister, I plan to go back to my place next week and settle in. I will let you know if Lisa decides to give me a second chance. I really want this to work. I'll stop by your house and say goodbye before I fly out." Jake mentioned.

* * *

The day after being back in the Northwest, Jake decided to stop by Lisa's place to talk with her. He was hoping she was there, but to his surprise, she was out for the night.

"Hi Max, so your mom went out with some guy tonight. Can you have her call me when she gets home if it's not too late? Could you relay this message for me? Tell her I really need to talk with her and I was hoping she'd call me. I left my phone number on a note under your porch mat the morning that I flew back east and I haven't heard from her since. Do you know if she got the message I left on the front porch a few weeks back?" Jake asked.

"She never told me about any envelope or card from you. Why did you leave without telling us anything? I was really disappointed and now she's going out with that Blaine guy practically every weekend." Max stated.

"Hey, I'm really sorry that I left so abruptly this past month. I had to take care of some very important business and visit my father at the same time. I want to make it up to you both. Do you and your neighbor friend want to come by and play with my dog, Blue' this week?" Jake asked.

"Maybe, I'll see what he's doing tomorrow. His folks don't want him going into the woods anymore. You know, when he got lost that day we followed you on the trail. Do you mind if I bring Blue' over to see him at his place instead?" Max asked.

"Not a problem. I'm going to lift up your porch mat to see if my note is still there." Jake bent down and picked the welcome mat up to look under it. "Well, what do you know? It's still here, but it looks like someone shoved it further under the mat to hide it from plain sight. When I dropped it off on your porch I stuck it partially under the mat and made sure that a part of the white envelope was showing." He looked over at Max and forced a smile on his face. "I could use your assistance in giving this note to your Mom. It's really important that she gets this message. Ask her to read my note please. Max, I like you and I want to get to know your mom more if she'll give me a chance to explain what happened. I'm hoping you will believe me and help me out one more time." Jake said.

"Ah, alright, Mr. Jake, I can give her this message and I will tell her what you showed me about the card being shoved further under the porch mat too. Someone definitely tried to keep her from calling you by hiding the envelope." Max replied. "Thanks for stopping by to check on us. When I come by to get Blue' I will let you know what my mom says. Heck, it's so obvious that someone moved it."

"Great, I really appreciate your help in this matter. See you soon, Max." Jake replied.

* * *

The following day Max walked over to the cabin in the woods to look for his neighbor, Jake. The dog wasn't lying on the front porch when he arrived onto the property so he wondered if they'd gone into town. He hustled up the front steps and knocked twice on the front door and then waited. Just as he was turning to leave, Jake appeared at the door holding a cup of coffee in his hand. He told Max to wait on the front porch while he searched for Blue's leash. After he hooked the leather leash onto his dog's collar, he motioned to the boy to follow him down the steps and he smiled at the kid as he handed the leash to him.

"Okay have a good time with Blue Boy and bring him back here in time for his dinner meal."

"Hey, Mister Jake, your dog looks like he lost some weight while you were gone on that trip. Did he miss us?" Max asked.

"Well, now that you mention it, Blue Boy' did actually miss you two youngsters. He wasn't happy that I left him with my cousin, Daniel and his two rowdy boys. They apparently provoke my dog and pulled on his tail too much. My cousin told me that he didn't seem that happy there and he whined at lot because I wasn't around to take him for walks. So it would really help if you or your friend could come over and take Blue' for a long walk more often."

"Sure, do you think that maybe in August we could all go to the lake and teach Blue Boy' how to swim and fetch a stick out in the water?" Max asked. "Don't most dogs like to play in the water and fetch a stick?"

"Yes, my dog loves to run and fetch a stick. I don't see why we couldn't go to the lake if things work out with your mom and me. Tell me what did she say when you mentioned that I wanted to see her this week so I could explain why I left town?" Jake inquired.

"Mom said she couldn't believe that someone had tried to hide your envelope like that. She was glad to actually have your card in her hands to read and we think we know who might have hidden it. She said to tell you that she wouldn't mind if you came by this Thursday evening around seven o'clock to talk with her."

"That's really good news! Thanks buddy for letting her know that I wanted to explain myself in person. Max, I really like your mother and I am hoping that she will be interested in spending more time with me. Would that be alright with you as well?" Jake asked.

"Yeah, sure, I guess. Do you want to take her on a date if she accepts your apology?" Max asked as he dug his shoe in the dirt and then he looked back over at Jake.

"Yes, I do. So tell your mother thanks for seeing me this Thursday and keep your fingers crossed that she will believe me when I say I am truly sorry for the mix up. It was definitely my mistake. I should have tried to talk to her in person instead of dropping off a card." He said.

"Yep, Mister Jake, you messed up big time because she was really sad and she moped around the house after that. Gosh, you should have seen her. She finally invited Mrs. Braden over for tea and I overheard them talking about you. My mom was really disappointed in the way you left without saying a thing to anyone." Max declared.

"Okay, you've made your point. I deserve to be horsewhipped for messing things up so badly. I plan to make amends to your mother and then see about making a plan which includes the three of us."

"Okay, see you later." Max said.

Jake watched the eleven year old boy and his dog walking away from his front yard. The two looked like quite a pair as they sauntered off down the beaten path. He was glad that this neighbor kid lived close by and could come over to play with his dog. He had plenty of things to fix on the cabin still and he needed to replace an old, rusty latch on the pump house door.

CHAPTER
Thirty-Five

The following afternoon, Max showed up at Jake's cabin to relay a message from his mom. She said he could come by for a brief visit to explain things. Thursday arrived and Jake was feeling a bit nervous about having this talk with Lisa. She may or may not decide to forgive him and the worst case scenario would be that she refused to be anything more than neighbors. He'd do whatever it took to convince her that he wasn't going anywhere. She was too important to him to risk hurting her again. He ran his fingers through his hair and grabbed a clean shirt to wear. Next, he searched through his luggage and a few boxes until he found the only sports jacket he owned. He brushed his teeth a second time and pulled on the lightweight jacket as he whistled for Blue Boy' to come inside from chasing squirrels and wild rabbits. He glanced one more time in the mirror and then at the last second decided to bring his dog with him to entertain Max while he made his apology.

Making his way along the well-worn path, Jake came upon the two neighbor's country properties. He approached Lisa Johnson's house after first passing by the Braden's place and he paused momentarily to take a deep breath before walking up to the porch steps. After inhaling one more good breath of fresh air, he whispered a quick prayer for help for this upcoming conversation with this captivating woman. Jake knocked on the front door and then he waited there while feeling unsure of himself and yet, with an air of expectancy and excitement at the thought of seeing this beautiful woman again. He wanted to pull her into his arms the moment he saw her, but instinctively; he knew she wasn't anywhere close to allowing this to occur after he'd caused her so much grief. Finally, he heard footsteps coming and then Max opened the door to welcome him inside where he chose to stand instead of sit down. Then surprisingly Max winked at him as if to encourage Jake in his endeavor to make amends with his mother. His dog jumped up on Max and they both raced out the door to play in the yard. For the last two days Jake had been feeling as if he deserved a major reprimand from this woman for his stupid behavior. Would she forgive him and be willing to give this relationship a second chance? He could only hope for the best.

He paced back and forth as he waited for her to come down the stairs. Jake nervously eyed the wall clock and wished this apology could be over and he might see her smile again. At last, Lisa walked into the room looking exactly as he'd imaged she might, a picture of loveliness and beauty before him. His first instinct was to close the distance between them and pull her into his arms, but he resisted this temptation and remained where he was. Then Jake cleared his throat and gave her a weak smile.

"Lisa, you look beautiful as ever. That color of that dress really suits you and accentuates your eyes nicely. I missed you while I was away visiting my father. I hope you will find it in your heart to give me another chance. I need to explain why I left for so long and why I chose to leave you a quick note with the hopes that you'd call me. When you didn't call me I figured you didn't care to talk to me." Jake said as he ran his fingers through his hair again and stood feeling awkward as he waited for her response.

"Jake, I thought we had a special connection the night you came over for the family dinner and I was expecting you to want to be more than just a neighbor who needed me to care for his dog. When you left the area and didn't let me know anything about your trip or plans, well, I figured that you didn't want to continue seeing me or Max for that matter. Why did you leave here without talking to me? She demanded.

"Lisa, I am sincerely sorry for making you feel like it was . . ."

"Jake Walker, listen to me and don't interrupt me right now! I'd asked myself these two questions for the first three days of your abrupt disappearance, what had I done to cause you to leave and were you ever coming back here again." Lisa remarked with a stern look on her face.

Jake stood there watching her face as she folded her arms across her chest. He thought maybe she was trying to speak without getting too emotional and he was right.

"Jake, I was ready to give my heart to you that night after we'd talked under the stars and in the moonlight. I felt as if our few times together had been special and I was beginning to think we could share a future together. Can you imagine how happy I was after you left that night? No, you probably can't know this. Well to be honest, I went inside to sit in the quiet of my home as I pondered the events of that week and how you'd rescued my son and how you had made me feel so alive again. I'd thought that I would never fall for another man after losing my husband. Marshall died so suddenly without saying goodbye to me or Max and for the next few years I felt helpless and sad a lot. My life has not turned out the way I'd planned. How could you leave me like you did and then come here and expect me to just simply say- oh that's okay. What were you thinking Jake Walker? You hurt me more than I thought I could hurt again. I didn't know what to think. Why did you leave?" Lisa demanded.

"You are absolutely right. It was the dumbest thing I've ever done. I want an opportunity to show you how much I truly care for you and for your son. Please Lisa, I'm asking you for another chance. I see clearly now how this must've made you feel and I really want to make it up to you. I will do anything to show you that I am truly sorry for disappointing you. I didn't mean to cause you this kind of grief or sadness. I thought that by shoving a note inside of an envelope with part of it sticking out from beneath the porch mat that you or Max would surely see it. I waited for you to call me so I could tell you what was going on in my life. I was wrong in how I handle this!" Jake declared passionately.

"Yes, you did make a big mistake by not asking for my phone number before leaving town. You made another huge mistake by not getting the Braden's phone number as well. What if something had happened to your cabin or we were worried that your dog had gone off and got lost in the woods? We certainly had no way of getting a hold of you or your family members." Lisa retorted. "By the way what did happen with your dog? Max told me it has been gone for a few weeks." She asked.

Jake made a slight move to get closer to Lisa. "Um about the dog, I asked my aunt to take him to my cousin's place for awhile." He replied.

"Alright, then tell me what you're really thinking at this moment before I say goodnight and head to bed without another thought about you." Lisa replied.

"I really like you, Lisa and I want to have a future with you. I will make you a promise to never leave without telling you my plans. I want to be a good influence in your son's life if you will let me. I need you in my life. I only went away in order to get healthy so I could be someone you could feel safe with while not being afraid of how I'd react at certain stressful times. Please give me ten more minutes of your time so I can explain why I had to go back to Dayton for those three weeks." Jake said.

"Fine, you have five minutes exactly!" Lisa exclaimed.

She stood there taping her foot on the floor with her arms still crossed over her chest. She was literally trying to keep Jake Walker from breaking through her wall of resistance. If only he was smart enough to know this: She was merely trying to protect her heart from being broken again like what had happened just three weeks before. However, her heart was not as stubborn as her mind appeared to be for at that precise moment she could sense that she wanted to truly believe in what Jake was saying to her. Watching this ex-Marine struggling to share with her, she knew she needed to calm down and listen with an open mind. Lisa started to relax as she vowed silently to trust her heart to make the right decision.

"I have been suffering from PTSD symptoms after being stationed in Afghanistan for a year. I was having trouble sleeping properly at night and I would wake up from nightmares about the war. I realized after going through this recent gun fight in the woods that I needed some professional counseling so I could hope to have a healthy mindset and a better ability to handle life's stressful situations. I was concerned that I might hurt someone I cared about if I didn't go get help. I wanted you to feel safe around me and not be afraid of any unpredictable reactions I may have in the future." Jake said.

"Well, I can see how you might feel that way. I was so hurt by your leaving without saying goodbye that it's possible your leaving us may've pushed an emotional 'trigger button' response from me. I went through the same emotions after you left town as I'd felt when my husband, Marshall, died suddenly and I was left alone to raise my young son. I felt so alone and sad for weeks after his funeral. So when you left here without any explanation or a phone call, I started to feel like I'd been abandoned again. Your absence and lack of communication caused me to feel as if I was suffering another lost all over again. I'm not sure I can trust you to stay put here and to not disappoint Max or me again in the future. You say that you struggle because of you traumatic experiences during the war. So what's to prevent you from flipping out around us someday in the future? I'm not sure I can handle that kind of worry. What if you disappoint my son again? I have to consider his well-being too." Lisa remarked.

"You are right. I had these same questions. That is why I flew back to see a professional counselor. I realized that I needed the help this therapist uses called CPT or cognitive processing therapy. This therapist also used a second method to relieve me of the stressful memories and insomnia trouble which is called PE or prolonged exposure therapy. They both worked in a short amount of time and I was able to process my trauma and get free of the inability to cope with stressful or loud sounds. I'm sleeping better now and I am no longer as easily irritated as I was before seeing the counselor. If you want me to I will fly back there in a few months to enlist this counselor's help again to relieve you of anymore concerns. I will spend more money to undergo any other therapy if I'm not well and stable enough to be in your life." Jake replied with a heavy heart. "Lisa, my main concern is to keep you and Max safe and to be the kind of person you want around for a good while."

"Jake, I understand now why you felt that you had to go back to Illinois recently. I appreciate your military service overseas and I want to support you in your recovery efforts." Lisa said.

"Thank you. I need to share one more thing with you before you give me your answer about our friendship and the future." Jake stated.

"I've applied for a job opening as a patrol officer at the Canadian-American border. My captain had recently mentioned my name to the Homeland Security office and they want me to come in next Monday for an interview for this position. If I don't get that job then I will open up my own business in Randall teaching people self-defense. I used to be involved with this kind of training while I was attending community college and working part-time in my father's business. It would just take some capital to get this kind of business started. So I plan to stay in this area for a long time." Jake mentioned.

"Okay, this is good to hear. I was concerned about what a few people have said concerning the idea that you could be selling the cabin and living in another state one day." Lisa remarked.

"Hear me out Lisa; I am not planning on selling the property or moving away. I am asking for the opportunity to show you that I can be someone you can trust completely." Jake said.

"I guess I could consider a trial basis for a couple of months. I have already talked to Blaine and confronted him about hiding the card and message which was intended for only me to read. He had a lame excuse for opening up the envelope and then shoving it further than necessary under our porch mat. I told him that I didn't want to see him for awhile since I needed to sort out my feelings for him." She replied.

"Thank you, Lisa. I appreciate you giving me a chance to explain and to prove how much I care for you. I want to make you happy. In fact, could I get you cell phone number right now? I will go over next week to visit with the Braden's and get their phone number like you suggested. I am grateful for your understanding and for an opportunity to continue getting to know you better. If there is anything in the future where you might need my help fixing something around your home just let me know or if Max wants to come by and take the dog for a walk then call me. We can keep our relationship on a friendly basis for as long as you need, Lisa. I promise to be available for you and Max." Jake said.

"That sounds like a plan that I am comfortable with. Jake I am sorry that you had to endure the hardships of war. It must've been very difficult for you. Helen Braden mentioned that sometimes men who make it through the war experiences also have to deal with a thing called 'survivor guilt' and she advised me to try and make an effort to be more understanding because of this fact. She was very insistent during our recent conversation that I should give you a chance to explain yourself. I am glad that I listened to her. I understand that as war veteran, you've dealt with a lot of pain and grief too." Lisa replied with a slight smile crossing her lips.

"Yes, I did lose my best friend, Josh, during one of our unit's awful conflicts and it rocked my world. I wanted to retaliate in the worst way! I didn't share this part of my grief and anger with the counselor and so maybe if I take the time to journal about my experiences, it will help me to stop blaming myself for not being there that day when he was killed. Thanks for understanding my situation. I am grateful that you've given me another chance to make things up to you, Lisa. I really care about you and Max." Jake exclaimed wholeheartedly.

"I realize that now, Jake Walker. My son needs a hero in his life and I think that you are just the kind of man we might both need, but more than a hero in my life, I need someone I can trust and who makes me feel safe again." Lisa whispered softly.

This was the opening Jake had been hoping for with this amazing woman and he couldn't hold back his feelings for her any longer.

"Alright, I would love to be the only man in your life for a very long, long time. You are the best thing that has come into my life lately, Lisa Johnson!" Jake spoke emphatically.

Stepping closer until he was standing in front of Lisa, Jake pulled her slowly into his warm embrace. Then he tilted her head slightly and kissed her until she had to pulled away to catch her breath. She smiled and grabbed his shirt as she pulled him back in close for a longer kiss. He realized suddenly that she was definitely the woman with the soulful eyes in his vision. He couldn't stop smiling at the thought that just maybe he was the man in the vision who'd managed to extend his hand to the woman who was falling though the air. Jake had been haunted by those sad eyes for the last four years and now all he wanted to do was to bring joy and hope to this actual, living woman nestled in his arms.

Maybe his grandmother, Eunice, was right after all. She'd believed that Jake had been given an ability to see into the future. It seems that he actually did receive important dreams and visions and therefore, he'd better pay closer attention to these unusual dreams. In the meantime, he was so grateful to be a part of this beautiful woman's life and of course her son too. He was excited about the thought of taking Max on fishing trips to the lake and teaching him self-defense. It was becoming more evident to Jake that he'd been kept alive as a youngster during his battle in the hospital for a divine reason. Maybe Lisa and Max were part of the divine purpose for his life just like the angelic presence had referred to so long ago. Jake would have to stop ignoring his unusual gift of seeing the future for people just as his grandmother had advised him before she passed away.

"Lisa, let's walk outside to enjoy the warm evening breeze." Jake said.

"I'd like that, Jake. It is great watching Max play with your dog, Blue." Lisa responded.

Taking her hand in his, he walked out onto the front porch where they both stood not speaking but simply lost in thought. Jake remained still as he marveled at the magic of the night and the glow of joy permeating the atmosphere around them. Then without saying a word, he pointed at the orange and red sunset filtering between the Evergreen trees standing resolutely in the far distance. Lisa smiled as she glanced over again at her son playing with Blue Boy' and she felt happier than she'd remember feeling for the past two years. Standing next to this marvelous woman with the promise of a wonderful future together, Jake smiled more than he had done in years. Reaching tenderly for her small, delicate hands, he pressed them to his chest. Breaking the quiet stillness of the moment, this rough ex-Marine officer began to speak from his heart.

"I want to be your hero, Lisa Johnson. I was thinking that if you'd like, we could all go out for hamburgers at Roscoe's and ice cream. Would you and Max consider joining me this coming Thursday?" He asked.

"Oh, Jake, you are certainly a true hero to the folks around here! And you are the best thing that has happened to me in a long time. Thank you for coming over here tonight to talk. I feel so safe and happy in your arms at this moment. I can't wait to tell Max our plans. I know he will be excited; he loves ice cream and more importantly, he likes any chance to spend time with you." Lisa remarked.

Jake smiled down at her and realized that he couldn't be any happier than he was at this very moment. He was holding such a wonderful woman in his arms and he found that he didn't want to say goodnight or leave her standing there alone. However, Jake realized that he should say goodnight since he'd see her in a few more days. He kissed her once more, but this time only on the cheek as he told her to expect him to come over around six thirty on Thursday evening to take them both for the special treat. Lisa smiled and said goodnight too. Then she turned reluctantly to go inside the house to sit awhile in her living room as she waited for Max to come inside. As she sat in the dimly lit room, she knew that her heart was softening towards this ruggedly handsome man. *Is it possible that she could be to falling for this handsome and intriguing ex-Marine she wondered?*

Nothing in life is certain and yet, Lisa felt confident that Jake would certainly keep his promises to her and to Max. After all, he'd stayed to protect her son during an awful situation in the woods and he could've been killed that day. She smiled again as she recalled his passionate kiss which was still lingering on her mouth. Yes, she knew deep within her soul that she had made the right choice to continue seeing Jake. She was lost in thought as she wondered if she could trust this ex-military man to protect heart just as he'd protected her son that awful day in July. Her next thought was of a phrase she'd heard once: Lightening doesn't usually strike twice in the same place. Could she find true, lasting love twice in her lifetime? Only time would tell she realized as she stood up and walked into her bedroom to get ready for the night.

At the same time, Jake was letting out a big sigh of relief as he walked back to his cabin in the dark. He paused for a moment to gaze up at the dark sky. The night seemed full of stars which seemed to sparkle and wink at him. He felt a new sense of joy. As he turned slowly around to observe the entire celestial panorama, he spied one brilliant sparkling planet which appeared to be bigger than the other starry planets on display overhead. Why was that one star so much bigger and brighter than the rest of the stars tonight he wondered? Was he imaging this sight?

Feeling as if both of their names were being written mysteriously in the kaleidoscope of stars above, Jacob Walker smiled broadly and couldn't stop smiling it seemed. Reflecting on the light radiating from that brilliant star brought back a memory of the fiction story he'd listened to as a young boy. In the story, his aunt had referred to the main character as the Light Star Hero. This made him recall the dream that Crash' Braden had that night he'd spent in the forest. Jake was glad he'd stumbled onto these two youngster that day he'd been hiking in the woods. Was it fate that had brought him here to heal and meet these two families? As he approached his uncle's property line and saw the cabin in the distance, he whispered a prayer of thanksgiving for this marvelous inheritance gift from his uncle. What if he'd decided to sell this property and remain back in his hometown? He'd never have met this beautiful woman and realized what had been missing in his life. Jake could no longer contain himself as he gave out a shout of sheer happiness. Stepping onto the front porch of his cabin, Jake remembered to whisper a prayer heavenward for extra help with this new, exciting friendship with Lisa Johnson. He wanted to believe that she might be missing him right now too. Little did he know that back inside of her quiet home, Lisa was sitting alone and smiling as she voiced similar words of thanksgiving for her real life hero, Jake Walker, who'd managed to sweep her off her feet and make her feel like a woman again.

WORK CITED

https://www.akc.org/ Australian cattle dog article, viewed on the internet at 10: 42 on August 16, 2010.

Holy Bible, King James Version, scripture verse located in Psalm 118: 17.

www.ingramcontent.com/pod-product-compliance
Lightning Source LLC
Chambersburg PA
CBHW021457110726
47899CB00001BA/192